Praise for Lenora Worth
and her novels

"This heartwarming romance will draw readers in."
—*RT Book Reviews* on *A Certain Hope*

"*A Leap of Faith* is a sweet and enchanting romance between two flawed but redeemable characters."
—*RT Book Reviews* on *A Leap of Faith*

"Her best story yet, it is filled with spiritual depth and hidden meaning."
—*RT Book Reviews* on *Heart of Stone*

Praise for Glynna Kaye
and her novels

"This is a wonderful story of teenage attraction given a second chance to succeed as adult love."
—*RT Book Reviews* on *Second Chance Courtship*

"A wonderful story of misconceptions, misunderstandings, undeserved guilt and love the second time around."
—*RT Book Reviews* on *At Home in His Heart*

"A warm and deeply engaging story."
—*RT Book Reviews* on *High Country Hearts*

With over seventy books published and millions in print, **Lenora Worth** writes award-winning romance and romantic suspense. Three of her books were finalists in the ACFW Carol Awards, and her Love Inspired Suspense novel *Body of Evidence* became a *New York Times* bestseller. Her novella in *Mistletoe Kisses* made her a *USA TODAY* bestselling author. Lenora goes on adventures with her retired husband, Don, and enjoys reading, baking and shopping…especially shoe shopping.

Glynna Kaye treasures memories of growing up in small Midwestern towns—and vacations spent with the Texan side of her family. She traces her love of storytelling to the times a houseful of great-aunts and great-uncles gathered with her grandma to share candid, heartwarming, poignant and often humorous tales of their youth and young adulthood. Glynna now lives in Arizona, where she enjoys gardening, photography and the great outdoors.

A Certain Hope

Lenora Worth

&

Second Chance Courtship

Glynna Kaye

HHARLEQUIN® LOVE INSPIRED®

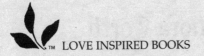

LOVE INSPIRED BOOKS

ISBN-13: 978-1-335-00669-1

A Certain Hope and Second Chance Courtship

Copyright © 2017 by Harlequin Books S.A.

The publisher acknowledges the copyright holders of the individual works as follows:

A Certain Hope
Copyright © 2005 by Lenora H. Nazworth

Second Chance Courtship
Copyright © 2011 by Glynna Kaye Sirpless

www.Harlequin.com

Printed in U.S.A.

CONTENTS

A CERTAIN HOPE

Lenora Worth

To the Ricks family—
Barbara, Bob and especially Jordan.

You all hold a special place in my heart.

Now faith is the substance of things hoped for,
the evidence of things not seen.
—*Hebrews* 11:1

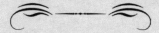

Chapter One

You've got mail.

Summer Maxwell motioned to her cousin Autumn as she opened the letter in her computer. "Hey, it's from April."

Autumn hurried over to the teakwood desk by the window. The Manhattan skyline was etched in sun-dappled shades of steel and gray in front of them as together they read the latest e-mail from their cousin and roommate, April Maxwell.

I'm at work, but I'll be leaving for the airport in a few minutes. I'm so nervous. I'm worried about Daddy, of course. And I'm worried about seeing Reed again. What if he hates me? Never mind, we all know he does hate me. Please say prayers for my sweet daddy, and for safe travel. And that my BMW makes it there ahead of me in one piece.

"That's our April," Summer said, smiling, her blue eyes flashing. "Her prayer requests are always so practical."

"Especially when they come to that car of hers," Autumn said through the wisp of auburn bangs hanging in her eyes. "She's not so worried about the car, though, I think. She's got a lot more to deal with right now, and that's her way of dealing with it. She's not telling us the whole story."

Summer tapped out a reply.

We're here, sugar. And we will say lots of prayers for Uncle Stuart. Tell him we love him so much. Keep in touch. Oh, and let us know how things go with Reed, too. He doesn't hate you. He's just angry with you. Maybe it's time for him to get over it already.

Summer signed off, then spun around in her chair to send her cousin a concerned look. "Of course, he's been angry with her for about six years now."

Reed Garrison brought his prancing gray-and-black-spotted Appaloosa to a skidding stop as a sleek black sports car zoomed up the long drive and shifted into Park.

"Steady, Jericho," Reed said as he patted the gelding's long neck. He held the reins tight as he walked the horse up to the sprawling stone-and-wood ranch house. "I'm just as anxious as you, boy," he told the fidgeting animal. "Let's go find out who's visiting Mr. Maxwell on this fine spring day."

Reed watched from his vantage point at the fence as a woman stepped out of the expensive two-seater convertible. But not just any woman, oh, no. This one was very different.

And suddenly very familiar.

Reed squinted in the late-afternoon sun, then sat back to take a huff of breath as he took in the sight of her.

April Maxwell.

It had been six long years since he'd seen her. Six years of torment and determination. Torment because he couldn't forget her, determination because he had tried to do that very thing.

But April was, as ever, unforgettable.

And now she looked every bit the city girl she had become since she'd bolted and moved from the small town of Paris, Texas, to the big city of New York, New York, to take up residence with her two cousins, Summer and Autumn. Those three Maxwell cousins had a tight bond, each having been named for the seasons they were born in, each having been raised by close-knit relatives scattered all over east Texas, and each having enough ambition to want to get out of Texas right after finishing college to head east and seek their fortunes. Not that they needed any fortunes. They were all three blue-blooded Texas heiresses, born in the land of oil and cattle with silver spoons in their pretty little mouths. But that hadn't been enough for those three belles, no sir. They'd wanted to take on the Big Apple. And they had, each finding satisfying work in their respective career choices. They now roomed together in Manhattan, or so he'd been told.

He hadn't asked about April much, and Stuart Maxwell wasn't the type of man to offer up much information. Stuart was a private man, and Reed was a silent man. It worked great for both of them while they each pined away for April.

Reed walked his horse closer, his nostrils flaring

right along with Jericho's, as he tested the wind for her perfume. He smelled it right away, and the memories assaulted him like soft magnolia petals on a warm summer night. April always smelled like a lily garden, all floral and sweet.

Only Reed knew she was anything but sweet.

Help me, Lord, he thought now as he watched her raise her head and glance around. She spotted him—he saw it in the way she held herself slightly at a distance—but she just stood there in her black short-sleeved dress and matching tall-heeled black sandals, as if she were posing for a magazine spread. She wore black sunglasses and a black-and-white floral scarf that wrapped like a slinky collar around her neck and head. It gave her the mysterious look of a foreign film star.

But then, she'd always been a bit foreign and mysterious to Reed. Even when they'd been so close, so in love, April had somehow managed to hold part of herself aloof. Away from him.

With one elegant tug, she removed the scarf and tossed it onto the red leather seat of the convertible, then ran a hand through her short, dark, tousled curls. With slow, deliberate steps he was sure she'd learned during her debutante years, she did a long-legged walk across the driveway, toward the horse and man.

"Hello, Reed."

"April." He tipped his hat, then set it back on his head, ignoring the way her silky, cultured voice moved like rich honey down his nerve endings. "I heard you might be coming home."

Heard, and lost more sleep than he wanted to think about right now.

"Yes," she said, her hand reaching out to pat Jericho's muzzle. "I drove from the Dallas airport."

"Nice rental car."

"It's not a rental. It's mine. I had it shipped ahead so I'd have a way to get around while I'm here."

Reed didn't bother to remind her that they had several available modes of transportation on the Big M Ranch, from horses to trucks and four-wheelers to Stuart Maxwell's well-tuned Cadillac. "Of course. You always did demand the best." *And I wasn't good enough*, he reminded himself.

"I like driving my own car," she said, unapologetic and unrepentant as she flipped a wrist full of black-and-white shiny bangle bracelets. They matched to perfection the looped black-and-white earrings she wore. "I hope that won't be a problem for you."

"Not my problem at all," Reed retorted, his gaze moving over her, a longing gnawing his heart in spite of the tight set of his jaw. "Looks like city life agrees with you."

"I love New York and I enjoy my work at Satire," she said with a wide smile that only illuminated her big, pouty red lips. Then she glanced around. "But I have to admit I've missed this ranch."

"Your daddy's missed you," Reed said, his tone going low, all hostility leaving his mind now. "He's real sick, April."

She lifted her sunglasses. "I know. I've talked to the doctors on a daily basis for the last two weeks."

In spite of her defensive tone, he saw the worry coloring her chocolate-brown eyes and instantly regretted the reason she'd had to come home. But then, he had a lot of regrets. "Seeing you will perk him up, I'm sure."

She nodded, looked around at the house. "Nothing has changed, and yet, everything is changing."

"You've been gone a long time."

"I've been back for holidays and vacations. Never saw you around much." The questioning look in her eyes was full of dare and accusation.

But he wouldn't give her the satisfaction of knowing he'd deliberately made himself scarce whenever he'd heard she was coming home to visit. Until now. Now he didn't have a choice. He couldn't run. Her daddy needed him here.

He shrugged, looking out over the roping arena across the pasture. "I like to go skiing for the winter holidays, fishing and camping during the spring and summer."

"Still the outdoorsman." She shot him a long, cool look. "That explains your constant absences."

"That and the fact that I bought up some of the land around here and I stay pretty busy with my own farming and ranching."

"You bought up Maxwell land," she said, her chin lifting in that stubborn way he remembered so well.

"Your daddy was selling, and I was in the market to buy."

She looked down at the ground, her fancy sandal toeing a clog of dirt just off the driveway. "He wouldn't want anybody else on this land. I'm glad you bought it."

For a minute, she looked like the young girl Reed had fallen in love with. From kindergarten on, he'd loved her—at first from a distance, and then, up close. For a minute, she looked as vulnerable and lonely as he felt right now.

But that passed. Like a light cloud full of hope and

sunlight, the look was gone as fast as it had come. When she looked up at him, the coolness was back in her dark eyes. "I expect you to take care of this land, Reed. I know I can count on you to do that, at least."

"Thanks," he said, and meant it, in spite of the accusing tone in her last words. "You know I'd never do anything to hurt your daddy. He taught me a lot and he's given me a lot—me and my entire family, for that matter."

"Y'all have been a part of this land for as long as I can remember," she responded, her eyes wide and dark as she stared up at him.

Reed wondered if she was remembering their times together. He wondered if she remembered the way he remembered, with regret and longing and a bitterness that never went away, no matter how sweet the memories.

"I'll be right here, as long as Stu needs me," he told her. He would honor that promise, in spite of having to be near her again. He owed her father that much.

"I guess I'd better go on inside then," she said, her tone husky and quiet. "I dread this."

"Want me to go in with you?" Reed asked, then silently reprimanded himself for offering. He wouldn't fall back into his old ways. Not this time.

"No. I have to do this. I mean, he called me home for a reason, and I have to accept that reason."

Reed heard the crush of emotion in her voice and, whether out of habit or sympathy, his heart lurched forward, toward her. "It's tough, seeing him so frail. Just brace yourself."

"Okay." She nodded, turned and walked back by the stone steps to the long wraparound porch, headed for her car. Then she turned back, her shiny gamine curls lifting in the soft breeze. "Will we see you at supper?"

"Probably not." He couldn't find the strength to share a meal with her, not tonight.

"Guess I'll see you later then."

"Yeah, later."

Reed watched from across the fence as she lifted a black leather tote from the car, her every step as elegant and dainty as any fashion plate he'd seen on the evening news. But then, April Maxwell herself was often seen on the evening news. She worked at one of the major design houses in the country—in the world, probably. Reed didn't know much about haute couture, but he did know a lot of things about April Maxwell.

His mother and sisters went on and on about how Satire was all the rage both on the runways and on the designer ready-to-wear racks, whatever that meant. April was largely responsible for that, they had explained. Apparently, she'd made a good career out of combining public relations and fashion.

She was just a bit shallow and misguided in the love and family department. She'd given up both to seek fame and fortune in the big city.

And he'd stayed here, broke and heartbroken, to mend the fences she'd left behind. Well, he wasn't broke anymore. And he wasn't so very heartbroken, either.

Why, then, did his heart hurt so much at the very sight of her?

She hurt all over.

April opened the massive wooden double doors to her childhood home, her heart beating with a fast rhythm from seeing Reed again. He looked better than ever, tall and muscular, his honey-brown hair long on his neck, his hazel-colored cat eyes still unreadable. Reed was a cowboy, born and bred. He was like this land, solid and wise, unyielding and rooted. After all this time, he still had the power to get to her. And she still had regrets she couldn't even face.

Before she could delve into those regrets, she heard footsteps coming across the cool brick-tiled entryway, then a peal of laughter.

"Ah, *niña,* you are home, *sí?*"

April turned to find one of her favorite people in the world standing there with a grin splitting his aged face.

"*Sí,* Horaz, I'm home. *¿Como está?*"

"I'm good, very good," Horaz said, bobbing his head, his thick salt-and-pepper hair not moving an inch.

"And Flora? How is she?"

"Flora is fine, just fine. She is cooking up all of your favorites."

"That sounds great," April said, hugging the old man in a warm embrace, the scent of spicy food wafting around them. She wasn't hungry, but she'd have to hide that from Horaz and Flora Costello. They had been with her family since her father and mother had been married more than thirty years ago. And after her mother's death when April was in high school, they'd stayed on to take care of her and her father. She loved them both like family and often visited with their three grown children and their families whenever she came home, which was rare these days. The entire Costello clan lived on Maxwell land, in homes they'd built themselves, with help from her father.

"You look tired, *niña,*" Horaz said. "Do you want to rest before supper? Your room is ready."

April thought of the light, airy room on the second floor, the room with the frilly curtains and wide, paned windows that allowed a dramatic view of the surrounding pasture land and the river beyond. "No, I don't want to rest right now. I want... I want to see my father."

Horaz looked down at the floor. "I will take you to him. Then I will instruct Tomás to bring in the rest of your bags."

"Yes, I left them in the trunk of the car." She handed him the keys. "And how is Tomás? Does he like high school?"

"He's on the football team," Horaz said, grinning again. "My grandson scored two touchdowns in the final big game last fall. We won the championship."

"I'm glad to hear it," April said, remembering her own days of cheerleading and watching Reed play. He'd been a star quarterback in high school and had gone on to play college ball. Then he'd gotten injured in his senior year at Southern Methodist University. After graduating, he had come home to Paris to make a living as a rancher. She had gone on to better things.

Not so much better, she reminded herself. You gave up Reed for your life in New York. Why now, of all times, did she have to feel such regrets for making that decision?

"Come," Horaz said, taking her by the arm to guide her toward the back of the rambling, high-ceilinged house.

As they passed the stairs, April took in the vast paneled-and-stucco walls of the massive den to the right. The stone fireplace covered most of the far wall, a row of woven baskets adorning the ledge high over it. On the back wall, over a long brown leather couch grouped with two matching comfortable chairs and ottomans, hung a portrait of the Big M's sweeping pastures with the glistening Red River beyond. Her mother had painted it. The paned doors on either side of the fireplace were thrown open to the porch, a cool afternoon breeze moving through them to bring in the scent of the just-blooming potted geraniums and the centuries-old climbing roses.

As they neared the rear of the house, April felt the cool breeze turn into a chill and the scent of spring flowers change to the scent of antiseptics and medicine. It was dark down this hall, dark and full of shadows. She shuddered as Horaz guided her to the big master bedroom where the wraparound porch continued on each side, where another huge fireplace dominated one wall, where her mother's Southwestern-motif paintings hung on either side of the room, and where, in a big bed handmade of heart-of-pine posts and an intricate, lacy wrought-iron headboard that reached to the ceiling, her father lay dying.

Chapter Two

The big room was dark, the ceiling-to-floor windows shuttered and covered with the sheer golden drapery April remembered so well. When her mother was alive, those windows had always been open to the sun and the wind. But her mother was gone, as was the warmth of this room.

It was cold and dark now, a sickroom. The wheelchair in the corner spoke of that sickness, as did the many bottles of pills sitting on the cluttered bedside table. The bed had been rigged with a contraption that helped her weak, frail father get up and down.

April walked toward the bed, willing herself to be cheerful and upbeat, even though her heart was stabbing with clawlike tenacity against her chest. I won't cry, she told herself, lifting her chin in stubborn defiance, her breeding and decorum that of generations of strong Maxwell women.

"Daddy?" she called as she neared the big bed in the corner. "It's me, Daddy. April."

A thin, withered hand reached out into the muted light. "Is that my girl?"

April felt the hot tears at the back of her eyes. Pushing and fighting at them, she took a deep breath and stepped to the bedside, Horaz hovering near in case she needed him. "Yes, I'm here. I made it home."

"Celia." The whispered name brought a smile to his face. "I knew you'd come back to me."

April gasped and brought a hand to her mouth. He thought she was her mother! Swallowing the lump in her throat, she said, "No, Daddy. It's April. April…"

Horaz touched her arm. "He doesn't always recognize people these days. He has grown worse over the last week."

April couldn't stop the tears then. "I… I'm here now, Daddy. It's April. I'm April."

Her thin father, once a big, strapping man, lifted his drooping eyes and looked straight into her face. For a minute, recognition seemed to clarify things for him. "April, sweetheart. When'd you get home?"

"I just now arrived," she said, sniffing back tears as she briskly wiped her face. "I should have been here sooner, Daddy."

He waved his hand in the air, then let it fall down on the blue blanket. "No matter. You're here now. Got to make things right. You and Reed. Don't leave too soon."

"What?" April leaned forward, touching his warm brow. "I'm not going anywhere, I promise. I'm going to stay right here until you're well again."

He smiled, then closed his eyes. "I won't be well again, honey."

"Yes, you will," she said, but in her heart she knew he was right. Her father was dying. She knew it now, even though she'd tried to deny it since the day the family doctor had called and told her Stuart Maxwell had taken a turn for the worse. The years of drinking and smoking had finally taken their toll on her tough-skinned father. His lungs and liver were completely destroyed by disease and abuse. And it was too late to fix them now.

Too late to fix so many things.

April sat with her father until the sun slipped behind the treeline to the west. She sat and held his hand, speaking to him softly at times about her life in New York, about how she enjoyed living with Summer and Autumn in their loft apartment in Tribeca. About how much she appreciated his allowing her to have wings, his understanding that she needed to be out on her own in order to see how precious it was to have a place to call home.

Stuart slept through most of her confessions and revelations. But every now and then, he would smile or frown; every now and then he would squeeze her fingers in his, some of the old strength seeming to pour through his tired old veins.

April sat and cried silently as she remembered how beautiful her mother had been. Her parents had been so in love, so perfectly matched. The rancher oilman and the beautiful, dark-haired free-spirited artist. Her father had come from generations of tough Texas oilmen, larger-than-life men who ruled their empires with steely determination and macho power. Her mother had come from a long line of Hispanic nobility, a line that traced its roots from Texas all the way back to Mexico City. They'd met when Stuart had gone to Santa Fe to buy horses. He'd come home with several beautiful Criollo working horses, and one very fiery beauty who was also a temperamental artist.

In spite of her mother's temper and artistic eccentricities, it had been a match made in heaven—until the day her mother had boarded their private jet for a gallery opening in Santa Fe. The jet had crashed just after takeoff from the small regional airport a few miles up the road. There were no survivors.

No survivors. Her father had died that day, too, April decided. His vibrant, hard-living spirit had died. He'd always been a rounder, but her devout mother had kept his wild streak at bay for many years. That ended the day they buried Celia Maxwell.

And now, as April looked at the skeletal man lying in this bed, she knew her father had drunk himself to an early grave so he could be with her mother.

"Don't leave me, Daddy," April whispered, tears again brimming in her eyes.

Then she remembered the day six years ago that Stuart had told his daughter the same thing. "Don't leave me, sugar. Stay here with your tired old daddy. I won't have anyone left if you go."

But then he'd laughed and told her to get going. "There's a big ol' world out there and I reckon you need to see it. But just remember where home is."

So she'd gone on to New York, too eager to start her new career and be with her cousins to see that her father was lonely. Too caught up in her own dreams to see that Reed and her daddy both wanted her to stay.

I lost them both, she thought now. I lost them both. And now, I'll be the one left all alone.

As dusk turned into night, April sat and cried for all that she had given up, her prayers seeming hollow and unheeded as she listened to her father's shallow breathing and confused whispers.

* * *

Reed found her there by the bed at around midnight. Horaz had called him, concerned for April's well-being.

"Mr. Reed, I'm sorry to wake you so late, but you need to come to the hacienda right away. Miss April, she won't come out of his room. She is very tired, but she stays. I tell her a nurse is here to sit, but she refuses to leave the room."

She's still stubborn, Reed thought as he walked into the dark room, his eyes adjusting to the dim glow from a night-light in the bathroom. Still stubborn, still proud, and hurting right now, he reminded himself. He'd have to use some gentle persuasion.

"April," he said, his voice a low whisper.

At first he thought she might be asleep, the way she was sitting with her head back against the blue-and-gold-patterned brocade wing chair. But at the sound of his voice, she raised her head, her eyes widening at the sight of him standing there over her.

"What's the matter?" she asked, confusion warring with daring in her eyes.

"Horaz called me. He's worried about you. He said you didn't eat supper."

"I'm not hungry," she responded, her eyes going to her sleeping father.

"Okay." He stood silent for a few minutes, then said, "The nurse is waiting. She has to check his pulse and administer his medication."

"She can do that around me."

"Yes, she can, but she also sits with him through the night. That's her job. And she's ready to relieve you."

April whirled then, her eyes flaring hot and dark in the muted light from the other room. "No, that's *my* job. That should have been my job all along, but I didn't take it on, did I? I… I stayed away, when I should have been here—"

"That's it," Reed said, hauling her to her feet with two gentle hands on her arms. "You need a break."

"No," she replied, pulling away. "I'm fine."

"You need something to eat and a good night's sleep," he said, his tone soft but firm.

"You don't have the right to tell me what I need," she reminded him, her words clipped and breathless.

"No, I don't. But we've got enough on our hands around here without you falling sick on us, too," he reminded her. "Did you come home to help or to wallow in self-pity?"

She tried to slap him, but Reed could see she was so exhausted that it had mostly been for show. Without a word, he lifted her up into his arms and stomped out of the room, motioning with his head for the hovering nurse to go in and do her duty.

"Put me down," April said, the words echoing out over the still, dark house as she struggled against Reed's grip.

"I will, in the kitchen, where Flora left you some soup and bread. And you will eat it."

"Still bossing me around," she retorted, her eyes flashing. But as he moved through the big house with her, she stopped struggling. Her head fell against the cotton of his T-shirt, causing Reed to pull in a sharp breath. She felt so warm, so soft, so vulnerable there against him, that he wanted to sit down and hold her tight forever.

Instead, he dropped her in a comfortable, puffy-cushioned chair in the breakfast room, then told her, "Stay."

She did, dropping her head on the glass-topped table, her hands in her hair.

"I'm going to heat your soup."

"I can't eat."

"You need to try."

She didn't argue with that, thankfully.

Soon he had a nice bowl of tortilla soup in front of her, along with a tall glass of Flora's famous spiced tea and some corn bread.

Reed sat down at the table, his own tea full of ice and lemon. "Eat."

She glared over at him, but picked up the spoon and took a few sips of soup. Reed broke off some of the tender corn bread and handed it to her. "Chew this."

April took the crusty bread and nibbled at it, then dropped it on her plate. "I'm done."

"You eat like a bird."

"I *can't* eat," she said, the words dropping between them. "I can't—"

"You can't bear to see him like that? Well, welcome to the club. I've watched him wasting away for the last year now. And I feel just as helpless as you do."

She didn't answer, but he saw the glistening of tears trailing down her face.

Letting out a breath of regret, Reed went on one knee beside her chair, his hand reaching up to her face to wipe at tears. "I'm sorry, April. Sorry you have to see him like this. But…he wants to die at home. And he wanted you to be here."

She bobbed her head, leaning against his hand until

Reed gave in and pulled her into his arms. Falling on both knees, he held her as she cried there at the table.

Held her, and condemned himself for doing so.

Because he'd missed holding her. Missed her so much.

And because he knew this was a mistake.

But right now, he also knew they both needed someone to hold.

"It's hard to believe my mother's been dead twelve years," April said later. After she'd cried and cried, Reed had tried to lighten things by telling her he was getting a crick in his neck, holding her in such an awkward position, him on his knees with her leaning down from her chair.

They had moved to the den and were now sitting on the buttery-soft leather couch, staring into the light of a single candle burning in a huge crystal hurricane lamp on the coffee table.

Reed nodded. "It's also hard to believe that each of those years brought your father down a little bit more. It was like watching granite start to break and fall away."

"Granite isn't supposed to break," she said as she leaned her head back against the cushiony couch, her voice sounding raw and husky from crying.

"Exactly." Reed propped his booted foot on the hammered metal of the massive table. "But he did break. He just never got over losing her."

"And then I left him, too."

As much as he wanted to condemn her for that, Reed didn't think it would be kind or wise to knock her when she was already so down on herself. "Don't go blaming yourself," he said. "You did what you'd always dreamed of doing. Stuart was—is—so proud of you. You should be proud of your success."

"I am proud," she said, her laughter brittle. "So very proud. I knew he was lonely when I left, Reed. But I was too selfish to admit that."

"He never expected you to sacrifice your life for his, April. Not the way I expected things from you."

"But he needed me here. Even though she'd been dead for years, he was still grieving for my mother. He never stopped grieving. And now…it's too late for me to help him."

"You're here now," Reed said, his own bitterness causing the statement to sound harsh in the silent house.

April turned to stare over at him. "How do you feel about my being back?"

Her directness caught him off guard. Reed could be direct himself when things warranted the truth. But he wasn't ready to tell her exactly how being with her made him feel. He wasn't so sure about that himself.

"It's good to have you here?" he said in the form of a question, a twisted smile making it sound lightweight.

"Don't sound so convincing," she said, grimacing. "I know you'd rather be anywhere else tonight than sitting here with me."

"You're wrong on that account," he told her, being honest about that, at least. "You need someone here. This is going to be tough and I… I promised your daddy I'd see you through it."

That brought her up off the couch. "So you're only here as a favor to my father? Out of some sense of duty and sympathy?"

"Aren't those good reasons—to be helping out a friend?"

"Friend?" She paced toward the empty fireplace, then stood staring out into the starlit night. "Am I still your friend, Reed?"

He got up to come and stand beside her. "Honestly, I don't know what you are to me—I mean, we haven't communicated in a very long time, on any level. I just know that Stuart Maxwell is like a second father to me and because of that, I will be here to help in whatever way I can. And yes, I'd like to think that we can at least be friends again."

"But you're only my friend because you promised my father?"

"Since when did this go from the real issue—a man dying—to being all about you and your feelings?"

"I know what the real issue is," she said, her words stony and raw with emotion. "But since you practically admitted you're doing this only out of the goodness of your heart," she countered, turning to stalk toward the hallway, "I just want you to know I don't expect anything from you. So don't do me any favors, okay? You're usually away when I come home. You don't have to babysit me. I'll get through this somehow."

"I'm sure you will," he said, hurt down to his boots by her harsh words and completely unreasonable stance. But then he reminded himself she was going through a lot of guilt and stress right now. It figured she'd lash out at the first person to try to help her, especially if that person was an old flame. "Guess it's time for me to get on home."

"Yes, it's late. I'm going to check on Daddy, then I'm going to bed." She started for the stairs, but turned at the first step, her dark head down. "Reed?"

He had a hand on the ornate doorknob. "What?"

"I do appreciate your coming by. I feel better now, having eaten a bit." She let out a sigh that sounded very close to a sob. "And…thanks for the shoulder. It's been a long time since I've cried like that."

He didn't dare look at her. "I'm glad then that I came. Call if you need anything else."

"I will, thanks." Then she looked up at him. "And I'm sorry about what I said. About you not doing me any favors. It was mean, considering you came here in the middle of the night just to help out. That was exactly what I needed tonight."

Reed felt his heart tug toward her again, as if it might burst out of his chest with longing and joy. He wanted to tell her that he needed her, too, not just as friend, but as a man who'd never stopped loving her.

Instead, he tipped his head and gave her a long look.

"I'll be here, April. I'll always be right here. Just remember that."

Chapter Three

April pressed the send button on the computer in her father's study, glad that she had someone to talk to about her worries and frustrations. Then she reread the message she'd just sent.

Hi, girls. Well, my first night home was a bad one. Daddy is very sick. I don't think he will last much longer. I sat with him for a long time—well into the night. Then Reed came in and made me eat something. Okay, he actually carried me, caveman-style, into the kitchen. Still Mr. Know-It-All-Tough-Guy. Still good-looking. And still single, from everything I can tell, in spite of all those rumors we've heard about his social life. He was very kind to me. He held me while I cried. And I cried like a baby. It felt good to be in his arms again. But I have to put all that aside. I have to help Daddy, something I should have been doing all along. Today, Reed and I are taking a ride out over the ranch, to see what needs to be done. I hope I can remember how to sit a horse. Love y'all. Keep the prayers coming. April.

That didn't sound too bad, she thought as she took another sip of the rich coffee Flora had brought to her earlier. She'd told Summer and Autumn the truth, without going into the details.

Oh, but such details.

After the devastation of seeing her father so sick, April hadn't wanted to go on herself. But Reed had made her feel so safe, so comforted last night. That wasn't good. She was very weak right now, both in body and spirit. Too weak to resist his beautiful smile and warm golden eyes. Too weak to keep her hands out of that thick golden-brown too-long hair. Too weak to resist her favorite cowboy. The only cowboy she'd ever loved.

You're just too emotional right now, she reminded herself. You can't mistake kindness and sympathy for something else—something that can never be.

Yet, she longed for that something else. It had hit her as hard as seeing her father again, this feeling of emptiness and need, this sense of not being complete.

Thinking back on all the men she'd met and dated in New York, April groaned. Her last relationship had been a disaster. All this time, she'd thought she just hadn't found the right one. But now she could see she was always comparing them to Reed.

That had to stop. But how could she turn off these emotions when she'd probably see him every day? Did she even *want* to deny it—this feeling of being safe again, this feeling of being back home in his arms?

No, she wouldn't deny her feelings for Reed, but right now, she couldn't give in to them, either. They had parted all those years ago with a bitter edge between them. And he'd told her he wouldn't wait for her.

But he was still here.

He's not here because of you, she reminded herself. *He's here because he loves your daddy as much as you do.*

She couldn't depend on Reed too much. She had to get through this one day at a time, as her mother used to tell her whenever April was facing some sort of challenge.

"One day at a time," April said aloud as she closed down the computer. But how many days would she have to watch her father suffering like this?

"Give me strength, Lord," she said aloud, her eyes closed to the pain and the fear. *"Give me strength to accept that with life comes death. Show me how to cope, show me how to carry on. Please, Lord, show me that certain hope my mother used to talk about. That hope for eternal life."*

Turning her thoughts to her father, April got up to take her empty coffee mug into the kitchen. She wanted to watch to see how the nurse fed him, so she could help. She wanted to spend the morning with him before she went for that ride with Reed. Actually, she didn't want to leave her father's side. Maybe she could stall Reed.

He'd called about an hour ago, asking if she wanted to check out the property. Caught off guard, and longing for a good long ride, April had said yes. Then she'd immediately gone to check on her father, only to find the nurse bathing him. April had offered to help, but the other woman had shooed her out of the room. At the time, a good long ride had sounded better than having to see her father suffer such indignities. But now she was having second thoughts.

"Finished?" Flora asked, her smile as bright as her

vivid brown eyes. Flora wore her dark red hair in a chignon caught up with an elaborate silver filigree clip.

April put her mug in the sink, then turned. "Yes, and thanks for the Danish and coffee. You still make the best breads and dainties in the world, Flora."

"Gracias," Flora said, wiping her slender hands on a sunflower-etched dish towel.

"And how you manage to stay so slim is beyond me," April continued as she headed toward the archway leading back to the central hall.

"Me, I walk it all off, but you? You need to eat more pastry," Flora said, a hint of impishness in her words.

April turned to grin at her, her eyes taking in the way the morning sunlight fell across the red-tiled counters and high archways of the huge kitchen. Even later in the year, in the heat of summer, this kitchen would always be cool and tranquil. She'd spent many hours here with her mother and Flora, baking cookies and making bread.

"I guess I walk mine off, too." April shrugged, thinking how different life on the ranch was from the fast pace of New York. Here, she could walk for miles and miles and never see another living soul, whereas New York was always full of people in a hurry to get somewhere. Wanting to bring back some of the good memories she had of growing up here, she said, "Maybe I'll make some of that jalapeño bread. Remember how Daddy used to love it?"

"Sí," Flora said, nodding. "He can't eat it now, though, *querida.*"

"Of course not," April said, her mood shifting as reality hit her with the same force as the sunbeam streaming through the arched windows. "I'm going to talk to the nurse to see what he can eat."

Flora nodded, her brown eyes turning misty with worry. "He is a very sick man. I keep him in my prayers."

"I appreciate that," April said. "I guess our only prayer now is that God brings him some sort of peace, even if that means we have to let him go."

"You are a very wise young woman."

"Mother taught me to trust in God in all things. I'm trying to remember that now more than ever."

"Your *madre,* she loved the Lord."

"Yes, she did," April said. Then she turned back to the hallway, wishing that she had the same strong faith her mother had possessed. And wishing her father hadn't ruined his health by drinking and smoking.

As she entered his room, she heard him fussing with the nurse. "I don't…need that. What I need…is a drink." Stuart's eyes closed as he fell back down on the pillow and seemed to go to sleep again.

The nurse, a sturdy woman with clipped gray hair named Lynette Proctor, clicked her tongue and turned to stare at April. "Man can barely speak, and he still wants a drink." She gave April a sympathetic look. "His liver is shot, honey. Whatever you do, don't give him any alcohol."

"I don't plan on it," April retorted, the woman's blunt words causing a burning anger to move through April's system. "And I'd like to remind you that this man is my father. You will show him respect, no matter how much you agree or disagree with his drinking problem."

Lynette finished administering Stuart's medication, checked his IV, then turned with her hands on her hips to face April. "I apologize, sugar. My husband was an alcoholic, too, so I've seen the worst of this disease. That's one reason I became a nurse and a sitter. I feel for your daddy there, but I just wish…well, I wish there was something to be done, is all."

"We can agree on that," April said, her defensive stance softening. Then she came to stand over the bed. In the light of day, her father looked even more pale and sickly. "This isn't the man I remember. My daddy was so big and strong. I thought he could protect me from anything."

"Now it's your turn to protect him, I reckon," Lynette said. "Do you still want to go over his schedule?"

"Yes," April said. "Show me everything. I'm going to be here for the duration." She stopped, willing herself to keep it together. "However long that might be."

Lynette touched a hand to her arm. "Not as long as you might think, honey. This man ain't got much more time on this earth. And I'm sorry for your pain."

"Thank you," April said, wondering how many times she'd have to hear that from well-meaning people over the course of the next few weeks. *How much can I bear, Lord?*

Then she remembered her mother's words to her long ago. *The Lord never gives us more than we can bear, April. Trust in Him and you will get through any situation, no matter the outcome.*

No matter the outcome. The outcome here wasn't going to be happy or pretty. Her father was dying. How could she bear to go through that kind of pain yet again?

She turned as footsteps echoed down the hallway, and saw the silhouette of a tall man coming toward her.

Reed.

He'd said he'd be around for the duration, too.

April let out a breath of relief, glad that he was here. She needed him. Her father needed him. Maybe Reed's quiet, determined strength would help her to stay strong.

No matter the outcome.

Reed listened as the very capable Lynette told them both what to expect over the next few weeks. It would get worse, she assured them. He might go quietly in his sleep, or he might suffer a heart attack or stroke. All they could do was keep him comfortable and out of pain.

With each word, told in such clinical detail, Reed could see April's face growing paler and more distressed. He had to get her away from this sickroom for a while, because he knew there could be many more days such as this, where she could only sit and watch her father slipping away.

When Lynette was finished, Reed motioned to April. "He's resting now. Good time to take that ride."

At the concern in her dark eyes, he whispered, "I won't keep you out long. And Lynette can radio us—I have a set of walkie-talkies I bought for that very reason."

"I'll take my cell phone," April replied, watching her father closely. Then she turned to Lynette and gave her the number. "Call me if there is any change, good or bad."

"Okay," Lynette said. "He'll sleep most of the afternoon. He usually gets restless around sundown."

"We'll be back long before then," Reed said, more to reassure April than to report to the nurse.

Seeming satisfied, April kissed her father on the forehead and turned to leave the room. Once they were outside in the hallway, she looked over at Reed. "I don't think I should leave him."

He understood her fears, but he also understood she needed some fresh air. "A short ride will do you good. It'll settle your nerves."

"Just along the river, then."

"Whatever you say. You're the boss."

April shot him a harsh look. "Don't say that. I'm not ready to be the boss."

"Well, that's something we need to discuss," Reed replied. "A lot of people depend on this land for their livelihoods." He hesitated, looking down at the floor. "And...well, Stu let some things slip."

"What do you mean, let some things slip?"

"Fences need mending. We're got calves to work and brand. Half our hands have left because Stu would forget to pay 'em. Either that, or he'd lose his temper and fire 'em on the spot."

April closed her eyes, as if she was trying to imagine her father roaring at the help. Stuart had a temper, but he'd always handled his employees with respect and decency. When he was sober, at least.

"You keep saying 'our' as if you still work here."

Reed placed his hands on his hips, then raised his eyes to meet hers. "I've been helping out some in my spare time."

Groaning, she ran a hand through her bangs. "Reed, you have almost as much land now as we do. Are you telling me you've been working your ranch and this one, too? That's close to fifteen hundred acres."

"Yeah, pretty much. But hey, I don't really have anything better to do. Daddy helps, too. And you know Stu's got friends all over East Texas. Your uncles come around as often as they can, to check on things and help out. Well, Richard does—not so much James. But they have their own obligations. We've all tried to hold things together for him, April."

She let out a shuddering breath. "I'm just not ready for all of this."

"All the more reason to take things one day at a time and get yourself readjusted."

"There's no way to adjust to losing both your parents," she said. Then she hurried up the hallway ahead of him, the scent of her floral perfume lingering to remind him that she was back home, good or bad.

Reed watched as April handled the gentle roan mare with an expert hand. "I see you haven't lost your touch."

April gave him a tight smile. "Well, since you told Tomás to bring me the most gentle horse in the stable, I'd say I'm doing okay."

"Daisy needed to stretch her legs," he replied.

"I still go horseback riding now and then."

"In New York City?"

She laughed at his exaggerated way of saying that. "Yes, in New York City. You can take the girl out of the country—"

"But you can't take the country out of the girl?"

"I guess not." She urged Daisy through the gates leading out to the open pasture. "Who's that other kid with Tomás?" she asked as the two teenagers waved to them from where they were exercising some of the other horses.

"That's Adan Garcia. They're best friends and they play football together. He helps Tomás with some of the work around here. Just a summer job."

"Why is he staring at us?" she asked. "He looks so bitter and…full of teenage angst."

Reed shrugged. "Guess he's never seen a woman from New York City before. Maybe that ain't angst, just curiosity about a 'city girl.'"

"Will you please stop saying that as if it's distasteful?"

"Not distasteful. Just hard to imagine."

"You never thought I'd make it, did you?"

"Oh, I knew you'd give it your best."

She kneed Daisy into action, tossing him a glare over her shoulder.

Reed followed on Jericho, anxious to know everything about her life since she'd been gone. "So what's it like in the big city?"

She clicked her boots against Daisy's ribs as they did a slow trot. "It's exciting, of course. Fast-paced. Hectic."

"Your eyes light up when you say that."

"I love it. I enjoy my work at Satire and it's fun living with Summer and Autumn."

Reed turned his head to roll his eyes. What kind of name was Satire, anyway? But right now, he didn't need to hear about her fancy threads workplace. So he asked the question that had been burning through his system since she'd come home. No, since she'd left. "And how about your social life? Dating any Wall Street hotshots or do you just hang with the Hollywood types?"

She slanted him a sideways look. "Honestly, I rarely have time to date."

His gut hurt, thinking about all the eligible bachelors in New York. "I don't believe that."

"Okay, I've had a few relationships. But… I've found most of the men I date are a bit self-centered and shallow. They're so involved in their careers, they kind of rush their way through any after-hours social life. I don't like to be rushed."

That made him grin. In his mind, she'd just described herself. Her new self. But then, maybe he'd misjudged her. "You never did like to be rushed. Maybe the city hasn't changed you so much after all."

"No, I haven't changed that much. I know where I came from. And besides, most of my colleagues tease me about my Texas drawl."

Reed could listen to that drawl all day long. "You have that edge in your voice now. That little bit of hurried city-speak."

"City-speak?" She grinned. "I can't imagine what you're talking about."

"Oh, you know. Fast and sassy."

As they walked the horses toward the meandering river, she gazed out over the flat grassland. Red clovers and lush bluebonnets were beginning to bloom here and there across some of the pastures. "Well, fast and sassy won't cut it here, unless I'm roping cattle. But at least I can apply my business skills to detangling some of the mess this ranch is in."

"How long do you plan on staying?"

Her eyes went dark at that question. "I… I told my supervisor I'd be here indefinitely. I have three weeks of vacation time and she agreed to let me use my two weeks of sick days. I've never abused my benefits at Satire, so she knew I was serious when I came to her asking for an extended leave of absence."

"And when…things change here, you'll go back?"

"That's the plan."

Reed didn't respond to that. But his silence must have alerted April.

Pulling up, she turned to stare over at him from underneath her bangs. "You do understand I have to go back?"

He nodded, pushed his hat back on his head. "I understand plenty. But tell that to your daddy. He has other plans, I think."

She shook her head. "I'm not even sure he realizes I'm here."

"Oh, he knows. It's all he's talked about for the last week. Every time he'd wake up, he'd ask for you. I kept telling him you were on your way. I think he's been waiting for you to get home just so—"

She looked cornered, uncertain. "Just so what? What do you mean? That he's going to give up and die now? After seeing him, I've accepted that, Reed."

"Yeah, well, that's something we can't help, but there's more to it."

Her eyes widened with fear and confusion. "Why don't you just explain everything, then? Just give me the whole story."

Reed didn't want to have to be the one to tell her this, but somebody had to. Stu had revealed it in his ramblings and whispered words. And Reed had promised the dying man he'd see it happen. "April—your father—he thinks you've come home for good."

Chapter Four

"Home for good?"

April stared over at Reed, a stunned wave of disbelief coursing through her system.

Reed nodded, looked out over the flowing river. "He has it in his head that you'll just take over things here. I mean, it's all going to be yours, anyway. It's in his will. And Richard and James both know that."

"My uncles have agreed to this?"

"They'll get their parts—a percentage of the oil holdings and mineral rights, things like that. But for the most part, the land and the house will belong to you."

April swallowed the pain that scratched at her throat. "I thought… I just figured he'd delegate things to Uncle James and Uncle Richard. I thought I'd get only my mother's part of the estate." She shuddered, causing Daisy to go into a prance. "Honestly, Reed, I've tried not to think about that at all."

"Well, start thinking," he said, the words echoing out over the still pasture. Then he waved a hand in the air, gesturing out over the landscape. "Pretty soon, all of this will be yours, April. And that means you'll have a big responsibility. And some big decisions."

She didn't want to deal with this today. "Could I just get settled and—could I concentrate on my father, just for today, Reed? I'll worry about all of that when the time comes."

"Okay," he replied, his tone as soft as the cooing mourning dove she could hear off in the cottonwood trees. "I won't press you on this, but I just thought you should know."

"I'm not sure what I'll do," she admitted. "I just don't know—"

"We'll work through it," he said, a steely resolve in his words.

"You don't have to help me, Reed." She could tell he didn't want to be tied down to the obligations her father had thrust onto his shoulders. And neither did she.

"I don't mind," he said, turning to face her as he held the big Appaloosa in check.

"Well, maybe I do," she retorted.

And because she felt herself being closed in, because she felt as if she were back in college and Reed was telling her what was best for her all over again, she spurred Daisy into a fast run and left Reed sitting there staring after her. She had to think, needed to feel the spring wind on her face. This was too much to comprehend all at once.

Way too much for her to comprehend. Especially with Reed sending her those mixed messages of duty and friendship. She didn't want his pity or his guidance if it meant he was being forced to endure her. She could handle anything but that. So she took off.

Again.

* * *

Reed caught up with her at the bend in the river where a copse of oak saplings jutted out over a broken ridge. Just like April to take off running. She'd always run away when things got too complicated. She was doing the same thing now that she used to do whenever they'd fought. She'd get on her horse and take off to the wild blue yonder. Sometimes she'd stay gone for hours on end, upsetting her parents and the whole ranch in general with her reckless need to be away from any kind of commitment or responsibility.

Well, now she was going to have to stop running.

"April," he called as he brought Jericho to a slow trot beside her. "Slow down and let's talk."

"I don't want to talk," she said over her shoulder.

But she slowed Daisy anyway. Even April wouldn't run a poor horse to the grave.

Reed pulled up beside her as they both brought the horses to a walk. "Let's sit a spell here by the water. Then we'll head back and I'll point out some of the most urgent problems around here."

"I think I know what the most urgent problem is," she retorted as she swung off Daisy. "My father is dying."

Reed allowed her that observation. He knew all of this had to be overwhelming. He hopped off Jericho and stepped over to take Daisy's reins. "I understand how you must be feeling, April. That's why I'm here to help."

She turned on him, her brown eyes burning with anger and hurt. "But you don't want to be here. I can see that. I don't want you to feel obligated—"

Reed tugged her close, his own anger simmering to a near boil. "You don't get it, do you? I *am* obligated.

To your father, and to you. What kind of man would I be if I just walked away when you both need me?"

"You mean, the way I walked away, Reed? Why don't you just go ahead and say it? I walked away when my father needed me the most. I was selfish and self-centered and only thought of myself, right?"

He nodded, causing her to gasp in surprise. "I reckon that about sums things up," he said. "But if you aim to keep on punishing yourself, if you aim to keep wallowing in the past and all that self-pity, then maybe you don't need me around after all. You seem pretty good at doing that all on your own. That and running away all over again."

He handed her Daisy's reins and turned to get back on Jericho, to wash his hands of trying to be her friend. He could just concentrate on being nearby when the time came. He could hover around, checking on things, without having to endure the double-edged pain of seeing her and knowing she'd be gone again soon.

"Reed, wait."

He was already in the saddle. It would be so easy to just keep going. But he didn't. He turned Jericho around and looked down at April, his heart bolting and bucking like a green pony about to be broken. Just like his heart was about to be broken all over again.

"I don't want to fight you, April. I just want to help you." He shrugged. "I mean, don't we have that left between us at least? When a friend needs help, I'm there. It's just the way it is."

She stared up at him, her brown eyes soft with a misty kind of regret, her short curls wind-tossed and wispy around her oval face. She was slender and sure in her jeans and T-shirt, her boots hand-tooled and well-worn.

"It's just the way *you* are, Reed," she acknowledged with her own shrug. But her eyes held something more than the regret he could clearly see. They held respect and admiration and, maybe, a distant longing.

He still loved her. So much.

"I need… I do need your help," she admitted. "I don't think I can handle this on my own. You were here when my mother died. Remember?"

"I remember," he said, nodding. He remembered holding April while she cried, right here on this spot of earth, in this very place, underneath the cottonwoods by the river. They'd watched the sun set and the stars rise. They'd watched a perfect full moon settle over the night sky. And he'd held her still. Held her close and tight and promised her he'd never, ever leave her.

Would he be able to keep that promise this time?

Reed knew he could keep his promises.

But he also knew April hadn't learned how to do the same.

But he got down off his horse and took her hand anyway. He didn't dare hope. He didn't dare think past just holding her hand. "I'll be right here," he told her.

"Thank you." She smiled and took his hand in hers, a tentative beginning to a new truce.

They stayed there, in what used to be their special spot, for about an hour. April had called the house twice to check on her father, so Reed decided maybe he'd better get her home. At least he'd been able to fill her in on some of the daily problems around the ranch. They'd somehow made a silent agreement to concentrate on business. Nothing personal.

"How about we head back?" Reed asked now. April

seemed more relaxed, even though he could tell she was concerned over this latest news of her becoming full owner of the Big M. "I'll show you the backside of the property. Should be home just in time for vittles."

That made her laugh at least. "You truly will always be a cowboy, won't you, Reed?"

He nodded, flipping his worn Stetson back on his head. "I was born that way, ma'am."

She laughed again at the way he'd stretched out the polite statement. "I hear you bought one of our guest houses for yourself."

"Yep." He got back on Jericho, noting the animal was impatient to get moving again. "A right nice little place. Three bedrooms, two baths, oak floors, stone fireplace and a game room that begged for a new billiards table."

April slipped back on Daisy with ease. She always had been a grand horsewoman.

"I'm glad someone is occupying that house. It always seemed silly to me to send guests to another house when we have so much room in the big house."

"Ah, but that's the way of the Texas cattlemen. Showy and big. The bigger, the better in Texas."

They trotted along at a reasonable pace, back over the rambling hills of northeast Texas. Reed took in the dogwoods just blooming in the clumps of forest at the edge of the vast pastureland, their blossoms bright white amid the lush green of the sweet gums and hickory and oak trees. Here and there, rare lone mesquite trees jutted at twisted angles out in the pasture, like signposts pointing toward home.

"It's funny how small our apartment is in New York, compared to all this vast property," April said.

"I would have thought you'd feel stifled there amid

all the skyscrapers and traffic jams," Reed said, then wondered why he'd even made the comparison.

"I did at first," she replied, the honesty in her eyes surprising him. "The city took some getting used to. But now…well, I like being a part of that pulse, that energy. In a way, New York is as wide-open and vast as this land. You just have to find the rhythm and go with it."

"Too fast-paced for me," Reed said, thinking they were straying back into personal territory. To lighten things, he asked, "How do Summer and Autumn like it?"

"They love it, too," April replied, laughing. "We all joke with our friends about how we left small towns with such big, famous names—Paris, Athens, and Atlanta—only to wind up in the biggest city of all—New York."

"I guess your friends do get a kick out of making fun of our slow, country ways."

"No, we don't allow that," she quickly retorted, an edge of pride in her tone. "Reed, you never did get that we loved our lives here in East Texas, but we all felt we had to get away, in order to…to become independent and sure-footed."

That statement had his skin itching, as if barn fleas had descended on him. "Seems you could have done that right here on the Big M."

"No, no, I couldn't," she said, giving him a slanted look. "I felt stifled *here,* Reed. I feel free in the city."

"Well, that just doesn't make a lick of sense, April."

"I know," she replied, her head down as Daisy picked her way over a bed of rocks and shrubs. "It's hard to explain, hard to reason, but Daddy depended on me so much. I couldn't replace my mother, Reed. And I knew he'd never marry again. I had to get away."

Hearing the fear in her words, hearing that soft plea for understanding, Reed got it for the first time. April hadn't been running from him, necessarily. She'd been trying to spread her wings and get out from under the grief her father had carried in every cell of his being. "It must have been hard for you, having to see him that way, day in and day out."

"It was. So when Summer and Autumn jokingly suggested we all head east, I jumped at the chance. I was the one who convinced them to just try living in New York with me for a while."

He wanted to ask her why she'd turned to her cousins instead of him, the man she supposedly loved. But he guessed staying here with him would only have moved her from one dependent man to another. Maybe she was afraid because of what she'd seen happen to her father. Reed told himself he wouldn't have smothered her, but in his heart he knew he certainly would have cherished her, and he probably would have been overly protective.

Instead he only nodded. "New York—about as far away from East Texas as a body can get. And you've all been there ever since."

"Yes, although I think they'd both like to come home more than me, truth be told. They don't say that, but I've gotten hints that Summer has been thinking about that for a while. She had a very bad relationship end recently and I think she's longing for the safe structure of her hometown and her family. Or at least the structure her grandparents gave her, growing up."

"Why didn't she come home with you? She could visit Athens easily."

"Work. She's a counselor at our neighborhood YWCA in New York. She loves her work, but it's so easy to become burned out, dealing with inner-city families on a daily basis. Their lifestyles are sure different from what we're used to."

"I can only imagine," Reed replied. Then he asked a question that he hoped April wouldn't take the wrong way. "Do y'all have a church in New York?"

April quickly nodded. "Oh, yes. We all attend a lovely brownstone chapel not far from our apartment."

"I'm glad to know you kept the faith, even in big ol' New York City."

She gave him a measuring look. "Preaching to me, Reed Garrison?"

"No, just checking to make sure you haven't completely changed on me."

"I'll have you know there are lots of Christians in the big city."

"Glad to hear it."

She gentled Daisy to a slow walk. "Reed, I've never lost my faith in the Lord. Summer and Autumn and I all know that God is in control of all things. We don't hide our Christianity. We celebrate it. That's why Summer just broke things off with her boyfriend. He resented her faith, used it to taunt her. She wouldn't allow him to undermine something so important in her life. None of us would do that."

Reed nodded, sensing from her strong tone that maybe April had been through a similar situation. But he refused to ask her about that. "Summer always was the most sensitive of all of you."

"Yes, and Autumn is the most practical. Which leaves me, the shallow one, right?"

He turned to face her, then reached across to hold Daisy's rein. "I never said you were shallow, April. I might have thought that at one time, but now—"

"Maybe now you're finally seeing the real me, at last."

Reed was just about to comment on that and tell her that he'd like to get to know the real her, when suddenly Daisy whinnied and started kicking her front legs in the air. "Whoa, there, girl," Reed said, glad he still had a grip on the mare's reins.

"What on earth?" April said, settling the horse down with soothing words and a tight tug on the reins.

Reed dismounted and stared down at where Daisy had landed. "Glass," he said, shaking his head.

"Daisy must have stepped in it," April replied, hopping down to stand beside him. "Is she hurt?"

Reed calmed the animal, then stood facing Daisy. He moved his hands down the mare's front right leg to the fetlock, then leaned in to support the animal as he pulled Daisy's right front foot up. "Yep. Got a chunk of bottle glass embedded, right there." He pointed to a tender spot just inside Daisy's shoe. "No wonder she got spooked." Then he motioned toward Jericho. "I've got a farrier's knife in my saddle bag. If you don't mind getting it for me, I'll try to see if I can clean her foot at least."

April did as he asked, quickly finding the instrument and bringing it to Reed. She watched as he moved the knife around Daisy's hoof and shoe. As Reed worked, a rounded piece of thick gold-colored glass fell out from Daisy's hoof. "Looks like the chunk hit her right against the frog, then got stuck near the shoe. She's gonna be bruised for a few days."

"We need to get her home and let someone look at this."

Reed nodded his agreement. "I can put some duct tape over it for now. Then I'll call the vet."

April searched his saddlebag for the tape. "You travel prepared, Mr. Garrison."

"Yes, ma'am. You never know what you'll need out here alone. Have to take care of our horses."

April gave him a proud look. "I feel good, knowing you've been watching out for things around here. I'm sure my father appreciates it."

"Just doing my job," Reed replied, embarrassed and touched by her compliment. He'd jump through fire to help Stuart Maxwell. And his daughter.

"I guess we'd better walk her home," April said, patting Daisy on the nose. "It's gonna be okay, pretty girl."

Reed glanced around. "Looks like someone has been camping out here. And maybe drinking something stronger than a soda. They must have had a good time, breaking up all these empty bottles."

"Trespassers, just one more thing to worry about," April said. Then she glanced up at him. "I'll need to ride home with you."

Reed heard the hesitancy in her words. "Well, if you'd rather walk—"

"No, no. It's a long way. I don't mind riding shotgun."

His gazed moved over her face. "Are you sure?"

"Of course I'm sure. How many times have we ridden double over the years?"

Reed remembered those times. Too vividly. "Well, let's get going," he said, the edge to his voice making him sound curt. "We'll have to go slow for Daisy's sake."

When he had April settled behind him in the saddle,

he tried to ignore the sweet smell of her hair and the way her hands automatically held to him. Instead, he concentrated on the mess they'd just left.

"We'll have to find out who's been having field parties out in our back pasture," he said over his shoulder. "Probably kids out for kicks."

"Yes," she answered, her tone so soft, Reed almost didn't hear it.

He had to wonder—was being this close causing her as much discomfort as it was him?

Discomfort and joy, all mixed up in the same confusing package. But then, that described his feelings for April exactly.

Lord, I need your help. I need to show restraint and self-control. Please help me to do and say the right things. Lord, just help me out here in any way you can.

The spring wind whipped across the open pasture in a gentle whispering, as if in answer to Reed's silently screaming prayers.

Chapter Five

⌒

While Reed took care of Daisy's foot with a medical boot until the vet could get there, April immediately went to see her father. As she left the warm sunny day outside and waited for her eyes to adjust to the dark recesses of the back part of the house, she said a prayer for her father.

"Lord, he never...my father never went to church with my mother. Show him the way home, Lord. Don't let him go without accepting You into his heart."

Lynette Proctor stepped out of the bedroom. "Oh, I thought I heard a voice out here. Are you okay, honey?"

April looked at the husky nurse, wondering if she could trust the woman. "I was saying a prayer for my father."

"Oh, how sweet." Tears pricked at Lynette's brown eyes. "If it makes you feel any better, I read to him from the Bible every night. I don't know if he can hear me or not, but I read anyway. Helps to pass the time, and it sure can't hurt for both of us to get a lesson."

"I appreciate that," April replied. "And I'm sorry about yesterday."

Lynette ran a work-worn hand over her clipped gray hair. "What in the world are you talking about?"

"I was rather rude to you—"

"Think nothing of that, sugar. You wouldn't believe what I've seen. Death brings out a lot of emotions, both good and bad. And when it's like this, where we have to wait—well, I've seen catfights right over a dying soul, people arguing over the will already, things like that. Family is very important, but some families just don't realize what they've got until it's too late."

April looked into the darkened room. "We've only got each other, my father and I."

Lynette's big eyes widened. "Oh, I wouldn't say that. Your father has had a host of friends coming and going since word got out that he's in a bad way. They say a man can tell how rich he is by his friends. He might be dying, but he was a very wealthy man, friend-wise. He can't take all his millions with him, but he sure can take those kind words and the way his friends have held his hand and told him how much they love him. He can take that to his grave."

April felt hot tears filling her own eyes. "Thank you, Mrs. Proctor. That's very reassuring."

"Call me Lynette, honey." Then she pulled an envelope out of her pocket. Oh, I almost forgot. Flora told me to be sure and give you this."

April took the cream-colored envelope, recognizing the fancy paper and the engraved address. "An invitation to the Cattle Baron's Ball. Daddy always loved this event when my mother was alive."

She thought back over the pasture full of longhorns she and Reed had seen while riding the land. The lanky herds of spotted cattle had milled around, getting fat off the bounty of the lush range, their droopy eyes and elegant long horns giving them a distinctive, sullen look. Reed had pointed out Old Bill, their senior sire bull, and several calves who'd been born recently. The Big M was famous for its quality, pure-bred longhorns. Just one more thing that tradition demanded of April. She'd have to keep that going long after her father was gone.

"I suppose I'll have to get used to attending such events," she said, wishing her father could guide her on what to do.

Lynette squinted at her. "Well, Flora said something about your attending in honor of your father."

April frowned and shook her head. "Oh, I couldn't. Not with Daddy so sick."

Lynette patted April's hand, then shrugged. "Just passing the message on. Flora really wanted you to have this. Maybe you should talk to her about it."

"I will," April said, rubbing a finger over the envelope. "And I'll send my regrets."

So many regrets, April thought as she went into her father's bedroom and sank down in the chair next to his bed. Stuart was sleeping, his breathing labored and irregular. The doctors had explained his condition, and how he would slowly deteriorate, but April still had a hard time accepting that the frail figure lying in this bed was her father.

"Hi, Daddy," she said, her voice squeaky and husky. "It's April. I went for a ride with Reed." She reached over to grasp her father's hand, noticing the bulging veins and the age spots covering his hand. "We have such a beautiful place here, Daddy." She looked at his hand and felt it move slightly. Maybe he could hear her. "I don't know what to do, Daddy. I'm not sure I'm up to the task of running the Big M. But I won't ever let it go, I promise. Somehow, I'll find a way. I promise you that."

Tears spilled from her eyes as she realized the implications of the promise she'd just made. Leaning over, April laid her head on her father's soft, clean-smelling cotton blanket. "Don't leave me, Daddy. If you'd only get well, I'd do anything. I know I left you once, when you begged me to stay. And now…it's too late to change that. But…if we just had one more chance."

Holding her father's hand tightly with both of hers, April sobbed, her grief and her regret so overwhelming that she didn't think she'd make it through the next few weeks.

Then she felt Stuart's hand moving beneath hers. Surprised, she raised her head. "Daddy?"

With a ragged effort, her father tugged his hand away from her grasp. Disappointment surged through April's system. Was he turning away from her pleas?

But Stuart didn't turn away. Instead, he opened his eyes and reached up to her face, his bony fingers trailing through her dark curls like wisps of smoke. "Love you, Sweet Pea," he managed to say, the words coming long and hard and labored. "Trust you." Then he dropped his hand and fell back asleep.

April stayed at his bedside, a smile on her face in spite of the tears she shed.

Reed sat at the big oak desk he'd bought from an antiques store in Dallas. He'd put it in the roomiest of the extra bedrooms of what used to be the Big M guest house. This room had a view of the rolling green pastures and the well-stocked fish pond at the back of the property. He could see the big house from here, too. He could see the arched double window of April's upstairs bedroom, located right over the swimming pool. That window caused memories to come swirling back, like moondust caught in spiderwebs.

Maybe he was caught in a web, too. A web of need and longing for something that could never be. He turned to the big collie lying at his feet. "Well, Shep, old boy, she's back and I'm in big trouble. Any suggestions?"

Shep yawned, stretched his front paws across the Aztec-style rug covering the hardwood floor and grunted a reply.

"You're no help," Reed retorted. "No help at all."

The phone rang then, making Shep bark and Reed jump. "Man, I gotta get a grip."

"Reed, it's Richard Maxwell. I was just calling to check on things at the Big M."

"Hello, Richard," Reed said, glad to hear from Stuart's brother. "I guess you've heard April's home?"

"Yeah, the girls e-mail back and forth. They're pretty worried about her and Stu. How's she taking things?"

"Not too good. She's devastated about her father, of course. And she's not sure about the future."

"Who is, these days? How's my brother?"

Reed filled Richard Maxwell in, wondering why the man hadn't called April directly. But then, the Maxwell brothers had come to depend on Reed lately to give them the truth, straight-up, about the ranch and their brother. So Reed told Richard the truth. "I don't expect him to last much longer, Richard."

"We're making arrangements to come over," Richard told him. "I tracked James down and he and I hope to be there by the weekend. And I might tell the girls to come on down, too."

"That would be good. I know Summer and Autumn would be a big help to April. You know how close they all are."

"I sure do," Richard said, laughing. "Three peas in a pod, that's what we've always called them."

"It's hard on April, being here alone," Reed said.

"She's not alone, boy. She has you. You always could talk her down—and we all know how high-strung she can be at times."

"I hear that," Reed said, a smile creeping across his lips. "I'm just not sure I can be of much help—"

"You're solid, Reed," Richard replied. "Stuart knows that. That's why he's set such high store in you."

"I appreciate the vote of confidence," Reed replied, not feeling confident at all.

They talked a few more minutes about the day-to-day operations of the ranch, then Richard said goodbye. Reed didn't mind that Stuart's brothers were keeping close tabs on things at the Big M. He wouldn't have it any other way. After all, a lot was at stake here. The livestock, the land, the oil leases, the acreage, the house and surrounding buildings—it all added up to a big amount of responsibility and a huge amount of revenue. But it was more than the wealth. The Big M was home. It always would be home.

At least, to Reed.

But would April want to make it home again?

That question nagged at Reed as he worked at his computer, filing away bills and keying in information on the spring calving season. It was a busy time, both for him personally, with his spot of land and his own growing herd, and for the Big M.

"I sure don't need any..."

Distractions. He was going to say distractions. But April Maxwell was much more than a distraction. She was like that piece of glass that had found its way into Daisy's foot. April was embedded inside Reed's heart. And he had the big bruise to prove it.

Reed sat, watching the sun set over the hills. He sat there and prayed for guidance and strength as he stared up at those windows—windows that shielded the woman he loved.

"Hi, girls."

April typed the greeting to her two cousins back in New York. She knew that they'd read the e-mail together, as they did each night when they all gathered around the computer, taking turns checking their personal messages, then sharing the really good ones with each other.

What would she do without Summer and Autumn? She was the oldest by two years, but her cousins were both very sensible and mature. Summer was more temperamental and subject to fiery outbursts of temper, while Autumn was always calm and in control. But they both felt the Maxwell loyalty just as much as April did. She had to wonder how different their lives might be if she hadn't dragged them to New York with her all those years ago.

Wishing they were both here, she continued her update.

Daddy is about the same today. But he did something so very sweet. I was talking to him, crying, wishing he'd just get up out of that bed. And he heard me! He touched his hand to my face and told me he loved me.

It was so special. My daddy never was one for words, you know. I don't remember the last time he said that to me. It took all of his effort, but now I know he has forgiven me for leaving him. I should have never done that. I love my life in New York with y'all, but now I'm wishing I'd just stayed here and worked somewhere closer to home—Dallas had a lot of potential. I knew that. Houston, even. Why did I have to go all the way across the country? Okay, I did it because Reed was pressing me to settle down. He got too close, too fast. I needed to be independent. I felt closed in by so much grief and pain. I guess I was afraid to let go of my heart after losing Mother. I can see that now. Funny how time causes us to look back and just all of a sudden see things so much more clearly.

I know what you're saying to each other—that it was our plan, our dream. We had to stick together. We had to show our formidable fathers that we could strike out on our own, just as they all had. Even now, all these years later, it's so hard to admit that we were all running from something.

We succeeded, but is it enough? Is it enough that I left Reed and my daddy behind? Is it enough that Summer had to go through that terrible relationship with Brad Parker in order to realize her real worth? Or that she still can't make a commitment to anyone because of how her parents left her on her grandmother's doorstep? Is it enough, Autumn, that you always have to have concrete proof of anything—that you can't go on faith alone, even in your love relationships, even in knowing that Summer and I love and support you, no matter what? No wonder none of us can find a man. We've set our sights way too high and we've forgotten what really matters. I guess all of this has got me thinking about things—how do we know we've made the right choices in life? Have we really listened for God's voice, or have we just listened to what we wanted, what we thought we needed, whether it hurt others or not?

I walked away from Daddy's grief and Reed's overbearing love. Summer, you've been turning to the wrong men all your life because you don't want to be abandoned ever again. And yet, they've all let you down, especially Brad. And Autumn, well, girl, you have to have too many details, too many charts and graphs in life. We all need to loosen up and turn back to the Lord. We need to go on faith and let it all work itself out.

Oh, I didn't mean to preach. Really I didn't. I'm just so confused right now. Did I tell y'all I went riding with Reed this morning? Did I tell y'all that I think I still love him?

I have to turn in soon, but I want to go and sit with Daddy for a while. Don't take what I said the wrong way, please. I'll be okay. We will always be okay, because we have each other. I wish y'all were here, but I know you have work to do—other obligations.

Other obligations kept me away from home for so long. Now, I have only one obligation. I have to get through watching my father die. Summer, maybe you should call Uncle James. He is your father, after all. Maybe you could make amends, make your peace with him. Before it's too late.

"Wow." Autumn Maxwell turned to her cousin after she finished reading the e-mail from April. "I've never heard April talk like that. She must really be depressed."

Summer shifted on the deep-cushioned red couch they'd found at a second-hand store in Soho. "Yeah, to even suggest I get in touch with my daddy. She's obviously not thinking very clearly. She knows where I stand on that issue."

"But…she's looking at it from a different angle now, honey. Uncle Stuart is dying. April's thinking your daddy, or even mine, could die, too. And with so much left unsaid."

Summer tossed back her long blond hair. "Some things are better left unsaid. You know that, Autumn."

"But I'm beginning to wonder if that philosophy is so wise," Autumn replied, hoping she sounded encouraging. "What would it hurt—"

Summer hopped off the couch, her black yoga pants dragging against her bare feet. "It would hurt *me,* so let's change the subject, please."

Autumn sent her cousin a questioning look, but all she got in return was Summer's retreating back and the slamming of her bedroom door.

Autumn sighed, and turned back to the computer.

Hi, April. I don't think Summer's ready for any sage advice just yet, sweetie. But I understand how you must be feeling. It must be so hard to watch your father die. I am sending you hugs and prayers. And I promise, if you just say the word, we will both come home, whether Summer wants to do so or not. She might not want to face her parents yet, but she will do anything to help you get through this. Promise.

Now, tell me all about your ride with Reed. I want details, good and bad. And I want to know the exact minute you realized you still loved him. I want to know what that must feel like. I've never been in love, you know. I have to live vicariously through you, I reckon.

So, tell me everything. Is Reed as good-looking as ever? Or even better?

April had to laugh at her cousin's inquisitive nature. Autumn was all business during the day. She was a CPA at an exclusive Manhattan firm—a firm that her powerful father had managed to get her an interview with, an interview that Autumn had protested at first—that independence thing again. But Autumn had taken things from there and she'd fought hard to make her father proud. She worked long hours, as well as most weekends, and she barely had a social life. But Autumn said she liked things that way. April believed that Autumn secretly wanted to break loose and live a little, but she just didn't know how. Autumn was the quintessential good girl, right down to her oh-so-proper white cotton pj's. But Autumn was also a very good listener. Her cousin could be very precise in getting to the heart of a matter.

And right now, April's own heart was being torn apart by her father's sickness and the sure acceptance that she still loved Reed Garrison.

It's a long story, she typed. I hope you're not sleepy tonight. And yes, Reed is even more gorgeous than he was when I left him. He's mature and a bit weathered, but still very attractive.

And there's more. Daddy wants me to take over the Big M. On a permanent basis. That would mean I'd have to stay here. Near Reed. I don't know if I'm ready for that responsibility. I need advice, cousin. Good advice.

I don't know what to do.

April signed off the computer and stood up to look out the windows of her room. She looked toward the east. She could see the dark shape of the brick guest house Reed now lived in. It was so like Reed to buy a house that had a clear view of the Big M's main house. It was so like him to stand guard over this ranch.

She saw the light from a single lamp burning into the night, and she wondered if Reed was down there, looking up at her window. She wondered if he was thinking about her right now.

April turned from the window and crawled into the crisp, sweet-smelling sheets of her bed, secure in the warm feeling of knowing Reed was nearby.

Ever watchful.

He'd always been right here, waiting.

But how long could a man wait for a woman who was so frightened of giving her heart away?

Chapter Six

"Vandals?"

Reed nodded at his father's one-worded question.

"Yep. It's been happening a lot lately."

Sam Garrison held tightly to his stallion's reins, then glanced down at the leftover campfire. "Charred beer bottles. Cigarette butts. Kids, maybe?"

"Has to be," Reed responded, walking Jericho toward the broken fence wire near the main highway. "They must be sneaking in off the main road. Probably parking their cars in that clump of trees just around the curve to the Big M."

"How much damage have you found so far?" his father asked, squinting underneath his worn straw cowboy hat.

"April and I saw the same thing about two days ago, on our ride around the property near the river. Daisy got a sliver of glass from that little campfire. She's still bruised. Stepped on some broken, burned-out bottle glass. Now this. I'd say some of the locals are having field parties on Big M property."

"Did you ever do things like this when you were

young, son?" Sam asked, a grin splitting his bronze-hued face.

"Did you?" Reed countered, his own grin wry. Then he shook his head. "I didn't have to trespass, remember? I was lucky enough to live on the Big M."

Sam tipped his hat at that comment. "And lucky enough to be just about the same age as the heir apparent."

"I don't recall mentioning April," Reed said, his grin dying down into ashes, just like this campfire had.

"Didn't have to mention her. She's written all over your face."

"It shows that much?" Reed asked, dropping his head down in mock shame.

"Son, I'm not a rocket scientist," Sam said, "but your mama and I know you still love April. Your mother thinks that's why you've never found anyone else."

"In spite of Mom's efforts to hook me up with every single lady at church and beyond?"

"Yep. Your ma loves you and…well, she wants some grandchildren. So do I. You know, we ain't getting any younger."

"Look mighty fit and young to me," Reed said, hoping to sway the conversation away from April.

But he should have known better. His father was as shrewd as they came, a real cowboy poet of sorts, a literary man who could quote Emerson and Thoreau and could still ride a horse and herd cattle better than any other man on the Big M.

"I'm fit, all right," Sam replied, slapping a hand to his trim stomach. "But fit don't cut it when a man's wishing for the next generation to carry on."

"I'm carrying on for you just fine, I thought," Reed said, frowning.

"That you are. Working the Big M and your own place. Makes a man proud. But…you're kind of stubborn in the love department. You ought to go after that girl, show her that you were wrong all those years ago."

"Me?" Reed shouted the word so loudly, Jericho did a little prance of irritation. "Me?" he repeated with a low growl. "Maybe your memory is getting rusty, Daddy. April was the one who had to get away from this place and away from me. I couldn't very well hightail it to New York and kidnap her. I don't want a woman who won't come willingly to me."

"Then make her *want* you, boy," his father said. "I had to do that with your mama."

"Oh, really. And here I thought she was the one who caught you."

"I let her think that, of course. But your mama was as prim and proper as they come. Still is. Had to woo her all kinds of ways. By the time I got through courting her, she was as strung up as a baby calf on branding day."

"Not a pretty picture, Pa," Reed said, shaking his head as he chuckled. "Don't think Mama would appreciate being compared to a calf."

"Well, she's certainly called me a stubborn old bull a few times," his father countered in a testy tone. Then he tilted his head. "Besides, we were talking about your love life, not mine. Mine's been just fine for close to thirty-five years."

Reed pinched his nose with two fingers, willing the tension in his head to go away. "Whereas mine is nonexistent, right?"

"Got that right, yes sir."

"Would you listen if I told you with the utmost respect to kindly stay out of my business?"

"Probably not." Sam waved his hand in frustration. "You need to get on with it or get over it, son."

"I'm trying," Reed said in a ground-out tone that made him sound more mad than he really was. "I'm trying."

Sam shook his hat and put it back on. "Tough times, these. Hard to watch one of my best friends dying right before my eyes. And one of the finest men in all of Texas, at that. Guess I shouldn't be pushing you back toward April. That girl's got enough to worry about without having you underfoot."

"That's why I'm trying to play it safe," Reed said, glad his father understood that at least. "I can't push her or rush her, Daddy. Not now, when she's so scared and hurt. I tried that the last time, and she bolted like a scared pony. She's…well, I've never considered April as fragile, but right now, that's exactly what she is. I don't want to be the one to break her."

Sam urged his horse forward. "Then be gentle, son. Show some understanding. You always did go in with guns blazing, in any situation. Might want to curve that domineering gene you obviously inherited from your ma's side of the family."

"Yeah, right," Reed said, smiling at his father. "You can blame it on Mom, but we both know you're as mulish and demanding as they come when you want to be."

"Who, me?" His father feigned innocence by rising his bushy brows and scrunching up his ruddy nose.

"Guess I got it double," Reed reasoned as he followed his father back toward home.

"You could say that," Sam agreed, his laughter echoing out over the pastures and trees.

Reed loved his parents with a fierceness that made his heart ache, and he loved what they had between them, that strong sense of loyalty and friendship that had been tempered by faith and family, through hard times and good times. He wanted that kind of love, that kind of commitment for himself.

And he wanted it with only one woman.

As they neared the lane leading back to the big house, Reed couldn't help but look up at that arched window. He hadn't talked to April today. He'd wanted to give her some time with her father. Time alone. Precious time. He'd wanted to give her so much, but he'd held back.

He was learning restraint, at long last. He was learning patience, at long last. He was learning what his wise father had been trying to tell him. That old cliché was true. Sometimes, in order to win back something you loved, you had to let it go. Well, he'd tried that route. And he'd learned to be patient the hard way through all those years. It hadn't brought April back. But she was back now, under sad circumstances. And this time, he wouldn't make any mistakes. He'd be patient, he'd be gentle, he'd be steady and sure. Reed wouldn't use her grief and despair to bring her back to him. That would be wrong, so wrong. But he'd be nearby if she needed him.

Lord, let it be right. Let it happen in your own good time, as Mama would tell me.

Grief was no way to start a relationship, or to bring April back to his way of thinking.

So he'd keep on waiting. And hoping. It was the only thing he could do.

* * *

Laura Garrison busied herself with setting the table in the kitchen of the big house. April helped her, putting out silverware and tea glasses, glad for the quiet strength Reed's mother possessed.

"I'm so glad you came by," April said, remembering all the times Reed's mother had been a guiding force in her life, especially after April's own mother had died. "And I insist that you and Mr. Sam stay and help me eat all this food."

"I wouldn't mind visiting with you," Laura said, her big brown eyes lighting up. "That is, if you're up to company."

"I could use the company," April admitted. "I've spent all day with Daddy, reading to him, talking to him. Sometimes, he opens his eyes and…it's almost as if he's smiling up at me. Other times, he just sleeps."

Laura finished basting the baked chicken. "The rolls are almost ready," she said as she came to help April with the salad and vegetables. "I hate that you're having to go through this, sugar. Stuart has always been our rock, strong and steady, a good leader with a heart of gold."

"That heart is old and worn-out now," April said, her hands gripping the cool tiles of the counter. She'd sent Flora and Horaz back to their house to rest and enjoy their own dinner. They needed a good night's sleep and some peace and quiet. Sam Garrison was sitting with her father while she and Laura prepared dinner. "Everyone here is so devoted to him. That has brought me a lot of comfort."

"We all love your daddy," Laura said, her shiny bob of brown hair flowing across her forehead with a defined slant. "And we all encouraged him to give up that bottle. But he just didn't have the strength. It's been hard on all of us. That's why I wanted to come and see you. We're all in this together, April."

April reached out to hug her friend. "Thank you so much. And please, stay for dinner and…why don't you call Reed, too? It'll do me good to have y'all for company. I can't stand the loneliness."

"Are you sure?" Laura asked.

April knew what she was asking. Did she really want Reed there?

"I'm sure." April nodded. "You don't have to walk on eggshells around me, Miss Laura. Reed and I, we've made a truce of sorts. Now is certainly not the time to bring up past hurts and regrets."

"*Do* you have regrets?" Laura asked, her eyes clear and full of understanding. Then she put a hand to her mouth. "I'm so sorry. I shouldn't have asked that."

"It's okay," April replied. "And the answer is yes. I regret that I was selfish enough to leave my father when he really needed me to stay. And I regret that I hurt Reed."

"You had to do what you thought best," Laura said with a shrug.

It was so like Reed's mom not to pass judgment. But April knew Laura Garrison loved her son first and foremost.

"I had to get away, yes," April said, hoping to explain. "I had to grow and expand my horizons, so to speak. But mostly, I knew I could never make Daddy happy. Not in the way my mother made him happy. And I've never admitted this, but I was so afraid I'd never be able to make Reed happy, either. I… I didn't think

I could settle down and be a ranch wife. I'm not like you, Miss Laura."

Laura's chuckle surprised April. "Honey, do you really think any woman is prepared to be a ranch wife? It's a hard job. Being a wife and a mother are hard jobs, no matter where you live. But if you love someone enough—"

"You make sacrifices," April finished. "I wasn't ready for that sacrifice."

"Well, you know, Reed could have met you halfway."

April shook her head. "What? Should I have made him move to New York with me? I hardly think Reed would have been happy living in the big city."

"No," Laura agreed. "But he could have fought harder to…to try a long-distance relationship."

"It would never have worked," April replied, sure as rain that Reed would have been miserable. "I couldn't ask that of him."

"You never tried," Laura pointed out with a soft smile.

"I didn't want to force him to wait for me."

"Honey, he's still waiting," Laura said. "Think about that. And if I know my son, I think he'll keep on waiting, because he's not going to get between you and the grief you're feeling right now."

That revelation hit April with all the force of being thrown from a horse. *Was* Reed truly still waiting for her? She'd wondered that so many times, had even hoped that might be the case. Then another thought even more formidable hit her.

Was she still waiting for Reed, too?

That question nagged at April all through dinner. Reed's parents were pleasant and upbeat, keeping the conversation light. They talked about the warm spring weather, about the alfalfa growing in the pastures, about the livestock moving through the fields and paddocks. They talked about April's job in New York and asked questions about life in the big city.

And while they talked, Reed sat silent and still, a soft smile flickering across his wide mouth now and then. He toyed with his tea glass and ate his chicken with the relish of a hearty appetite, his eyes settling now and then on April.

Each time he looked at her, something shifted and slipped inside her, like river water gliding over a rockbed. She thought back over the years she'd been away and wondered how she'd ever managed to leave him. Was it the grief eating away at her? Or was it the regret?

I have to be sure, Lord, she thought. *I have to be sure that if I decide to stay here and do my father's bidding, that it's for all the right reasons. I don't want to hurt Reed again. And I can't take any more hurt myself. Help me, Lord. What is Your will in all of this?*

"Ready for some dump cake?" Laura asked now.

"I'm always ready for cake," Sam replied, winking at April.

Laura got up, but Reed put a hand on his mother's arm.

"I'll get it, Mom. Coffee, too?"

"Sure," Laura said, the surprise in her voice sparkling through her eyes.

"Want to help me?" Reed asked April.

She glanced up at him, wondering what he was up to. But his eyes held only a warm regard that made her feel secure and safe. "Yes. I'll bring the coffee if you get the plates for the cake."

"I think we can handle that," Reed said. She saw the warning look he sent to his two curious parents. "You two behave while we're getting dessert."

"Us? We'll just sit here and let your ma's fine cooking settle while you young folks do the rest of the work," his father replied, his eyes twinkling.

"They are so cute together," April said, not knowing what else to say.

The laughter and whispers coming from the table across the arched, tiled kitchen washed over her like a familiar rain. She loved Reed's parents and had always wished her own parents could have had such a solid, stable, long-term relationship. Instead, Stuart and his Celia had had more of a roller-coaster ride of intense love and obsession, followed by bouts of anger and fire— Until death had ended it all, leaving both April and her father shocked and devastated.

She could see now that her mother's sudden death had been at the core of her fears. She was beginning to realize that maybe that was the main reason she'd been so afraid to give in to her love for Reed. That was why she'd run away. She couldn't deal with something so rich and intense just after losing her mother. What if she lost Reed, too?

You did lose him, she reminded herself as she gathered coffee cups and cream and sugar onto a long porcelain serving tray adorned with sunflowers and wheat designs.

"You look mighty serious there," Reed said over her shoulder, grabbing the coffee carafe before she could put it on the tray. "I'll take this over, then come back for the cake and plates."

April watched as he set the coffee carafe on the table.

He had that long-stride walk of a cowboy, that laid-back easy stride of a man comfortable in his own skin.

And he looked good in that skin, too.

Stop it, she told herself as she looked away from Reed and back to the heavy mugs she'd put on the tray. When Reed came back to the counter, she looked up at him, then asked him in a low voice, "Why have you never married?"

From the look in his eyes, she wished immediately she could take that question back. But it was out there now, hovering over them like a swirl of dust, stifling and heavy.

If the question threw him as much as it had her, he hid it well behind a wry smile. But he didn't miss a beat in answering. "I reckon I'm still waiting for the right woman to come along," he whispered.

"Think you'll ever find her?"

He leaned close, the scent of leather and spice that always surrounded him moving like a wind storm through April's senses. "Oh, I found the right woman a long time ago. But I'm still waiting for her to come around to my terms."

April's heart banged hard against her ribs. Her hands trembled so much, she had to hold on to one of the mugs in front of her. "What…what are your terms, Reed?"

His voice whispered with a rawhide scrape against her ear. "I only have one stipulation, actually. I want that woman to love me with all her heart. I want her to love me, only me, enough to stay by my side for a lifetime and beyond."

April looked up at him then and saw the love there in his stalking-cat eyes—the love and the challenge. "You don't ask for much, do you, cowboy?"

"Doesn't seem like much if you look at it the right way."

Then he turned and sauntered back to the table where his parents waited in questioning wide-eyed silence.

And April was left to look at the scene with a whole new perspective. And a whole new set of fears.

Chapter Seven

$\sim$

April came into the kitchen the next morning only to find Flora slumped in a chair, crying.

"What's wrong?" April said, rushing to the woman's side. "Is it—is it my father?"

She'd sat with him late into the night, pouring her heart out to him, telling him that she still loved Reed, only now she didn't think she deserved to be loved back. Telling him all about her fears and her reservations, her hopes and her dreams. She'd checked on him just minutes ago and Lynette had assured her he was sleeping.

"No, no, *querida,*" Flora said, reaching up a hand to April. "It's not your papa. It's…" She waved the other hand in the air. "It's Tomás. That boy is giving us so much trouble lately."

April breathed a sigh of relief only to see the concern in Flora's rich brown eyes. "What's Tomás doing that's so bad it would make you cry?"

Flora shook her head. "He shows no respect. His parents—they both work all day long—they let him run wild. No restraint. And that Adan—*élse malo*—he's mean, very mean. He's going to get in big, big trouble, that one." She lapsed into a string of Spanish, then went back to wringing her hands.

From what April could glean from Flora's rantings, she gathered Tomás and Adan had taken Horaz's pickup for a joyride and had been stopped by the sheriff for speeding. There was a hefty ticket to pay. And Horaz would probably have to be the one to pay it, since Tomás's parents were heavily in debt from overextending themselves.

"I'm sorry, Flora," April said, patting the distraught woman on the shoulder. "Do you want *me* to pay the fine?"

"No," Flora said, getting up to wipe her eyes on her gathered apron. "That wouldn't help. The boy needs to learn how to fix his own problems. He will work it off. His grandfather will see to that, even if my son thinks Tomás can do no wrong. No wrong for big football star."

April knew enough to understand the implications of that. High-school football was a very popular sport all over Texas. And Tomás was a gifted athlete, she deduced from everything she'd heard since coming home, which meant his other, less noble traits would sometimes be overlooked for the sake of winning the game. Unless he pushed things too far. "If Tomás rebels against authority too much, he might get kicked off the football team next season."

"Sí, sí," Flora replied. "This is what I try to tell my son. This is what Horaz tries to explain to Tomás. Heads of wood, those two. Heads—stubborn heads. *Loco.*"

April smiled at Flora's sputtering condemnations in spite of the seriousness of the situation. "I could try to talk to Tomás," she offered.

Flora grabbed April's hand. "You have too much—

too much to worry with. Tomás, he is my responsibility. Mine and his grandfather's, since we've been put in charge of him for the summer. His own parents are too busy to see the problems." Another harsh string of Spanish followed.

"I love Tomás, too, remember?" April replied, remembering how she used to take the young Tomás horseback-riding when she was a teenager. "What if I get Reed to talk to him? He looks up to Reed, or at least he used to when he was little."

Flora's eyes lit up. "*Sí,* Reed. Everyone looks up to Reed. And Tomás has heard the stories of Reed Garrison. Now there was a football star, that one. He never gave his parents any trouble. And he was the best in his day."

"Yes, he was," April replied, her memories of crisp autumn nights so real she thought she could smell the smoke from the bonfires, hear the words of the high-school song. And she could clearly see Reed's smiling, loving face from the crowd of padded players on a green field. He'd always searched for her in the cheerleading line, giving her a wave for promise and hope.

What had happened to that promise and hope?

"Will you ask him?"

Flora's plea brought April back into the here and now, all the memories gone in the blink of an eye.

"Of course," April said, wanting to reassure Flora. But just thinking of having to face Reed again after he had thrown down the gauntlet last night made her want to run and hide away in her room.

But April was done with running and hiding. Her father wasn't going to get out of that deathbed. Reed wasn't going to back down. She had to stand up and take responsibility for her actions and her mistakes. It was up to her now to make sure the Big M kept on going. And if that meant she'd have to counsel one of their own— she and Reed together—then so be it.

At least dealing with Tomás would take her mind off her father and her feelings for Reed.

"I'll call Reed right now," she told Flora. "Just let me have a cup of coffee first."

Flora hopped up, her hands fluttering in embarrassment. "I'm so sorry. I should have—"

"Don't be silly," April said, waving the woman back down. "I'll get both of us a cup of coffee. And maybe some of that wonderful cinnamon coffee cake you always have stashed around here."

Flora smiled at that. "Better with melted butter on it. You can slip it into the microwave. Or I can do that."

"You sit," April commanded. "I'll take care of breakfast."

She wasn't sure if she could actually eat, but if Flora's cooking didn't entice her, nothing would.

She thought about Reed again. She'd thought about Reed for most of the night. She wondered if her father had heard her talking about him last night, had understood how strong her feelings were. How scared she was to make that final step toward Reed, that step that meant family and home, total commitment, total surrender.

She had a feeling Reed wouldn't want it any other way, and why should she blame him for that? She longed for that kind of love herself, even if she was terrified to try it.

On the other hand, what about her job at Satire? She had responsibilities there, too. And she loved what she did there, the things she'd accomplished. She was good at her job. How could she walk away from something that she enjoyed, a career that gave her contentment and a measure of accomplishment? A career, she reminded herself, that oftentimes took control over her entire life, leaving her alone at the end of the day. When she looked back, if she hadn't had Summer and Autumn there with her in New York, she probably would have been lonely and miserable, in spite of the friends she'd made at work.

No, April told herself with a fierce denial, *coming home has just brought too many things to the surface. I can't just abandon my career. I can't do that.*

Bringing the coffee and food to the table where Flora sat, April put her own turmoil to rest for now and managed to smile over at the other woman. "I guess being a grandparent is just as hard as being a parent."

Flora nodded, took the coffee with a *"Gracias."* "You think once you raise them, everything will be okay. It's never okay. You worry." She pressed a hand to her heart. "You worry here, you hold them close, here, always."

"I guess my father worried about me, even when he knew I was doing all right in New York."

"Sí. He always talked about you. Very proud, that one. Always longed to see you. Especially when—"

She stopped short.

"Especially when he was drinking?" April asked, finishing Flora's unspoken thoughts.

Flora nodded, tears brimming her eyes again. "A good man, a very good man. But the drink—it made him say things he couldn't take back. Very sad."

April felt that sadness down to her very bones. So much time wasted, so much love lost. She didn't think she wanted that kind of love, the kind that made a powerful, virile man turn into a wasted-away skeleton of himself.

Did she love Reed too much? Could she ever accept that love, with all the stipulations it required?

Then she remembered Reed's words to her last night. *I only have one stipulation... Doesn't seem like much if you look at it the right way.*

I don't know the right way, Reed, she thought. *I don't know how to look at love without seeing the pain involved.*

She glanced over at Flora and found the woman's eyes closed and her lips moving. "Flora?"

"I pray," Flora said, her eyes still closed. "I pray for you and Mr. Stuart, and Reed and my Horaz. And especially for my Tomás." Then she opened her eyes and smiled. "God has already answered part of that prayer. You and Reed, you will see to my grandson, *si?*"

"*Sí,*" April replied, lifting her eyes to the heavens. "*I hear you, Lord,*" she said out loud.

Flora smiled and took a long sip of her coffee.

April wanted to see him.

Reed let that bit of information settle into a simmering stew inside his gut. It hurt to think about her. The physical pain of loving her was getting to him. It had been okay when she was off far away, across the country. Time, bitterness and distance had faded his pain, and the soft rage he'd felt at her leaving, into a kind of mellowed photo album of memories. Memories he'd hidden away until now.

And he hadn't helped matters by challenging her last night. He'd practically asked her to stay, right there in the kitchen, with his well-meaning parents watching in rapt awe. He'd almost blown it. Again.

"I'm needing some guidance here, Lord," he said aloud as he pulled his rumbling pickup into the sprawling side yard of the big house. *"I've got a nice, easy thing going here. I have my bit of land now, a place to call my own. I've worked hard these last few years. You have blessed my life, Lord. Only one thing was missing."*

And that one thing was now waiting for him out by the crystal-blue waters of the swimming pool. Ending his prayers on a silent plea for strength and restraint, Reed opened the wrought-iron gate leading to the back of the property. He found April waiting for him right where she said she'd be. For once.

She was wearing a golden-beige sleeveless pantsuit of some sort. Linen, his mother might say. Soft linen that flowed around her like a summer wind. Her jewelry reflected the same gold of her clothes, simmering and rich against her porcelain skin.

Reed had to stop and take in a breath. She looked like some noble ancient princess, sitting there on the chaise. Until he looked into her dark eyes.

"What's wrong?"

April gestured to the cushioned chair beside the umbrella table. "We need to talk."

Oh, boy. He didn't like that look in her eyes. The last time she'd told him they needed to talk, she'd already packed her bags for New York and just wanted to tell him goodbye.

He sank down in defeat, took off his hat and said, "So, talk."

"It's about Tomás," she said, letting out a breath with each word.

"Tomás?" Confused but relieved, Reed leaned forward. "What's up with Tomás?"

She handed him a glass of lemonade, then settled back on the chaise. "Flora is very upset with him." She told him the whole story then. "She wanted me to ask you to try to reason with him, tell him to take it easy and be careful. You know, a kind of man-to-man talk."

"Why me?" Reed asked. "And why do you look so sad and serious?"

She shrugged, causing her chunky jewelry to settle back around her neck. Reed eyed the pretty stones and glowing gold. "Everyone around here looks up to you, Reed. Flora thought you'd be the natural choice for the job. And if I look sad, well, I am. But that's not something for you to worry about. Flora needs your help right now."

He got up and paced around the rock-encrusted pool deck. "That's me. Good ol' Reed. Salt of the earth. The go-to man." For everyone except her, of course. Shrugging, he started to leave. "I'll talk to Tomás. He's supposed to be helping me with some fence work today anyway. Give us a chance to have a nice long chat."

"Are you angry at me?"

She was right behind him, so close he caught the whiff of her floral perfume. "No," he said with a long sigh. "I'm not angry at anyone. Just tired and confused, is all. And sad, just like you." He turned to face her, looked down at her dark curling hair, her big brown eyes, and her beautiful mouth, and felt the flare of that old flame, burning strong inside his heart.

Then he did something he would later call very stupid. He kissed her, right there in the broad open daylight, by the swimming pool, with the many windows of the long, rambling house open for all inside to see. It was a stupid move because he'd steeled himself to go slow, to take things easy. He didn't want to spook her.

She didn't seem spooked in his arms.

She kind of melted against him, her hands touching his hair as a soft sigh drifted between them. Her sigh. Or maybe it was his. Reed couldn't be sure. But he was very sure of one thing. And that one thing made his hard heart turn to mush.

April still loved him, too. This he knew with the instinct of a man who always knew what he wanted, even when he wasn't sure how to go about getting it. He aimed to find the right way to go about winning April back. For good.

With that declaration pumping through his head, he let her go and stared down at her, hoping he didn't seem too triumphant. "That…that wasn't supposed to happen," he said with a ragged breath. "I mean, we were discussing this situation with Tomás, right?"

She managed to nod. "Right. I'm not sure how—"

"I know how," he interrupted, one finger tracing a wayward curl of rich brown hair that had managed to find its way across her cheek. "One look, April. That's all it takes. One look and I remember everything. And I want to hold you, and protect you and kiss you."

He saw the fear rising up in her eyes like a mist coming in over the river. "We shouldn't—"

"I know. It's the wrong time. It's not fair to either of us. But there it is. We kissed each other, and, unless I'm mistaken, you enjoyed it just as much as I did."

She lowered her head, staring at the gently moving water in the serene pool. "Reed, we need to concentrate on my father right now. And all the problems on this ranch. The vandalism, and now this with Tomás." Then she looked back up at him. "But I've learned something, coming home. This place doesn't just run itself. A million little problems crop up each day. And I want to thank you for always…for helping my father through all of this. I know it hasn't been easy for you. You could have left—"

"I wanted to stay," he said, the old anger coming back to numb the joy he'd felt at having her back in his arms. "I will stay. No matter what happens. *This* is my home. This will always be *my* home. Is that clear, April?"

His own anger was reflected back at him through the haze of anger in her eyes. "Very clear, Reed." Then she turned to head back inside the house. "Just talk to Tomás. Flora and Horaz don't need to be worrying about him right now."

"Yes, ma'am." He tipped his hat and headed back to the gate.

So much for thinking she still loved him. She did, he knew that. But she wouldn't admit that to him, or to herself, either. She'd watch her father die, bury him, then she'd go right back to New York. Running scared again.

And she'd leave Reed here waiting, all over again.

Chapter Eight

You've got mail.

Summer called out to her cousin. "Hey, April's sent us an update. Want me to read it out loud?"

"Sure," Autumn said, distracted by the mound of paperwork in front of her. Tax time. It was a killer, but it paid the rent. And being a CPA for one of the largest accounting firms in New York meant she was right in the thick of things. Just the way she liked it. She liked numbers and charts. She liked proof. Everything had to add up, make sense. Only two more days of this intense tax season frenzy, and then she could relax a bit. Not that she ever actually relaxed.

"Go ahead, I'm listening," she called to Summer.

"Okay."

"'Daddy is about the same. Uncle Richard called Reed the other day, then called me. He hopes to come and visit this weekend. He said I should ask y'all to come home, but Autumn's surely busy right now. Maybe in a few weeks, if Daddy can last that long. If not, well, I guess y'all will have to come when things change, when he's gone. He looks so frail, so old. How did I let things get this bad?'"

Summer stopped reading. "No mention of *my* daddy, huh? No mention of Uncle James and Aunt Elsie. Of course, they're probably off on the yacht, unaware of anyone else but themselves."

"Your bitterness is showing," Autumn called.

"You think?"

"Just read me the rest, so I can get back to work."

Summer turned back to the computer.

"'Reed kissed me this morning.'"

That brought Autumn careening across the big lofty living room so fast, the magnolia-scented candles Summer always kept lit flickered from the stirring of air. "What?"

"Says so right here," Summer replied, pointing at the words on the screen. "Reed kissed April."

"Oh, my." Autumn sank down on a cushioned polka-dot footstool near Summer's chair. "What else does she say?"

"'We were by the swimming pool. It was mid-morning. He kissed me right there in the sunshine. And it felt as if we'd never been apart. I don't think this is smart right now, even if it felt so right. I have to think about Daddy. And did I tell y'all that Daddy thinks I'm home for good, that he expects me to stay here and run the Big M?'"

"Makes sense," Autumn murmured. "She will inherit it after he's gone. I mean, Daddy and Uncle James will get their parts, but they both gave up running the Big M long ago. And Uncle Stuart is the oldest. She's his daughter. Makes sense to me that he'd leave the majority of the ranch holdings to his only heir."

"Shouldn't we be jealous or something?" Summer asked.

Autumn slapped her on the arm. "Of what? Our parents have just as much loot as Uncle Stuart. And we're not hurting, either."

"I was just teasing," Summer said, sticking out her tongue. "I don't want any of it, anyway. Besides, my parents are too busy spending their part to worry about actually thinking about *my* future."

Autumn scowled at her cousin. "You need therapy."

"I don't need some overpaid shrink to tell me that my parents don't care about me," Summer retorted. "Now, can we get back to worrying about April?"

"Sure," Autumn replied, more worried about Summer. She had a chip on her shoulder that seriously needed shaking. But Autumn wouldn't be the one to do it. "Go on," she said, nudging Summer. "Keep reading."

"'I don't know what to do. I planned to return to New York and Satire. I've built up a career there and I have a good chance of getting a promotion when we break into ready-to-wear this fall.'"

"Head of ready-to-wear marketing," Summer said, nodding. "She'd be so good at getting Satire's ready-to-wear off the ground. Trendy new threads and upscale department stores—stock should go right through the roof. Glad I invested early."

"It would mean lots of traveling to all the various stores," Autumn said. "All over the country and around the world. And I'm the one who told you to invest early, so you're welcome. We both should make some money off this one."

"How can she run the ranch and do that, too?" Summer shot back, ignoring her cousin's other remarks.

"What does she say?"

"'I don't think I can do both—run this place and keep my job, let alone get a promotion.'"

Summer jabbed the computer. "Told you."

"Just keep reading," Autumn said, scanning the words on the screen. "I've got to get back to work."

Summer turned and started reading again.

"'I'm in such a fix. But all of that aside, I have to be near Daddy right now. I talk to him every night, tell him all the things I wished I'd said before. I'm not sure he can hear me, but it feels so good to pour my heart out to him. Why did I wait so long? Why did I let myself fall back in love with Reed? I've realized that all this time, he's been waiting for me to come back, and now that I'm here, it's for all the wrong reasons. I'm home to watch my father die. So Reed is being kind and patient and undemanding, but I've also realized that maybe, just maybe, I've been waiting for Reed all these years, too. I guess I always thought he'd come for me, you know? That somehow, he'd come to New York and tell me he wanted me back home, with him. Isn't that silly?'"

"She's completely stressed," Summer said, finishing the e-mail. "Maybe I should go there, be with her. She's getting too caught up in memories of her first love. That's dangerous. She shouldn't get her hopes up."

Autumn stared at her cousin. "What's wrong with a little hope? Uncle Stu is dying. And she still loves Reed. What's wrong with hoping that they might actually get to be together?"

Summer jumped up, headed for the kitchen. "I just wouldn't pin too much hope on a happily-ever-after," she called over her shoulder. "She's been through enough."

Then she came back to the sofa with a container of yogurt. "Maybe I should just go there and help her get her head straight."

"You could go to *lend her your support,*" Autumn said, "not shatter her illusions. You have gobs of vacation time accumulated." She started back toward her desk. "Then as soon as tax season is over, I could come, too. If—"

"If it's not too late," Summer finished. "I'll see what I can arrange at work. Take a few days. I could use a vacation anyway."

"That's an understatement," Autumn replied. "But if you go and your parents do show up, don't make a scene, all right? It's not the time to make a big deal out of past hurts, Summer."

"Yes, ma'am," Summer said, saluting her cousin, her frown pulling her oval face down. "You're so calm and collected, Autumn. How do you do that?"

"Do what?"

"Always stay in control. I mean, I blow up, shout, fight, pout. But not you. Always got it together."

"You make that sound like a sin."

"It is, if you can't ever let go and just—react."

"I don't recall reading about that in the Bible."

"I do," Summer countered. "Something in Psalms, about asking the Lord to cleanse us from our secret faults."

"I don't need cleansing and I don't harbor any secret thoughts. I'm just fine."

"Well, I guess I do—harbor secret thoughts, that is," Summer replied, her eyes downcast. "I guess I got me a lot of cleansing to do. I cry out, just as King David did, but sometimes I don't think the Lord is listening."

Autumn touched her cousin's arm. "Well, just don't do it when you get to the Big M. I mean, don't cry out at your parents or raise a ruckus. Ask God to ease your famous temper. April needs us to be strong and supportive."

"If I go, I won't make a scene, I promise," Summer replied.

Autumn hoped her volatile cousin meant that. It would be bad if Summer lost her cool while Uncle Stu lay dying.

"You know Mr. Stuart is dying, right?" Reed asked Tomás as they rode the fences the next morning.

Tomás held on to the dash of the hefty red pickup with one hand while he worked on adjusting the radio dial to a hard-rock station. "Yeah."

Reed pushed the boy's hand away and turned the radio off. "And you understand that we all need to rally around the family right now, not cause any hassles?"

Tomás glanced over at him, his dark eyes slashing an attitude a mile wide underneath the fringe of his silky black bangs. "You mean, like I shouldn't get speeding tickets and cause an uproar with my grandparents?"

"Yeah, I mean that," Reed said with a sigh. "Want to talk about it?"

"I wasn't going that fast."

"You just got your license. You might need to take it easy until you're a little more experienced."

"I *am* experienced, Reed. I've been driving all over this ranch since I was twelve."

Reed nodded. "I did the same thing. Best place to learn to drive. But driving on these dirt lanes is a whole lot different from driving out on the highway or up on the Interstate. I'd hate for something to happen to you or your buddies. And I don't think Adan's parents would approve of this kind of behavior, either."

"We're okay, Adan and me. Or we would be if everybody would just leave us alone."

Reed stopped the truck near a sagging barbed-wire fence, then got out. "It's our job to hassle you, man. Keep you in shape. We wouldn't want the star of the football team to get in trouble."

"I'm covered there," Tomás said with a twist of a grin as he slammed the truck door. "Coach understands me."

"I'm sure he does," Reed said, wondering when things had changed so much in high-school sports. His coach had kept a tight rein on all the players—curfew, good grades, no late-night shenanigans, no drugs or liquor. A long list of no-nos. Nowadays, it seemed as long as a boy could throw a ball or run fast, he could get away with indiscretions of all kinds. "Listen," he said as he and Tomás rounded the truck, "we all care about you. If we didn't care, we'd just let you run loose."

"My parents let me do whatever I want," Tomás retorted. "*They* trust me."

Reed stared over at the young boy. Tomás was handsome in a dark, brooding way. A way that could lead to trouble down the road. And from the pained expression on the boy's face, Reed decided Tomás wished his parents did care a little bit more. A whole lot more.

"Do your parents know about the ticket?"

"Yeah, sure. No big deal."

"Uh-huh." Reed could only guess what his own father would have done in the same situation. It would have been a *very* big deal. "Well, your grandparents think differently. So… Horaz is giving you yard duty on top of your other chores."

"What?" Tomás threw down the coil of wire he had gathered from the back of the truck. "I have to mow that big yard? That is so *not* fair."

Reed shrugged. "Life is so not fair at times. But you have to roll with the punches. You got the speeding ticket. Now you get to do the time."

"But Grandpa said he'd help me pay it."

"Yes, and because he's doing that, he expects you to work off some of the price."

"That's just not right."

"Neither is going sixty-five in a thirty-five-mile-per-hour zone. Can't have it both ways, Tomás."

"My dad says I can have it all, if I just keep playing football. He says one day, I can own a ranch like the Big M."

"Your dad is proud of you, I reckon," Reed replied, shaking his head. "But first, get a good education, and stay out of trouble. I sincerely hope you become a success in football, Tomás. College and pro. But don't count on that. Have a backup plan."

"Did you?" Tomás asked, his expression clearly stating the obvious. Reed had had the same dream and it ended when he messed up his knee.

The boy's pointed question should have hurt, but Reed knew in his heart he was content with his lot in life. He could deal with it. Well, almost. "As a matter of fact, I did have a backup plan," he told Tomás. "I always wanted to have my own spot of land, right here near the Big M. And now I do."

"Yeah, and look how long you had to work to get that," Tomás remarked, his tone smug and sure.

Reed grabbed Tomás by one of his thick leather gloves. "Hey, I'm proud of my land. I worked hard to get it. I wouldn't have it any other way. And you'd better learn right now, son, there aren't any shortcuts in life."

"You sound like my *abuelo*. But then, both of you have spent most of your lives catering to the whim of the big man, right?"

Reed wanted to smack the kid, but he held his temper in check. "We weren't catering to anyone's whims, Tomás. We were making a living—an honest living. Your grandparents have had a good life here on the Big M. Stuart Maxwell has made sure of that. And he's always helped my family, too. Don't bite the hand that feeds you, and don't ever disrespect Stuart Maxwell again."

Tomás looked down, his sheepish expression making him look young and unsure. "I just want a better life, Reed. I just want more."

"We all want that, kid. But…just make sure you go about getting the good in life in the right way. Remember your roots, your faith in God. Remember where you come from. Don't do anything stupid, okay?"

Tomás looked doubtful, then shrugged. "Yeah, sure. I'll be careful."

"I hope so," Reed said. He'd have to pray that Tomás had listened to him. Really listened.

April tried to listen to what the preacher was saying in church the next Sunday. But her mind wandered off in several different directions, maybe because Reed and his parents were sitting right behind her. She could almost feel his catlike eyes on her.

He'd been standoffish and quiet since their kiss. He'd been avoiding her. He came by and called to check on her daddy and give her updates on the ranch. That was something at least, since he could send any one of the many hands they had on the Big M to do that job.

But then, Reed had always been a meticulous details man. He'd always been thorough in anything he did—from playing football to starting a vegetable garden to dating the rich girl from the big house. In fact, she had to remind herself, he'd been so complete in his love for her, in what he hoped their future would be like, that he'd spelled it out in detail for her over and over again.

And she'd let him believe she wanted the same things.

She looked up at Reverend Hughes. What had he just said? His mercy endures forever? Did God show mercy to those who turned from him? Would God show mercy to her dear, dying father? Would God show her that same mercy?

I was scared, Lord. I was so scared.

She could understand now. Her heart and her head had matured a hundred times over. If she had married Reed back then, she would have made his life—the simple life he'd always wanted—miserable.

Because I was miserable.

Why couldn't she just be happy? Why had she gone so far away to find her own brand of happiness?

Because I was scared. I'd lost my mother. I'd watched my father deteriorate into a mire of grief. Even going away to college hadn't helped. The weekends at home only brought the pain back into a sharply focused kaleidoscope of anger and grief.

That grief had been so overwhelming, so thick with despair, April had felt as if she were drowning. And she felt that same pulling feeling now, which was why she'd taken a precious hour away from her father to come to church.

I had to get away, to find some peace, some space. Back then, and now, for just a little while.

But she didn't want to repeat the same mistakes, follow the same path again. *Not this time, Lord.*

All those years ago, she'd hurt Reed. And she'd never wanted to hurt Reed. She loved him. Loved him still.

I need Your mercy, Lord.

April thought about her father. Asked God to show all of them His tender mercies. She had to take it one day at a time. That was all she could do at this point. She couldn't think beyond her father and what lay ahead— Even if she did feel Reed's eyes on her, willing her to think of him and their future.

When April got home an hour later, Flora greeted her in the kitchen. "I just got here myself. Lunch is in the oven, *querida*. Oh, and you have a message from a Katherine Price. Phone was ringing when I came in. Lynette can't hear it back there. We've got that phone turned off, so we don't disturb your father."

"Katherine called?" April took the note Flora had scribbled. "Urgent."

"Sí," Flora said, taking off her church hat so she could serve up the pot roast she'd left in the oven on warm. "Is she someone from your work?"

"My supervisor, the CEO of public relations," April said, reaching for the phone. "She's probably wondering why I haven't called in to work."

"You have enough to worry about."

"Yes, but I also have responsibilities back in New York. Although I pretty much cleared my desk before I left."

"You should eat first," Flora said, concern marring her tranquil eyes.

"I will later. You and Horaz go ahead. Are any of your family joining you for Sunday dinner today?"

"No," Flora said with a sigh as she tied her apron. "My son, Dakota—you remember him—he took his wife on a weekend to Dallas. Left us in charge of Tomás, of course."

Her fingers on the phone, April asked, "Did Reed talk to Tomás?"

"*Sí,* but the boy was very angry still. Blamed us for his troubles. He's not happy to be doing yard work."

April had to smile at that. "It's going to get hot out very soon. But then, Tomás should be used to sweating, what with football practice all the time."

Flora nodded. "He's just not used to authority. *Obstinado,* that one."

April shook her head. "I hope things get better. Now, you get your lunch ready while I make this call."

She left Flora humming a gospel tune. Heading out onto the long tiled verandah by the swimming pool, April dialed Katherine Price's home number.

What did her boss want on a Sunday afternoon?

Her stomach twisting in knots, April waited for the phone to ring. Just one more thing to deal with. She didn't need problems at work while she had so much going on here at the Big M.

But then, she'd already decided she couldn't handle both.

She once again prayed for that mercy Reverend Hughes had talked about. Mercy, and strength. She needed both for the long days ahead.

Chapter Nine

"April, darling, how in the world are you?"

Hearing the lilt in Katherine's voice made April breathe a sigh of relief. If her boss was in a bad mood, she wouldn't have called April "darling."

"I'm okay, all things considered," April replied into the phone. "I got your message. Is everything all right?"

"First, how's your father?"

April could envision the sophisticated leader of Satire public relations and marketing worldwide sitting on a chaise lounge on the sprawling balcony of her Park Avenue apartment, sipping an espresso and eating biscotti. But she was touched that Katherine had thought of her father before rushing headlong into business.

"My father is about the same, Katherine. The doctor comes by each day and tells us there is nothing else to be done. He hasn't opened his eyes for days now."

"You poor dear," Katherine said. "I wish there was something *I* could do."

April couldn't take any sympathy. She'd fall apart and she didn't want to do that in front of fashionable, together Katherine Price. "You can tell me what's happening at Satire. Why you called with an urgent message."

"Oh, right. Well, darling, you know we're in the midst of getting prepared to launch the ready-to-wear this fall. And of course, you've done such a great job with the preliminary marketing. You left things in good shape and the marketing and public relations departments are following your guidelines to the letter."

"But?" April asked, hearing the worry in Katherine's voice. "Is there something else that needs to be done?"

"Well, darling, you know I wouldn't ask if it weren't really important."

"Just tell me," April said, dread making her words sound sharp.

"Darling, is there any way you can fly back to New York for a couple of days? It's just a glitch or two with one of the department stores. They're trying to renege on the original contract. They want to cut back on their advance orders for the fall line."

"The contracts are ironclad," April replied, thinking there was no way she could leave her father right now. It was ironic how her whole perspective on work had changed.

"We know that, April," Katherine said through a long-suffering sigh. "But the store in question is giving us grief. Frankly, I think they're about to declare bankruptcy and they're trying to clean house, so to speak, before this goes public. That's why we need you here to negotiate—through our lawyers, of course. You always know what kind of spin to put on this type of crisis."

A crisis. Katherine Price, the head of PR for one of the most successful fashion houses in the world, thought that one department store trying to go south was a crisis.

April wanted to tell her that she now knew what a real crisis was like, but it wasn't Katherine's fault that her father was so ill. "Which store is it?" she asked, wondering how she was going to take care of this without going back to New York.

"It's Fairchild's," Katherine replied. "You know they've already had to restructure and lay off employees nationwide. They were banking on Satire to help them get back in the thick of things—they haven't had a winning label in their stores for a very long time now, just mediocre stuff all around—but it looks as if someone within their ranks got cold feet about overextending the stores with this massive order."

"Would that someone be Danny Pierson, by any chance?" April asked, the pieces of the puzzle beginning to come together in her mind.

"Why, as a matter of fact, he's the one who called me personally," Katherine said, surprise echoing out over the phone line. "Is there something about him I should be aware of?"

"Only that I dated him last year and it ended rather badly," April replied. "He didn't take the breakup very well."

"Oh, my. How long did you two date?"

"About six months," April said, remembering what a pompous control freak Danny had been. "He…made certain demands I couldn't meet."

"And now he's making those same demands on Satire," Katherine said. "Darling, you know not to mix business with pleasure. How could you let this happen?"

April held a finger to her forehead and pushed at the bangs covering her eyes. "I didn't let anything happen, Katherine. He didn't work for Fairchild's when we were an item. He went with them right after the beginning of the year, this year. And I'm sure he's just now discovered our contract with them. I can't imagine he'd be doing this to get back at me, though. He could jeopardize not only Fairchild's reputation, but his own."

"Then you agree you should come back and handle this?" Katherine asked, her tone firm.

"I didn't say that," April replied. "I think all we have to do is tell our lawyers to meet with Fairchild's and explain how things stand. That should get Danny to back off."

"And what if he doesn't? Darling, you know how important this ready-to-wear launch is. We've been working on this for eighteen months straight."

"I realize that," April said, "but, Katherine, I can't leave my father right now. He's…he's not going to last much longer."

Silence. Then a long sigh. "I understand. And you have my utmost sympathy, dear. But we need someone who can sweet-talk the powers at Fairchild's. And that would be you."

"What if I call Danny?" April asked. "Maybe I can nip this in the bud before it goes any further."

"You'd be willing to do that?"

"I can try. It's a start, at least. And I'll call all my contacts at Fairchild's and find out if this is something Danny just cooked up, or if it's really serious."

"Well, I guess if that's the best we can do right now—"

"I'll take care of it," April said, her insides recoiling at the idea of having to deal with slimy Danny Pierson again. But then, it was part of her job to negotiate tricky situations with clients. And there was a lot riding on this deal, as Katherine had reminded her. "I have

Danny's number in my business files. I'll call him first thing tomorrow."

"Thank you so much," Katherine replied. "And keep me posted on this."

"I will, of course," April said. "I'll get this cleared up. Don't worry."

"I know you will. And darling, I really am so sorry about your father."

"Thank you," April said.

When she hung up the phone, she turned to find Reed standing in the doorway.

He looked sheepish. "Sorry, I didn't mean to listen in. Flora told me you were here in the den."

"It's okay," April said, raising a hand in the air. "Just a problem at work."

"You don't need a problem at work. You have enough to worry about right here."

"I know, I know. And I don't need everyone reminding me of that, either."

He stalked into the room. "Sorry. Is everything all right at work?"

"Just a little mixup with one of our clients. I'll get it straightened out."

"Do you need a break from all of this?"

"No," she said. "I'm afraid to leave the house. He's so frail and quiet." Right now, she really wanted to just run away from everything and everyone. Especially Reed. He was hovering and that made her nervous. "Did you need to talk to me?"

"No. Just wanted to check in. See how you're holding up."

"How do I look?" she asked, the words snapping out like a whip against hide.

"Like you need a break, just as I said."

He moved toward her, but she backed away. "I don't need a break. I'm fine. I just need to think about how to take care of this problem without having to go back to New York."

The silence between them told her he was weighing her words. Weighing and judging, she imagined.

"So you want me to go?" he finally asked.

"That's entirely up to you, Reed." She looked up at him, the hurt in his eyes making her wince at her harsh attitude. If she could be honest with him, she'd rush into his arms and beg him never to leave. But she wasn't ready to take that step. "I just need some time alone," she said.

"Okay. Mom wanted me to invite you over to supper tonight."

"I can't leave the house, Reed. You know how things are."

This time, he watched her back away again, then moved after her until he had her in his arms. "Hey, I do know how things are. We can have supper here again. Or we can just send something over, if you don't want company."

"I can't eat," she said, hot tears brimming in her eyes. "I can't think beyond his next breath."

"I know," he said, kissing the top of her hair. "I wish there was something I could do."

His gentleness almost did her in, but she took a calming breath and let out a shaky laugh. "Funny, that's what my boss just said, right after she practically ordered me back to New York."

Reed lifted her chin with a finger. "You're not going back right now, are you?"

Offended at his possessive tone, she pulled away. "No, of course not. But I'm going to have to make some calls, fight some fires. I still have a job—or at least I did when I left New York."

She could feel the condemnation again, see it in his eyes as he spoke. "Yeah, I guess you can't just forget about your work."

"No, I can't. But I'm not leaving my father." At his raised eyebrows, she added, "Does that surprise you, Reed? If so, then I guess you don't know me as well as you think you do."

He stepped back. "I thought I knew you, but the old April would probably have taken off by now. This April, the woman I'm looking at right now… I think she has staying power."

"Impressed?"

"No, proud," he said before turning to leave. Then he whirled at the arched doorway. "I am proud of you, April. You're doing the right thing."

Before she could think of a mean, smart retort, he left the room, the sound of his cowboy boots clicking with precision against the tiled floor.

"I don't know the right thing to do," April said, her plea lifting up to the heavens. "I don't know what I should do or say."

She silently prayed that God would give her the grace to do what she had to do. And that Reed would continue to be proud of her, no matter what decisions she had to make over the next few weeks.

He wasn't very proud of himself, Reed decided later that night. He was trying. Heaven help him, he wanted to do and say the right things when it came to April.

But the woman just brought out the worst in him.

As well as the best.

So the subject of New York City was definitely a sore spot between them. But then, Reed couldn't understand why anyone would want to leave a place like the Big M. The rolling pastures and hills, the trees and ponds, the rows and rows of crape myrtle growing all over Paris, the Red River nearby, all the work a big ranch required—all of this was his lifeblood. His family had lived and worked on this ranch for generations. He was as rooted here as the cottonwoods and the *bois d'arc,* or bow dark trees, as the locals called them.

He just couldn't understand why April didn't feel the same toward her home. What had driven her away from the place she'd always seemed to love.

Grief.

The one word echoed around him like a dove's soft coo. He remembered April telling him that her father's grief had stifled and scared her. But what about her own grief? Maybe she hadn't actually worked through her own pain after her mother's death.

No, instead she'd run from it. And she was still running. But she was being brave in coming back to her home, no matter the horrible memories and the sadness that seemed to shroud the big house these days. Maybe she was home in the flesh, but her spirit was somewhere far away. Her spirit was lost in maybes and what ifs and what-might-have-beens. Just as his own seemed to be, Reed decided.

When he coupled her immense grief back then with the fact that he had been constantly hovering with unsolicited advice and unwelcome demands, asking her about marriage and family, well, no wonder the woman had escaped. He shouldn't have pushed her so hard. But he'd wanted a future with her so very much. He still did. But she was grieving yet again.

The phone rang, jarring him out of the troubled thoughts that were pounding at his brain.

"Hello," he said, his tone full of irritation.

"Son, are you all right?" his mother asked.

"Just dandy. What's up?"

"I wondered why you didn't come by for dinner. You and April."

His mother's words were full of questions and implications.

"April wasn't in the mood for company, Mom. And I don't think she's been eating very much at all, either. I think she's lost even more weight."

"That girl eats like a bird. Always did."

"Well, I guess her appetite is taking a hit these days."

"Did you offer to stay there at the house with her?"

Reed lifted his gaze to the heavens for support. "Mom, she didn't want me there."

"Oh, I think you're wrong there," his confident mother responded. "I think she wants you there, but she's afraid to voice that."

"Well, I can't second-guess her. Never could."

"The Lord has a plan for you two. I've always believed that."

"Well, then let's just let the Lord show us the way," Reed said, his tone lighter this time. He knew his mother meant well, and he loved her for caring. But he also knew that if he and April were ever to have a life together, then it would have to be something they both wanted, regardless of how strongly his mother felt about it.

It would be up to God to intervene.

Reed thanked his mother for calling, then hung up the phone. He was just about to go to bed when Shep started barking and pawing at the back door. "Need a walk, old fellow?" Reed asked as he swung the door open.

He stepped outside and heard the noise at about the same time Shep took off toward the small storage shed behind the house.

Someone was out there.

Shep barked with renewed frenzy as he galloped toward the shed. Reed hurried after the dog.

"Who's there?" Reed called, hoping it was just an armadillo or a possum.

When he heard footsteps echoing out behind the building, he knew the intruder was human. He ran toward the shed, listening as Shep's angry, agitated bark filled the quiet night.

Reed reached the shed just as a shadowy figure cleared the wooden fence behind the shed. "Hey, you," Reed called, "too chicken to show your face?"

All he heard was the sound of hurried footsteps and then the roar of what sounded like a four-wheeler taking off. And Shep, barking at the fence.

When he was sure that the intruders were gone, Reed called to his dog. "Let's go get a flashlight, boy."

Reed got a high-beam light out of his truck, then inched his way around the outbuildings. He saw footprints near the back of the shed, but couldn't find anything else.

Apparently, he'd caught the culprits just about to jimmy the locked door.

"I wonder what they thought they'd get out of there,"

Reed said to Shep. The dog barked back, still anxious to chase his quarry.

Reed thought about the equipment in the shed. The riding mower was stored in there, along with some tools and other garden supplies. He usually kept an empty gas can in there to use to refuel the lawn mowers. Maybe whoever it was wanted to get some free gas.

"Strange," Reed told Shep as they circled the yard. "We've never had burglaries or vandalism on this place before."

But someone was stirring things up now. The campfires in the pastures, the damaged and broken fences all along the highway, and now this.

Someone was trespassing on the Big M and on his land, too. And Reed aimed to find out who that someone was.

Chapter Ten

April finished helping Lynette turn her father, so they could change the sheets and give him a sponge bath. He hadn't responded to their touch or their words in days. He was beyond eating or taking in fluids. All the equipment and machines had long ago been removed from his room.

Now it was just a matter of time.

Tucking the fresh-smelling sheet over his clean pajamas, April leaned down to kiss him. "Okay, Daddy, you're all set for the day. You might have some visitors today. Uncle Richard's scheduled to arrive. He's going to stay a few days, help us out around here."

Stu's breath barely left his chest. His skin was wrinkled and spotted with age. His hair, once thick and crisp brown, now consisted of a few grayed wisps.

"He looks at peace, honey," Lynette said, shaking her head at April. "I think he's ready to make his journey home."

April hated hearing that, but seeing her father this way, she would almost welcome such peace for him. For his soul. "I hope... I hope he's having pleasant dreams."

Lynette came around the bed and patted her hand. "I reckon he's making his way to your mother's side right now. She'll be there to greet him, you know. Her and your grandparents, everyone who's gone on ahead of him."

April swallowed back the hot tears burning at her throat. "That should bring me some comfort, shouldn't it?"

"It should," Lynette replied. "But death is hard on the living. We have to stay behind, missing them. I guess you've missed your mother for a long time now."

"More than I can say," April replied, weariness overtaking her as she swayed against the bed.

She was so tired, she felt chilly and numb, and a bit disoriented. When she wasn't sitting here by her father's side, she barricaded herself inside his big office on the other side of the house, going through files and calling ranch workers for reports. The work was endless, and supervising it had taught her much more than she'd ever learned growing up here.

She'd also been in touch with her department at Satire, hoping to clear up the mess with Fairchild's. And she was still trying to reach Danny Pierson. She'd left her cell phone and home numbers with his secretary, but Danny was playing hard to reach. Why he'd pick now of all times to stall out on this deal was beyond April's comprehension. But Danny had always been a grandstanding, arrogant businessman. At first, his assertiveness and confidence had attracted her. Now they repelled her. There was healthy ambition, and then there was ruthless ambition. April appreciated the first but no longer wanted to be a part of the latter.

She decided she didn't have the energy to worry

about that right now. Danny knew how to reach her, and he knew what she wanted to talk to him about. He'd always been good at tracking *her* down when he wanted something.

She turned as the door creaked open. Flora stuck her head inside. "I'm sorry to interrupt, April. But Mr. Reed needs to speak with you."

April nodded, then turned back to touch her father's hand. "I'll be back in a little while, Daddy."

She came out of the dark room, her eyes hurting at the brightness of the morning. She'd lost track of the days. They'd all started merging into one big dark vortex of longing and prayer, coupled with late hours of work and bedside visits. She rarely left her father's side, rarely left the house even to go outside, unless one of the workers needed her advice on something. She had to be there with him, coaxing him to go to her mother, telling him it would be okay, telling him that God would take him home.

Lord, let him find his way back to her and You.

She saw Reed at the end of the long hallway. "Hi," was all she could manage to muster.

"Hey there. You look exhausted."

"Thanks, so do you."

"Yeah, well, I guess neither of us is getting much sleep."

"I have my reasons, but what about you?" she asked, puzzled by the serious expression on his face. "What now?" she asked, sensing that something else had happened.

"The vandalism," he replied. "It's getting worse. Had someone snooping around my garden shed two nights ago."

"Really? Why didn't you tell me sooner?"

He looked toward the closed door of the bedroom. "You know why. Anyway, Daddy and I have been patrolling the ranch at night. We take shifts with some of the other hands."

"Thank you," April replied, not sure whether to be appreciative or angry that he'd taken matters into his own hands. "You don't have to do that, though. We can call the sheriff."

"I don't mind," he responded, scooting her out onto the dappled tiles of the long back patio. "C'mon. You need some fresh air."

"I think I've forgotten what that is."

"All the more reason to sit in the sunshine."

She did that, finding a wrought-iron patio chair to fall against. The soft floral cushions were warm and welcoming, just like Reed's gentle eyes. "Tell me all about this trespassing and vandalism."

"It's the strangest thing," Reed began, only to be interrupted by Flora at the door with lemon cookies and freshly brewed iced tea. *"Gracias,"* he told her with a big smile.

April didn't miss the smile or the way Reed had so thoughtfully asked for refreshments. "Thank you," she told him when Flora had gone back inside.

"Eat a cookie," he suggested, shoving one in her hand.

She took a bite, felt it begin to stick and grow in her tight throat, then grabbed her glass of tea. "Talk," she said, motioning with her hand.

"Oh, as I was saying, they don't take anything on these nightly excursions. And they don't do much damage. Just seems to be kids having parties on our property. Now, why they'd want anything from me—that's what I don't get."

"Have you actually caught anyone?"

"No, no. We can't seem to place where they're coming in. They move around a lot, so it's hard to pinpoint 'em. But we always find traces, can tell that they've been on the property. They don't even try to hide the messes they leave."

"So what can we do?"

"Well, I'm going back out tonight. And I've told Richard all about it. He's going on rounds with me tonight, too."

April was too tired and worried to get mad that Reed was going over her head to her uncle. After all, she had no right to question his actions or his motives. Uncle Richard had been helping out with the daily routine of this ranch for several years now.

"Well, just be careful," she said, hoping her tone didn't sound too irritated. "I can't deal with something happening to you or Uncle Richard on top of everything else." She shrugged, threw down the cookie, and looked away from his questioning gaze. "I've got this problem at work I'm trying to deal with, and no one will return my calls on that. And Daddy is getting worse by the minute. I don't know—"

He shifted forward then, taking her hand. "You know you can lean on me."

She could only nod, staring out at the tranquil flow of the swimming pool. She blinked back tears. "Look at this place. It's so beautiful. The sun is still shining. The land is thriving, growing, changing, providing. This place provides for all of us. Why did it take me so long to understand that? And to see just exactly how much work goes into a place I've taken for granted all my life? Why now, Reed, when he's dying? Why couldn't I see what he saw—what you tried to show me?"

"Hush," Reed said as he dropped to his knees and put his hands on her face. "Hush, now. It's gonna be all right."

She pushed away from him and got up to pace. "It will never be all right again, Reed. My mother is dead. My father is dying. I've made such a mess of things. I don't have any immediate family left."

"You have me." He was there, urging her to be still. "Hold on to me," he said. "Hold on or hit me or scream at me. But don't push me away again, April."

She bit her lip, trying to hold back the pain. But she was so very tired. So she turned to him, fell against him, let him wrap her in that same warmth the sun was providing.

He felt as strong and formidable as this land. He felt like the earth and the sky and the wind all wrapped up in one comforting, gentle blanket of warmth. She wondered what it would feel like to have such assurance, such security with her always. To have Reed holding her at night when she was afraid, to have him there with her each morning with the sun shining so brightly. Could she even dream of such a hope?

I am with you always.

The words from the Bible verse echoed in her head.

The Lord was with her, April realized. But did the Lord have enough grace to give her a second chance?

Always.

She looked up at Reed, saw the assurance there in his eyes. "I need… I need you," she said, the words husky and thick with tears. "I need you, Reed."

"I'm here, darlin'. I'm right here."

She let him hold her while she cried. Then she raised her head and smiled as she sniffed back tears. "You were right. I did need some fresh air."

"Want me to come in and sit with you and your daddy for a while?"

She thought about that. She hadn't allowed others inside her father's room with her. She'd wanted to be alone. But this morning, she needed some company and some comfort. "Would you?"

"Of course."

She took his hand and turned toward the house. Then she turned around and grabbed her half-eaten cookie. "Thank you again," she told him as they went back inside. "For everything."

Reed squeezed her hand and guided her back to her father's side.

They sat there with Stuart until Flora came in to tell April that her Uncle Richard had arrived and lunch was ready in the kitchen.

"Thank you," April said, her voice hoarse, her throat tight. "We'll be there in a minute."

She turned to Reed. He'd sat here without complaining, without idle small talk. He'd barely said two words, but he'd held her father's hand the whole time. And her hand. He'd held her hand. He was holding it now.

"Will you stay for lunch?" she asked, wondering when she'd decided to quit fighting her feelings for him. Suddenly, instead of wanting to avoid him, she wanted him here beside her. Was it a sign of weakness or a sign of acceptance? She couldn't be sure.

"I'll stay," he said in a soft whisper. "It'll give me a chance to update Richard."

She nodded. "Let's go get Lynette to relieve us then. She's doing Daddy's laundry, I think."

"She's a good nurse. Goes beyond the call of duty."

"Yes, she is. At first, I wasn't so sure about her. But she's very devoted to Daddy."

"We all are," Reed added as they left the room. "I'll go find Lynette while you greet your uncle."

"Okay."

April watched as he headed toward the other end of the house, where the combination laundry room and mud porch was located behind the garage. She turned left into the kitchen.

"Uncle Richard!"

Her handsome uncle turned and gave her a bitter-sweet smile. "C'mere, girl, and give your ol' uncle a hug."

April rushed into his arms, her breath leaving her body in the big bear hug he gave her. Uncle Richard smelled of spice and leather, which only reminded her of her father.

"It's so good to see you," she told him as she managed to extract herself from his embrace. "And you're just in time for lunch."

"Can I go in and see Stu first?"

"Of course." She glanced over at Flora, then back to her uncle. "But I have to warn you. He doesn't look the same as you probably remember."

"I understand," Uncle Richard said, his dark eyes going misty. "I'll be right back."

While he hurried toward the back of the house, April helped Flora put ice in the tea glasses. Together, they set the table and got the food dished up. Reed came in and poured the tea, as natural and comfortable here as he would be in his own house.

Uncle Richard came back a few minutes later, his eyes watery, shock creasing his tanned face. "Hate to see him like this. You know, he was always our big brother. We could turn to Stu for anything, anything at all, and he'd move heaven and earth to see that we got it. Just wish I could do the same for him now."

"I know." April glanced from her uncle to Reed, then pushed at the salt-and-pepper tuft of curls falling across Richard's forehead in a rakish style. "Have you heard from Uncle James?"

Richard shrugged, shifting his weight, and stomped his handmade snakeskin boots. "Your other uncle is not available right now. Taking a cruise down to the Keys on the Maxwell yacht. I've sent him word, but I've yet to hear back from him."

"Some things never change," April said, amazed that the middle brother of the Maxwell clan could be so shiftless and uncaring, considering they'd all been raised by wonderful parents with a strong set of values. Uncle James and his wife, Elsie, liked the good life. And they'd taken advantage of all the Maxwell holdings in three counties to make sure they had a grand lifestyle. While they'd lived that lifestyle, Summer had spent most of her time with her mother's parents, in a house that had been standing for over a hundred years. Even though her grandparents had loved her with a strong foundation of faith, Summer had an empty place in her heart, a place still waiting to be filled by her parents. An empty place and a bitterness the size of Texas.

"What exactly does James do?" Reed asked. "I mean, when he's not traveling around."

"He's supposed to be in charge of our oil leases," Richard said as they all sat down to eat. "But I have to stay on him all the time. I've got people in place to make sure things are handled, if you get my drift."

Reed nodded, shooting a glance at April. "April's been checking the books here at the ranch. Everything seems to be in order now. April's done a good job of catching things up. Stuart has a lot of people working on the details of the day to day activities."

Richard nodded his approval. "Stu always was thorough. Now, James…he just wants to keep having a good ol' time. I've tried to tell him his rodeo days are over and he's not getting any younger, but that boy won't listen to reason. He should be here with Stu."

No wonder Summer rarely talked to her parents. April remembered how they'd left Summer behind in the small town of Athens, Texas, time and again, so they could travel the world and be seen at all the right places, cashing in on the lucrative endorsements Uncle James had made during the heyday of his rodeo career.

How could they do that to their daughter? How could Uncle James stay away now, when his brother needed him?

"Do you think he'll come home at all?" she asked Richard after they'd said grace over the food.

"Who knows?" Richard said, shaking his head as he took a corn pone from the basket Flora had put on the table. "Flora, honey, you've outdone yourself. Fresh peas and fried chicken, mashed potatoes. Gayle will have my hide for going off my diet, but I can't resist."

Flora beamed with pride. *"Gracias."*

"Flora, sit down and join us," April said, urging the woman down into a chair. "Where's Horaz today?"

Flora looked embarrassed. "In town with Tomás. Taking care of some business."

"Oh, okay." April figured that business had to do with the traffic ticket Tomás had been issued. "I hope everything works out."

"Sí," Flora replied as she absently dipped herself a big helping of steaming peas. Then she gave Richard a bright smile. "Teenagers."

"Tell me about it," Richard said, laughing. "These girls—remember them, Flora? Growing up here on the Big M and running loose all around half of Texas. We sure had our hands full, didn't we?"

"Sí," Flora said again, grinning. "And how is Autumn? She is a good girl, that one."

April smiled as she sampled the creamy mashed potatoes. Everyone loved Autumn, even if her cousin was a bit set in her ways and as straitlaced as an old shoe.

Uncle Richard chewed his chicken, then laughed. "Autumn is still Autumn. Born with a calculator attached to her hand. Always after the bottom line, that one. Have you talked to her lately, April?"

"Only on e-mail," April admitted. "I haven't made many phone calls to New York. I'm usually in with Daddy and I don't want to disturb him. But Summer and Autumn e-mail me daily, and me, them. They've offered to come down, but I told them not yet."

"Modern technology. I'll never get the hang of it," Uncle Richard said. "In fact, I'll let y'all be the first to know a big secret. I'm retiring in the fall."

April put down her fork. "You're closing the firm?"

"Nah, now, I'll never close Maxwell Financial Group.

We've got clients all over Texas, honey. But I've hired me a hotshot financial advisor to take over. He knows all about computers and technology, and he's as sharp as a tack when it comes to making people money. The man is a genius."

"Have you told Autumn about this?" April asked, wondering how her cousin would take her father's retirement.

Autumn had always had this dream of one day returning to Atlanta, Texas, to work with her father. But her father probably didn't know about Autumn's dream, since Autumn refused to stray from her ten-year plan. And that plan included working in New York for a few more years.

"Not yet," Richard admitted. "Your Aunt Gayle knows, of course. And I've already put Campbell on the payroll—that's one of the reasons I was able to come here to be with y'all. Campbell can hold down the fort."

"You hired this… Campbell to take your place?"

"Not necessarily. He will be chief financial advisor, but I'll always be the boss, retired or not. Campbell Dupree understands how things work. He won't be any trouble for the family. None at all. He grew up in Louisiana, but he got a top-notch education at Harvard. He's traveled the world, got a real handle on how international finances work."

Richard said this with the kind of pride and confidence that April's daddy used to exude. The Maxwell men were nothing if not arrogant and self-assured. She had to wonder if Campbell Dupree fit that mold, too. And how Autumn would react to such a man taking over the family business.

"Maybe you should tell her, Uncle Richard," April

said with a gentle plea. "I mean, she's going to be so surprised."

"Well, I don't know why. That girl knows I can't work the rest of my life. If James can travel the world without a care, then why can't I?"

"You deserve some downtime, that's true," April replied, "but Autumn—well, she cut her teeth at Maxwell Financial Group. She sat at your knee, right there in the company you built from the ground up, and learned everything she needed to know about money and finances."

"That's right and one day, it will all be hers," Uncle Richard reasoned. He dipped more peas and grabbed another corn pone.

"She might be upset that you've hired someone, though."

"Now, why?" Uncle Richard sent April a sharp look. "Unless you're trying to tell me that Autumn might have wanted the job."

"Well, she's hinted that she'd love to one day move back home and—"

"Well, bless Bessy, why didn't the girl tell me that?"

"It's not set in stone," April said, hoping Autumn wouldn't be angry at her for spilling this secret goal. "I guess she's just afraid of…of disappointing you. You know, if something went wrong."

She glanced over at Flora and Reed, but found no help there. Flora kept her eyes glued to her plate and Reed tried hard not to look too curious and amused.

Uncle Richard stared across the table at her. "Autumn could never disappoint me. She's my baby. I'm so proud of her. You know, she's sent some big clients my way over the years. That girl's got contacts all over the world. She's about the only person who could match Campbell, I reckon."

"She's very good at her job, that's for sure," April said, pushing her fork around in her food.

"Well, Sam Houston and Custer, too," Uncle Richard said as he sat, shock-faced. "You just never know about people. I'll have to think about this and see what I can do."

"Well, you can't fire your new hotshot financial genius," April said. "That wouldn't be right."

"No, that wouldn't do," her uncle agreed. "The man's got an ironclad contract. But I might have another solution." He beamed at April, then winked. "A solution that just might be a win-win situation for all of us."

April wondered what her lovable but impulsive uncle had suddenly concocted for his only daughter. Maybe she should warn Autumn. Later, she decided. Much later. Right now, she didn't have time to get caught in the middle of a family squabble. And right now, Autumn was deeply and gleefully caught up in tax season.

She'd find the right time to explain things to her stubborn cousin. But much later.

Chapter Eleven

"Did you ever find out what your uncle has cooked up?"

Reed asked April later that night.

"No. He's as stubborn and tough as an old barnyard rooster, and just as unpredictable."

"Do you think Autumn's gonna pitch a fit about him retiring and hiring this new fellow?"

"Oh, yes," April said. "I guess I should warn her, but honestly, I don't have the energy right now to handle putting out yet another family fire."

"It's between them, anyway," Reed said. "Might be best to let Richard tell her."

"I thought about that, but I can't keep this from Autumn. We tell each other everything. I just have to find the right time to break it to her," she whispered back, careful not to bother her father.

Not that their quiet chatter could bother him. He hadn't responded to anything they said. His body was slowly shutting down. So now April could only wait and pray.

So many people had been by to see him. April had

tried to keep a list of everyone, so she could thank all of them later.

"You have a remarkable family," Reed said, his words soft-spoken. "You know, when we were growing up, there was this one big old oak tree right near the back fence of y'all's yard. I used to climb up in that tree and watch—"

"You spied on me?"

He shook his head. "Not spying so much. Remember those grand parties your parents would have out on the back lawn?"

"Oh, yes. Mother loved entertaining, loved having a crowd here. Sometimes, she'd have the whole Cattle Baron's Ball committee here for a 'planning' party. They loved attending that big event, mingling with all the other ranchers and oil people. Of course, I had to decline Daddy's invitation to the ball this year, even though Flora said I should go in his place." April stared at her father, then asked, "So, you wanted to come to the parties?"

Reed nodded. "I wanted to be a part of something big like that. But it wasn't the glittery parties I wanted to see." He turned in the muted light, his gaze falling across April's face, washing her in longing. "It was you."

April felt the heat of her blush down to her toes. "But you saw me every day, Reed. We ran around this entire ranch like a couple of wild heathens."

"I know that," he said, and she could see the memories in his eyes. "But at those parties… you'd walk out, all dressed up in fluffy party gowns and I'd just about fall out of that tree." He shrugged. "I reckon somewhere around my fourteenth birthday, I started seeing you as a real live girl. I remember the party your parents had for you when you turned sixteen."

"You were invited to that party, Reed Garrison."

"I know I was. And I came."

"But you didn't stay," April said, the memories rushing over her, reminding her of that warm spring night years ago. She remembered seeing Reed in his church suit. He'd looked so uncomfortable, and so very handsome. And she remembered the way he'd looked at her. "I wore a white dress."

"It was the most beautiful thing."

"You wouldn't talk to me. I thought you were mad about something."

"I wasn't mad. I wanted to kiss you."

"But you were afraid?"

"Very afraid."

"You acted so funny, as if you had a frog in your throat."

"I did. I saw you through the open doors, and then you came down the back verandah stairs in that white dress and your mother's pearls. I'd already lost my heart to you, but that night, I knew something was different. That things would be different between us if I did kiss you."

"Oh, Reed—"

Stuart moaned, causing both of them to jump up as if they'd been caught.

"Daddy?"

April felt her father's hand squeezing hers. "I think he wants to tell us something, Reed."

"Stuart? It's Reed. What is it?"

Stuart moaned again, lifted his other hand.

"Daddy, do you hurt? Can I get you anything?"

Both Reed and April leaned forward, trying to hear the raspy words. But April heard only one word.

"Happy."

She looked up at Reed. "Did I hear him right?"

Reed glanced back down at Stuart with a frown. "You're happy?" he asked.

Stuart nodded, a slight movement of his head. He didn't open his eyes. "For you two."

Then he fell back into the deep sleep April had become so used to seeing.

Reed motioned April to follow him to the door. "Uh, April… I think he believes we're, uh—"

"Back together," she finished. "I didn't think he could hear anything we say, but I guess he can."

"And we've said a lot lately."

"But we never said we were back together."

Reed pulled her close, planting a soft kiss on her cheek. "Some things don't need to be voiced to be seen, April."

Shocked, she could only stare up at him. Could her father, as sick as he was, see what she couldn't admit with her own heart? "I don't know—"

"I do," Reed replied. "But I don't have time to go into this now, and besides, I can tell you're not ready for it yet. I have to meet Richard down at the stables. We're going out on patrol, remember?"

"Yes. Flora was supposed to wake him at ten. Is it that late?"

"Yes, it is. Why don't you go to bed and let Lynette take over?"

"I will in a little while. I'm just going to sit with him a little longer. See if he says anything else."

Reed gave her a soft grin. "Stuart believes in us, April. Maybe you should try doing that, too."

April watched him saunter up the hallway, her heart drumming a beat of longing and pride. Her father hadn't been able to talk to her very much, but he'd told her all the things that were important. He loved her, and he was happy to see her back with Reed. Her dying father believed she was home for good and everything was as it should be.

Why couldn't she believe that, too?

"I don't believe you finally took the time to call me," April said into the phone an hour later. "Danny, do you know what time it is here in Texas?"

"I know exactly what time it is," Danny Pierson said into the phone, his tone smug and pleasant. "That's because I'm sitting in a hotel in downtown Dallas."

"You're in Dallas?" April moved through the house, the mobile phone at her ear. She'd left Lynette with her father so she could take this call. "What are you doing there?"

"Checking up on our store at the Galleria," Danny said. "It's one of our top producers, you know."

"I've heard things weren't going so well with Fairchild's," April shot back, unwilling to deal with his spin on things.

"There are always rumors in our business. You should know that, April."

"Why are you blocking our contracts with Fairchild's, Danny? It's a bit late in the game to shut things down now."

"I'm just concerned," Danny replied. "This is a risky

move for Satire. And it's even more risky for Fairchild's. You know how exclusive our stores are, April."

"Yes, I do. That's why I think this is a good move. Satire will bring in hordes of customers. You have to agree with that. Fairchild's certainly knew that when these contracts were being negotiated."

"Yes, but I didn't work for Fairchild's then. And that was—well, that was when I thought I could trust you."

"You can trust me now, Danny, past differences aside. Don't do this. Just because *we* didn't work out, don't make this personal."

"Is that what you think I'm doing?"

"That's it exactly," she said, fatigue making her snap. "And I really don't have time to go into that now. Just know that our contract is tight and you can't back out on the deal now."

"Meet me in Dallas and we'll go over the details."

"I can't do that. My father is very ill."

"I'm sorry to hear that. Your family has quite an impressive name around these parts, highly respected. I know this is hard on you."

"Very hard. Which is why I don't need this problem with Fairchild's right now. Just back off and honor the original agreement, Danny."

"Only if you meet me to discuss it."

"I can't do that."

"Then I'll drive up to Paris. It's not that far from Dallas. I checked the map. Always did want to see that replica of the Eiffel Tower with the red cowboy hat on top you always talked about. Didn't you tell me it's near the Civic Center?"

"Don't come here," April said, panic bubbling through her system. "It's not a good time."

"But business is business and I'm sure you don't want this deal to go sour."

"Danny, my father is dying. Just do what you can to make this happen. I can't worry about this right now."

"We'll see," Danny replied, his tone less threatening now. "I understand about your father, April. I'll try to go back to the board of directors and see what I can do to clear this problem. But I'd like to see you."

"Another time," April said. "Just call me tomorrow with the details."

She hung up, then glanced out the big windows at the back of the house, a sense of dread filling her soul as the night grew dark and cloudy. She did not need Danny Pierson here, harassing her about business or personal matters. Not now.

So much to worry about. Her father. Reed and Uncle Richard out there hunting down trespassers. Danny and business pushing at her. So much to think about, to take care of.

"I need You, Lord. I need Your strength."

She waited, staring out into the dark night. But the silence of an empty, desolate house was her only answer. That and a distant rumble of thunder and lightning out over the trees to the west.

April turned from the darkness and walked down the long hall toward her father's room.

"Mighty quiet night," Richard said as he adjusted the black Stetson over his wiry salt-and-pepper hair. "Too quiet. But looks like a little bit of rain might blow in."

"Yep," Reed answered in a whisper. "Maybe if a storm comes, our vandals will give up this game for tonight."

"I doubt that," Richard replied, chuckling. "If it's kids out for kicks, they won't know when to quit. Probably don't have sense enough to get in out of the rain."

"Until we catch 'em," Reed said. "Then they'll have more to worry about than wet clothes. Want some more coffee?"

"Nah. I'm getting too old for all that caffeine. I tell you, son, old age ain't no picnic."

"I hear that." Reed was silent for a while, then added, "Stu spoke to April and me tonight."

"He did? Well, that's something, I reckon."

"He said he was happy. For us."

Richard let out a grunt that merged with another rumble of thunder in the sky. "A dying man's last wish. He wants you and April together. He's always wanted that."

"He's not the only one."

"When are you gonna make that happen, son?"

"That all depends on April."

"How's that gonna work, with you here and her back in New York?"

"You think she'll go back?"

"Well, I'm thinking she has a life there. No need for her to waste away on this old ranch, unless, of course, that's what she wants to do."

"It'll be her choice."

"So you'll let her go again?"

"I don't want her to stay here and resent me for it."

"What about if she stays here and loves you for it?"

"Now that would be a different matter."

"You need to learn the fine art of persuasion, Reed."

"I'm not a salesman like you, Richard. I don't have the right words."

"Oh, I think you do. I can talk a good game myself,

as far as people's finances. But when it comes to understanding women—"

"Zero?"

"You got it. But I do know this. You have to persuade women sometimes. They want to be wooed. They want to know they're loved and treasured. They like security."

"You sound just like my daddy. He pretty much told me the very same thing. By my reasoning, April should see that she'd be secure with me."

"Women like that old-fashioned kind of romance," Richard replied sagely. "Why, I don't know. But Gayle is always telling me that. So I romance her as often as I can, just to be on the safe side."

"April is a modern woman, Richard. She has a mind of her own. She's very independent. And very secure in her own way. I'm not so sure romance can compete with that."

"Maybe not. But I think she loves you just as much as you love her. She just needs some reassurance."

"Don't we all?"

"Yes, we do. That's why we have to keep the faith, through good and bad."

They fell silent again. Reed could hear the cicadas singing, the fluttering melody of the alfalfa swaying in the damp wind. He smelled a hint of honeysuckle, reminding him of April's sweet-smelling hair. He closed his eyes in a prayer—not his will, but God's plan.

And then he heard the snapping of trees, the crackle of heat against branches, and he smelled a different kind of scent, this one acrid and smoky. He saw the fire rising up out of the copse of bow dark trees nestled along the fence rail.

"Richard?"

"I see it. Somebody's gone and set fire to that wooden gate out there."

Reed hopped up. "With this wind, that could spread to the fields."

"I'm right behind you," Richard shouted as they rushed toward the growing fire.

Too late to worry about an ambush or a surprise attack. Whoever was doing this had grown bolder. And much more dangerous.

"Hey!" Reed called as two shadowy figures took off running through the trees. "Hey, stop right there!"

"Did you bring a rifle?" Richard shouted as he stomped at the fire. He took off the lightweight jacket he was wearing and hit at the trees.

"I did," Reed answered as he searched the trees. "But I left it in the truck. I didn't think things would turn this nasty."

"Go after them," Richard called. "I'll get this little brushfire out in no time."

"You sure?" Reed asked, stepping on embers and hitting at the fence with a broken tree limb.

"Yeah. It's almost out now."

Richard was right. They'd managed to subdue the fire that had been leaping up the fence and through the small trees. And thankfully, Reed felt a few big, fat raindrops hitting his hot skin.

Rain. God had sent rain.

I think it's going to rain.

April typed the words on her laptop, careful to keep an eye on the nearby bed and her silent, sleeping father.

She continued the e-mail to her cousins in New York.

Things are getting tough here. Summer, I appreciate your trying to get away, but I understand when things come up. You are needed at the center, so please don't worry about rushing down here. You both will be here soon enough, I know. And you'll be here when I need you. And I will need you. Reed has been so sweet. He sat with Daddy and me tonight. He sat and held my father's hand and prayed and talked to me in soothing, comforting words. I've changed since coming home. I now know that this is home. But I'm still afraid of making that final commitment—to Reed and the future he could offer me. I want to love him. I do love him. And I need him now more than ever. But I'm so tired and so afraid. I'm afraid to love him. Isn't that the silliest thing? I can see him reaching out to me, can feel his eyes on me. But it's as if I can't move toward him, as if something is holding me back. My heart is too heavy to hold all the feelings I have for Reed.

She stopped typing and closed her eyes to that heaviness for a brief moment. Then she finished the e-mail.

I'll talk to y'all later. I'm going to sit here and wait for Reed and Uncle Richard to come back.

She shut the laptop and stilled, listening to the wind and the thunder, her gaze moving over her father's shadowy profile.

Then she closed her eyes again and fell asleep, her dreams lost in a gossamer time of happiness and laughter, a time of a young boy in his church suit and a young girl in her white dress and pearls, smiling at each other on a perfect spring night.

* * *

April heard the rain hitting the roof at about the same time she heard something crashing on the other side of the house.

Jumping up in disoriented, wide-eyed shock, she checked on her father, then stumbled across the room and creaked open the door of the bedroom. "Lynette?"

No answer. Flora and Horaz had gone home right after dinner. And April had sent Lynette to bed down the hall hours ago. Glancing back at the digital bedside clock, she saw that it was well past midnight.

She called out again, afraid Lynette had fallen. "Is anyone there?"

The rain came down in a wash of gray that danced across the yard like a sheet waltzing in the wind. The sky lit up with the glare of brilliant golden lightning and the banging of angry thunder. She watched it through the many windows around the patio, her breath coming in little shallow gasps as she stayed in her spot at the bedroom door.

Worried that something had happened to Lynette, April decided she couldn't just hover here like a ninny. She hurried toward the front of the house, hoping to find the nurse. "Lynette, are you all right?"

And that's when April saw the figure of a man standing at the other end of the hall.

Chapter Twelve

April squinted into the darkness, thinking maybe Reed and Richard had returned. But she could tell by the stance of the intruder and by the hooded jacket he wore to hide his face that this wasn't either of those two men.

The locked gun cabinet was behind the intruder, in her father's office, and her cell phone was upstairs in her bedroom. No help there. She didn't dare go back in the bedroom. The intruder might follow her there and hurt her father.

Trying to think which way to go and what to do next, April called out. "What do you want?"

"I won't hurt you," the man said, his voice shaky and raspy. "I just need to get some stuff and leave."

"What do you want?" April asked again, moving back toward the front of the house. If she could run up the central hall to the front door, she'd be able to grab a phone or escape. But she couldn't leave her father alone.

"Just turn around and go back in your daddy's room."

Surprised, April realized this intruder knew the layout of the house—and apparently knew *her*. As her eyes adjusted to the darkness, she saw that the man was dressed in dark clothes, making it hard to even guess at his identity. "Who are you?"

"Just go back inside the room and you won't get hurt."

He had a Spanish accent.

April felt the hair on the back of her neck standing up. "What are you after?"

"Lady, you ask way too many questions." He waved his hand at her and advanced toward her. "I don't want to hurt you."

"Then just leave. Now." She hoped he didn't have a weapon. "No one will have to know you were even here. But you need to hurry. My uncle will be back soon."

He fidgeted and glanced around behind him. "I can't do that."

He sounded resigned to his dirty work.

And he sounded young and frightened.

April moved a step closer, determined to get him away from the back of the house and her father. She checked again, squinting in the darkness, but still didn't see any type of weapon on him. And then she looked around for one of her own.

Because she wasn't going to let whoever this was get away. Not without a fight, at least.

Reed ran through the rain like a man being chased by hounds. He could see one of the vandals just up ahead. Apparently, this time they'd hidden their means of escape near the very back of the property line, probably on one of the riding trails.

"Stop," Reed called, his words lost in the wind and the rain. "You'll only make this worse if you keep running."

Whoever it was kept right on running anyway. Reed hurried after them, his bum knee sending signals of protest with each step.

They were nearing the fence along the property line now. The pasture gave way to uneven, weather-worn gullies and terraces. Reed hopped over a muddy terrace, the rain falling in his eyes and blinding him. He winced as his leg twisted, but he didn't stop.

The lone figure hesitated just enough at the fence line to give Reed an edge. He surged forward with all the power of a linebacker, tackling the man in a groan of pain and exertion just as he tried to climb over the fence.

They rolled and tussled in the wet mud and grass, but Reed had more strength and muscle than the other guy. It took Reed only a few seconds to realize this wasn't even a grown man.

He was wrestling with a kid.

April said a prayer, hoping that her father would sleep through the ruckus and that Lynette was safe in her room. "Just take what you want and leave," she said, watching the shadowy figure for any signs of flight or fight.

"I don't want to hurt anyone."

The man—make that *boy*—seemed jittery and skittish, but then he was breaking and entering into her house, so she figured that gave him the right to be a little nervous. It also gave her an edge.

"That's good that you don't want to hurt me." She stood perfectly still, her gaze fluttering over a huge clay vase sitting on a dark console in the center of the hallway. If she could get to that vase...

He didn't speak, didn't move.

"So are we just going to stand here all night?" she asked, her breath sticking in her throat.

"No, I don't think so."

"Good. Just turn around and leave the way you came and we'll call it even. Please, I don't want to disturb my father."

"I can't do that."

"Why not?"

The dark figure stalked toward her, his hand held out. "C'mon, my friend is waiting by the road. You'll have to come with me."

"Got you," Reed said as he landed his quarry flat on his back, mud and rain sliding off both of them. He held the captive down with both hands, his breath coming in a great rush of air. "Now you can explain what you're doing on Maxwell land," Reed shouted.

The kid kept his face turned away. And he wasn't talking.

Reed grabbed him by the chin, turned him around, and in a flash of lightning saw the face he would have least expected to be doing damage to the Big M.

"Tomás?"

The boy winced, closed his eyes, then moaned. "Let me up, Reed. So I can explain. Before it's too late."

"What do you mean, too late?" Reed said, loosening his grip on the boy.

"The house," Tomás hollered. "They went to the big house. I don't want them to hurt April."

Reed held the boy by his shirt collar. "Who? Who's up at the house?"

"My friends. Two of them. They had this plan—to

take money from the safe—that's all we wanted, just some money."

Reed's blood went cold as realization hit him. "So you planned this whole thing? You distracted everyone just so they could break in?"

"Sí," Tomás said, his voice shaky, his expression filled with shame and remorse.

"You messed with the wrong people, son," Reed said angrily. Then he yanked Tomás up and half dragged him along, mud sluicing at their feet as he hurried back to his truck. "You'd better hope it's not too late, Tomás. You'd better pray that nothing's happened at that house."

"I'm not going anywhere with you," April said, her pulse throbbing at an alarming rate in her ear. But she refused to be afraid. Suddenly, everything was very clear in her mind. This was her home, and that was her father lying in that bed. She'd been afraid of loving Reed too much; she'd been afraid of coming home to death and grief. But she wasn't afraid now. She wasn't about to let this little twerp get the best of her. "Did you hear me? I'm not leaving this house with you."

He shifted his feet, his gaze darting here and there. "Look, I don't want any trouble. We'll just drive you out to the highway and let you go."

"You said, there's someone with you?"

"He's waiting in the car. But I promise we won't hurt you. We don't want any trouble. We just wanted some easy cash. This was supposed to be easy."

She breathed a sigh of relief at his words, but didn't believe him. "Well, this is not easy for either of us, is it? My father is very ill, but then, you probably already know that. And yet, you still just wanted some easy cash? Does it make you feel good, breaking into the home of a dying man?"

"I'm sorry," he said, his head bent. "It wasn't supposed to be like this—"

April listened, her heart skipping and skidding. This was just a kid! And his voice seemed so familiar.

This new knowledge made her bold, took away some of her initial shock and fear. She stared at the stranger, thinking it was time to end this standoff. Making a split-second decision, she rushed for the table to grab the vase.

But the kid was faster. He ran smack into her and pushed at her grasping hand. April caught hold of the lip of the heavy vase, then aimed it for his head. He ducked, but not before she managed to lift the vase just enough to nick his temple with a hard blow. Screaming, he grasped at her hand, sending the vase crashing to the tile floor. The echo of the crash startled the kid, giving April time to push him away. Expecting him to come at her, she quickly grabbed a fractured piece of the broken clay to use as a weapon. But the boy backed away, then turned and ran up the wide hall.

And right into Lynette Proctor.

Reed and Richard both rushed inside the gaping door leading from Stuart's office to the back verandah.

"Somebody sure broke in," Richard said, his breath heaving, his hair plastered with rain and mud.

Reed pushed Tomás ahead of him, careful to keep a firm grip on the teenager's wet, dirty clothes. "Yeah, but then, our friend here had already told us that." He gave the frightened kid another shove as they entered the house. Tomás had talked a lot in his nervousness. And Reed still couldn't believe what the boy had told them.

But now, he saw it with his own eyes.

The office was ransacked, drawers left open and empty, files tossed to the four walls.

"I'll deal with this, and you, later," Reed told Tomás.

"Where is our help?" Richard whispered as they heard a commotion on the other side of the house. He headed for the gun cabinet.

"The sheriff should be sending someone," Reed said. They'd called 911 from the truck. He shoved Tomás at Richard. "Watch him."

Richard nodded toward the gun cabinet. "Don't you need protection?"

"I'll manage," Reed replied. He didn't want to accidentally shoot April or Lynette, or anyone else for that matter. "You just make sure Tomás stays put."

"Be careful," Richard said, his grip on Tomás's shirt collar making the boy grimace in pain.

Reed rushed out into the dark hallway, the sound of rain and thunder mingling with the sounds of angry voices emanating from the front of the house.

"April?" he called, a rippling fear causing him to see red. "April, are you all right?"

He ran to Stuart's room and was relieved to see that Stuart was sleeping and undisturbed.

But where was April? Where had that noise come from?

When he heard sirens out on the road, Reed sent up a prayer of thanks for that, at least. "April?"

"We're in here."

He followed her voice, hoping he wouldn't find something horrible in the next room.

He found them in the den. Lynette Proctor and April stood over the trembling figure they had cornered on a chair by the window.

"Are y'all all right?" Reed asked as he hurried to April.

"We're fine," she said, falling into his embrace and getting herself all wet in the process. "We're okay."

She sounded a bit shaken. Reed looked her over, taking in the fear and resolve in her big, dark eyes. "Are you sure?"

Lynette grunted, then held a hand toward the man in the chair. "We snared us a burglar. I tackled him right there in the hallway, after April tried to ping him with a vase."

"They tried to kill me," the teenager said, his voice shrill, his tone whining and afraid.

"You broke into my father's office," April shouted down at him. "You could have hurt someone, or worse, you could have gotten shot."

"If I'd had me a gun," Lynette said, her tone smug and firm, her eyes flashing. "I heard him rustling around in there. Left a mess, that's what he did."

Reed stared down at the dark-headed boy. "You're a friend of Tomás's, right? Adan? You're Adan."

The boy didn't answer. He just sat there glaring.

Richard came in then, pushing Tomás ahead of him. "Looks like we found our vandals." He thumped Tomás on the head. "Kid, have you lost your mind, trying to break into the Big M?"

Tomás crumpled into a heap on a nearby chair, then shot an accusing look at his partner in crime. "You told me nobody would get hurt."

"Nobody did," April said. "But you're both lucky we didn't shoot first and ask questions later."

"He was only supposed to take some cash from the safe," Tomás said, his defiance almost comical. Except this was no laughing matter.

"I couldn't find the safe," his friend wailed. "Then she came down the hall toward me." He pointed to April, then swallowed hard. "They're gonna put us in jail, Tomás." He lapsed into Spanish.

Reed thought he heard a very sincere appeal to God in there somewhere. "You need to pray, both of you." He turned to Tomás. "Tomás, why would you be a part of this?"

Tomás shrugged. "They dared me."

"They dared you?" Richard echoed, shaking his head. "Son, haven't we been good to you?"

Tomás glared up at him. "*Sí*, but… I feel like a loser. The hired help, getting handouts. Always only handouts."

April leaned close. "Tomás, your grandparents are a part of this family. We don't give handouts. We have loyal people on our land, people who work hard and make a good living. We consider all of them family, even you." She grabbed him by the arm. "Now tell me why you did this?"

"I told you—they dared me. I had to show them I wasn't scared. But…my ride left me out there in the pasture." He frowned at the other boy. "They were only supposed to take a little money."

Reed winced, shook his head. "You're gonna have to tell the sheriff the whole story, Tomás. And I have to call your family."

Tomás groaned. "It started out as a game. A dare.

We had some fun, hanging out in the pastures. Then we started leaving things here and there, just to—"

"Just to make us think it wasn't serious," Reed finished. "I guess that's why you tried to break into my toolshed, too, right? Just to throw us off?"

"We didn't mean any harm."

Reed glanced at April. "Until someone suggested robbing the big house, huh? Then you had to distract us one more time, so your friend here could do his dirty work, right?"

Tomás glared across at the other boy. "He said it would be for kicks, to get some cash, just for fun. He said no one would ever trace it back to us."

"Are you both dumb as dirt?" Richard asked, his hand holding on to Tomás's friend with a firm grip. "What's your name again, son?"

"Adan," the boy mumbled, his head down.

"Well, Adan, I hear the sheriff coming. Might as well give me your parents' number, so we can call them, too. And whoever was waiting to give you a ride out of here—well, I reckon they're long gone by now. We'll have to let their parents know. It's gonna take a while to straighten all of this out."

Reed looked at April again. "Are you sure—"

"I'm fine," she said. "Just a bit dazed."

"You sure didn't need this."

"No, I didn't. But at least now we know who was behind the vandalism."

He nodded. "Yeah, we solved it."

"Together," she said, her smile bittersweet.

"With me out there, chasing down a kid, and you in here, trying to—what was that Lynette said?—*ping* another one on the head with a vase." He felt the shudder passing through his body. "April, when I think of what could have happened—"

"It didn't."

"At least we got through this without too much trouble, and nobody seriously hurt."

"We're quite a pair."

"Yeah," Reed said, relief flooding through his system. "Quite a pair." He couldn't tell her that he'd been in a dark fear out there, wondering if she had been hurt. He couldn't show her just how relieved he really was. "Let's go let the sheriff in and get this night over with."

"Flora, we're not going to press charges," April said the next day.

Flora was inconsolable. "*Gracias,* April, *gracias. Lo siento. Lo siento.*"

"It's not your fault," April said, taking Flora into her arms. "It's going to be all right."

"What will become of my grandson?" Flora asked, her eyes watery and red-rimmed.

"Community service," April replied. "Reed and I thought it was the best way to teach these boys a lesson."

"They could have gone to jail," Flora replied, shaking her head. "*Por qué?* Why would Tomás do such a thing?"

April had wondered that herself during the sleepless hours of the long, rainy night. "From what we could gather, his friends pressured him. They saw an opportunity and they took it. They talked Tomás into creating a distraction, so one of them could sneak into the house and get whatever cash they could find. Cash and other valuables, according to the sheriff."

"There is no excuse for this," Flora said, wiping her eyes. "His parents—they finally sat down with us and Tomás and had a long talk. At least, that is something good."

"That *is* something good," April agreed. "Maybe now they will pay more attention to Tomás."

"He might not get to play football this fall," Flora said. "Serves him right, *el niño loco*."

Reed came into the kitchen, followed by Horaz. "It's all taken care of," he told April.

Horaz took his wife into his arms, talking to her softly in Spanish.

"What was decided?" April asked.

"There will be a hearing, closed, because they're juveniles, of course. But from what we could gather and from what the sheriff could promise us, they'll probably have to pick up trash up on the main highway for the rest of the summer, then do volunteer work at the local food bank and a couple of other charities for a long time to come."

April nodded. "Do you think that's a fair punishment?"

Reed let out a frustrated breath. "I don't know. What they did was wrong, but in the end, nobody got hurt, thank goodness. They were more stupid and scared than dangerous. It could have been much worse."

"You're right. I don't know who was more scared last night, me or that boy."

"He came here with Tomás," Reed said, disgust evident on his face. "He had meals right here in the kitchen, swam in the pool, fished, rode horses."

"And saw a lot of things he could pawn or sell for

profit," April reminded him. "Will they be on probation for a while?"

"I'd say a good long while," Reed replied. "And they're both off the football team for the next season."

"You tried to warn Tomás," she said, taking Reed's hand in hers.

"I should have done more."

"Reed, you can't take care of all of us. You're only human, you know."

"More human than I realized," he said. "My knee is still protesting my midnight run."

"I'm proud of you."

"Oh, yeah?"

She felt the heat of his gaze, the longing in his question. "Yeah."

"Proud enough to have dinner with me tonight?"

"I can't leave—"

"Here, in the dining room?"

She glanced around. "Do you think that's wise? I mean, after all the commotion last night?"

"Don't you think we deserve a nice dinner for our crime-solving abilities?"

That made her smile. "I don't know. I wouldn't feel right—"

"It's just dinner, April. Just you and me."

Confused, she stared up at him. "What do you have in mind?"

"Just some time together, alone. We'll be right here, if your dad needs us."

"Who's cooking?"

"Not me," he assured her. "And certainly not Flora. She needs some time off."

"I agree."

"My mom will provide the food."

"Reed, she's already done so much."

"She doesn't mind. It's part of her matchmaking skills."

That made her smile. "Everyone's determined to bring us together."

"And I'm the first one in line."

"Is that what this dinner is all about?"

"Maybe."

April smiled up at him. "Should I dress for this dinner?"

"Yes, ma'am. Dress up. Get all glamorous."

"For you?"

"Will you, for me?"

"I think I can find something in the back of my closet, if I can just find the energy to actually get dressed."

"Good." He leaned forward and gave her a kiss on the forehead. "You rest up and I'll see you around seven."

"Okay."

April watched as he left the room, then turned back to Flora and Horaz. They both looked miserable and embarrassed.

"It's okay," she told them as she rushed forward to give them a hug. "I love you both so much. You know that, right?"

"Sí," Horaz said. "We feel the same."

"Let's go visit Daddy," April suggested, needing to be near her father.

Taking them both by the arms, she led the old couple down the long hallway, refusing to let the scare they'd had last night bother her anymore.

She'd learned what really mattered, since she'd been

back at the Big M. And right now, seeing her father and being with the people she loved was all that mattered.

And those people included Reed Garrison.

Chapter Thirteen

"Can you believe this?" Summer said as she finished reading April's latest e-mail. "Vandals and a break-in at the Big M? That's just what April needed."

"Doesn't sound too good," Autumn said absently from her paper cluttered desk. "I'm just glad everyone is okay."

"Yes," Summer said as she shut down the computer and took her empty teacup to the sink. "I'm surprised April didn't shoot that Adan."

"April hasn't been near a gun since she left Texas," Autumn reminded her overly zealous cousin.

"She still knows how to use one, though," Summer replied. "We all do."

"Don't remind me," Autumn countered. "I don't like guns."

"Necessary in today's world."

Autumn glanced up at her cousin. "You must have had a bad day at work."

Summer ran a hand through her long hair. "Yeah, if that's what you call helping three more battered women find the strength to stay away from their husbands, then I guess I did have a pretty rotten day."

Autumn dropped her ink pen. "I'm sorry you didn't get to go visit with April."

"Well, work has to come first."

"You need a vacation, Summer."

"So they tell me." She shrugged. "Let's not worry about me. Just think—right about now, Reed is getting dinner ready for April. That's so nice." Then she let out a gasp that made Autumn jump.

"What?"

"I just remembered. Today is April's birthday."

Reed figured April had forgotten that today was her birthday. But he hadn't, which was why he'd tried so hard all day to get things in order for their special dinner.

The house was back to normal. Reed had hired two ranch hands to help him get the office cleaned up. Adan hadn't found the safe, which was tucked behind a small book cabinet, but he'd done a good bit of damage. His parents had readily agreed to pay for that. All three of the boys were put on probation and community service, their parents ordered to supervise them strictly. The driver had bolted and run, but his parents had been just as upset as Tomás's and Adan's, and the authorities agreed he was just as guilty. They'd been planning this all summer by deliberately messing up the land so everyone on the ranch would be distracted just enough to allow the break-in. And they'd waited for the perfect night to do it.

It had been calculated and perfectly timed, but they'd failed anyway, because they were young and hadn't thought of the consequences or all the things that could go wrong. Well, they'd be thinking about that for a long time to come now.

The judge had also suggested they all attend church on a regular basis. Reed didn't think that would be a problem.

He glanced around the formal dining room one more time, making sure everything was ready for his evening with April. When he thought about what might have happened last night, he thanked God for protecting April and Lynette and April's father. Things could have taken a bad turn, but that was over now and Reed was glad. He only wanted to give April some time away from all of it, a chance to put all the bad stuff out of her mind.

The long glistening pinewood table was set with the abstract sunflower-etched china and matching crystal. Two golden glazed hurricane lamps sitting on the massive sideboard sparkled with the fire of vanilla-scented candles. The big, glass-paned doors were thrown open to the tiled patio and the pool beyond, allowing the cool night breeze and the scent of fresh blooming jasmine and gardenias to waft through the big room. Soft, soothing Spanish guitar music played in the background.

"It looks real nice, son."

Turning to give his mother thanks and a hug, Reed said, "You go on home and rest now. I appreciate everything y'all did. And thanks for inviting Richard over for the evening so we could have dinner by ourselves."

"Anything to help April get through this." She kissed him on the cheek. "And to help you and April find your way back to each other."

"Think good food will win her over?"

"Couldn't hurt. That and my handsome son."

"Thanks again, Mom."

She'd had Reed's daddy grill them two juicy rib-eye steaks, and she'd fixed fresh steamed vegetables and chocolate mousse, knowing April loved chocolate.

Reed watched his mom leave, then turned to check himself in the mirror over the long buffet. He wore a tuxedo—something his mother had suggested. His hair was combed and he smelled fresh and clean. "Guess I'll do."

"Oh, you'll do just fine."

He turned to find April standing at the arched door to the dining room; his breath caught in his throat as he took in the sight of her.

She wore a creamy satin sleeveless dress with a big collar that framed her slender shoulders and showed off her long neck. The dress flared out at her waist in a full-skirted halo that dropped almost to her ankles. She wore matching cream-colored shoes, and pearls on her ears and around her neck.

Reed had always loved April in her pearls.

"You'll do, too," he said, his voice husky and intimate. "Come here and let me look at you."

She whirled into the room like a ballerina, smiling over at him. "It was my mother's. I found it in the storage closet where Flora put all her clothes."

"Pretty as a picture," he said, holding her out away from him as he looked her over. Then he leaned close and gave her a peck on the cheek. "Happy birthday, April."

Her eyes widened, first in surprise, then in a dark sadness. "It is my birthday, isn't it?"

"Yes. That's what this party is all about."

Her eyes turned misty then. "Thank you."

Reed kissed her again, then gently touched her cheek. "No tears tonight, okay?"

"Okay," she said, the one word shaky.

He tugged her toward the table. "C'mon in."

She glanced around the room. "Reed, this is so nice."

"How's Stuart?"

"He's the same. Lynette promised to call me if anything changes, good or bad."

"So we can have an hour alone, just to talk?"

She nodded, glancing back out toward the hallway. "I have to admit, I feel a little guilty, all dressed up like this, with him so sick."

Reed came around the table to pull her close. "We're right here, sugar. Right here nearby. Your daddy wants you to be happy. You can take a little time to eat and relax."

"I hope so. I'm not sure I have an appetite, but everything sure looks good."

He smiled, touched a hand to her curling bangs. "We missed the Cattle Baron's Ball. It's tonight, in Dallas."

"You could have gone—to represent the Big M."

"Not without you."

"That's so sweet."

Reed tugged her close, taking in the scent of lilies and honeysuckle that seemed to float around her. "Right now, I don't feel very sweet. I feel selfish, because I just wanted some time with you all to myself."

"At least you're honest."

"I'm trying…and I'm trying to be patient."

She pulled away and turned toward the table. "Why don't we eat this wonderful food?"

"Okay." He backed off, knowing she was still skittish. Knowing and wondering when she'd just give in and love him the way he loved her. Or let him love her the way she should be loved.

"Let's say grace," April said, then she bowed her head and thanked God for the bounty of the Big M. *"And for keeping all of us safe. Give my father some peace, the peace that he needs right now. And help Tomás and his family, Lord. We ask this in Your name."*

"Amen," Reed said. "Here you go," he told her as he adjusted her chair. "Want some mineral water?"

"Sure." She watched as he poured sparkling water from a green bottle chilling in the ice bucket. "Thanks."

He waited as she took a long drink. "Good?"

"Tingly. That hit the spot."

Reed fell for her all over again, simply because she seemed nervous and fragile. And she looked so young and pretty, just like on that night of her sixteenth birthday.

"Ever wish we could turn back the clock?" he asked.

She took up her knife and fork. "Of course. I wish I could make Daddy well, and…that Mama was here with us. I wish I could understand why death has to separate us."

Reed saw the sadness in her dark eyes. "I don't know how you handle it, knowing he's dying. I think about my parents and how much I love them. It's just hard to imagine, even when we know we'll see them all again one day."

"It is hard," she said, nibbling on her vegetables. "I haven't handled it very well. I want to blame God, you know. But I understand it's a part of life and no one's to blame. Death is just part of the journey. It's really another part of life, just in a different place."

"You're very wise to think that."

"My mother taught me to have faith, always."

"Do you have faith in me, April?"

He watched the play of emotions on her face, saw the joy, the fear, the pain, the hope. And waited for her answer.

"You've been so kind, Reed. So much a part of my life. I couldn't have made it this far without you here, helping me out. I didn't want to admit that, didn't want to look weak and helpless. But I've come to realize that turning to someone for help isn't a sign of weakness. It's a sign of strength, a sign of how much I do believe in you."

Reed leaned back in his chair. "Wow, that was some speech."

"But it wasn't what you wanted to hear?"

He threw down his fork. "You know what I want to hear, but I don't have the right to ask you that, not now, when Stuart is so sick."

April leaned forward and grabbed his hand. He saw the tears brimming in her eyes. "Are you willing to wait for me, Reed? Are you willing to give me some more time?"

Reed got up and pulled her out of her chair. "I've been waiting all my life. What's a little more time?"

Then he kissed her, to show her that he was more than willing to wait. But on his own terms. "I want you to love me again, April. I just want that—whenever you're ready."

He saw in her eyes that she did love him. He felt in her kiss that she had always loved him.

Patience. He had to learn patience. But he'd been so very patient, for so long.

April looked up at him, touching his face. "I don't deserve you."

"You deserve to be happy. You deserve…whatever can make you happy. I hope I can help in that department. I promise I'll try."

"I just need to get through this. And then, I'll decide what to do…about everything."

That wasn't exactly what he wanted to hear. "About us, you mean?"

"Yes, about us. About the ranch. Everything."

Then she kissed him again, feathering his face with little butterfly touches. "Can we break into that chocolate mousse now?"

Reed had to laugh at that. "You're trying to distract me."

"Will it work?"

"No. I can't be distracted from getting what I want. You should know that about me."

"I do. It's one of the things I love—"

"One of the things you love about me?"

"Yes."

"I guess that'll have to do for now," he said as he handed her a dessert dish full of the creamy mousse.

She smiled and grabbed a spoon. "It's a start."

The dinner ended way too soon for Reed. They'd finally settled down to small talk and laughter. He loved the way April laughed. When she was truly happy, her whole face lit up, her creamy porcelain skin glowing with an inner light.

He wanted to make her laugh for all the days of their life.

"Thank you again," she told him as they carried their

plates into the kitchen. "This evening was so lovely. And it did help me to relax. It was a very thoughtful birthday present."

"Good," he said. "Let's take a stroll around the backyard before we say good-night."

She raised her dark brows. "Okay."

"Don't worry. It's just a friendly walk—to fight off the calories in that chocolate mousse."

She laughed at that. "I guess that would be smart."

He took her out by the pool. "Look at those stars."

April followed his gaze, lifting her head to the dark heavens. "A clear night, after all that rain last night."

Reed pulled her back against his chest, then wrapped his hands around hers at her side. "The good Lord always sends us signs of His beauty and His bounty, even after a bad storm."

"It was a bad night all the way around," April said, a long sigh leaving her body. "I still can't believe Tomás would be involved in such a thing."

"He's young and misguided," Reed replied, resting his chin on top of her silky curls. "And his parents have always allowed him to kinda run wild. They left things up to Flora and Horaz."

"And they tried, they really did," April added. "But Tomás isn't their responsibility, no matter how much they want to help him."

"I think things will change now. Some good should come of this bad. We've given those boys a second chance. I just hope they don't mess up again."

"I don't think Tomás will. At least he has all of us behind him." April turned to face him then. "You are a good man, Reed. You always look for the good in others, too. And you're always willing to give people another chance."

He touched his forehead to hers. "Hush, you're making me blush."

"I just want you to know—"

The ringing of the doorbell pealed through the house, stopping April in midsentence. "Now who could that be this late? Maybe Uncle Richard forgot his key."

She hurried inside, her skirts swishing. Reed followed her. "Hey, wait up." After last night's break-in, he didn't want her answering the door without him right there.

The bell rang again just before April opened the big door. "I'm coming." Turning to look back at Reed, she whispered, "Someone sure is impatient."

When she turned back to face the visitor, Reed heard her sharp intake of breath. Then he felt a definite chill as her body stiffened.

"Danny, what are you doing here?"

The man standing at the door had sandy-blond hair and an attitude, from what Reed could tell. Reed hated him on the spot. Something about the arrogant way the man slanted his gaze possessively over April brought out Reed's protective instincts.

And his jealousy.

"May I come in?" the man asked, waving a hand in the air. "The bugs in Texas are just as big as everything else around here."

April shot Reed a confused, shocked look. "Of course. Come in." She motioned to Reed. "Reed Garrison, meet Danny Pierson."

"Reed?" Danny's icy-blue eyes glazed over as he

stared at Reed. "Well, I've certainly heard a lot about you. You and April…grew up together, right?"

"That's right," April interjected before Reed could explain how things were. She gave Reed a warning glare as she closed the door.

"And who are you?" Reed asked, shaking the hand the other man extended. After all, his mama had taught him manners. But his daddy had taught him how to fight.

And he sure smelled a good ol' fight coming on.

Apparently, so did April. "Danny is—"

"Her ex-boyfriend," Danny finished. "But I hope to change that." He put an arm around April's shoulder, then smiled over at Reed. "Know what I mean?"

"I think I do," Reed said, a slow rage burning its way through his system. Then he glanced at April and saw the distress on her face. "Maybe you should have called first. This isn't a good time. April's father is ill."

"I'm aware of that." Danny scanned them both with a puzzled look. "Is that why you're both so dressed up?"

Reed curled his fists at his side. "We were having dinner. A *private* dinner."

"Oh." Danny shrugged, tightening his grip on April. "Hope I didn't interrupt anything important. But April and I have some unfinished business."

Reed stepped forward. "I don't think—"

"Reed, it's okay," April said, coming between them. "Danny's company—Fairchild's Department Stores—is under contract with Satire. We just need to work out some of the details."

Reed glared at the other man as if he were a nasty bug. "Is *this* the problem you were telling me about?"

April nodded. "Yes. I mean, Danny and I have some problems to clear up. It's just business."

"Did you invite him here?"

"No, not really. But since he's here, I think I should talk to him."

"Yeah, man," Danny said, clearly triumphant. "We're just going to talk. About old times and a bright new future."

Reed felt the pulse throbbing in his jaw, felt the tension flaring through his head as he clenched his teeth.

"April, are you sure?"

"Yes," April said. Then she turned to Danny. "Why don't you wait in the den?" She pointed across the hall. "I'll just show Reed out."

"See you, Reed." Danny grinned, then turned to go into the other room.

April took Reed by the arm. "Can we talk?"

"About what?" he said as they went into the kitchen. "About that fancy city fellow coming here to win you back? April, I won't—"

"You won't what, Reed? Let him near me? Let him flirt with me?" Her eyes were snapping a dark fire, but Reed wasn't sure just which one of them she was mad at—the ex or him. Maybe both. "I'm a big girl, remember? I've lived out on my own for a very long time now."

He closed his eyes. "I don't need to hear the rest. You've had other relationships, same as me."

"Yes, but you've jumped to the wrong conclusion here, same as always. Danny and I are over. We've been over for a very long time."

"So what's he doing here?"

"He was in Dallas on business. When he finally returned my calls, he asked to come here."

"And you told him he could? I can't believe that! Your father—"

"Stop it," she said, her face flushed, her eyes black with rage. "Just stop it. And leave, now. After everything…after all we talked about tonight, you still think the worst of me."

"April, I—"

"Just go, Reed. I can't take any more of this. Don't you see? No matter what we feel for each other, you will always, always think of me as the shallow little rich girl who broke your heart. You don't even believe what I've tried to explain to you. You think you know what's best for me. I can't go through that again."

Broken and baffled, Reed slowly nodded his head. "Well, neither can I."

He turned and stomped through the house to the open doors leading out to the pool. And he didn't look back.

He couldn't look back.

He'd just used up the last of his patience. There was nothing left. Nothing but an aching emptiness that was as vast and deep as the beautiful starry sky over his head.

"I guess nothing good is gonna come out of this particular situation after all, Lord," he said, his questioning prayer echoing out over the night.

When he reached his truck, he turned and looked back at the glowing lights from the house. And he felt like that teenager all over again, on the outside looking in.

Chapter Fourteen

April held her hands to her temples, massaging away the nagging headache that seemed to be coming on strong. This night had been just about perfect, but now it was going downhill very fast.

"Feeling bad?" Danny asked as she came back into the den.

April dropped her hands to stare at him. He looked every bit as handsome as she remembered him. But now she could see through all that charm. And besides, he'd ruined her night with Reed. She'd have to deal with *that* one later. Now she just wanted Danny gone. "I'm not feeling at my best, no. Danny, why did you come here?"

He shrugged and picked up a small crystal bowl from the coffee table, moving it from hand to hand. "I thought we had some business to discuss."

April grabbed the bowl before he managed to drop it. "The only business we have is this—we're over, through, finished. And you didn't have to create this little snag in the contracts between Satire and Fairchild's just to get back at me."

"Oh, you think that's what this is all about?" he

asked, coming so close she could smell his expensive aftershave. That scent had at one time made her all giddy. Now she just wanted to be sick.

"Isn't it?" she asked. "I told you not to come here. My father is dying, this ranch is in a mess, and I don't need you to complicate things."

"Nothing complicated about me, babe," he said, one finger trailing down her face to her neck. "I just wanted to see you again."

"So you did plan this whole thing?"

He smiled, shifting closer. "Of course I did. The contracts are pretty standard, but I managed to find a couple of loopholes. So I used that as an excuse. That and a quick trip to Dallas. Then it made sense to swing by here and see you."

April backed away. "This is ridiculous. You're not only wasting my time, but you're using Fairchild's perks to take a side trip to Paris, Texas? Danny, not only is that risky, it's downright stupid. You could lose your job."

"I have the authority to do whatever I see fit regarding the Satire line. My employer knows what I'm doing."

"But I bet you put a really good spin on things, just as you've always done."

She turned, but he grabbed her by the wrist, twisting her back around. "Don't walk away from me, April."

"Let me go," she said, her resolve giving way to the warning moving through the pain of her headache.

"Oh, no. I didn't come all this way to be ignored."

"Danny, I don't know what you expected, but I can't help you. Not with the contracts, and certainly not with us. The contracts can't be changed without a big, ugly battle, and I'm not interested in anything you have to say regarding us."

"Without a big, ugly battle there, too, you mean?" he said, his eyes flaring a white-blue. "Is it because of *him?*"

April yanked her arm away, then rubbed the spot where he'd held her. "If you mean Reed, it has nothing to do with him. But it has everything to do with *you.* I don't feel the same about you as I once did."

"Oh, yeah, I remember. Because I'm ruthless and cutthroat and I don't play fair?"

"That and other things," she said, remembering his quick temper and his refusal to compromise on any issue at all, including her faith. "I think you just need to leave."

"Not yet," he said, coming toward her.

April turned just as he grabbed her around the waist. He tried to kiss her, but she pushed him away. "Danny, stop it."

"Oh, don't play that game."

He tried again, but April was too quick this time. She scooted around a high-back chair. "I asked you to leave and I mean it. Do you want me to report your behavior to the CEO of Fairchild's?"

"You'd do that, just to get even?"

"I'd do that just to get rid of you."

"You know, I can stall on these contracts, hold up the entire shipment of Satire ready-to-wear."

"You go right ahead," April said, weary with all his threats. Weary to her very bones. But she had more backbone now than she'd had when they were dating. "I'd like to see you explain that to the higher-ups. Fairchild's is already in a heap of trouble. It wouldn't do to miss this chance to make a comeback. I don't think it would sit well with all those people you're trying to impress. And I know how hard you try to impress, Danny."

She saw the anger flaring in his eyes. He came at her, trying to grab her arms, but she was ready for him. April swung around and picked up the nearby cordless phone. "Just touch me again and I'll have the whole ranch down on your head."

He stepped back, hands up. "I guess I misjudged you, April. I thought you'd come begging."

"I don't beg anyone."

He stood silent, staring at her for a moment. Then he let out a defeated sigh. "Okay. I don't want a fight. I just wanted to put things right between us."

"Things will be fine if you leave now. But if you ever try to pull something like this again, Danny, I'll have to report you. And I don't want to have to do that."

He shrugged, checking the anger she could see pulsing in his jawline. "It would be your word against mine."

"Yes," she said, remembering how they'd been happy together at one time. But it had been a false happiness, and it hadn't withstood the test of time. Not the way her friendship, her love for Reed, had. Maybe God had sent Danny here for that very reason, so she could see what a real love between a man and a woman should be like, even with time and separation between them.

Why had she sent Reed away? He would have made quick work of getting rid of Danny Pierson for her. But April knew it was better this way. This was her battle, not Reed's, no matter how much Reed would want to protect her. If she couldn't stand up to Danny, she'd never be able to face Reed or anyone else again. She wanted Reed's respect and she wanted him to see that she wasn't that spoiled socialite he'd accused her of being the day she left.

She looked over at Danny, feeling nothing for him.

That, and knowing that her love for Reed could be a blessing instead of a fear, gave her the courage she'd never had before. "It would be your word against mine. But I think you know which one of us people would believe. After all, you haven't exactly been discreet and tactful in how you treat people."

"I guess I haven't at that." He slumped against a chair, scowling. "And you've been a model of propriety."

His sarcasm and criticism didn't sting the way they should have. April had been through so much since the last time she'd seen him. He had no idea just how strong she'd become. But he was about to find out.

"I don't have to justify myself to you, Danny. Now, I think it's time for you to leave—"

"April!"

Lynette's frantic call from the hallway stopped April in midsentence. She whirled and hurried down the hall. "What is it?"

But when she saw Lynette's tear-streaked face, she knew. She knew.

"Is he—"

"It's bad," Lynette said, taking both of April's hands in hers. "You'd better come. I'll call Richard, too."

April gave Danny a helpless look. "I have to go."

Danny nodded, his face going pale. "I understand."

April didn't have time to make sure he left the house. She rushed to her father's room, dread coursing through the erratic pulse beating its way through her system.

Reed entered the house from the back. The dining room was dark, but a light burned from the kitchen and the long hallway. He went into the kitchen and found Flora sitting at the counter, her hands clasped in prayer.

She looked up at the sound of his steps. "Reed! It's so sad. So sad."

Reed could feel the weight of death pushing through the house. Just hours ago, he and April had laughed and talked, walked through the gardens. Then he'd gone and gotten all riled up and ruined things. Again.

He wouldn't hurt April again. And he wouldn't allow himself to be hurt again. He'd just about decided that maybe she would never love him the way he loved her, that maybe she'd changed but he'd stayed the same. He'd been in the same holding pattern since the day she'd left. Maybe she was right in getting angry with him each time he tried to step in and save the day.

But wasn't that what being a life partner, a helpmate, was all about? Shouldn't he be the one to always be by her side and hold her up in her time of need? He was just an old-fashioned country boy who loved a sophisticated, very modern city girl. But it wouldn't matter, if he couldn't make her love him back.

He might just have to accept that and let her be.

When Richard had told them it was near the end, Reed hadn't hesitated to come here and be nearby. Just in case she needed him.

"I know, Flora," he said now, taking the woman's withered hand in his. "It's tough. But you and Horaz, you know you mean the world to him, and to April. She'll need you both now."

"Sí," Flora replied, nodding. "Horaz is in the den with that other man. Waiting."

"What other man?"

"That stranger who showed up."

"Oh, Danny Pierson? He's still here?"

She bobbed her head again. "He said he no leave

with April's father dying. He said he wanted to stay in case she need him."

"I'll take care of him," Reed said. Then he stalked across the entranceway, determined to throw that no-good out on his ear.

But the sight he saw made him stop and stare—and feel ashamed for his take-no-prisoners attitude. No wonder April had kicked him out earlier.

Horaz was talking quietly to Danny Pierson, talking and nodding his head, a gentle smile on his face. And Danny seemed to be listening. Gone was all the arrogance and the bluster Reed had witnessed on meeting the man earlier. Danny seemed intent on what Horaz was saying, his expression one of concern and respect.

Both men looked up as Reed entered the room.

"Hola," Horaz said, getting up to shake Reed's hand.

"Hey," Reed said, puzzled down to his boots. "What's going on?"

Danny stood then and extended his hand. "I'm so sorry about April's dad. Horaz was just telling me about him. He sounds like a decent man."

"He is," Reed said, wondering if this night could get any more confusing. "And what are you still doing here?"

Danny raised a hand. "Hey, now, I know I came on a little strong before, but April set me straight. I was wrong to come here, but now that I'm here, well, I can't just leave her. I have to make sure she's okay."

"Do you even care about how she feels?"

"Of course I do," Danny said, sincerity making him look a whole lot younger than Reed had first believed. "I—I just wanted to see if there was any chance—"

"Not a chance," Reed said.

"She told me that." Danny let out a breath. "She's changed. She seemed more sure of herself."

"April has always been very self-assured."

Danny came to stand face to face with Reed. "Now that's where you're wrong. At times, she seemed very insecure to me. And she let me walk all over her. But she didn't do that tonight. Tonight she stood up to me and told me how things are. I thought I could just come in here and get her back with threats and my old condescending routine, but it didn't work this time."

Reed let that soak in, thought seriously about punching the guy, then asked, "And do you understand now? How things are?"

"I think I'm beginning to," Danny said, some of the old smugness coming out again. "It's you, man, all the way. I think it was always you. But, hey, I can't fight all that's going on here. I just didn't want to leave. Not yet."

Reed wanted to toss the man out the door, but how would that make him look? April was already steamed at him. He didn't want to make a scene, not tonight. Danny was right. April had changed, even if Reed still saw her as that beautiful sixteen-year-old socialite. She was stronger now, still determined, still beautiful, but a whole lot more courageous. Or maybe she'd been courageous all along and Reed just hadn't seen it. He'd always thought she'd been a coward for running from their love. But didn't it take courage to do what she'd done? To move across the country to a strange place and start a new life? Didn't it take courage and strength to leave everything and everyone she loved, in order to overcome her father's grief? And her own? She'd had to start over in order to become the best person she could be. But surprisingly, she'd never lost her faith in God in all that time.

Why was that so very clear to him now?

Reed suddenly realized that maybe he'd changed, too. Normally, he would have fought a cad like Danny Pierson with all his might, no questions asked. But in spite of his jumping to conclusions earlier tonight and making April mad at him all over again, Reed had shown restraint. He'd left quietly, if reluctantly.

If only he'd kept the faith, as April had done. He'd never given her the benefit of faith. He'd never actually believed in her. And that was part of the reason she hadn't turned back to him now.

"You want me to go?" Danny asked.

"Sit down," Reed told Danny. "I'm going back to check on her."

Danny sank back down in the chair then glanced over at Horaz. Horaz nodded and lowered his head, silent but sure.

Reed decided Danny was in good hands with Horaz, so he headed toward the back of the house, his footsteps sounding against the tiled floor. He dreaded going into that room, dreaded seeing April and her father. But she needed someone to be there with her. She needed someone to believe in her.

He wanted to be that someone. This time, he wouldn't let her down.

Chapter Fifteen

April stood over her father's grave, the mist of a silent rain falling in a gentle dance all around her. April didn't feel the cool mist or hear the soft rumble of thunder in the distance. She couldn't smell the sweet, clinging scent of so many flowers covered with the tears of rain. She was lost somewhere in the past.

She was remembering all the good times. She'd had a blessed life, growing up here on the Big M. She'd had parents who loved and cherished her. They'd given her the world. Her mother had taught her always to have a life of faith, always to put God first in all things, no matter how privileged their life had been. And even though she'd tried to do that, April had never understood the responsibility that came with vast wealth, or the obligations that came with a deep, abiding faith, until now.

Now, all of this belonged to her. And she didn't know if even her strong faith could sustain her.

She could feel the weight of that responsibility on her shoulders, could hear her mother's laughter, could see her father's brilliant smile.

"What am I supposed to do now, Daddy?" she asked,

the chill of the spring day causing her to wrap her arms around herself. "I miss you already. I miss you so much and, now, I miss Mama all over again. I'm all alone."

"No, you're not."

She turned to find Reed standing there with a raincoat and an umbrella, his eyes washing over her in the same misty way the water was washing over the cemetery.

"We missed you back at the house," he said as he stepped forward. "Had a feeling you'd be here."

She turned back to stare down at the flower-covered grave. "I guess everyone thinks I'm incredibly rude."

"They all understand," he said as he draped the coat around her shivering body and held the umbrella over both of them.

He didn't speak again and April thanked him for that, her heart brimming with love for him and this land. If she could just let go enough to accept that love.

Finally, she cleared her throat and pushed away the tears. "Is the house still full?"

"Just the family now," Reed said, one arm holding her steady. "Summer and Autumn are doing a good job with supervising the food and the visitors. They were even nice to Danny before he left. But they were worried about you."

"I just needed some air." Then she sent him a soft smile. "You were nice to Danny, too. Thanks for letting him stay at your house."

"It was interesting—two of your exes talking about old times."

"I guess y'all compared notes?"

"No, I'm just teasing about that. I told him he was welcome to stay as long as he didn't mention anything about your time with him, or ask me anything about you and me now. He understood and he was a perfect gentleman."

"Imagine that. I think this trip has changed him."

"It's changed all of us."

"Yes, I guess it has."

She felt the tug of his hand against the coat. "Remember that verse from Isaiah? 'The grass withers, the flowers fade, but the word of the Lord stands forever'?"

She nodded, thinking these flowers were too beautiful ever to fade. But they would. They would.

"I've always loved that particular verse."

She let out a struggling laugh. "And why are you telling me this?"

He kissed the top of her head. "Just to remind you that some things withstand the test of time. That love surpasses pain and death. I understand that you're scared about a lot of things, but God's love and grace will get us through this, April."

She laid her head on his chest, seeking the warmth and security that he offered. "I know. That's what I keep telling myself. It's just so hard to understand, to accept. We should have had a good life together, my parents and I. I wanted them to see their grandchildren, to live to be very old. I wanted so much for them. Now that will never happen."

"They will see it all, April. They'll be watching over you."

"I have a lot to think about," she said. "Too much to think about."

"Take your time. The Big M is functioning. We all know what needs to be done."

"You've been taking care of things for a long time

now, Reed. Thank you for that. And for being there the other night, when…when—"

"Shhh." He kissed her again, a soft whisper against her temple. "I'm not going anywhere."

"Uncle Richard will be a big help," she said, gaining strength with that reassurance. "I'm not so sure about Uncle James. He couldn't wait to leave today. Probably afraid Summer would light into him and her mother, the way she kept glaring at them."

"Yep." Reed became quiet again, then turned her to face him. "April, about the other night when Danny showed up—"

"Look, Reed, I was a bit stressed out that night. I mean, all that with Tomás, then Danny."

"I know. But there is no excuse for how I reacted to Danny Pierson being here. I'm sorry I jumped to the wrong conclusion. I seem to do that, where you're concerned."

"It's water under the bridge," she said. "We've been through worse."

"Yeah, like me always doubting you. I can see now why you bolted and went to New York. It wasn't just about your father's grief. It was because I was smothering and demanding, right? And I never believed in you enough to show a little faith."

April raised her head to stare over at him. "Reed, none of that matters now."

"Yes, it does. It matters more than ever. I don't want that to happen this time."

April could feel the weight pressing at her heart. "Things are different now. I'm not that young girl who clung to your every word."

"No, ma'am, you are not that. You're a woman. But you're still the only woman I want."

April pulled away, her breath catching in her throat. "I can't think about this right now. I've got so much to consider, so many things to decide."

She watched as Reed stepped back. "Okay. I guess I thought that part had been decided—that you and me belong together."

"Belonging together and *being* together are two different things," she said. "I've got to decide what's best for my future. Do I stay here or go back to New York? I don't know."

She could tell that wasn't what he wanted to hear, but she wasn't going to fight with Reed right here over her father's grave. "Can we talk about this later?" she added.

He nodded, a gentle resolve in his eyes. "C'mon. You're freezing. Want me to drive you back to the house?"

"I did walk," she said, shaking her head. "I took off before the rain came and I just sort of wound up here."

"We could take the long way home."

She raised an eyebrow. "Oh, yeah?"

"Let's go for a long drive around town."

"That sounds nice. I'm not ready to face everyone back at the house just yet."

"Okay, then. Let's go."

Reed drove his mother's car through Paris, Texas, past the Culbertson Fountain in the historic district. "Did you know this is considered the prettiest plaza in all the state of Texas?" he asked April, hoping to make her laugh.

She did laugh. But she still sat slumped over in her corner of the car. "Well, it *is* lovely."

He drove by the old railroad depot, then on past some of the old homes lining the streets. "This rain is nice. We needed a good rain."

"Yes, I guess we did."

"I called Mom and told her we were going for a drive, so no one would worry about you."

"Thanks."

"Want to see the Market Square Mural? That's always a crowd pleaser."

"Reed, I know what Paris looks like. No need to be my tour guide."

"Sorry. Guess you do remember some of it, even if you never took that fancy convertible of yours for a spin."

"I remember all of it." She smiled over at him. "Remember that summer my mother insisted we have our picture taken in front of the Eiffel Tower—our Eiffel Tower?"

He laughed, hoping she was at last beginning to feel better. "I sure do. She made me wear a red cowboy hat just like the one up on the tower. I think my mom has a copy of that picture somewhere."

"And I had on red boots. My mother wanted to do an abstract—with the picture all black and white, except for the hats and my boots. She said that replica was truly a Texas treasure and that the red hats and boots would represent the heart of Texas and us. And she said that we didn't need Paris, France. Not when we had Paris, Texas."

"Your mother was amazing."

"Yes, she was. So talented."

"You know, I have one of her abstracts hanging in the den at my house."

"Yeah?"

"Uh-huh. When your dad decided to sell me the guest house, he gave that picture to me as a house-warming gift."

"I haven't even seen your house."

"I know. One day, I'll give you the tour."

"One day."

Reed noticed the crape myrtles blooming all over the place. Along the roadsides, the red clover and Indian paintbrush were beginning to spring up. Out in the field, the bluebonnets tipped their heads to the rain.

"It's almost summer," he said. "Lots of work to do."

April sat up and looked over at him. "Stop the car, Reed."

Concerned, he pulled the car over at a small park. "You okay?"

She bobbed her head, then turned to look at him.

"I have to go back, you know."

His heart did a quick thud, then sank down. "To New York, you mean?"

"Yes. I have to take care of some things."

"Is that your way of telling me you won't be back here?"

"I don't know," she said. The honesty in her eyes hurt him. It was too bright, too expectant.

He turned toward her. "April, I know today was hard on you. The funeral, all the people, everything. You've got a lot of burdens to bear, and I don't want to be one of them. If you need to go back to New York, then I guess all I can do is kiss you goodbye."

"Just like that?"

"Just like that. What do you expect me to do, beg you to stay? You know I want that, but only if you want it, too."

"You'd let me go, and not condemn me or resent me?"

"I've never condemned you. I resented that we couldn't be happy together. But happiness has to come with certain sacrifices. I can see that now."

"But Reed, is it fair for you to sacrifice *your* happiness while you wait for me to decide about things?"

"I'm happy. I was happy."

"Until I came back."

He tugged her into his arms. "Listen, I love you. I have always loved you. You can see that. Anybody with two eyes can see that. I can't hide it. But...we've both changed. I've learned to be patient, but I've also learned to be less demanding and more understanding."

"So you won't be angry when I leave again?"

"I'll be hurt, but not angry. I wish... I wish I could just sweep you up and take you home to the life I've always dreamed about us having. But that wouldn't be right. It wouldn't be fair. You had to go away once. And now it's time for you to go away again. We both knew it was coming."

She hugged him close. "I won't neglect the Big M. I promise. I won't let anything happen to the ranch."

Reed held her tight, shutting his eyes to the reality of her leaving him again. "I know you won't. And we'll all be here to help."

"You've always been right here."

"Yes, ma'am." He held back the pain. Was he crazy to hold on to such an uncertain hope? To cling to that dream of having her as his wife? "Maybe it's time for me to throw in the towel, though."

She raised her head. "What does that mean?"

"Maybe it's time for me to accept that you might not feel the same way—about us, I mean."

She touched a finger to his lips. "Don't say that. I can't keep expecting you to wait. But I don't want to lose you, either. I don't know what's wrong with me."

Reed knew what was wrong. "You've just lost your father. You're dealing with so much pain and grief. I won't push you for anything else right now. But when you're ready, I'll be here. Right here. Will you remember that, and…just call me if you need me?"

She fell back into his arms, her tears pouring out like the rain shrouding them inside the car. Reed held her as she cried, the gray of the dreary afternoon turning to the darkness of a rainswept night. He held her and accepted that he might not ever be able to hold her again.

"Hold on, I'm coming."

April ran to the ringing phone, dropping bags as she went. It was one of her co-workers from Satire, wanting to see how she was doing and if she wanted to go out to dinner with the gang. In the couple of weeks she'd been back, she'd had all sorts of invitations.

"Thanks for the offer," April said, her eyes scanning the New York skyline. "But I'm just going to stay in tonight and catch up on some work."

"That's what you tell everyone who calls here," Summer said from the doorway after April hung up. "You should get out more."

April started putting away the groceries she'd picked up around the corner. "I don't want to go out."

Autumn came out of the bathroom draped in her old

terry robe, with a towel on her head. "Did I hear the phone ringing?"

"It was for April," Summer said, making a face. "She declined a fun night on the town, from what I could gather."

"I don't want to go out. End of conversation," April said, annoyed with her well-meaning but overbearing cousins.

"Have you heard from Reed?" Autumn asked as she fixed herself a cup of tea.

"No. And I don't expect to hear from Reed. Why should Reed call me? I left him. Again."

"You didn't leave *him,* technically," Summer pointed out. "You just left Texas. Again."

April turned to face her cousins. "Do y'all ever wish we could just pack up and go home?"

"I knew it," Summer said, stomping her sandal-clad foot. "You *want* to go home, don't you, sugar?"

April sank down on a high stool at the counter. "I think I've finally made up my mind. But I had a little help from a most unlikely source."

"Tell us," Autumn said, getting out two more tea bags and cups.

April pushed at her hair, tugging the silk scarf away from her throat. "Katherine fired me today."

"What?"

"Well, she fired me, then she offered me another position with Satire."

"Katherine is a strange bird," Autumn said, shrugging. "So what kind of other position?"

"Western region director of Satire ready-to-wear. I'd be based in Dallas."

Summer plopped on the couch. "As in Dallas, *Texas?*"

"Yes. That would be the one."

Autumn hopped around the counter. "That would mean you'd be near home, honey! Near—"

"Near Reed," April finished. "I'd be able to work *from* home, according to Katherine. It would involve some traveling and time spent in Dallas, but for the most part, I'd be able to work from the Big M."

Summer twisted her lips, a sign that her mind was racing. "Does Katherine know about this thing between Reed and you?"

"I told her some of it when I got back a couple of weeks ago." She shrugged. "Katherine knew something was wrong. She thought I was just depressed about Daddy, but when I started telling her, everything kind of spilled out."

"I think Katherine is compromising," Autumn said with a practical tone. "She doesn't want to see you go, so she's come up with a way to keep you and let you go home, too."

"Amazing," Summer said.

"Amazing," April repeated.

"Are you going to accept?" Autumn asked.

April sat there, her heart thudding a beat that told her at last she could have it all. "What if I do and…it's too late for Reed and me? I've held him away for so long. I was so afraid. And the funny part is, now I'm not afraid of loving him, but I *am* afraid to tell him that. Because I think I've waited *too* long."

"Oh, I don't think it will ever be too late for that, honey," Summer said. "That man is so in love with you."

"And I love him," April said, thinking the words sounded strange, being said out loud. "I love Reed."

"Well, amen," Summer shouted. "Admitting it is the first step, you know."

"The first step to what?" April asked, still scared silly.

"To being happy," Autumn finished. "Now, why don't you call Reed and tell him?"

"I can't do that yet," April said. "I have to find the courage."

"You could just surprise him and show up," Summer replied.

The thudding in April's heart changed tempo, began a new, hopeful beat. "Maybe I will."

"You ought to just call the woman," Richard said. "It's been over two weeks. Don't you worry about her?"

"Every hour on the hour," Reed admitted.

They were standing near the roping arena, watching one of the hands work with a feisty colt. It was a clear day with a powder-blue sky full of promise.

"I've talked to her, of course," Richard replied, his hands slung over the fence. "I'm kinda keeping things going until she can get back down here."

"Did she say she was coming back anytime soon?"

"I think she'll want to check on things from time to time."

"And that's why I'm not going to call her. I don't like long-distance, time-to-time relationships."

Richard let out a chuckle. "You two cut the cake, you know that? You dance all around the issue here."

"Oh, and just what is the issue here?"

"That you love that girl and she loves you."

"Then why am I here and why is she there?"

Richard leaned close. "I don't know. But you're a

Texan through and through, Reed. And Texans never back down from a fight."

"I don't want to fight with her anymore."

"Then don't. Just go and get her and bring her home."

"It's not that easy."

"How can you say that when you've never even tried?"

Reed stared over at April's uncle, his thudding heart changing tempo. It begin to beat with a little more strength and confidence. "You know, you're right. I've never been to New York City."

Richard slapped him on the arm. "Well, son, I'll fire up the company jet and you can be there by morning."

"Let me just go pack an overnight bag," Reed said. "This time, instead of letting her run away from me, I'm gonna run *to* her."

"Now you're talking."

Richard was right. Maybe if he went after April, she'd finally believe in their love.

"I need you to meet me by Central Park," Summer said.

April made a face at her cell phone. "Right now?"

"As soon as you can get there. I have a nice surprise for you."

"Summer, I told you I can't do lunch today."

"Just meet me," Summer said, impatience crackling through the line. "It's a beautiful day and you need some sun. And I need to talk to you."

"Where are you?"

"Fifth Avenue and 59th Street, at the fountain."

"Okay, that's not very far. I guess I can make it."

"Good. See you."

April hung up, let out a sigh toward all the files on her desk, then grabbed her purse. Summer seemed so insistent. Wondering what her cousin needed to talk to her about and what the big surprise was, April walked out of the building, then headed toward 59th Street. "This had better be good."

"This is going to be good," Summer told Reed just before she gave him a peck on the cheek. "You were smart to call me first, buddy. Because you know she'd just bolt again if you didn't have the element of surprise on your side."

"Are you sure?" Reed asked, glancing around the busy streets. His hotel was right up the street from April's office, but he'd called the apartment first and talked to Summer. Summer had cooked up this crazy meeting at the park. Now Reed wasn't so sure.

"Trust me," Summer said. "Now, she'll be coming from that way." She waved her hand, her bangle bracelets making a soft medley. "I'm going back to work." She started walking backward in her high heels. "Don't mess this up, Reed."

Helpless, Reed watched her go, then glanced around the plaza and over at the hills and trees of the park. "Who knew something this big and green could be in a city?"

The fact that he was talking to himself didn't seem to bother the many people passing by. They all looked serious and businesslike, and they mostly ignored him.

So he waited, enjoying the warm sunshine and the blooming flowers and the brilliant summer-new trees.

And then he saw her.

April hurried up the street, her huge baby-blue

leather tote bag slung over her arm, her short hair wafting out around her face. She wore a floral print dress with tight, elbow length sleeves and a full skirt that hit just below her knees. And she had on those infernal tall sandals like Summer had been wearing.

She looked so fresh and pretty, Reed had to glance around to make sure he wasn't dreaming.

He waited, watching as she looked toward the park. Watching as her expression changed from purposeful to surprised…to confused…to happy.

Maybe Summer was right. The element of surprise seemed to be working.

"Reed?" she said as she hurried across the intersection separating them. "How—"

"Don't ask," he said as he pulled her into his arms. "Just don't ask."

She didn't. She hugged him tight. "Can I ask *why,* then?"

"Because I love you," he said as he held her away. "Because I decided it was time for me to do the running." He kissed her forehead. "I've never gone chasing after a woman, and since you're the only woman I've ever wanted…well, here I am."

"You came for me." It was a statement filled with wonder and endearment. "You came here, for me?"

"Yes, ma'am. Why else would I be standing in the middle of Manhattan in the middle of May?"

"I was coming back, you know."

"Really, now?"

"Yes. I have a new job, in Dallas. I can work from home."

"And where would home be?"

"The Big M, with you."

"So I could have spared myself this trip to the Big Apple?"

"Oh, no. Seeing you here, well, that seals the deal. Now I know you really do love me."

"You doubted that?"

"No, but you doubted me. You coming here, I think it means you don't doubt me anymore."

"No, I don't."

"Good, because I'm not afraid anymore. I love you," she said.

Reed's heart beat faster with each impatient car horn, with each tread of feet against asphalt. "I love you, too."

"Want to go home now?"

"Not just yet," he said, holding her face in his hands.

"I want to see the rest of this big park. And your city."

"I'll be glad to show it to you. And then we can go home. Together."

"Together," he said. He kissed her, the certain hope of their love coloring his world with blessings and thankfulness.

* * * * *

Dear Reader,

Death is never easy to accept, but it is a part of life. As Christians, we are taught that this life is just a part of eternity. We know that a better life is still to come. But still, we weep when we lose a loved one. So we have to keep the faith and hold fast to that certain hope that will bring us eternal life.

April had to learn this lesson as she watched her father dying. She also had to learn that sometimes the things we fear the most are the very things that we need the most. She needed Reed's love, but she was afraid to embrace that love. She didn't want to be hurt. Reed was steadfast and strong, but he wanted her on his own terms. Together, they had to move toward a faith of things hoped for. They found that hope in their love for each other.

My hope for you is that your faith will always be strong enough to get you through the worst of times, and that it will bring you comfort and strength in all things.

Until the next time, may the angels watch over you always.

Lenora Worth

SECOND CHANCE COURTSHIP

Glynna Kaye

To my sister and best friend, Sheryl, who faithfully
reads all my drafts—and never complains
even during the third or fourth round.

Acknowledgments

Thank you again to Love Inspired senior editor
Melissa Endlich for enthusiastically allowing me
to share Canyon Springs with the world.

Thanks also to my agent, Natasha Kern, for her
words of encouragement and vote of confidence.

And as always, an extraspecial thank-you to my
"Seeker Sisters" at www.Seekerville.blogspot.com.
I'm still amazed at how God brought us all together.

I run in the path of your commands,
for you have set my heart free.
　　　　　—*Psalms* 119:32

Chapter One

Cowboys ain't nothin' but trouble.

The oft-heard parental warning echoed through Kara Dixon's head. No surprise, for in the dim light and blowing snow outside a Canyon Springs, Arizona, restaurant, her eyes had fastened on the back of a broad-shouldered, dark-haired specimen of the cowboy variety. The Western hat and shearling jacket might be mimicked by wannabes, but the horse trailer hitched behind a big, silver Ford pickup vouched for his authenticity.

A cowboy. Yet another reason she had to get out of this town and back to Chicago. The sooner the better, too. She'd yet to run into a bona fide wrangler on the streets of the Windy City, which suited her just fine.

But how could she not take pity on the poor man? A man who valiantly endeavored to hand-brush fast accumulating snow from his crew cab pickup—while juggling a wailing toddler in one arm and making frequent grabs for a wandering preschooler with the other. Poor guy. Women shouldn't send their helpless men out into the world without adequate kid training. And back up.

She sighed. She didn't have time for this tonight.

Customers straggling in late with cross-country ski rental returns had delayed the closing of her mother's general store, Dix's Woodland Warehouse. Much longer and Mom would start wondering why she hadn't brought home the promised Friday night dinner from Kit's Lodge. A quick call would put her mind at ease, but being accountable to Mom again was already getting old. It was bitter cold, too, with wind whipping out of the northwest in buffeting gusts. No, it wasn't a good night to stop and offer a helping hand.

Nevertheless, she returned to the SUV she'd borrowed from her mom and retrieved a heavy-duty snowbrush. Then, securing her jacket's insulated hood, she approached the struggling male and raised her voice over that of the squalling child.

"Could you use some help?"

He swung toward her, his face in shadow.

She waved the snowbrush.

"Oh, man, thanks." His own raised voice held a note of grateful surprise as he endeavored to calm the unhappy little girl now flinging herself back and forth in his arms. "Didn't know it snowed so much while we were inside."

"That's mid-January in mountain country for you."

Before Kara could register what he was intending to do, the man stepped forward and thrust the flailing toddler at her. *What?* She didn't want to hold the kid. All she'd intended to do was help clean off the guy's truck. But the bundled-up, squalling tyke was stretching out arms to her. Even though she was irritated with "Daddy," Kara reluctantly relinquished the snowbrush and gathered the tiny screamer into her arms. Lovely.

The man snagged the sleeve of the older child and

gently pushed her toward Kara as well, then turned to the truck and set to work. Through the passenger-side front window, she glimpsed a lop-eared, mixed-breed mutt taking in the outside activity with interest. Almost as if laughing at her.

Kara awkwardly jiggled the bawling little one and fished in her pockets—in vain—for a tissue to wipe the miniature nose. She winced as slobber-wet fingers brushed her face. Where was the kid's mitten? Kara glanced at the snow-covered ground but saw no sign of it, then caught the tiny, sticky hand in her own.

Hurry it up, Cowboy.

As she warmed the little hand, she caught the older child staring at her. Even in the dim light it was clear she didn't think this stranger was handling her sibling with any degree of expertise. Kara bestowed a weak smile. It was hard to tell through the dim light and pelting snow, but the face peeping out from under a hood looked familiar.

Kara made shushing sounds at the youngster in her arms, then raised her voice over the howls. "What's your name?"

"Mary."

"Mary what?"

"Mary had a little lamb." The preschooler giggled and danced away.

Kara forced another smile. A comedian. She turned her attention again to the toddler who, for whatever mysterious reason, had abruptly quieted. Thank goodness. She'd pulled her tiny hand free, rubbed her nose and was now studiously exploring Kara's facial features with the tip of a moist finger. The girl giggled. Sniffled. Then hiccupped.

Kara turned her face aside to see what had happened to Cowboy. She shifted the kid and squinted through the steadily falling snow. Oh, there he was. On the far side of the pickup.

"Uh, you about done over there?"

"Almost. Hang on." He said something else but the wind snatched away the words.

Cowboy made a few more swipes with the brush, then limped around the front of the truck to open the passenger-side back door. He motioned to the older girl. "Hop in, Mary."

With a boost from him, the child obeyed. Then, tucking the snowbrush under his arm, he leaned inside the truck to harness her in a car seat.

"What's your phone number, sweetheart?" he called over his shoulder to Kara. "9-1-1-Kid-Help?"

He chuckled.

Her heart dipped. Then stilled.

She knew that laugh.

She shook her head, in part to loosen the toddler's fingers now snaking into the hair under her hood, but mainly to dash away the foolish imagining. Being back in Canyon Springs made her jumpy. Paranoid. And at the present moment, a little sick to her stomach.

It couldn't be *him*. No way. She'd have heard if he was back in town, wouldn't she? Then again, for the past six weeks she'd been buried alive managing the Warehouse for her mom. Taking on the household tasks and transporting her parent to out-of-town physical therapy appointments. There hadn't been a single moment to catch her breath, let alone catch up with in-the-know locals.

But maybe that's why the little girl looked familiar? He'd returned after all—had kids now? Her mind flashed back a dozen years to a tall, lean high school senior who'd moved to town her sophomore year. He'd had her female classmates swooning over a slow, lazy smile that she remembered well. T-shirt. Jeans. Western boots. Attitude.

But although she'd lain awake far too many nights dreaming about him, she'd steered clear. Mostly anyway. After all, he was a cowboy. Just like her no-good dad. That "troublemaking preacher's kid" the towns-people had labeled him.

Thanks mainly to her...

Please, God, don't let it be him.

"Ouch!" Cringing, she grabbed her earlobe and pried away tiny fingers. "Not the earring, kid."

The child pulled back and frowned, studying her a long moment. Big dark eyes. Another hiccup. Then the tiny face crumpled and the wailing began again.

Kara stepped to the open truck door. "Okay, Daddy, time to reclaim your kid."

"That's not Daddy," the older girl objected from the backseat, her tone indignant. "That's Uncle Trey."

Kara's breath caught.

The man backed out of the truck and turned to her, both of them now illuminated by the vehicle's interior light. Steady blue eyes met hers. In that flashing moment his gaze reflected the surprise of mutual recognition. A recognition that rocked her to the core, all but knocking the wind right out of her.

He'd changed. Filled out. Matured. Laugh lines crinkled at the corners of his eyes. The crooked nose he'd broken from a fall off a horse still imparted a rugged, reckless air to his countenance. Same strong jaw, now in need of a shave. Every bit as handsome as he'd ever been. And then some.

"Kara?"

Her gaze riveted, struggling for breath, she could only nod. He didn't try to jog her memory as to who he was. He knew she'd remember. He'd have read it in her eyes.

Oh, yes, she remembered Trey Kenton.

After a too-long moment, he gave a wry chuckle. "Didn't figure I'd ever run into you again."

She swallowed and held out the now-whimpering child. "I don't imagine you did."

He accepted his niece and handed over the snow-brush, but his eyes searched Kara's. For what? Confirmation that she was sufficiently ashamed of the cowardly lurch she'd left him in those many years ago?

Oh, yes, she remembered. Would never forget. Or forgive herself. So why should he?

She broke eye contact and motioned to the child fussing in his arms. "She lost her mitten."

How lame. She owed him an apology, not an evasive, impersonal observation.

He dug out a handkerchief and wiped the sniffling toddler's nose, then enveloped the tiny bare hand in his large gloved one. "She hasn't had a nap in days and now we're all paying for it."

Could he be as uncomfortable as she was? After all, the last time they saw each other… Her cheeks warmed at the memory.

"Come on, Uncle Trey. Let's go home."

"Hang on, Mary."

He focused again on Kara with a look she could only interpret as wary. Couldn't blame him.

"So, Kara, you're back in Canyon Springs."

She tightened her grip on the snowbrush. "Not for long. Helping my mom get back on her feet. She hasn't been well."

"Heard about that. Sorry."

Was he? Sharon Dixon and Trey Kenton hadn't exactly been a match made in heaven. Cowboy types didn't easily endear themselves to her mom. Or her.

The wind kicked up again, swirling a stinging mix of snow and ice pellets into their faces.

"Need to get these kids home and tucked into bed." He turned to the truck and eased the toddler into the empty car seat next to that of her sister.

Kara stepped away on unsteady legs. Was he visiting? Just babysitting for his brother and sister-in-law? Surely he hadn't moved back to Canyon Springs. No way. From the moment he'd set a booted foot inside the city limits as a teen, he'd been determined to put the mountain community in his rearview mirror.

With speed that likely rivaled his best record at roping and tying a calf, Trey buckled in his niece. Then he shut the back door and turned to Kara once more, his face again shadowed. "Thank you kindly for your help."

With a brisk nod and a tip of his hat, he limped around the front of the truck to the driver's side and climbed in.

He didn't have a limp in high school.

Heart pounding in an erratic rhythm, she could only stare stupefied at the pickup as another gust of wind slammed into her. She hardly felt the cold creeping in around the neckline of her jacket or the wind-driven snowflakes pelting her face.

That was it? A coolly polite "thank you kindly for

your help"? She took another step back, absently glancing down at the frosty ground—and spied a pint-size mitten lying half-buried in the snow. She knelt to pick it up with a trembling hand.

But before she could return it to its diminutive owner, the truck started—and the man whose life she'd all but ruined drove away.

Whoa. Trey gave a low whistle as he and the girls headed out of town to his brother and sister-in-law's place, the windshield wipers battling the pummeling snow.

Kara Dixon. Hadn't bargained on that one tonight.

He'd been in and out of Canyon Springs the past several months and knew she'd returned at Thanksgiving. Heard she was an interior designer with some big firm in Chicago. Had even glimpsed her a few times, helping her mother out of a car at the grocery store. Unloading boxes at the Warehouse. Dashing coatless across the street to Camilla's Café.

He'd intentionally kept his distance—even stayed away from town most weekends—but she wasn't a woman who'd be easily overlooked. Not with that toned figure and long, red-blonde mane of hers caught up in a ponytail, Strawberry blonde. That's how his sister-in-law described it. And Kara was model-tall and leggy, too, like a thoroughbred. He'd forgotten how it initially amused his seventeen-year-old self that ill-fated night when, in a sassy show of bravado, she'd walked right up to him, all but able to look him straight in the eye.

Just like her old man did to him now.

Well, maybe not *just* like. Her father's blustery shot at intimidation didn't send his heart galloping off like a wild mustang or his brain hurtling into a bottomless, fog-filled canyon. Didn't make his mouth go as dry as the Sonoran desert before summer monsoons kicked in.

Trey took a deep breath, still reliving the shock of turning to face her. No, he hadn't bargained on running into Kara up close and personal. And he sure hadn't bargained on feeling as if he'd collided with rock-hard Mother Earth, compliments of an irritable bronc. Even after all this time, even after what she'd done to him, he couldn't shake the impact of those beautiful gray eyes.

He let out a gust of pent-up breath. What was wrong with him anyway? He wasn't a kid anymore with a crush on the prettiest girl he'd ever seen—yet his heart was doing a too-familiar do-si-do, the rhythm beckoning him back through time.

He slammed the heel of his hand into the rim of the steering wheel, startling his dog, Rowdy, who rode shotgun on the seat next to him. He gave the Gordon setter-collie mix a reassuring pat and a feathered tail wagged in understanding.

Kara. No way was he going down that road again. He'd come back to town to lay the past to rest, not resurrect it. Thank the good Lord it sounded like she didn't plan to linger much longer. Just popping in to check on her mom. He needed to stay focused on the business at hand. Business, in fact, that Li'l Ms. Dixon wasn't going to be much pleased about once word got around. Which it eventually would in a tiny place like this.

In spite of himself, his mind's eye drifted to that long-ago night that now once again seemed like yesterday. The look in her eyes. The sweet scent of her hair. How she felt in his arms…

"Uncle Trey, why did you drive past our road?"

The accusing voice of his older niece carried from the shadowed recesses of the backseat, jerking him into the here and now.

"Just takin' the scenic route." He glanced into the rearview mirror at Mary, all the while racking his memory as to how much farther he'd have to drive to turn around with the empty trailer hitched to the back.

Kara Dixon was already messing with his mind.

"It's dark." Mary's petulant voice came again. "I want to go home."

She sounded as tired as he was. Three days playing both Mom and Dad had just about done him in. One more day to go.

"Your wish is my command, princess."

"I'm your princess?"

"You know it."

He glanced again at Mary, then over his shoulder at Missy and smiled. Sound asleep. He'd drive all night if it would keep her snoozing. What a day. He shouldn't have dragged them all the way to Holbrook this afternoon to look at that pony.

Seemed like a good idea at the time, but that was before a stronger cold front plowed into the region. Before he'd discovered the advertised pinto was an ill-tempered beast, certainly nothing he'd want his nieces having anything to do with. Then there had been the diaper dealings. A lesson learned the hard way. No, not a day he cared to relive anytime soon. His sister-in-law would laugh her head off.

It was just as well, though, that the trip was a bust. His brother would have killed him if he'd bought the girls a pony. With the parsonage remodel in town coming along on schedule, Jason and his wife wouldn't be staying at the cabin and acreage out in the boonies much longer. Which meant, too, he needed to give serious thought about what to do with himself. There wouldn't be any space at the parsonage for a tagalong brother.

At least he'd soon be able to move his horses to the equine center he and a group of investors were renovating. Last week his working-from-home office assistant had submitted the final documents for a permit to board his horses, so at least he didn't have to worry about that. Just needed to find office space until the facility's remodel was completed—and a place to throw down his bedroll until a house caught his fancy.

A couple of miles farther on, he pulled into the snowy, graveled lot of a long-abandoned bait and tackle shop. He got himself turned around and headed back in the right direction.

"What was that lady's name, Uncle Trey?" Mary piped up again.

"What lady is that? The pony woman?"

"No. The pretty one. Who was holding Missy."

He tightened his grip on the steering wheel. "Her name's Kara Dixon. We went to high school together."

"Did you kiss her?"

Memory flashed with an accompanying kick to his gut. Yes, he'd kissed her. Once. And fool that he was, a million other times in his dreams.

"Mommy said Daddy kissed *her* in high school when they were sixteen—on Valemtime's Day—and then they got married."

He smiled at her mispronunciation of the holiday.

"How old are you, Uncle Trey?"

"You're awfully full of questions tonight, squirt."

"Mommy says you need to kiss a girl and get married so you'll stay in Canyon Springs."

"Your mommy—" He stopped himself. Nothin' he'd like better than to settle down close to "his girls." That was the plan, but he didn't want to set Mary up for disappointment if it didn't work out. No point either in attempting to enlighten a four-year-old on his thoughts regarding the relentless mission of his sister-in-law. Except for the one date he'd managed to pull off behind her back, he'd steered clear of Reyna's matchmaking, and females in general, since his return to town.

He didn't need her hounding him about Kara Dixon. *No siree.* He wanted no part of the grown-up version of the girl from his past. The gray-eyed gal with a kissable mouth—who'd left him sittin' high and dry when the cops showed up.

Chapter Two

"Where'd you get this darling little thing, doll?"

"What?" Jerked from her Trey-troubled thoughts, Kara looked up from the breakfast table. Her mother, Sharon Dixon, stood in the kitchen doorway waving the Kenton girl's pink mitten.

She must have dropped it when she'd hung her coat on the enclosed back porch last night. Or had Mom been rifling through her pockets for cigarettes or other incriminating evidence of misbehavior, just as she'd once caught her doing when Kara was a teen? She cringed inwardly at the memory, thankful that even though their relationship wasn't always warm and fuzzy, they'd come a long way in the past decade. Or so she'd thought.

"Found it last night. Belongs to one of Pastor Kenton's kids, so I'll need to return it." No need to divulge how she knew who it belonged to. Hopefully Mom wouldn't ask.

"I may see Reyna this morning. If she's back from the retreat." Her mother spoke in the raspy fragments of a former heavy smoker. "Ladies' tea at the church. I'll take it to her."

Over and over throughout the night Kara had waded through possible scenarios of returning it. Of using the opportunity to ask Trey's forgiveness. But of course her mom could return the mitten. That made the most sense. She couldn't face the child's uncle again anyway. How could she apologize without telling him the truth? A truth that she wasn't free to tell?

What am I going to do, God?

Her grip tightened on the fork in her hand. Why couldn't stupid choices made in the past be left *in* the past? And why did she keep wasting her breath, crying out to the Heavens about it? Hadn't she learned when Dad walked out that God had more important things to deal with than her?

Aware that Mom was watching with a curious tilt to her head, she set her fork on the stoneware plate and glanced out the paned windows of the cozy cinnamon-scented kitchen. A frosty blanket coated the towering ponderosa pines, lending the trees a holiday-ish flocked appearance. But she wasn't in a holiday mood. A blustering gust shook the powderlike crystals loose, flinging them into the air and sending a fairy dust cascade earthward. Sleet pecked on the window above the sink.

She shivered. Why'd Mom always keep it so cold in the house? "Is someone picking you up for the church thing, Mom, or do you want me to drive you? I don't want you walking in this. That wind's nasty."

"Peggy's coming by. You should come with us." Her mom brushed a hand through her layered auburn hair. "Lindi's giving a talk on community service. I think it's one of those 'it's not what Canyon Springs can do for you, but what you can do for Canyon Springs' spins. I know she'd love to see you."

Since returning to town she hadn't heard a peep out of her once-upon-a-time friend and cousin, Lindi Bruce. Did she know Trey was back?

"Unfortunately, there's nobody to cover for me." She folded her napkin and placed it on the worn wooden table by her plate. "Meg's visiting a hospitalized friend in Phoenix and won't be back until this afternoon. Roxanne has out-of-town company and asked for the day off."

"Then give Lindi a call next week. You haven't had a chance to catch up with any of your friends. Been too busy taking care of your feeble old mom."

"That's what I'm here for, Feeble Old Mom," she teased, then drained the last of her orange juice. "In case you've forgotten, if I wasn't helping you I wouldn't even be in town."

Her mother's lips tightened and Kara's heart sank. She'd said the wrong thing again. If only she could get along with Mom as well as her friend, Meg McGuire, got along with her. Every time she saw them together, laughing and on the same wavelength, jealousy stabbed. But then, Meg was everybody's sweetheart.

"Nevertheless," her mother continued, "with Lindi running for city council, you have lots of catching up to do. She's a dream candidate, even as young as she is—sure to give Jake Talford a run for his money. Her granddad's about to pop his buttons. You two girls make your families proud."

That was debatable.

She stood, then carried her plate and glass to the sink where she rinsed them off. The only time Mom was proud of her was when she was doing exactly what Mom wanted her to do. Like coming back to Canyon Springs.

She glanced at her watch. Seven-thirty. "Guess I'd better brush my teeth and head over to the Warehouse. With fresh snow, the more adventuresome types may look for outdoor activities. Maybe ski rentals will do a good business today."

"We can hope. The recession's lingering effects have hit the high country hard."

Kara frowned. Her mother and an accountant in Show Low looked after the books for Dix's Woodland Warehouse. Kara didn't have a clue about anything on the business side of her mother's store. "We're doing okay, though, aren't we? I mean, turning an adequate profit, right?"

Mom smiled. "Tightening the belt a bit. But don't go worrying about that."

"Well, you don't need to be worrying about stuff like that either. Did you sleep okay last night? You look tired."

While her mom had only turned fifty-six last month, she'd gradually put on excessive pounds through the years. Which led to borderline diabetes and knee damage, and put her on a walker on bad days. But she'd lost considerable weight in the aftermath of her November heart attack and no longer had the round, merry face all had grown accustomed to. When Kara returned at Thanksgiving, it had been like coming home to a ghost of her mother.

Which scared her.

"I'm fine, doll."

"You have to be honest with me, Mom." She folded her arms in an attempt to feel in control, when all she wanted was to slip into the comfort of her mother's arms like she'd done when she was a little kid. Everything coming all at once—Mom's illness, taking leave from her job, Trey's return… It was too much. "If you're not feeling well, we need to get you checked out before things get out of hand again."

"I'm fine. Goodness knows you're not letting me do anything around here." Her mom chuckled. "Between both you and Meg helping, I've plumb become a lady of leisure."

"Take it easy today, okay? Get some rest. Going to that tea isn't a priority."

"Does me good to see everybody. Laugh a little."

She fixed a glare of mock reprimand on her parent. "Catch up on gossip?"

"Mercy me, at a church event?"

Laughing with Mom felt good. Why couldn't it be like this between them all the time?

"Speaking of gossip—" She paused, preparing to ask if her mom was aware that Trey Kenton had returned to town. Then she thought better of it. Should her mother confess, it would only lead to an argument. "Never mind."

If God had the time and inclination to take mercy on her, she'd be out of town in a couple of weeks and never have to see Trey again.

Trey kept his voice low as he spoke into his cell phone.

"Sure wish you'd stop talking about my love life in front of the girls, Reyna."

His sister-in-law's whoop echoed in his ear. "And what love life would that be?"

He pictured the wide smile of his brother's pretty, plump wife. White teeth flashing in contrast to her creamy Hispanic skin tone, her dark eyes dancing. Not only lovely, but her husband's number one fan, a great mom and a woman of deep faith. How'd his little brother rate such a catch? Must have extra pull in the heavenly realms.

"Very funny, Rey. But I'm serious."

"Ooh, serious, huh?" She giggled. "As in you're going to do what if I don't stop?"

"If you want me to stay here like you keep saying you do, knock it off. Mary's too young to be fixating on kissing and romance and marriage and stuff."

"Kissing and stuff?" Reyna giggled again. "Were you dealing with birds and bees issues this week, Uncle Trey?"

Fighting a smile, he walked sock-footed across the cabin's hardwood floor to the living room, then pulled back one of the insulated drapes. Still snowing. "Put Jason on, will you?"

His sis-in-law laughed again, then he could tell she'd covered the mouthpiece to bring his younger sibling up to speed. They were in Tucson for a pastoral retreat, enjoying cactus and warm sunshine. Lucky dogs.

"Yo, bro." The voice of Jason Kenton, pastor of Canyon Springs Christian Church, greeted him. "Reyna giving you a hard time?"

Trey's smile broadened as he continued to stare at the wind-shaken ponderosa pines. "Is there ever a time she doesn't?"

"So, what's up?"

"Just checking in. You still planning to get home tonight?"

"Last session's over around noon. Hope to be home before dark." Jason paused. "But we're willing to stay another night if you'll cover the worship service tomorrow morning. And devotions at the care facility in the afternoon."

"Dream on, preacher man." His brother had been on his case for months to take a more active role in the family "business."

"Unless, of course, you think your congregation can ferret out a deeper meaning in a ridin' and ropin' demonstration."

Jason chuckled, and Trey envisioned him scrubbing a hand alongside his neatly clipped beard, facial hair he'd grown in recent months in hopes of looking more mature.

"So, the girls behaving themselves this morning?"

"Still in bed." Trey raked a hand through his sleep-matted hair. "Hey, while I have you on the line—I was wondering if you remember the name of a guy who was in your graduating class. The one with the big ears and funny laugh. Couldn't even wait to get off school property before he'd pull out a cigarette and light up. Was always wanting to borrow my lighter."

"Pete. Pete Burlene." Jason paused for a moment. "Why? You think he's the one?"

"Grasping at straws is more like it."

"You know, Trey—" His younger brother let out a huff of air, then continued in his best pastoral tone that for some reason always irritated Trey. Even after four years in ministry in Canyon Springs, it remained a stretch for Jason to sound older and wiser than his twenty-eight years. "You have to ask yourself, bro, is it worth it? Worth getting tied up in knots trying to uncover the real culprit's identity?"

"Look, Jason—"

"If this is what it's going to do to you, maybe settling back in Canyon Springs isn't the best move after all." He lowered his voice. "In spite of what my wife thinks."

Trey's jaw tightened. Jason still didn't get it. "I don't think there's any harm in trying to clear my name."

"But look what it's doing to you. And you're no closer to finding out who left your lighter at the scene of that fire than when you first hit town. Face it. It's been twelve years."

"Every man needs a hobby."

Jason scoffed.

"Look, Jas, injury cost me my livelihood. Then my new job brings me back here. You're the one who's always saying there's no such thing as coincidence. Doesn't it sound to you like God's providing an opportunity for resolution? Justice?"

"'Fraid I can't speak for the Man Upstairs on this one, dude."

What he meant was he thought his big brother was chasing after something better left alone. Well, he could think whatever he wanted. He wasn't the one locals looked at with suspicion. Nobody questioned his honesty. His integrity. They didn't whisper behind *his* back.

"It's a shame," Jason continued, "that you were such a loner—and that our folks had taken me to Phoenix to catch a plane for that spring break mission trip. You didn't have anyone to confirm you were nowhere near Duffy's place when the property caught fire."

Trey's lips tightened. It didn't do you any good to have a rock-solid alibi if your star witness refused to come forward.

"Well, Jas, I'll let you get back to your retreat. I have to pick up my toys, then hit the shower before the girls wake up." He glanced around at the cabin strewn with kid stuff. A diaper bag toppled on its side. Stuffed animals and dolls in various stages of dress piled on the sofa. Pint-size shoes and socks under the coffee table. Yesterday's dishes still in the sink. How'd it get to be such a disaster in only three days?

Jason barked a laugh. "Why do I have a feeling the girls will have lots to tell us when we get home?"

Trey groaned. "Yeah, well, just remember you owe me one."

"You got it, buddy."

"Take it easy coming up the mountain. Snowing."

"Will do."

Trey shut off the phone and again stared out the window at the swirling, wind-whipped flakes, making no move to wrestle his surroundings to order.

He shook his head as memories he'd fought all night resurfaced. Kara Lee Dixon. If he wasn't mistaken, she'd been as surprised to see him last night as he'd been to see her. Maybe more so. Hadn't she known he was back in town? Not from the look on her face. The fear in her expressive eyes.

What did she think he'd do after all these years? Chew her out on a public street? Make a spectacle of himself in front of the girls? Call the cops? No, he'd long ago forgiven her.

He hadn't handled their reunion well. Caught off guard, he'd been every bit as tongue-tied around her as he'd ever been as a teen. Practically threw Missy in the truck, then climbed in and hit the gas. That must have impressed the former girl of his dreams.

But like it or not, he and Kara needed to have a little chat.

Chapter Three

"I can't believe you didn't tell me you went out with Trey Kenton last fall." Kara looked up from where she knelt mopping a front corner of the Warehouse floor and leveled a disbelieving stare at her old college roommate.

Meg McGuire, soon to be Mrs. Joseph Diaz, had stopped by mid-afternoon Saturday to collect a trunk full of flattened cardboard boxes. Now here she stood, handing Kara another old bath towel and delivering the dismaying confirmation that Trey was indeed considering moving back to town. He was heading up a renovation of Duffy Logan's old horse facility, a property that had closed and fallen into disrepair almost a decade ago when Duffy suffered a debilitating stroke and his wife moved him out of town for better medical care. But why would Trey come back here of all places? Right smack-dab on top of the scene of the crime that drove him from town as a teenager?

"How would I know you had any connection to Trey?" Meg's eyes narrowed with interest beneath the fluffy bangs of her short, brunette hair. "When your name came up one time, I couldn't tell if he even remembered you."

Oh, he remembered her all right.

"He definitely recalled that old car of yours," Meg continued with a teasing tone.

Kara's memory flashed to the infamous '63 Mustang. The sporty, cream-colored car her daddy had lovingly restored and left behind when he took off for new adventures. He'd had the gall to transfer the registration to her as a sweet sixteen birthday gift. It still sat in the garage behind her mother's house.

"I sense a story here." Meg's eyes sparkled with a speculative gleam. "Were you and Trey sweeties? Hmm?"

Warmth crept into Kara's cheeks as she wiped the wooden floor with a fresh towel, then got to her feet. She'd told her mom about the leak last spring, yet the trickle again coursed down the wall from ceiling to floor. From the looks of the warped plaster and paint discoloration above, the summer monsoon season had added to the damage. Now the snow. So much for the expertise of repairmen.

"Trey and I were friends. Sort of." How could she explain the mixed-up adolescent relationship she didn't even understand herself?

"Friends, huh? Your mom mentioned you had a crush on my Joe once upon a time, but she never mentioned Trey."

Kara laughed. "Mom talks too much."

She crossed the rustic, wood-beamed room to spread soppy bath towels on the bricked portion of the floor in front of the woodstove. "Joe was my crush of the moment in middle school—when I found out his mom walked out on him like my dad did me. Besides, there wasn't anything to mention about Trey—except Mom didn't like him."

She lifted an insulated carafe from its perch next to the coffeemaker and poured a mug of spiced cider for Meg. She'd kept her more-than-friends feelings for Trey a secret from the world those many years ago. Seemed strange to be openly teased about him now. And why did her heart tap-dance at the mere mention of his name, just like it had at sixteen?

"She didn't like him because of the cowboy connection? Because of your dad?" Meg cupped the mug in her hands and inhaled the fragrant brew. "Or because, you know, of that other thing?"

Kara stiffened, the carafe poised above another mug. "You've heard about that?"

Meg nodded, her expression curious.

"Mom always said cowboys were trouble." Kara filled the second mug to the brim. "But he didn't do it. So don't believe anything you hear to the contrary."

"I didn't learn about it until after I went out with him. But I wasn't about to believe it. I'm glad my instincts were on target." She took a sip of cider. "So, then, if you weren't sweethearts, why are you all bent out of shape that he could be moving back to town?"

"I'm not bent out of shape." Kara met her friend's gaze, doing her best to keep her voice from betraying the turmoil inside. Meg wasn't trying to be nosy. They'd been open with each other in college, sharing all the secrets young women held dear. Except the one having to do with Trey. "I'm surprised, that's all. Didn't expect to run into him last night. You might find this hard to believe, as enamored as you are with Canyon Springs, but he hated this town."

"He's never mentioned that to me."

"You've talked a lot?"

"Some."

Was Meg being deliberately obtuse, trying to draw her out? To get her to say more than she had any intention of saying?

"He's so sweet," her friend rambled on, a playful twinkle in her eye. "And single. Never married."

"If he's such a great catch," Kara fired back with a grin, "why aren't you marrying him instead of Joe?"

She couldn't picture Meg and Trey as a good match, but nevertheless a fleeting tingle of envy pierced her consciousness. After all, Meg had dated him not long ago. What had that been like? Trey, all grown up. A man.

"I was falling for Joe by the time I met Trey." Meg's eyes went dreamy, so at least she hadn't been forced to come to a heartrending decision between the two men.

"Just remember, Meg—" she took a sip of cider before setting down the mug "—if you want to make it to your wedding day alive, don't even think of trying to set me up with him."

"Vannie Quintero, the teen who works at my future father-in-law's campground, is thrilled to be teamed up with an ex-cowboy." Meg winked. "Maybe you would be, too."

"Don't count on it." Kara gave in to a smile and tossed her ponytail over her shoulder. She'd hardly believed it when Meg had told her Trey agreed to mentor a high school kid. Or that no one, considering his own teenage track record, voiced objections. "Besides, there's no such thing as an *ex*-cowboy."

"You never can tell. With the right woman…" Meg gave her a mischievous poke in the arm. "Now that I'm going to be more than a temporary resident of Canyon Springs, I wish you'd move back, too. Think of all the fun we'd have."

"Fun?" she countered with a grin of her own. "Like watching you and Joe cuddling up on the sofa, eyes glued to each other like at the New Year's Eve party a couple of weekends ago?"

"Hook up with Trey," Meg said, wiggling her eyebrows, "then go thou and do likewise."

Kara shook a finger at her. "I'm warning you—"

Her friend had all but bubbled with happiness since she and Joe got engaged. Must be nice. Not that she resented her friend's good fortune to find a guy like the ex-navy corpsman with a cute kid. Meg more than deserved a happily-ever-after. But if Kara had the misfortune to return permanently, she'd likely seldom see her old friend. With Meg's full-time teaching job, a soon-to-be husband, new stepson—and probably future kids—that didn't leave much time to hang out.

Besides, Canyon Springs wasn't in her future. Never had been. Never would be.

She held up her hand, thumb and forefinger pressed together. "I'm *this* far from that promotion. And I'm sure my supervisor wouldn't appreciate my ditching him right now. Not after he's gone out of his way to cover for me while I'm checking in on Mom. I promised to be back in two more weeks, and I take my promises seriously."

Her memory flickered to the last conversation she'd

had with her supervisor and mentor, Spencer Alexander. He'd laughed, but not in a derogatory way, when she'd let it slip that her father had been a rodeo cowboy. He'd called her his "little cowgirl."

"And don't forget," she continued. "I came back here for a few weeks last spring when that new medication got Mom's system all out of whack. And when she fell last summer. Unpaid time off isn't helping my professional reputation—or my savings account. I'm still covering my quarter of the rent and utilities on the apartment even when I'm not there. Making car payments, too."

Meg gave an exaggerated sigh. "I'm thrilled you're getting a chance to live your dream. But I can dream, too, can't I?"

"Dream away. But don't hold your breath."

Meg glanced at her watch, then set her mug down before snatching her jacket off the back of a nearby chair. "Thanks for helping me load the boxes. I'd better get going. Have a few things to finish up before we start carting things over to the new place tonight. Joe's dad let us store my Phoenix furniture at the RV park's rec center until we got the house livable."

With another twinge of unexpected envy, Kara recalled the cute little place Meg and Joe bought last month and where Meg would now be living prior to the wedding. She'd helped her spruce up the kitchen last week. A little paint and a lot of elbow grease. New floor tile laid and curtains hung.

"You're still having a move-in party tonight? Even with the snow?"

"Yeah. It'll be messy, which is why I want to cut up boxes to protect the hardwood floor." Meg zipped her coat and dug gloves out of her pockets. "Joe starts official paramedic training Monday and he wants me settled in before he leaves."

Kara motioned to the ceiling. "Even though you weren't in the upstairs apartment for long, I'm going to miss you."

"I'll miss you, too. It was great not to have to spend the past six weeks in the RV. Your mom wouldn't even take rent money—said to consider it an engagement gift. Can you believe it? But I'm sure she could use a paying tenant."

"She wouldn't have offered it if she'd needed the money."

Meg's smile widened. "Now I have a wedding to finish planning, don't I? Spring break will be here before we know it. Speaking of which, Joe's Aunt Rosa started sewing your maid of honor dress. Hopefully she'll be far enough along for a final fitting before you leave."

Bells above the store's front door tinkled, sounding merrier than Kara felt, and the pair glanced at a bundled-up couple entering the welcoming warmth of the general store.

"Looks like I'd better let you get back to work." Meg stepped forward to give her a hug. "Good luck on getting the leak fixed. See you tonight?"

Kara nodded, but it was with a heavy heart that she watched her friend out the door. Even though Meg didn't seem to sense it, she didn't like the invisible wall that reared itself between them with Trey's return. But there was no way she'd attempt to explain to her what she'd done to him. Meg was so enthralled with Trey, she'd never understand. She'd certainly think far less of her college friend if she knew.

Already dreading an evening where Trey might show up, Kara grabbed a dust cloth and gave the checkout counter a swipe, then paused to gaze around the familiar expanse of the Warehouse. The paned windows. Plank floors. Well-stocked grocery items and other general merchandise. Displays of mountain country souvenirs and outdoor gear.

The knot in her stomach tightened. Why hadn't her cousin Lindi alerted her to Trey's return? Lindi. The reason she couldn't tell Trey the truth. Beg his forgiveness. It was twelve years ago this very spring that her confused and scared, barely sixteen-year-old self had made the promise. Pledged that she wouldn't tell a soul her best-friends-forever cousin had confessed to accidentally setting the forest on fire.

By the time she'd found out Trey had been accused... it was too late. She'd already made that impulsive vow that still reached out to haunt her. Just one more sign that while God may have set her world in motion, kept it spinning, he was most often off in another sector of the universe.

"Hey, Trey!" Meg grabbed his snow-covered, jacketed arm, hauling him and his nieces off the porch and into the house she and Joe would soon be calling home. "You're just in time for pizza."

He stepped onto the rug by the door, Missy in his arms and Mary clinging shyly to his leg. He gazed around a room full of people helping themselves to the savory, mouthwatering contents of cardboard delivery boxes. He glimpsed a few familiar faces—Meg's fiancé and his dad and son. A dozen or two others he guessed to be church friends or teacher pals of Meg. Some of Joe's buds.

Recognition flickered in the gazes of several guests. That was to be expected in a small town. Warm interest reflected in the smiles of a few of the younger women. That was usually to be expected as well—wherever.

But no Kara.

Thank you, Lord.

He almost hadn't come, thinking she might be here, that it might be awkward, but he hated to back out on Meg. The perky newcomer to town had held a special place in his heart ever since they met last September. If it wasn't for that hotshot Diaz guy, it might be him settling down with the pretty schoolteacher. Or at least that's what he told himself on poor-pitiful-me days. But by the time he'd gotten her to go out with him, she was already falling for the ex-navy guy, one of Reyna's cousins. Meg hadn't realized it yet, but Trey had, and he backed off.

"Sorry I'm late, Meg. I've been babysitting the past few days and Jason and Reyna still aren't home yet."

A chorus of soft *aahs* echoed from female throats and inwardly he chuckled. It hadn't taken long to figure out that if you wanted to score interest with the local ladies, babysitting by far outweighed the classic walking-the-pup routine.

"Yeah, yeah," Joe's father, Bill Diaz, taunted, his mustached mouth widening in a smile. "Timed it just right so all the heavy lifting's done."

"Guess you cowboys aren't as dumb as you look." The dark-eyed Joe cast him an appraising glance, a look he'd become accustomed to during the months Joe'd been courting Meg and keeping an eye open for rivals.

Relax, dude. She's all yours now.

"Don't listen to them, Trey," Meg said as he toed off his boots at the door. "You can make yourself useful bringing in the sodas—which my loving fiancé forgot to do."

A slice of pizza halfway to his mouth, Joe made sounds of protest.

"Consider it done." Trey would rather do something constructive than stand around making small talk with people he didn't know. People who may have formed judgments about him based on rumor. Coming back to Canyon Springs held more than its share of challenges. But God opened doors and he was gonna be man enough to walk through them no matter what it took.

Meg reached out for Missy; then he knelt to divest Mary of her coat. He peeled out of his own jacket and tossed their stuff on a folding table piled high with outdoor wear. Not trusting the guests to know a genuine Stetson when they saw one, he hesitated to top off the mound with his felt hat. But his ever-alert hostess snatched it from him and slid it onto a peg by the front door, then pointed in the direction of the kitchen.

With Mary gripping the welted side seam of his jeans, he made his way through the crowd, following the cardboard carpet past the staircase and into the kitchen. Looked like new floor tile. Fresh paint job on the cabinets, too. Curtains at the windows. Nice. Meg's doing? Or Kara's?

He'd have to figure out something homey like that when he bought a fixer-upper of his own. Having scrimped and saved every spare dime of his rodeo winnings for a hefty down payment, he had his heart set on a little house, some acreage. Had been looking forward for years to a day when he could settle down, start a family. A place like this, on the edge or outside of town, would be ideal. That is, if he cleared his name and made a go of the business. Old Reuben Falkner, city councilman, wasn't making the latter an easy effort.

He headed to an open door where Meg had indicated he'd find the laundry room. A light was on, but when he stepped to the doorway of the miniscule room, he halted. A familiar red-blonde ponytail dangled half-way down the back of a trim female dressed in figure-skimming jeans and a blue wool sweater.

Kara.

With her back to him, she wiped off soda cans arranged on the clothes dryer's surface. He had a second to catch his breath. But no time to back out the door before, head down and lost in thought, she whirled in his direction. Ran smack into his chest.

"Oh!" Her long-lashed gray eyes met his as she took a startled step back, pulling away from his hand that had instinctively reached out to steady her. For a long moment their gazes held. Every bit as close and as beautiful as she'd been that long-ago night. The night she'd sashayed up to him. Slipped her arms around his neck…

But tonight her eyes were that of a filly fixin' to bolt.

"I didn't hear you." Face flushing, she took another step back and glared at his socked feet as if he'd deliberately shed his boots to sneak up on her.

"Sorry. I was put on soda duty."

Kara frowned, apparently irritated Meg hadn't thought her capable to handle the task on her own. Then she spied Mary clutching his leg and her expression softened. She motioned to the cans.

"You can haul some of these to the living room if you'd like. Or break up that bag of ice in the chest there."

"Ice or sodas, doesn't matter to me." He chuckled, hoping to catch her eye and put her at ease, but she kept her focus on anything but him.

"Ice then."

He nodded and they did an uneasy tango as he and Mary maneuvered around her, the air charged with an unmistakable, mutual awareness. Had twelve years really gone by?

She took a sidestep toward the now-vacated doorway, but without thinking he shot out his arm to block her. Wary eyes met his. His breath caught at the light scent of her woodsy perfume.

"We need to talk, Kara."

Where'd that come from? He'd been hangin' out with his sister-in-law too long. Starting to sound like a girl. But all he needed was a lousy five minutes. He'd ditch Mary and make Kara understand he didn't hold anything against her. That she could stop looking at him like he was going to haul her into court.

Her brows lowered. "I—"

"Trey, did you bring Rowdy with you?" the familiar voice of five-year-old Davy Diaz called from across the kitchen.

Trey stared at Kara a long moment, his heartbeat counting off the seconds. Then he lowered his arm and turned to the youngster who trotted across the floor toward him and Mary. *Bad timing, kid.* But he'd sensed Kara's relief.

He gazed down at the black-haired, brown-eyed boy and smiled at the youngster's reference to his canine sidekick. Kids loved Rowdy. "We can't stay long, so he's out in the truck. That woolly coat of his keeps him toasty warm."

"Daddy wouldn't let me bring my puppy." Davy's shoulders slumped as he crammed his hands in his jeans pockets in an adultlike gesture. A miniature little man. His dark eyes brightened as he studied his cousin, Mary, who'd loosened a grip on Trey's pant leg and taken a hesitant step forward.

"Kara's already seed it," the boy continued, "but do you guys wanna see my new room? I'm gonna live here when we marry Miss Meg."

Mary looked up at Trey, hope in her eyes.

How could he turn down such cool kids? He glanced at Kara, but she again avoided his gaze. "I'd like to, Davy, but after I finish up here, okay? You two go on without me."

"No, go right ahead," the woman next to him insisted, all but shoving him out the door. "I can handle things here."

All I need, Lord, is five stinkin' minutes.

Granted, the other thing he needed to explain would likely take more than five minutes—if she'd hear him out at all. Her father had told him the two of them still weren't on speaking terms. Hadn't been for fifteen years. But he'd need to get her old man's permission to discuss it with her anyway.

He hauled Mary into his arms and Davy stepped forward to grab his free hand. Glancing back as the little boy pulled him along, he caught Kara's skittish gaze. Gave her a nod.

"We still need to talk, darlin'."

Chapter Four

We need to talk.

Ugh. Kara rummaged in a laundry room drawer until she found a small, metal mallet; then she knelt by the insulated chest to break up the bag of solidifying crushed ice. No wonder men hated that phrase when women accosted them with it.

So he thought they needed to talk? Until he walked into the room and she literally ran into him, she'd have agreed. She'd intended, at some point, to apologize as best she could. But not here. Not now. And certainly not after seeing the mutual memory of her immature teenage behavior spark in his expressive eyes. Heard his breath catch when their gazes held for a too-long moment. No, not the shared memory of his being abandoned to the law. Rather, an even more vivid memory of her boldly stepping up to him. Thoroughly kissing him. Making a suggestion she had no business making.

He'd rejected it on the spot.

She gave the ice another series of whacks that sent shattered fragments flying, then stood. She'd been young and stupid back then. Probably every bit as stupid even now because every fiber of her being cried out to dash into the cold, dark night as far from Trey as she could get.

She shouldn't have come this evening. She'd anticipated a few awkward, public moments if he showed up for Meg's party. Steeled herself for superficial greetings. Self-conscious small talk. But she hadn't anticipated him hunting her down, corralling her in the laundry room for one-on-one time. Wanting to settle old scores. Here. Tonight.

With shaky hands she dumped the contents of the plastic bag into the cooler with a resounding clatter.

"What's taking so long?" Meg appeared in the doorway of the laundry room, Trey's niece, the infamous screamer, in her arms. Thank goodness the contrary little thing seemed content enough tonight. Maybe her uncle had gotten her down for a nap.

"Where's Trey? I sent him to help you."

So much for warning her old friend not to matchmake.

"Davy dragged him upstairs to look at his room."

"Men." Meg made a silly face, then frowned. "You okay? You look kinda funny."

Hope sparked. Now was an ideal opportunity to make her getaway. "A little tired, I guess. Everything from the past weeks is catching up with me. Think I'll cut out early. Get to bed at a decent hour for a change."

"You sure?"

She nodded, anxious to retrieve her coat and boots and get out of there. But she'd no more thought it than light footsteps followed by heavier ones clambered down the staircase. Glancing past Meg, she saw Davy and Mary head to the living room and a frowning Trey step into the kitchen, a finger poked in one ear and his cell phone pressed to the other.

He moved to the French doors leading to the patio, flipped on the exterior light and peered into the night. "You're kidding. Yeah, it's snowing harder up here, but—"

He turned as Meg and Kara entered the kitchen as well, then covered the mouthpiece. "Jason. DPS won't let anyone come up the mountain tonight."

"Oh, no," Meg whispered, giving Missy a hug.

But Missy paid her little attention, her wide dark eyes fixed on Kara, a dainty hand reaching toward her. Kara managed a weak smile in the child's direction, hoping Mighty Mouth wasn't fixing to treat them to a replay of last night's deafening rendition. She tossed her ponytail over her shoulder and cautiously eased away.

Trey continued to listen to his brother, his expression broadcasting dismay with the Arizona Department of Public Safety. He cleared his throat. "Sure, I can cover the care facility stuff. But come on, I don't know how to preach."

Kara and Meg exchanged a glance. Jason wanted Trey to preach tomorrow?

"No, no. Don't lose any sleep over it. I'll figure something out." He switched the phone to his other ear. "What? Naw. I don't think it's gonna get that bad."

He again glanced out the glass panes. Snow whipped out of the darkness, piling up at the base of the door. "Well, if it comes to that, maybe we can get a motel room. Don't want to impose on anybody. But I don't think—"

Meg and Kara exchanged puzzled glances.

"No, don't worry. I'll handle it. Yeah. Yeah. You, too."

He shut off the phone and let out a gusty sigh. Then

he looked over at them, his smile tight. "He says if we get what DPS says we're going to get, there's no way I can dig out from his place in the morning in time to cover at the church."

Meg's face crinkled in sympathy. "They had to stay overnight with her folks a few weeks ago when we got that foot and a half of snow. I've been out there—that forest service road is super-primitive. So you're covering for Jason tomorrow?"

"Looks like it. He says it's too late to call a member of the congregation to fill in. Unfortunately," Trey continued with a glance in her direction, "Reyna's folks are out of town and I don't know her siblings well enough to show up on their doorsteps. So I guess we'd better get moving if I'm going to get the girls settled in at a motel."

He took Missy from Meg's arms, but the little girl's brown eyes remained fixed on Kara. "I'm totally unprepared except for a truckload of diapers, but that snow's accumulating fast."

"Oh, forget the motel, Trey. I'm sure Joe and his dad would put you up for the night." Meg motioned to the interior of her house. "The girls can stay with me. Plenty of room here for Rowdy, too."

"Thanks, but I couldn't—"

Meg cut him off with a snap of her fingers, her eyes brightening. "No, no, wait. I have a better idea. Kara and I have the perfect solution to your predicament."

"You do?" His voice held a note of wariness.

Kara didn't like the sound of her friend's proposal either. "We do?"

"Sure we do." Meg stepped across the kitchen, then pulled her purse from a lower cabinet shelf. A moment later she swung around, dangling a key from a fluorescent pink pom-pom key ring.

"Ta da! Remember the apartment I just vacated? Dix's Woodland Warehouse Bed-and-Breakfast to the rescue."

From the look on Kara's face an hour ago when Meg extended the unexpected invitation, he was in the doghouse for sure. Their mutual friend's enthusiastic offer had caught both of them off guard. He'd done his best to protest, to give Kara an out, but an oblivious Meg insisted it was the ideal solution. Caught in the middle, Kara had done the only thing she could do—echoed her old friend's generous suggestion. Assured him she was more than happy to put him and his nieces up at the Warehouse.

But he knew better.

Nevertheless, here he was in the second-floor apartment, ready to get the girls settled in. Meg kept Rowdy for the night, and Kara indicated she'd be by shortly to make sure they had everything they needed for the unplanned sleepover.

He watched his giggling nieces explore the unfamiliar space, looking none too sleepy if he was any judge. It was a church night, though, so he had to get them tucked in soon. Then he had to figure out a plan for tomorrow's worship service. And the visit to Pine Country Care.

But first things first.

When Kara showed up, they'd have that little talk he'd promised, even if he had to lasso the little lady to do it.

She'd throttle Meg later.

Lodging a complaint, insisting her friend withdraw

the offer, would have made her seem petty. Tightening
her grip on the overflowing fabric shopping bag, she exited by the Warehouse's front door and locked up. Then,
scurrying through the deepening snow, she made her
way toward a recessed door between the stone-fronted
Warehouse and the adjacent bakery.

She didn't appreciate Meg's interference—especially
after she'd asked her not to set her up with the cowboy.
Even if they didn't have a canyon-size gulf from their
past yawning between them, she and Trey didn't know
each other anymore. Had never known each other. Not
really. He'd moved to town in November of his senior
year. The fire had been in late March, after a series of
drought-ridden years. So five months max. Yet she'd
spent over a decade bound to him. Chained by guilt.

Gathering her courage, she pulled open the glass-
paned door and started up the steep, dimly lit stairs
like a condemned prisoner heading for the guillotine.
She'd do her best to drop off the bag and make a hasty
exit. But what if he tried to corner her as he'd done at
Meg's? Demand an explanation of her cowardice and
a long overdue apology?

He had every right. She owed him that.

But not tonight.

At the sound of little girl giggles, running feet and
Trey's cowboyish whoops coming from a door left
ajar at the top of the stairs, she paused. The Trey she'd
known in those few short months hadn't been criminally
rebellious like some of their peers. No, he just went
quietly about his business doing whatever he wanted
to do, whether it was not completing homework, skipping school so he could spend more time with the horses
at Duffy's or sneaking an occasional cigarette. In all

honesty, it was her own cowardice that sealed his troublemaker image in the mind of the community. Now here he was a dozen years later, a guy with a toddler in his arms and another curtain climber hanging on his leg. A regular family man. No, they didn't know each other. At all.

At the top of the stairs it was tempting to leave the shopping bag looped over the doorknob and make her escape. But curiosity won over and she gave the door a push. Peeked inside as a giggling Missy, her chubby little legs pumping as fast as they could go, dodged Trey's outstretched hands.

The apartment's unobstructed, hardwood expanse made it much too appealing for an active toddler. In fact, except for the bathroom and kitchen, the nonstorage portion of the second floor consisted of a single room divided by a wide, bolted-down bookcase that separated the sleeping quarters from the front area. Perfect for an energetic little kid, as Kara remembered from her own childhood.

She stepped inside as Missy sped by.

"Don't just stand there laughing, woman, catch her!" Trey lunged again, sliding on the polished wooden floor in his socks. Then he righted himself and in a few quick steps swept the still-giggling toddler into his arms for a bear hug.

Kara couldn't help but clap her approval of the child's antics—and Trey's agile performance. She should have known a cowboy, once he got the hang of it, could round up a kid as easily as a calf.

Still clutching the shopping bag, butterfly wings hammering against the wall of her stomach, she carefully wiped her boots on the rug by the door. "My mom said I did exactly the same thing in here when I was little."

A grinning Trey approached, Missy squirming in his arms. "You lived up here?"

"From birth through preschool. This was my folks' first place in Canyon Springs, right above their new business."

Trey assessed the space with a critical eye. "Now that Meg's moved out, does your mom have any plans for it?"

Uh-oh. That sounded like a more-than-casual query. She didn't want Trey upstairs. Didn't want him in Canyon Springs at all. Mustering a benign smile, she cut him off at the pass. "She'll need the extra storage space for inventory expansion. Besides, as you can probably tell, it's not that well insulated. Cold in the winter and hot in the summer."

The dark-eyed Missy stretched out a hand to her but she pretended not to notice.

"Meg didn't have any complaints." He glanced toward Mary who'd wandered to the far side of the room. He took a step closer to Kara and lowered his voice, apparently wanting to make sure the little girl was out of earshot. "Don't want to talk about this in front of Mary—"

She tensed. Was he going to call her on the carpet? Right here and now?

"—but I've already worn out my welcome at my little brother's place. They'll be moving back to the parsonage soon, so I need an office and a place to bunk. This would be just the ticket."

"Don't think Mom would go for that."

The slow smile that still made Kara's heart skip a beat surfaced. "Why not?"

She glanced at the boots standing at attention by the door. A hat nestled on a bookcase shelf, out of reach of the girls. Then looked him over. Worn jeans. Tooled leather belt with a silver buckle. Western-cut burgundy shirt unbuttoned at the collar. Just like in high school, only a more muscled, more grown-up version of the senior classmate she remembered.

"I don't think she'd go for, you know, a cowboy type."

"No cowboys, huh?" He pried Missy's fingers from his earlobe, but his amused gaze didn't leave Kara's face. "That's discrimination, Kara."

"What I mean is, if Mom was looking for a renter—which she's not—she'd be expecting a steady income. A stable tenant who'd stick around awhile."

"Then we're in business." He slapped his left leg, the apparent source of the limp. "Busted myself up so many times my surgeon's washed his hands of me. Says I'd better not get on another bronc or bull or I could end up in traction the rest of my life. I'm grounded for good. So I'm your man."

Her breath came a little quicker. Her man? Maybe in her dreams. Unfortunately, cowboying wasn't the only drawback to Trey Kenton. She might as well be blunt. "Mom will remember you as you were in high school."

"Boys grow up." A friendly but assessing gaze slid over her and a smile quirked again. "Girls do, too."

Their gazes met. How easy it would be to fall back into that old flirtatious teenage banter they used to share. The chemistry had stood the test of time, but she couldn't risk it.

"Well, since Mom's not looking to rent—"

"Maybe I'll give her a call."

He wouldn't, would he? She lifted the shopping bag still clutched in her hand and held it out to him. It was time to make her escape.

"I stopped off at the Warehouse and got you a few things. Breakfast cereal and a half gallon of milk. T-shirts for the girls to sleep in. Toothpaste. Toothbrushes. A comb. Razor."

Eyes twinkling, Trey caressed Missy's soft cheek with the back of his hand. "Noticed the girls need a shave, did you?"

"Right." Heart pounding, she handed off the bag and dragged her gaze from the firm jaw that once again showed evidence of a dusky shadow. "Snow's still dumping, so I need to get going. Bedding's in the chest over there. Meg said she'd washed it up. Washer and dryer behind the louvered doors." She glanced at him again, still avoiding Missy, who now leaned forward in his arms, hands outstretched toward her. "Do you need any help with anything?"

She hoped not. But as the hostess for his overnight stay, she had to at least offer.

"No, you've been more than generous." He set the bag on a nearby upholstered chair, the expression in his eyes becoming serious. Searching.

Oh, no. "Well, I'll see you later then. Sleep tight."

She turned toward the door, but he stepped forward to catch the upper arm of her coat sleeve.

Not now. I need to apologize. Beg his forgiveness. But not tonight. Not now.

He tugged on her sleeve and she momentarily closed

her eyes, willing her heart to quiet. Even ventured a prayer. Then took a quick breath and faced him again.

He released her arm but held her gaze. "I know you need to get going, but I'm sorry Meg put you on the spot—offering the apartment without asking you first."

"Happy to help out." Happy? What a liar she was.

He glanced down at the floor, then back at her as if uncertain how to proceed. "Look, Kara, for whatever reason, we seem to have gotten off on the wrong foot at Meg's tonight. Maybe even last night in the parking lot at Kit's."

She clasped her still-gloved hands. "Guess we were both caught off guard."

He shifted Missy in his arms and thrust out a hand, his gaze penetrating hers. "What do you say then? Truce?"

Chapter Five

*N*ow. *Apologize now.*

But she hesitated, her jaw tightening as their gazes held. She nibbled her lower lip, then took a ragged breath.

A truce.

"I guess it all depends." She lifted her trembling chin.

Trey withdrew his outstretched hand, his expression uncertain. "On what?"

She swallowed. *Now. Say it now.* "On if you can forgive me for not coming forward after the fire. For not—"

Trey held up a hand to halt her, then nodded to Mary who was now checking out the contents of Kara's shopping bag only a few feet away.

She'd totally forgotten about the little girl's presence.

"Honey—" he smiled at his niece "—why don't you trot on into the bathroom and get ready for bed? Kara's got something in the bag for you to wear to sleep in. I'll be in to help you in a few minutes."

Moving to crouch down by the child and shopping

bag, Kara pulled out an adult-size, pink *I Love Arizona* T-shirt. She'd hoped the girls would like the shimmery trim and the satin ribbon threaded along the hem, a delicate bow tied off to the side. Judging by the delight on Mary's face when she handed it to her, she'd guessed right.

Eyes wide, Mary glanced at her uncle, then smiled at Kara with that same slow smile Trey sported. "How old are you, Kara?"

"No, Mary." Trey shook his head at his niece. "Don't start with that again."

The preschooler giggled and clasped the T-shirt to her chest, her gaze intent as she took in Kara's hair, her face. Almost as if trying to memorize her every feature. "Thank you, Kara."

"You're welcome."

Then without warning the black-haired girl threw her arms around Kara for a hug. A tight one. Smelling of baby shampoo.

A warm whisper tickled Kara's ear. "I like you."

Kara hugged her back. "I like you, too."

Mary pulled away, then with another giggle and a conspiratorial look at Trey she trotted off to the bathroom.

Kara stood, shaken by the genuineness of the child's outburst of affection. Kids. She'd never had a clue around them, but Mary didn't seem to care. Maybe she should pass out pink T-shirts more often.

She caught Trey watching her. "I don't mind telling her how old I am. It's not like it's a secret."

"Take it from me, that's not where she was going with her question." He grimaced. "And don't ask."

She laughed at the chagrined look in his eyes.

"Thanks for reminding me she was there a minute ago. I'd totally forgotten. She's so quiet."

"Sometimes." A smile tugged at his lips as he patted Missy's diapered bottom. She was barely keeping her eyes open now, her head nestling into the crook of his neck. "I've learned the hard way that unless I want my brother and sister-in-law to get a word-for-word replay of everything I say, I'd better be alert to a miniature undercover operative in my midst."

The sound of water running in the bathroom sink echoed into the expanse of the room. Outside the Warehouse, wind buffeted. Ice crystals pecked at the windows. A floorboard creaked.

"Kara—"

"Trey—"

They both stopped. He nodded toward her. "Ladies first." *Please God, get me through this.*

"I'm sorry for not telling everyone that you were watching movies with me that night. That you were nowhere near the Logan property when it caught on fire. When I heard you'd been accused, arrested—" She took a ragged breath, voice quavering as her tear-filled eyes sought his. "Can you ever forgive me?"

"Already did, darlin'," his low voice assured her. "A long time ago."

She stared at him. Not comprehending the kindness reflected in his eyes. Wasn't this where he was supposed to pull out his cell phone and dial 911? Report her for withholding evidence in a criminal case?

"I knew you were scared." His words washed over her in a reassuring wave. "Understood why you didn't want anyone to know you were with me. Especially your mom."

"I'm so sorry." But not for the reasons he thought. There was so much more to the story of that night that he didn't know. So much more that she couldn't tell. "If I could go back, as I've done ten thousand times in my mind, I'd do it all over again. But right, this time. I hate myself for what you had to go through."

"No need for that." His eyes grew thoughtful as if mentally traveling back in time. "I admit juvenile detention wasn't any fun. Or the unending community service projects. Or summer school so I could get my diploma. But I know now it could have been worse."

She tilted her head, hanging on his every word. "How could it have been worse?"

"I could have been eighteen, not just shy of it," he continued. "It could have been national forest service property instead of Duffy Logan's, a forgiving church member. And my dad could have been the town drunk instead of a respected pastor."

She clenched her fists in an effort to warm ice-cold fingers. To stop their trembling. "Why didn't you rat me out? Make me come forward?"

He hadn't attempted to contact her in the days after his arrest. Not once.

"I knew you were mad at me, you know, for—" He swallowed. Glanced away.

"Having the guts to say no?" Heat burned her cheeks as the memory flared. How he'd responded to her kisses. At first. Then the look on his face when she made that inappropriate proposal. How he'd stepped back. Held her at arms' length. Apologized for getting carried away. Left without another word.

Don't deny his assumption. Let him think you sold

*him out to retain driving privileges and peace with your
mom. Sold him out for childish revenge.*

"It's all in the past." Gentle eyes echoed his smile.
"Let's leave it there."

Wonder filled her. "Thank you."

Missy moved restlessly in his arms, and Kara took a
step toward the door. She needed to get away. Come to
terms with what had just transpired. At long last she'd
apologized. And he'd forgiven. "I'd better let you get
the girls to bed. But—"

There was one more thing she needed to know.

He shushed the little girl, who was beginning to fuss.
"Yeah?"

"You never liked this town, even before the fire. Why
did you come back?"

He took a breath. "Guess you might call it unfinished business."

She shook her head, not following his train of
thought.

"Injury sidelined me from the rodeo circuit. Then
I was hired to relaunch the Logan facility. Planned to
get in and get out."

How was that old business? Restoring the place he'd
been accused of torching?

"Reyna's been dogging me to stay on. To settle
down here. A few months ago I'd have said no way."
He gazed down at Missy cuddled in his arms. "But the
place grows on you, you know? And with Missy and
Mary… Well, I've decided to clear my name and call
Canyon Springs home."

Her heart jolted. "How are you going to do that? Nobody's going to listen to me at this late date. Believe
that I'm your alibi."

"You're right. And I won't ask you to do that. This isn't your battle. It's mine."

"Then how?"

"I have to prove myself to the community. That I'm a man of integrity. A man to be trusted." He glanced down at the again-dozing Missy. "You see, Kara, you're not the only person who didn't come forward. Someone else knows I didn't set that fire."

Kara's fists clenched in her pockets.

"One other person knows, because they started it. Left my cigarette lighter there. And I intend to find out who that person is."

"He's *what?*"

Kara clutched her mother's arm as she helped her to the house's back door after church on Sunday. She'd hardly slept at all last night. No wonder, after Trey's bombshell. But surely she misunderstood what her mom said.

"You heard me, doll. Coming for lunch." Her mother grasped the railing to steady herself. "His nieces, too, of course."

Trey could be arriving any minute?

Last night he'd no more voiced his intention to find the real arsonist when Mary had trotted into the room to show off her T-shirt pj's. Avoiding Trey's gaze, Kara had oohed and aahed to the little girl's delight. Then made her escape.

But now this. Nowhere to run. Nowhere to hide.

Trey had forgiven her when he thought she'd just been a scared, stupid kid. One who immaturely reacted out of fear. Immature revenge. He had no idea she'd known this whole time who'd started the fire.

He'd hate her when he found out.

She held open the door to the enclosed porch for her mom, greeted by the tantalizing scent of a Crock-Pot pork roast and the lingering aroma of an apple pie baked earlier that morning. Mom knew that kind of thing wasn't on her doctor-mandated diet, but she'd stubbornly called the Warehouse yesterday afternoon and insisted Kara pick up the meat and other ingredients for a few of her many specialties. Said she felt like having company, which had long been a custom on Sundays before her late autumn heart attack. She'd always liked to see who God led her way to invite from church or the neighborhood.

But why Trey of all people?

When they'd divested themselves of coats and boots, they moved on into the kitchen where her mother laid out five plates and handed her a fistful of silverware.

"Kind of surprised you'd invite Trey Kenton, Mom." She kept her voice even as she arranged the utensils. Years ago Mom had expressly forbidden her to see him outside the church youth group activities. Not that she always obeyed. "I didn't even know he was in town until Friday night."

"Need to talk business with him."

"What kind of business?"

"Looks like he'll be renting the Warehouse apartment."

Several spoons slipped from her fingers and clattered to the hardwood floor. She knelt to pick them up with a trembling hand. She tossed the utensils into the sink, then opened a drawer for replacements. "Don't you think maybe we should have discussed this first?"

"Got to chattin' with him after you went off with

Meg this morning. Returned Missy's mitten, by the way." Mom winked. "He says he's indebted to you. Missy had already lost another mitten on his watch this week. He's down to the last spare pair and figured he'd be answering to Reyna if at least one of them didn't turn up."

She gave her mother a weak smile. She should have returned the mitten herself so Mom wouldn't have had an excuse to strike up a conversation with him this morning.

"But, Mom, for years you haven't wanted to deal with the headaches renters can bring." She smoothed a turned-up corner of the tablecloth. "Don't forget, I won't be here much longer to oversee a rental. Run interference if things don't work out."

"Haven't forgotten." Mom opened a cabinet and pulled out a serving platter. "But he mentioned you'd let him and the girls stay there last night. One thing led to another and, well, it seemed like the right thing to do. Him being the pastor's brother and all."

"But if you've decided to rent, wouldn't it be better to get the word out to your friends first? See if they know a nice, quiet, local girl who'd put up pretty curtains and keep the place neat and clean? I don't want to sound biased, but most guys are notoriously bad housekeepers."

Mom was okay with some clutter but a stickler for cleanliness, so throwing out that reminder was worth a shot.

Her mother shrugged. "He's going to use it as an office, too, so I assume he'll keep it presentable."

"But Trey Kenton? Mom, don't you remember how you—"

"Boys grow up."

Now where had she heard that before?

Kara opened a cabinet and searched for two plastic cups for the girls. No glassware for the wee ones. "You know what you always said about Dad. Cowboys ain't nothin' but trouble."

Her mother chuckled and dried her hands on the towel looped on the refrigerator door handle. "Guess I did say that a time or two, didn't I?"

"A time or two?" She stared in openmouthed disbelief. "It was a never-ending litany. You didn't want me to have anything to do with Trey even though he was the minister's son."

Her mother sobered as she opened the oven to peek in at the still-baking potatoes. "I was hurtin' bad back then, doll. Your dad leaving was a blow I wasn't prepared for. Takes time for even God to heal that kind of stuff."

"Sure, but—"

"Honey," her mom said, turning a frank gaze on her, "if you're afraid Trey might burn down the Warehouse, remember almost nobody accused him of deliberately catching fire to the forest. He was careless with a cigarette. But he doesn't smoke now. I made sure of that."

"It's not that, it's just—" She heard the rumble of a truck pulling around to the back of the house.

At the sound of an engine cutting off and the slam of a door, her mom handed her the salt and pepper shakers, then peeked out the window. "There they are. He sure seems to have those kids in tow quite a bit. I imagine that's one reason why he wants a place of his own in town. A little privacy."

So she *had* known Trey had been back awhile.

But why couldn't he rent a room at the Canyon

Springs Inn? A cabin at Mackey's? There were plenty of available places in the off-season. Why did it have to be the Warehouse? She joined her mother at the window to watch as Trey opened the back passenger-side door and leaned in to unharness the girls.

Think of something. Fast.

"You know he has a dog, don't you?" Mom never liked animals in the house. Wouldn't even let her keep so much as a hamster indoors. "What's he going to do with that big hairy dog?"

"Says Rowdy's house-trained, so I assume he'll take him on walks. Forest service property is just a few blocks away."

Her stomach did a rollover. *Rowdy?* Mom knew his mutt's name?

This was not looking good.

"Is this Kara's house, Uncle Trey?"

Mary strained to see over his shoulder as he bent down to unbuckle her harness.

"Sure is."

"I think I like her house." She bobbed her head with deliberate motion to make the wispy five-inch-long ponytail swish from side to side.

That morning she'd insisted her hair be put in a ponytail. Couldn't be talked out of it. He'd finally found a rubber band in the back of a kitchen drawer, but it was no easy chore. Came out off center, but she didn't seem to mind.

He glanced toward the familiar cream-colored house nestled under a canopy of ponderosas. Like Mary, he liked the Dixon place. Or used to. Until the night he had to make the hardest decision he'd ever made up to that point in his young life. And for more nights than he cared to admit, he wondered if it had been the right one.

He refocused on his nieces, ignoring the tension in his upper arms. Man, Kara's mom used to scare him to death. Even now, fixing to walk up to her door seemed no less a feat of raw courage than when a chute gate swung open and a near-ton of horned, hard-as-steel muscle leaped out from under him and into an arena. He chuckled at the comparison. That facing Kara's mom on her home turf was akin to gearing up for a bone-jarring, neck-snapping, eight-second ride.

"Why are you laughing, Uncle Trey?"

He pulled the zipper of Mary's coat up to her neck. "'Cause your Uncle Trey is still a big, overgrown kid."

Mary giggled.

He'd been pretty proud of himself talking to Mrs. Dixon at the church earlier this morning. Managed to carry on a conversation like the adult he was. Joked about Missy's AWOL mitten. But when he thanked her for last night's use of the Warehouse, mentioned his interest in renting it, he hadn't anticipated she'd be so open to the idea. She had invited him to lunch for further discussion. Maybe his efforts at integrating into the community were paying off, too. He must have presented himself well. Proved he'd matured. Was reliable.

Either that or she was desperate for rent money.

"Get those girls in here, young man." Mrs. Dixon waved at him from where she'd poked her head out the open back porch door. "Freezing out there."

"Yes, ma'am." He tipped his hat in her direction, then helped Mary out of the backseat before reaching for Missy. He negotiated the shoveled-out walkway, passing by the door of a freestanding, two-car garage. Did

Kara still have that classic '63 Ford Mustang in there? He'd have to check it out.

Inside the glass-paned porch, the enticing aroma of a hot-cooked meal greeted him. His stomach rumbled in anticipation. Except for a burger and fries at Kit's Lodge Friday evening and pizza at Meg's last night, he and his nieces had lived off soup and sandwiches the past several days. Cereal for breakfast.

It took some doing, but he got the girls and himself out of their winter wear, then joined Kara's mom in the kitchen. Did this room ever bring back memories. The white-painted cupboards, the wooden kitchen table with its ladder-back chairs, the faint scent of cinnamon. A still-familiar collection of sun catchers sparkled in the window. It was as if time had never passed.

"Go on in the living room, Trey." Mrs. Dixon waved him toward the arched doorway. "Make yourself and the girls at home. I'll change clothes, then we can eat in about twenty minutes."

She disappeared down a hallway, and he ushered Mary in front of him as he carried Missy to the living room. Kara, in jeans and a rose-colored sweater, knelt by a stack of split logs in the tiled entryway. Gathering an armful, she glanced at him with an uncertain smile, but didn't seem surprised to see him. Her mom must have told her he was coming.

She stood and, as she turned, one of the logs clattered to the floor.

"Here, let me help with that." He set Missy down in a nearby rocker and crossed the room to reach for the armload of wood.

"Thanks." Her fair skin flushed as she relinquished it to him, then bent to pick up the stray log. When she straightened, her long-lashed gray eyes met his. And as always, the impact staggered him.

He swallowed. "Thanks for telling your mom about my interest in the apartment."

"Don't thank me. That was her idea."

"Maybe. But I got to thinking about what you said about her remembering me from high school. So knowing how she felt back then, you can't convince me you didn't put in a good word."

With effort, he dragged his gaze from hers, then moved across the room to kneel in front of the stone fireplace. He checked the damper and arranged the wood in the iron grate.

Kara held out a few fire starter wedges to him, her soft hand grazing his, and an unexpected jolt of electricity shot up his arm. Man, what was his problem? This was worse than it had been in high school. Acutely aware of her, he shifted away.

"Pretty clever means, *Pastor* Kenton," her lilting voice teased, "of getting out of a sermon at the worship service this morning."

He grinned. It *was* ingenious, if he said so himself. "Hey, Vannie's a talented guitar player. And Cassidy sings so well."

"And everyone loved seeing those teenagers up there leading a song service, so you scored points with the whole congregation."

"Aim to please."

Amusement glinted in her eyes as she gave him a multipurpose lighter, her hand again brushing his. In spite of the distraction, in a matter of minutes he had flames licking the wood. He stood, dusting off his hands. "There you go."

"Just like old times."

Their gazes met again. Old times. How had he forgotten the afternoon he'd once helped her get the fireplace going? How they'd knelt side by side, groaning when each time they lit the match, got the kindling in flames, it would go out. Bumping elbows. Playfully pushing. Each vying to see who could get it started first.

He recalled it now like yesterday. How she'd leaned her shoulder into his, wedged her way in front of him, deliberately whipping her ponytail in his face to divert him from their playful competition. In retaliation, he'd slipped his arms around her waist. Pulled her back. Back into his arms where she'd turned, her face brushing his cheek. Her eyes laughing into his, her mouth only inches...

That's when her mom had walked in, and from the look on her face he'd known he'd worn out his welcome. From then on he was no longer ushered into the heart of the Dixon household unless accompanied by friends. As their gazes now locked in shared memory, he knew he was in trouble. Big trouble.

But...would that be so bad? Now that they had their misunderstandings out in the open? Could begin to relate to each other as adults? Maybe that was teenage foolishness, him still thinking he needed to steer clear of her. She'd apologized last night. Sounded plenty sincere, too. The tears in her eyes had about done him in.

Sure was a pretty little gal. All soft and good-smelling. Even his nieces liked her. Couldn't keep their eyes off her any more than he could. Maybe it wasn't *only* to prove his innocence that God had opened doors for a return to Canyon Springs?

He cleared his throat. Couldn't let his mind wander

down that road right now. Get his hopes up only to get the stuffings knocked out of him again. "I guess—"

The crash of ceramic hitting the entryway tile sent them both whipping around.

Chapter Six

"Oh, Missy!" His older, ponytailed niece pushed the startled two-year-old away from the pottery fragments littering the tiles. "Look what you did."

He frowned. Missy? No way could the toddler have reached up on the bookcase to pull a piece of Navajo pottery from its perch. But a four-year-old could.

He moved to kneel between the two girls, reaching out to block Missy from moving closer to the shards. She stared at the broken object, not comprehending what had happened. But at least she didn't cry as Kara led her across the room.

He slipped an arm around Mary's waist and gave her a hug. "You okay?"

She nodded emphatically, avoiding his gaze.

"Care to tell me what happened?"

With flustered movements, she pointed to the shattered pieces. "She, she—"

"She?"

Mary nodded. "Uh-huh. She didn't mean to do it, Uncle Trey. It slipped."

He pulled her in close to whisper in her ear. "You're sure it was Missy?"

She nodded, her soft hair brushing his face. Man, he hated her lying to him. When *anyone* lied to him, for that matter. He turned her to face him and brushed back dark curls that had come loose from her ponytail, framing the pretty little face. "You know I count on you to always tell me the truth, princess."

He glanced over at Kara, who still kept Missy occupied, and her eyes met his. Great. Her expression looked almost as stricken as Mary's. He could replace the pottery's dollar value, but not if it had a sentimental one.

A soft sob from his older niece drew his attention. Lower lip trembling, a tear trickled down a flawless cheek.

He ran a reassuring hand along her arm. "You have something you want to tell me?"

Face crumpling, she flung herself into his arms and sobbed into his shoulder. "I did it, Uncle Trey. I didn't mean to. I was holding it tight. I didn't mean to. I'm sorry."

An ache deep inside swelled as her tiny warm body clung to him for all she was worth. She and Missy were his heart's pride and joy. How'd they manage to worm their way in there so quickly? Got him thinking that clearing his name and elbowing his way back into Canyon Springs was an answer to his prayers?

When the tears subsided, he pulled a handkerchief from his back pocket and dried her face. Let her blow her nose. Sad brown eyes gazed into his. "I'm sorry, Uncle Trey."

"You're forgiven." He gave her another hug, then pulled back to study her. "Remember, you can always tell me the truth. You don't ever need to lie to me, okay?"

She nodded.

"Now you need to tell Kara you're sorry, too."

He gave her a little nudge to where Kara stood by Missy. The toddler's arms were outstretched to her, indicating she wanted to be picked up, but Kara hadn't taken the hint.

Hands clasped behind her back, the voice of his older niece quavered. "I'm sorry, Kara."

"I know you are." Kara knelt and Mary hurried forward for a hug.

Trey stood. "Sorry about the pottery. I'll replace it if it can be replaced."

"Don't worry about it." Mrs. Dixon's voice came from across the room. "Just a piece I bought from a roadside stand up on the Rez. Didn't cost much."

He glanced again at Kara for confirmation, but she didn't meet his gaze. Deliberately avoided it, if he were any judge. But why'd that avoidance weigh so heavily on his heart? Why'd he long for her to smile up at him, to let him know she felt the same connection he was feeling?

But maybe she wasn't feeling it, too.

Never lie to me.

Trey's soft, measured words to his niece echoed through Kara's mind throughout the entire meal as he and her mother chatted amiably like old pals. Came to an agreement about renting the empty Warehouse space.

You know I count on you to always tell me the truth.

No doubt where he stood on that issue. When she'd apologized last night and he'd forgiven her, her heart had soared. Even praised God for hearing her for a change. But no more. Trey only forgave her for a partial truth.

"Kara?" Mary pushed her plastic cup toward her with a shy smile. "Can I have more milk?"

"Please," Trey reminded her as he cut Missy's meat. Always as well prepared as any Girl Scout, Mom had produced a booster seat from who knows where for the toddler.

"Please?" Mary echoed, then propped her chin on fisted hands and swished her hair from side to side. "Do you like my ponytail, Kara?"

"I sure do." She reached for the cup and filled it halfway from the jug next to her.

"Uncle Trey did it." The little girl cut a look at her uncle. "He wanted it to be like yours."

"You wanted it to be like Kara's," he corrected as he wiped Missy's face, then cast Kara an apologetic glance. "I did the best I could. Didn't have a ribbon."

"I can get you a ribbon after lunch."

Mary's eyes brightened as she reached out for her cup. "She's got a ribbon for me, Uncle Trey."

"That's what I hear. And what do we say when someone does something nice for us?"

"We say thank you." Mary clasped her hands in her lap. "But I don't have it yet."

"She has a point there, Trey." Kara's mom chuckled. "You may have a budding lawyer on your hands."

He shook his head, a smile tugging at his lips.

"And speaking of legalities," her mother continued, "I'll have the rental paperwork drawn up by the end of the week. But if you need to move anything in before then, go right ahead."

Why was she being so accommodating? Maybe, like her daughter, she was feeling guilty? Feeling bad because she'd all but outlawed him from the house? Now with him being the current pastor's brother, she felt she needed to make it up to him?

Trey excused himself from the table, then disappeared into the enclosed porch. A moment later he returned carrying the pink pom-pom key chain Meg had passed on to him last night.

"Now that it's almost official, does anyone mind if I switch this out for something less feminine?"

His laughing gaze caught Kara's and she couldn't help but smile back. He was such a decent, good-hearted guy. Which made her hate herself even more. His kindness last night had freaked her out almost as much as his declaration that he intended to expose the real fire starter.

Trey glanced at his watch. "Almost time to give that devotion at the care facility. But thanks again for agreeing to the rental. And for inviting us for this award-winning meal."

Her mom stood and moved to the other side of the table to pick up Missy. Should she be doing that? Lifting that much weight?

"What are you going to do with the girls?" Mom gave the child a kiss on the cheek. "They aren't letting youngsters in at the care facility. No one under eighteen. Flu precaution."

Trey frowned. "Jason didn't mention that."

"Heard it was announced Friday. Leave 'em here. We'll find ourselves a book. Flake out together for a nap."

"You're sure, Mrs. Dixon? I might be able to—"

"Yes, I'm sure. The Pastor For A Day is entitled to a few perks. And," she added, "my name's Sharon."

Inwardly Kara groaned. Why was Mom taking such a shine to Trey? This was a bit extreme even if she'd been overcome with belated guilt.

"All right. Thanks. And Sharon it is." Trey picked up his and Missy's plates. "I can help clean up here. That's the least I can do for you ladies after such a fine meal."

"I'll take care of it." Kara took the plates from him.

Mom waved her away. "Just put everything in the sink to soak. You used to do Sunday visits at Pine Country with me. Trey could probably use some help. Show him the ropes. Play that piano pretty for them."

Thanks a lot, Mom. She had a ton of things to do this afternoon. Needed to check on Roxanne at the Warehouse. Spend some time in front of the computer catching up on Garson Design business. She hadn't spent much time this past week on the new project. What if Spence called to ask about its status?

Trey caught her eye. "You don't have to go. I imagine they'll take pity on me and not start any riots when Jason doesn't show up."

"Kara needs to get out," Mom insisted. "She's spent the last month cooped up with me or at the Warehouse."

"Actually, Mom, I—"

From behind Trey, her mom shook her head, a death ray all but shooting from her eyes. Why was she—? A cold chill spiraled up her spine.

A family-style meal. Renting the apartment. Babysitting his nieces. A warm welcome to the man she'd once warned Kara away from.

Was Mom trying to fix her up with Trey—to keep her from leaving Canyon Springs?

* * *

Self-consciously aware of his proximity, Kara gave Trey a furtive glance as they pulled out of the driveway to head to Pine Country Care. His pickup fishtailed as it momentarily fought for traction in the freshly plowed street, then straightened. Snow crunched under the tires in a soothing rhythm.

What she'd have given twelve years ago to have been openly riding through town beside him. With the handsome new boy. With somebody everybody didn't think they already knew everything about. What must it be like to grow up where everyone didn't know you from your diaper days? Didn't know you'd fallen off your bike on the way to school in third grade. That you'd bombed on middle school cheerleading tryouts. That your first date stood you up.

Didn't know your dad had run off and left you behind.

A neighbor drew her attention as he paused from shoveling his driveway for a friendly wave. She and Trey waved back, and from the satisfied look on Trey's face this was a hometown perk he liked. The recognition. Friendliness. But she imagined they wouldn't reach their destination before it would be all over Canyon Springs that they'd been spotted together. One of the many joys of small towns she'd be happy to do without.

She settled back in her seat and sneaked another peek at Trey. Despite his relaxed, smiling expression, tension tightened in her forearms. Now was the time to learn how he planned to uncover the real fire starter. If she didn't draw him out, there was no telling when she'd again have the opportunity.

"Meg said you're taking Vannie Quintero on to mentor. Sort of a youth coach. You're serious about this clearing your name and winning over the old hometown, aren't you?"

Trey nodded, keeping his eyes on the snow-packed road. "You bet. I'm also assisting with an affordable housing project. Sort of a Habitat for Humanity kind of thing. Donating supplies to fix up the local youth center, too."

She forced an encouraging smile. Put a teasing lilt in her tone. "Kind of overkill, isn't it, cowboy?"

He returned her smile with a genuine one of his own. "I can't move back here if I don't get the business up and running by summer, and to do that I need to gain the respect and cooperation of the community. As it is, one of the city officials is giving me the runaround. I can't believe how much authority is granted to city councilmen here."

"Small-town bureaucracy. Get used to it." She tucked a loose strand of hair under her faux fur hat. "So why not go where nobody knows you? Where you don't have to prove anything to anyone. Start fresh."

"Believe me, this wasn't my idea." He shook his head, wonder reflecting in his eyes. "God's been opening doors and nudging me through them."

Kara laughed. "Boy, am I glad God's not as hands-on in my life as He is in yours. No way would I voluntarily move back here. He'd have to drag me back kicking and screaming."

He shot her a questioning look. "I don't know which surprises me most. That you don't like Canyon Springs—or that you don't believe God's involved in your life."

"Well, He's not involved like He is in yours, apparently."

"What makes you think that?"

"Don't get me wrong. I totally believe in God. Joined His team when I was ten." She remembered well the preschool and thereafter days when Mom dropped her off for kids' programs on Sundays. Neither of her folks were into anything having to do with God back then, but it made a convenient day care one morning a week. "It's just that when Dad left and didn't come back, I realized God answers some people's prayers, but not others. I'm one of the not others."

Trey frowned, but it appeared he was smart enough not to argue. She turned to look out the side window as they drove through what passed in Canyon Springs for a downtown. Hovering at a population of just under three thousand, the off-the-beaten-path community nestled in the pines. Like her mother's general store, most shops were geared to luring in seasonal visitors. Bikers, hikers, campers and fishermen in the summer. Cross-country skiers and other lovers of winter sports during the snow-packed months. The place certainly looked quaint enough on a day like this, with a frosty layer on the ground and clinging to pine branches.

A nice place to visit, but…

Whoever would have thought a sensible guy like Trey would naively believe coming back to Canyon Springs was a God thing? "In my estimation, Trey, hometowns are highly overrated. People build up this cozy little fantasy about them, but they don't deliver."

He mustered a smile. "I can see how the attraction is hard to explain to someone who's had a hometown to come back to."

"So you've bought into the Mitford myth?"

"What's that?"

"You know, the glory, laud and honor hymn wistfully sung to small-town America."

Trey chuckled. "There's a lot to be said for a sense of belonging. Roots."

"Lots to be said for independence, too." She met his gaze in challenge. "Wings."

With an indulgent smile, he turned down another pine-lined side street, a hodgepodge mix of A-frames and ranch-style homes with roofs, decks and porch rails softened by a layer of white. "So you see those two values—roots and wings—as polar opposites? They can't complement and support each other?"

"Not here. Stick around and you'll see what I mean."

Canyon Springs probably did seem pretty idyllic compared to his on-the-road rodeo lifestyle. And he'd moved around a lot growing up, too, with his folks starting churches and filling in at small-town congregations that couldn't afford a full-time pastor. But life here would only disappoint him in the long run.

As they rounded another corner just inside the city limits, her startled gaze flew to the barren expanse of Duffy Logan's old horse property. The land where Trey was renovating the long-neglected equine facility.

The site of the fire.

Even now, a dozen years later, five once-forested acres stood barren except for blackened, knee-high stumps where the damaged trees had been cut down for safety's sake. They pushed up out of the snow like flat-topped shark's fins. Silent sentinels, witnesses to the foolishness of her past.

She cut a look at Trey. He came here every day.

Drove past it, then down the winding lane through the thick stand of remaining trees to the indoor arena and stables. Maybe he was used to seeing it by now, but she'd avoided the area all these years. Even now it made her sick to her stomach to look at it.

To her dismay, he slowed the truck in front of the barren stretch of land. "I've got a guy scheduled to come in here this spring to pull out all the stumps."

She twisted her gloved hands. "What will you use the land for?"

"Parking possibly. Or another workout arena. Maybe just pasture. Whatever we decide on, at least we'll clear out the remnants of the fire."

"I'm surprised nobody's already done that." Did her voice sound as wooden to him as it did to her own ears?

"It's not going to be cheap to clear it out, grade it, make sure it's contoured for good drainage. Fence it in. Duffy wouldn't have had the money for that. Then after his stroke, the property sat here, neglected. You know he died a few years ago, don't you?"

"Yeah. He'd think it was great you're fixing the place up. What are you going to call it?"

"High Country Equine Center." He gave her a lop-sided grin. "But I imagine locals will always call it Duffy's. You want to see it?" He braked the truck as they neared a double-wide entrance marked by two stone posts and a wrought-iron arch.

"Right now, you mean?"

Trey glanced at the dashboard clock. "Guess not, huh? Time for our visit. But afterward, maybe? Or some other time."

"Maybe another time." Nervous fingers toyed with the cuff of her sleeve. "Have a lot going on today."

"You've probably been to Duffy's before, right? So I think you'll appreciate the changes we're making." His voice held a note of pride. "Gutted the main stable section adjoining the arena and have redone that. Tore down peripheral buildings that had seen better days, too. Will replace those as time and money allow. Remodeling the office next."

He applied his foot to the gas pedal again, and three-quarters of a mile farther down the tree-lined road pulled the pickup into the plowed parking lot of Pine Country Care. A low-slung building with a steep-pitched roof, it hunkered down in the frozen expanse beneath a stand of ponderosa pines.

As they walked up the paved pathway to the facility, Trey touched her arm. "Thanks for helping me today. I felt like your mom kind of badgered you into it."

"She wants me to get out more. Thinks I've been pushing myself too hard since I came back."

And that if she throws me at you, Trey, I'll return for good. Not.

He opened the wooden double door at the entrance and, smiling her thanks, she stepped forward. Then stopped. For right in front of her, bundled up against the cold, stood the person she least expected, but most needed, to see.

Her cousin, Lindi Bruce. Not looking in the least bit happy.

Chapter Seven

With a quick "Hi, cuz," Kara stepped inside to give Lindi a hug. But her longtime friend didn't return it with much enthusiasm.

Trey joined them in the spacious lobby and Lindi, her dark brown hair glinting in the soft light, arched a delicate brow. "Surprised to see you two here."

Meaning together.

"Trey's brother," Kara said, not wanting her cousin to jump to conclusions, "is the pastor at Canyon Springs Christian. He got snowed out of town. So Trey's filling in and Mom wants me to show him the ropes. So, what brings you here? Nobody in the family's ill, I hope."

"No." Lindi glanced around the lobby, then lowered her voice. "Checking in on my future senior constituency."

"She's running for city councilman. Woman. Person." Kara jumped in to clarify for Trey. "Youngest in the city's history, if she gets elected."

Lindi straightened the handbag slung over her jacketed shoulder. "Uncle Ed's retired and Grandpa's ready to, but since no one else in the family wants to pick up where they left off, it falls to me to keep the family name in the city annals."

"And your grandfather is—?" Trey ventured.

He wouldn't have paid much attention to local politics as a teenager, know Lindi's connections. But he'd mentioned a city official giving him a hard time, hadn't he? That sounded a lot like the man who'd raised Lindi when her father and mother—Kara's mom's sister—had been killed in a car accident.

"City Councilman Reuben Falkner," the young candidate spoke with evident pride.

Trey nodded agreeably enough, but Kara noticed the hairbreadth lowering of his brows. A flicker in his eyes. Even after all these years she could tell something about the name of Lindi's grandfather had struck home in a not-so-pleasant fashion.

"City Council will take up a lot of time," Lindi continued. "Time I'd prefer to devote to my family and catering business, but how can I say no to Grandpa?"

Although she smiled, she wasn't joking. Nobody said no to her grandpa. While the council bylaws limited the length of an individual position to three years, that didn't stop anyone from running for office every other election. Councilman Falkner and his brother believed that as descendants of the community's founders they had a responsibility to govern.

"We need to get set up for the worship service." Kara caught Trey's eye, then turned to give Lindi a pointed look. "I'll be in touch. *Soon.*"

An hour and a half later, with a devotional, extended time of singing and a few dozen hugs behind them, Kara and Trey headed home.

Trey carefully steered the pickup around a four-foot

high berm of snow left by a plow at one end of Kara's street. "I thought things went well, didn't you?"

"They're always so appreciative of visits." She tossed back her ponytail. "But I can't believe you were asking Mr. Manter all those questions afterward."

"I told you I intend to clear my name."

"By interrogating some poor old man?"

"He was the vice principal of the high school back then. Don't you remember? Knew all the kids. Knows the town."

"But still—"

"I've been in and out of Canyon Springs the past year, semi-living here since September, and no one's come forward with tips or a confession. So I'm stepping it up a bit. Need to be more aggressive."

"I thought you wanted to worm your way into everyone's heart. Earn their respect. But asking a bunch of questions, making accusations—" Townspeople wouldn't like random finger-pointing. Unfounded allegations. They wouldn't like *him*. She had to put a stop to it before this went any further and caused even greater damage to his reputation. She couldn't just stand by and watch. Not a second time.

Trey pulled into the driveway next to Kara's mom's house and cut the engine. "I haven't made any accusations. I'm investigating."

She reached for the door handle. Maybe she could talk him out of further probing until she got things settled once and for all with Lindi. "It's going to get around that you're snooping. People won't like that."

"You don't understand why this is so important to me, do you?" His solemn gaze held hers. "Why I can't let it go."

"You could do yourself more harm than good." She opened the door, but before she could get out, he laid his hand on her arm.

"Then tell me you'll help me, Kara."

From the look on her face, you'd have thought he'd asked her to help him dispose of a body. The dread in her eyes told him all he needed to know. What he'd begun to suspect. Disappointment plunged a saber into his soul.

"You're not sure that I didn't set that fire, are you?"

With a quick intake of breath, her eyes widened. "What? No, no, Trey, I never thought that."

"You're thinking I could have started it before I came by your place. That it smoldered and flamed to life later that night."

She placed her hand over his, her grip tightening as her beautiful eyes pleaded. "That never crossed my mind. Ever."

"So you will help me?"

"I—"

The distress in her gaze belied the words of assurance. He'd thought all this time that she hadn't come forward because she'd been humiliated by his rejection. It never occurred to him she doubted his innocence.

"I didn't start that fire, Kara." He took a ragged breath and reached for his own door handle. He needed to retrieve the girls. Pick up Rowdy from Meg. Get out of here.

Her grip tightened again on his arm, her gaze intent. "I believe you, Trey. One hundred percent. But you already agreed no one would buy me as your belated alibi."

Hope sparked. "This is your hometown. You grew up here. You know everybody or know somebody who does. We can figure it out together."

"Don't you think your time would be better invested in your business? It'll bring a positive economic impact to the community. That's what will win the town to your side."

"It's not enough." *Please, Lord, it's important that she understand.* "Twelve years is a long time to live knowing no one believed me when I said I didn't do it. No one except my family."

"Nobody said you set the fire on purpose. Accidents happen."

"An accident didn't happen." His jaw tightened. "Someone tossed down a cigarette—and my lighter. It may not have been set deliberately, but someone implicated me. If it happened to you, wouldn't you wonder what you'd done to make someone want to get back at you like that? Want answers? Justice?"

"Whoever found your lost lighter may not even have known who it belonged to."

Maybe. But it had been distinctive. Silver with a turquoise stone embedded in the side. He gazed at her a long moment, a heaviness settling in his chest.

"I thought you'd understand. I mean, you took a lot of hassle about your dad." Guilt stabbed that he couldn't yet tell her about his connection to her father. "So you know what it feels like to be talked about."

"I know it doesn't feel good. Believe me, I haven't forgotten the time you stepped in when those kids were giving me a hard time. Speculating about what my father had done. Why he left Mom and me behind."

Why hadn't he thought of it before? "That's it."

"What?"

"Those kids. The ones I set straight. What were their names?"

Her expression darkened. "You're way off track. They were good kids basically. Just misguided."

"But it makes sense, doesn't it? That they'd want to get back at me?" He marveled that the answer had been there right in front of his face all this time. "I only went to school here a handful of months, so the names and faces are blurry. Was it Gord? Cord? What was the kid's name—the chubby one with the braces? You know who I'm talking about."

"He goes by Cordell now," she said with obvious reluctance. "He's a police officer."

"Like cops never did anything stupid when they were kids? And he had a couple of sidekicks. Little goth gal. Black hair. Purple sparkle nail polish. Tattoo on the back of her neck."

"Lark. She's a social worker for the county. Both have made decent lives for themselves."

"Of course they did." His voice hardened. "And they could do it because they weren't looked on with suspicion."

"Trey—"

"There were a couple of others, weren't there? Work with me here, Kara."

She looked him square in the eye. "No. If you want to win the community's favor, accusing some of its reputable citizens isn't the way to go about it."

"I told you I'm not accusing anyone."

"But the plan is to eventually, isn't it?" Her gray eyes wide with an alarm he didn't understand, she leaned toward him. "Do yourself a favor, Trey. Don't."

* * *

"I want a ponytail again." Mary pushed away her empty cereal bowl. "Like Kara."

"Kara who?" her mother asked, wiping the Wednesday breakfast table with a damp cloth.

"Uncle Trey's Kara."

Trey jerked his head up from where he'd had his nose buried in yesterday's newspaper, barely listening to the girlish conversation going on around him. What had she just said?

"Uncle Tway! Uncle Tway!" Missy banged the flat of her hand on the table.

"Uncle Trey has a Kara, does he?" Reyna raised her brows and glanced in his direction. "Interesting."

He scowled. "No, it's not interesting. So get that gleam out of your eyes. Kara Dixon has a ponytail and Mary's taken a liking to it."

Reyna laughed. "And why does that make you so cranky this morning?"

He shot her a warning glare. He wasn't cranky. He just didn't want her breathing down his neck. Pushing him at Kara the way she'd done Meg. She often pointed out that if he hadn't dragged his feet when he had first met the cute schoolteacher, it might not be her cousin walking Meg down the aisle in March.

Mary slid out of her chair and trotted around to him. "Uncle Trey?"

He focused on his pajama-clad niece. "What, princess?"

"You like ponytails, don't you?" She patted his arm. "And kissing?"

"Kissing?" Reyna laughed again. "By all means, Uncle Trey, please share the answer to that one."

He folded the paper, placed it on the table and stood. Almost tripped over Rowdy snoozing at his feet. "Talk to your mom about ponytails, Mary. The only ponytails I know anything about are on the back end of a pony."

He could still hear Missy's "Uncle Tway" chant and the threesome's giggles as he snatched his jacket and hat off hooks by the back door. He headed out with Rowdy into the still-dark morning to feed his horses. Now he'd never hear the end of this ponytail thing from Reyna. She'd dog him about her old high school classmate at every opportunity. The very thing he didn't need right now. Not with the way things ended with Kara Sunday.

So much for toying with the idea that God might have a happily-ever-after plan in the works there. Not only could she hardly wait to get out of Canyon Springs, but she thought his quest for justice would backfire on him. And her talk about God not being involved in her life? A red light for sure.

He slipped into the ice-cold, two-stall barn where his two American quarter horses, Taco and Beamer, had come in from the adjoining corral when they'd heard his approach. They headed into their respective stalls, waiting patiently for him to fill their feed buckets. Within minutes the barn echoed with contented horse sighs, swishing tails and the soothing sound of his equine friends rummaging in their buckets and chewing grain. He located a currycomb and, with Rowdy watching from the doorway, went to work on Taco.

It was plenty clear the root of Kara's beliefs about God stemmed from her dad's unwise choices. He'd known her father since his own early days on the rodeo circuit, when her dad was into rodeo promotion, not participation. And as Leonard "Dix" Dixon himself had explained it to him when Trey'd been chosen by the investors group to run Duffy's old place, he'd left rodeoing to settle down and raise a family. But he hadn't prepared well for that transition. Too restless. Wasn't cut out to be a shopkeeper at Dix's Woodland Warehouse.

Eventually, against his wife's objections, he'd been lured by an old acquaintance into a "sure thing" opportunity to make a killing off real estate speculation in the boom days of hotter-than-hot land deals in the West. Apparently the amiable, likable Dix, with all good intentions, sweet-talked trusting locals into investing with him. But he didn't have the experience or the business savvy needed, and promising deal after deal fell through. Cost his investors thousands. Turned more than a few local residents against him. Was the last straw that busted up his marriage to one of the town's favorite sweethearts. And under a cloud of shame, he'd left Sharon and thirteen-year-old Kara behind.

Which is why Dix didn't want his name mentioned as one of the equine center's investors. He'd come into some money in a later remarriage and wanted to invest it anonymously back into the community he'd let down. But that was something Trey needed to talk to him about now that Kara was home. Didn't sit right to keep it from her. As much as he himself hated deception, he didn't like being a part of Dix's.

Rowdy brushed up against Trey's leg, bringing him back to the present. As troubling as he found the situation with Dix, Kara's reaction to his plan for vindication disturbed him, as well. Were both she and Jason right? Had he misread why circumstances led him back to Canyon Springs? Was seeking to be exonerated a fool's errand he'd live to regret?

"She denied ever thinking I set the fire, Rowdy," he said aloud. "Sounded convincing enough. But maybe she thinks I'd blame someone else just to get out from under this cloud."

Trey scratched Taco behind the ear, his mind's eye drifting back through the years. A once-in-a-lifetime opportunity with the pretty teenager had presented itself that night and he'd turned it down flat. Even as enjoyable as the prelude had been, he'd known in the back of his mind she was acting out. Getting back at her mom. Her dad.

Shoving away the too-vivid memory, he gave Taco's winter-coated sides another round with the currycomb. "Don't know where I got the strength to get myself out of there, guys. Must have been the good Lord whispering in my ear." He chuckled. "Either that or my healthy fear of Sharon Dixon."

But all joking aside, he still had the here-and-now Kara to deal with. And steering clear seemed the best plan of action.

Chapter Eight

"You haven't forgotten your promise, have you?" Kara's cousin Lindi Bruce whispered from where she sat across the polished wooden table at Kit's Lodge.

Kara drew her gaze from the window. The winter morning stood out in stark contrast to the warm, rustic interior of the lodging and eating establishment. Even with a sparse morning crowd, she was comfortable that their conversation wouldn't be overheard above the breakfast chatter.

"I haven't forgotten. There's not a day that goes by when I'm back here that I'm not reminded of it."

She studied her cousin. Unbelievably, they hadn't talked about the promise since they were teenagers. Hadn't discussed the morning a terrified Lindi appeared on her doorstep, confessing she'd accidentally caught the forest on fire. Begging Kara not to tell, not to get her in trouble with her grandfather—or the law.

By unspoken agreement, they'd attempted to bury it so deeply that for a time they could all but convince themselves it never happened. That they'd dreamed it. But it was still very much alive, like a giant gorilla stuffed in the closet of both their lives. And since Trey's return, it rattled the bars of its cage with increasing frequency and forcefulness.

"How about you, Lindi? How often do you think about it?"

"Not much," she admitted. "Until each time you come back to visit. And now Trey. Freaked me out when I saw you with him."

"That's why I wanted to talk to you." Kara wet her lips. "He's determined to clear his name."

Lindi stiffened, her fork halfway to her mouth. "You haven't told him anything, have you?"

"No." Nor did she intend to mention that Trey asked her to advise him on what he called his investigation.

"What are we going to do?" Lindi set down her fork. "What if he puts two and two together? I was a smoker back then. At the very least I could be added to the list of suspects."

"You honestly want to know what I think we should do?"

Lindi nodded, interest sparking in her eyes.

"Come clean."

"What? Are you crazy?"

Kara met her cousin's look of alarm with determination. It wouldn't be easy to convince her, but there was no other way out. Even as she contemplated the difficult path ahead, a flutter of hope, the nearness of release, convinced her this was the right thing to do.

"We were both kids back then, Lin. Scared kids. Making that promise, keeping my mouth shut while Trey took the rap when they found his lighter—that *you* dropped—wasn't the smartest decision I've ever made. In fact, it was flat-out wrong."

The pitiful-little-girl look that had worked to Lindi's advantage for too many years to count focused on her full force.

"Do you have any idea what the fallout would be for me?"

"There's been fallout for Trey, too."

Lips compressed, Lindi again picked up her fork and stabbed a pineapple wedge. "Grandpa would have a heart attack if this came out in the middle of the campaign."

"Lindi—"

"It's not just about me." Her cousin cut a look around the room, then leaned forward. "If Jake Talford wins, he'll turn this town on its head. He's running on an economic growth platform that could destroy the way of life we've all come to love."

That *some* had come to love.

But although she didn't agree that Jake was such a danger to the community, she couldn't argue with her. A revelation that the natural-resource-protection-touting Lindi Bruce had not only set the forest on fire but kept her mouth shut and let someone else take the fall for it would be just the edge Jake needed.

"I know you have the town's best interests at heart, but—"

"What happened is in the past, Kara. What's done is done."

"There was a time when I wanted to believe that. But we can't let this go on any longer."

With shaking fingers, Lindi again set aside her fork, the pineapple still impaled on its tines. A fleeting cast of emotions flitted across her face. Indecision. Panic. Fear.

"There's more at stake here," she said, voice quavering, "than the city council spot."

The muscles in Kara's stomach tightened.

"James and I—" Lindi momentarily closed her eyes as if gathering courage. "Things are rocky, to say the least. Adding to it, he wants to take a job in Phoenix. But I don't want to raise the kids in the fifth largest city in the country. If we can't work things out, it will likely lead to divorce. And an ugly custody fight."

An invisible rope tightened around Kara's throat.

Lindi's tear-filled eyes bored into hers. "Do you know what all this coming out right now would do to my chances of getting sole custody of Craig and Kirk? I could forget it, that's what."

With her cousin's words, Kara's hope of freedom from the decade-long deception crashed with reverberating finality.

"I'm sorry, Lindi. I didn't know you were having marriage problems." She leaned forward with a final desperate appeal. "But don't you see? We can't continue to let Trey be blamed."

"*We* can't? Or you can't?" Lindi pulled a tissue from her handbag and dabbed at her eyes. "You probably had a thing for him in high school, didn't you? All the girls did."

Kara's throat tightened. She pushed back her plate. "We were friends."

"But finding him here again, you'd like it to be more than friends, wouldn't you?"

"I'm leaving town a week from Monday," she said, ignoring the probing question. "Seeing Trey again— realizing how what we did is still affecting his life—well, it's killing me."

"Then run off to your big-city fantasyland and forget about it. This isn't your home now. Stop dwelling on the past."

"Believe me, I've tried."

Balling the tissue in her hand, Lindi lowered her voice to an almost inaudible level. "You know, don't you, that we could wind up in jail? At the least, he'd probably sue me. You, too."

They'd been well under eighteen. Minors. What was the statute of limitations on covering up a crime?

Lindi's eyes narrowed with a speculative gleam. "And what do you think this out-of-the-blue revelation would do to your mother's fragile state of health?"

Kara thrust the alarming thought of her mother aside. "I want to be free, Lindi. I'd like your permission to tell Trey the truth."

"Well, you're not getting it. Haven't you been listening to anything I've said? What this could do to me?" Her friend pulled the napkin from her lap and slapped it down beside her plate. "You're not even thinking straight. You're letting a slow, lazy smile and flirty blue eyes trip you up."

"I can tell him without your permission, you know."

"No, I don't think you will." Tear-wet eyes triumphant, Lindi's trembling lips formed a faint smile. "You made a promise. And you don't want to be like your old man who couldn't keep one."

As she parked in the Canyon Springs Christian Church lot late that afternoon, a troubled Kara continued to mull over Lindi's words. The waitress at Kit's Lodge had stepped up just as Lindi had risen from her seat, so the breakfast conversation was terminated abruptly. Lindi even stuck her with the tab. How had their friendship deteriorated to this? All because of that stupid adolescent promise.

She dashed across the tree-lined street to the parsonage, then slowed down. This wasn't a Chicago thoroughfare where she had to dodge packs of pedestrians and impatient drivers. No reason to hurry around here, that was for certain.

Maneuvering around an SUV in the driveway as well as a car she recognized as Meg's, she entered the open garage door of the ranch-style house. A week or so ago her college friend, who was serving on the parsonage makeover committee, had brought her here for input on ideas she thought Reyna might like. They brainstormed together, did sketches, took measurements. So this is where she'd most likely left her tape measure.

But the missing device was the least of her problems. What was she going to do about Lindi? Yes, she could defy her cousin, break her promise and tell Trey the truth so he'd call a halt to his investigation. But that still seemed wrong. How well did she really know the grown-up Trey? What if he wouldn't keep silent? Wouldn't protect Lindi at the expense of his own reputation? The potential loss of the council seat didn't much matter to her, but could Lindi land in jail? Lose custody of her kids?

The door connecting the garage to the house was unlocked, so she slipped through the laundry room and into the kitchen. A radio in an adjoining room belted out an old toe-tapping country tune she hadn't heard in years. A night out at the symphony had become the preferred melodic choice. Still, she caught herself humming along to the familiar rhythm.

"Yoo hoo, Bryce! Meg! It's me, Kara."

She gazed around the kitchen in appreciation of Meg's earlier efforts. It was coming along nicely. Appliances had arrived since her last visit. Glass-fronted cabinets were now installed. Matching oak trimmed the granite countertop.

It reminded her of her mother's house, not so much because of the layout or color scheme, but the atmosphere. So cheery with sunlight spilling in the windows, playing across a caramel-colored accent wall. Cozy. Made you want to sit down at the as-yet-nonexistent table in the roomy new bay window and have a cup of coffee. A chat with a friend. Your spouse.

The image of Trey seated for breakfast flashed through her mind. Long, jeans-clad legs stretched out under the table. Booted feet. Broad shoulders squared as he brought a steaming mug of coffee to his lips...

With considerable effort, she refocused on the space around her. Unlike the palace-size interiors she'd helped design or decorate, this one was people-size. People-friendly. For more families than she cared to think about, the decision to build or buy seemed based on ensuring more than enough rooms to keep family members as far apart as possible. The economic slump might not be good for the design and construction business, but downsizing might do wonders for family dynamics. Not, of course, that a cute and cozy house had made one ounce of difference in her own family's case.

Thanks, Dad.

"Hey, Kara." Bryce Harding, who was supervising

the remodel in his free time, stepped into the room. Like her, he'd grown up in Canyon Springs. But unlike her, he'd chosen to come back. "What brings you here today?"

She smiled at the bearded, lovable bear of a man in his mid-thirties. Hard to believe he'd managed to stay single for so long. "I may have left my tape measure when I was here last time."

"Wondered where that came from." He pointed to the top of a box in the far corner where the fist-size metal device rested.

"Ah ha. That's it." She stepped across the room and slipped the measuring tape into her jacket pocket. "Thanks."

Bryce clapped his hands, then rubbed them together. "So, what do you think? Just the kind of place you'd like to raise your kids?"

"Looks great. Reyna and Jason will be thrilled."

"Hope so. Took your suggestion to paint all the walls the same light color. Carpet's set for delivery next week. Same shade throughout the house."

Kara laughed. "Glad to know that there's one man in the universe who can follow directions."

Meg appeared behind him, arms laden with D-ringed fabric samples, Joe's son Davy at her side. "You were right about the paint, Kara. It makes the whole place seem bigger, doesn't it? Not so chopped up like before with different colors of paint and carpet in every room. I'm going to remember that when we fix up the second floor at our new place."

"I get my own room," Davy piped up, his dark eyes sparkling as he slipped his hand into that of his soon-to-be mom. From the look on her face, Meg loved every moment of her new life. Funny how her friend's dream had always been to live in Canyon Springs—and her own had been to be anywhere but here.

Folding muscled arms across his broad chest, Bryce's gaze settled on her. "You're heading back to the big city, are you?"

"Week after next."

"Everyone sure misses you, gal. Thought maybe you'd be stickin' around this time. You know, considering."

"Mom's illness, you mean?"

"Mmm, not exactly." His tone held a teasing note, his eyes twinkling.

"Considering what?" Meg demanded, giving him a punch in the arm. "If you've figured out a way to keep Kara in town, spill it, you big lug."

"Oh, let's just say…" Bryce chuckled, his friendly eyes still focused on her. "A reliable source saw Kara riding around town with Trey Kenton Sunday afternoon."

Her heart jerked and a wave of heat pulsed through her. Meg's pointed gaze questioned silently.

Bryce winked. "But my informant didn't report if it was a case of sittin' courtin' close. Eh, Kara?"

With a deliberate show of banging the back door, Trey stepped out of the laundry room and into the kitchen. He shouldn't have eavesdropped like that, letting a rockin' country song cover the sounds of his entry. But when he'd heard Kara's sweet voice and Bachelor Bryce flirtatiously chatting her up, he'd paused a little too long in making an entrance.

A startled Kara turned in his direction, her face flushing.

"Good afternoon, folks." He nodded a greeting to Bryce, Meg and Davy, then focused on the pretty, flustered woman.

A nervous smile played over her lips. Probably wondering what he'd overheard. It did seem that small towns had eyes and ears open at all times. That would take some getting used to. But surely she couldn't have missed the wistfulness in Bryce's tone when he asked her if she'd be leaving town. Said "everyone" missed her. Any fool could hear the disappointment in his voice at her affirmative response.

Not surprising. Any single man in his right mind would find her departure disheartening news. Why was it, though, that every time he took a shine to a woman in this town, there was always a rival hovering in the wings? Whoa. *A shine to Kara?* Naw. Just the aftershocks of a teenage crush.

"Didn't see your vehicle outside." If he had, he'd have come back later.

"I parked at the church. Ran in to retrieve my measuring tape." She pulled it from her pocket as proof. "So you're working on the parsonage, too?"

"As often as I can."

She turned to Bryce. "I need to run. Errands to finish. But it sure was good seeing you again."

"Likewise. Get yourself back home more often. Don't be such a stranger."

She said her goodbyes to Meg and Davy, then glanced uncertainly at Trey. With a stiff smile she slipped past him, heading to the door, but he caught her upper arm and brought her to a halt. Startled eyes met his and he raised an inquiring brow.

"Have a minute to spare? We have a little business to discuss."

Chapter Nine

His words sent her heart plummeting. Why, whenever she saw him, did such an excruciating combination of guilt and teenage longing twist through her? Had he heard Bryce's comment about sitting courtin' close? Maybe he'd now recognize that small towns could be invasive if you valued your privacy. She'd already warned Mom against any further "making nice" with Trey in hopes that a little romance might persuade her to stick close to town. No way would she be willing to live in this fishbowl again.

With a tip of his hat toward Bryce, Meg and Davy, Trey motioned Kara toward the laundry room door, then followed her through the garage and into the driveway. No doubt she'd get a phone call from Meg tonight, demanding to know what was up with the Sunday afternoon cruise with Cowboy.

What business did he need to discuss right now? Hadn't she made herself clear that she wouldn't help him point fingers at Canyon Springs residents?

He walked her out to the street. "I talked to your mom."

"Sounds like I'm in trouble."

He pulled gloves from his pockets. "No, no trouble. I'm accepting her offer to move in before the rental papers are signed. Will transfer my office assistant into the apartment tomorrow."

Now she'd be tripping over him until she left town.

"Your mom said you could let me in through the back of the Warehouse." His gaze remained steady, as if watching for her reaction. "Said moving in by that route is easier than the street-side staircase."

"It's quite a bit wider. Has a landing so it isn't so steep. There's a better place to pull up a truck, too."

"So tomorrow afternoon? That's good with you?"

"Sure. Let Mom know when." She thrust her hands into her jacket pockets. "I'll make sure Roxanne's there to let you in."

Was that a flicker of disappointment in his eyes?

"Thanks. Appreciate it."

"So, you're moving only your office or yourself, too?"

"Office for now. Then as soon as I get my horses settled in at their new home, I won't have to run back and forth out to Jason and Reyna's to take care of them. Can stay here in town."

She motioned toward the parsonage. "House is looking good, isn't it?"

"I'm glad the church members decided on a complete remodel. Even without the summer monsoon winds knocking a tree into the chimney and ripping up the roof, it was due for an overhaul." He shook his head. "Sixty-year-old house. You should have seen it before they gutted the place in September. Fifties' tile. Sixties' fixtures. Seventies' shag carpet and eighties' wallpaper. The appliances were so ancient, I think they came by covered wagon."

"That's right, you lived in the parsonage for a while. Does it seem strange to see it again?"

"Not quite so much now that they busted out that wall between the kitchen and dining room, added the bay window. A master bath. But at first it was like stepping back in time." Which couldn't have been a good feeling.

She took a step into the street, then stopped. "I want to apologize for coming across so negative yesterday. About your investigation, I mean. It's just that I don't want the past hurting you even worse than it did the first time."

Surprise sparked in his intent gaze.

"You're not the first person to caution me." He kicked a booted toe at a snow clod. "Jason's put in his two cents' worth."

"You have your heart set on staying here, don't you?"

He pulled off his hat and ran a hand through his hair. "I reckon so. There's nothing I want more than to settle down in one place. Be a full-time uncle."

And eventually a full-time dad? He'd find a local girl who'd be into horses and kids and homemaking. Someone with whom he didn't share a muddled, mixed-up past. A warmhearted gal without a speck of deceit in her, who'd make up for all the post-fire years he'd endured.

Kara fisted her fingers in her pockets. The woman who'd eventually win his heart wasn't even in sight yet and already she resented her. Couldn't stand the thought of her cuddling in close to Trey. Being there for him. Encouraging him. Standing by him come what may.

Please, God, one little favor? Don't let her be any-one I know.

"I've been doing some thinking," Trey continued, oblivious of the internal hostility directed at his name-less future bride, "about what you and Jason said. And I realize I need to back off. Trust that God will open the doors He wants opened."

Was that her problem, too? That she hadn't yet waited long enough to see any good come from her father's departure? From the fire? The promise to Lindi? But look at things now—even worse than they'd ever been.

"Mom says God can work bad things out for the good." Here she was parroting words to encourage Trey that she wasn't sure she even believed. Or rather, words she believed for other people, but not herself.

His brows knit together. "I get too impatient. Some-times it feels like the whole town knows a secret and no one's letting me in on it."

"Everybody doesn't know a secret, Trey." She could say that with certainty.

"Maybe not. But someone knows."

Two someones to be exact. She'd call Lindi tonight. Trey deserved to hear the truth.

"What do you mean you quit? I just told you I'm let-ting you go." Trey stared at the sixty-something woman standing in front of his secondhand wooden desk, her chubby chin jutting in obvious defiance.

What a way to start a Monday morning.

"I don't abide by lying, Marilu." He kept his tone even. Nonthreatening. "Or dishonesty of any kind."

She shook a head of gray-streaked brown curls as she rummaged in her handbag. "Never you mind that.

You're the bossiest boss I've ever had and I'm not taking any more of it."

She slapped something down on the desk. His business credit card. As he watched, sensing his blood pressure rising with his every breath, she spun away to snatch her coat from the hook by the office-apartment door.

He stood. "In the business world things have to be done on the up-and-up. You have to pay your bills on time. Prove yourself trustworthy. You can't go—"

"Oh, yes, I *can* go." With a belligerent look she thrust her arms into the coat sleeves. "Watch me."

She headed out the door.

Trey maneuvered around his desk and followed her onto the landing above the stairs. "Just hold on a minute, Marilu."

"Ain't got the time, Mr. Kenton. You can mail me my check."

"About those charges—"

"Deduct 'em."

"Look, you can't walk out of here without—"

"Don't be telling me what I can and can't do, young man." She tipped her head to look at him over the top of her glasses. "I'm done with that."

She started down the stairs.

"Now hold on a minute."

"No time. Save your breath."

"But Marilu—"

"No time." She waved a dismissive hand, not pausing in her determined flight.

He watched her to the bottom of the steps, then swung around and reentered the apartment. Now what was he supposed to do? Never should have hired her in the first place, but Casey down at the gas station said she needed a job, had bookkeeping experience. That she could work from home until Trey had an office set up. He'd taken her on in early December.

After Rose quit.

You'd think with the way the economy was these days that people would appreciate a paycheck, even a part-time one. And what was she carrying on about? The bossiest boss. What did she mean by that? She'd lied right to his face. Then while arguing with him, he caught her in another lie. And another. He couldn't have any of that. Couldn't risk tainting his name, his new business. He didn't abide by lies, not even little white ones.

He returned to the desk to gaze at the clutter. Weeks ago she'd said she mailed the signed and notarized documents. The final ones that would give him the go-ahead to move his horses into the equine center property. But he'd found them on her desk Friday night, along with a paid invoice that showed *someone* had used his credit card to foot the bill for an extravagant purchase from an online cosmetics site. And a shopping channel charge. Could have been an accident the first time. Pulled out the wrong credit card or something. But twice? Did she think he wouldn't notice just because she handled the bookkeeping?

He wasn't that trusting.

Then this morning, before he'd even rolled out of bed, he'd gotten an irate call on his cell phone from the guy who was installing steel pipe fencing. The payment was a month overdue and he wouldn't show up again until the bill was paid in full.

Thank goodness he'd taken Sharon Dixon's offer to

get his office set up at the Warehouse last week before the final documents were signed. Mere hours after Marilu's departure on Friday, he'd made his discoveries.

Before she showed up this morning, he'd gathered enough evidence to prove she hadn't done much of anything the past month except cruise the internet. Had left bills unpaid. Racked up suspicious charges. Ignored unfinished documents with critical deadlines. Just what he didn't need right now. Not with a conference call with the investors scheduled for midmorning.

What he *did* need was coffee.

He glared at the little coffeemaker perched atop the filing cabinet. He'd had it for years, but the antiquated thing had given up the ghost that morning. He should have known the day would go downhill from there.

He headed to the floor-to-ceiling window to look out on the still-snowy street below. Well, he'd just have to find someone else. Sam Brooks, who ran the insurance office across the street, operated an informal job bank of sorts. Kept a bulletin board of job openings and job seekers in his entryway. He'd see who was hankerin' for office work and was willing to follow instructions. Someone who didn't cut corners and slide off into the dark side of what Marilu defensively termed "gray areas."

He called it dishonesty.

Thirty minutes later, he stomped back across the street from his visit to Sam's. Empty-handed. Nothing posted there was even close to what he needed in an office helper. He paused under the sheltering wooden porch outside the Warehouse, straightened his hat, then pulled his coat collar up around his neck to fend off the bitter wind.

Okay, he'd figure something out. He'd hand-deliver the signed permits to house his horses. And the pipe fencing payment. But first he'd call Reyna. See if she could fill in. It wouldn't be too many hours over the next few days to get those documents finalized. If she could meet the immediate deadlines, he'd have time to find permanent help.

He pulled out his cell phone and put in a quick call to his sister-in-law. But she reported that Missy had wakened complaining of a sore throat, so Reyna was a no go. The day was looking better and better.

He needed coffee. Badly.

And he knew where he could get it.

Spinning on a booted heel, he entered the toasty warm Warehouse, the little bells jingling a welcome. The gratifying aroma of fresh-brewed java met him at the door. None of that fancy flavored stuff here. Just good old-fashioned, hand-ground straight up.

He secured the door behind him, wiped his boots on the heavy-duty rug, then beelined across the hardwood floor to the coffeemaker. Tension dissipated almost tangibly as he filled a flat-bottomed insulated cup.

"And to what do we owe the honor of your presence this early in the a.m.?" Kara's lilting voice carried from behind the checkout counter and he turned toward her.

"Mornin', Kara." He lifted the cup to her in greeting, noting how the soft green, cable-knit sweater fit her trim figure to perfection. He hadn't seen her except in passing since last week. She'd kept herself scarce. Sent Roxanne to help him with anything he needed while settling into the space upstairs.

Was she avoiding him?

He took a sip of the steaming beverage. No sugar.

No cream. Just the way he liked it. "My coffeemaker croaked."

"Help yourself then. That's what it's here for."

"Thanks." He sauntered over to the counter; then something hanging off the front of it caught his eye. He reached down to unfasten the cheerful holiday reminder from its hook, then held it over his head. A cellophane-wrapped cluster of mistletoe. Red bow and all.

"Getting started early on the season, Kara?"

She groaned, then laughed and came around the counter to snatch it from his hands. "Don't you dare tell Mom you found it. She's superstitious about not getting all the Christmas stuff boxed up and put away before the new year."

"Out with the old, in with the new?"

"Exactly. Do you know how many times I've walked right by that without seeing it?" She returned to her spot behind the counter and stuffed the telltale evidence in a drawer, then put a finger to her lips. "Shh. Remember, mum's the word."

"You got it." He gripped his coffee cup, enjoying sharing a secret with Kara. Liking the way the smile lit up her face. Couldn't see that often enough to suit him. "Hey, you don't by any chance know anyone who'd like to pick up a steady paycheck doing office work, do you? Correspondence. Filing. Bookkeeping. Part-time right now, but eventually could go to forty hours—or more—when the place is up and running."

She frowned. "Don't tell me Marilu quit."

So she'd been paying enough attention to his comings and goings to know his office help's name?

"I fired her. Although she'll tell a different tale."

Kara's eyes widened. "What could that poor old thing possibly have done to get herself fired?"

"I'm not going into details." He hadn't decided if he'd press charges or let it go. Probably the latter. "But let's just say I can't abide a liar."

Kara turned away, her hand catching on a glass jar filled with stick candy, tipping it. She caught it before it rolled over the edge, then placed it back in a row with several others. Such delicate hands. Flitting like butterflies from one container to another as she straightened them.

He took a deep breath. "Can't have someone working for me that I can't trust."

"No, you can't have that." Kara focused on getting the jars arranged just right. Must be the designer in her. Looking for balance and composition.

"So did you fire Rose, too?"

He chuckled, remembering the gray-haired grandma who'd done typing for him when he'd first come to town. "Heard about Rose's departure, did you?"

She pushed one jar a half inch to the left. "And Liz."

"Now, you can't go counting Liz. Her husband got laid off and they moved out of town."

"I'm betting it would only have been a matter of time."

"Oh, you are, are you?" He cocked his head to the side and gave her an appraising look, warming to the unexpected teasing lilt to her voice. Hmm. It might be worth a shot. Maybe not smart, but what did he have to lose?

He lifted his coffee cup and took another sip, his eyes focused on her above the rim. "How are *your* typing skills, darlin'?"

Her startled gaze jerked up from the candy jars, and with a laugh she backed away faster than a ropin' horse once the loop landed 'round a running calf. "Oh, no. Not me. Get that look out of your eye."

"Just need help tomorrow. Maybe the next day or two. That's all. To tide me over until I can get a replacement. Have a deadline looming for responding to bids for arena seating. Contract prep, too. Payments need to go out. I'm up a creek without assistance."

"You've checked Sam's bulletin board?"

"Yep. And Reyna can't fill in. Missy's sick."

She frowned as she stepped back up to the counter. Gave one of the candy jars another push.

Undecided? Good sign.

"What exactly would I be doing?"

Easy boy. Don't spook her. He leaned casually against a pine support pole next to the counter and took another sip of coffee. "Entering data into the project database. Typing and proofing contracts. A little light bookkeeping. Getting everything to the post office before closing time Friday."

"That doesn't sound too involved."

"Fifteen bucks an hour." Now where'd that come from? Already giving her a hefty raise far beyond that of the other gals. But desperate times called for desperate measures, right?

She waved him off. "No pay. Roxanne says you've helped out around here this week while I've been tied up with Mom's physical therapy appointments. You've been unloading boxes. Moving shelving. Paying a vendor who was hassling her about cash on delivery. If I do it, it'd be as a favor."

If? Definitely considering it. He finished off the coffee, keeping a triumphant smile from reaching his lips. "I don't expect paybacks."

"I know you don't, but that way neither of us has to get into the tax paperwork for just a few hours employment."

"You have a point there."

"Roxanne's coming in tomorrow afternoon to give me a few hours break to run errands. But they don't have to be done right away. Just have to get them taken care of before I head back to Chicago next week."

"No pressure. I know you're busy here. I'm just a desperate man throwing out a wide loop."

"You explained why Marilu's gone. But why is it, again, that Rose departed?"

He hesitated, then came clean. "She bailed on me. Said I'm too bossy. Marilu says so, too."

Kara laughed and his heart again warmed.

"Are you? A micromanager, I mean?"

"I wouldn't go that far. But I do have standards. A quality of work I expect."

"Can't fault you for that. I'm the same way."

He waited, toying with the coffee cup, giving her time to think. Not wanting to push her. But seeing her now, eyes bright and the ponytail shimmering with her every move, doubts crept in at his impulsive bid for assistance. He'd promised himself again last night to steer clear of Kara, to keep his mind on his new project. But here he was charging in, inviting her right into the middle of his world. Not a smart move.

But she'd be working on her own most of the time. He had plenty of things to take care of elsewhere over the next few days. They'd hardly see each other.

Right?

She studied him a long moment as if similar doubts were sorting themselves out in her own mind. "Okay. I can spare a few hours. You can show me what to do in as much detail as you want to go into initially, but after that, no micromanaging."

He winked. "I promise to stay out of your hair."

And, oh, what beautiful hair.

He must be out of his mind to ask for her help.

Chapter Ten

"I can't risk it, Trey. You can't either."

Dix Dixon's gravelly voice carried clearly through Trey's cell phone.

"Telling her risks retaliation—that she'll deliberately tell someone who will tell someone and the next thing you know this promising enterprise goes down the drain because of its connection to me. And you along with it."

Trey gazed around his new Warehouse office. He didn't like this situation one bit, but he sure didn't need another strike against him, that was for sure. "It wasn't such a big deal before, but now that she's working for me—"

"She's what?"

"Yeah, I'm in a tight spot here with deadlines. Hired her to fill in when I fired Marilu yesterday. For lying. Now I feel like I'm lying by not telling Kara I'm working with you."

He'd spent an hour yesterday afternoon purging the files, both paper and electronic, of anything having to do with her father. Hated it. Felt like deception. But he hadn't been able to get ahold of Dix until this morning.

"You're not lying. You're keeping a promise, Trey. That's all. Believe me, telling that little gal will only upset her. She hasn't said much more than two words to me since she was thirteen. If this business means anything to you, keep my involvement under your hat."

"I don't know…." Trey ran a hand through his hair. He understood Dix's predicament. Trying to make good on investments gone bad years ago. Wanting to clean up his own reputation in the community. But surely he could trust his own daughter, couldn't he?

He heard a knock at the door. Light. Possibly feminine.

"Gotta go, Dix. I think she's here."

She shouldn't have agreed to it. She should have sent Roxanne to fill in instead, even if it meant paying her triple-time. But she hadn't thought fast enough. Had given in to the onslaught of guilt that plowed into her when he'd said he'd fired Marilu.

For lying to him.

She'd almost knocked a jar of candy to the floor when he'd uttered those words. Recovered just enough to pretend to rearrange the glass canisters. Couldn't bear to look up at him.

Why'd he have to keep being so nice to her? Helping out at the Warehouse. Even swinging by Mom's place this morning to shovel the driveway and sidewalks of a few inches of fresh snow so she wouldn't have to do it. Mom was thrilled.

Now here she sat in front of a flat-screen computer on Tuesday afternoon, typing away while Trey sat on the sofa, paperwork spread out before him on the coffee table. His afternoon meeting in Show Low had been canceled but, true to his word, he didn't micromanage. Not much anyway.

At least not once he figured out she could find her way around his word processing software and the spreadsheets and database. He'd finally settled down to review bids, Rowdy at his feet. Still seemed antsy, though. From the corner of her eye she sensed restless movement. Shifting. Heard the rustle of papers.

Knew he was looking at her. Again.

He cleared his throat. "So how are things going in the big city, Kara?"

She paused, fingers poised above the keyboard as she struggled to bring to mind Garson Design. Seven weeks she'd been gone now. It seemed fuzzy, light-years away. "Love it there. It would be perfect if I could just stay in Chicago long enough to land that promotion."

He gave a low whistle. "Promotion, huh?"

She placed her hands in her lap and turned to face him. "Not to a lead designer or anything of that magnitude. I'm still on the beginner rung. But it will be my first promotion. A step up. An increase in responsibility. Maybe in salary."

"Glad to hear they're treating you right." He scratched the late-afternoon stubble along his jaw as though deep in thought. "So you have what—like a condo or something back there?"

Her inner eye flew to the cramped, two-bedroom high-rise apartment she split with three roommates. "I'm not home that much, so I share a place with friends."

"Coworkers? Interior designers, too?"

"Actually, no. Just friends."

Sort of. She didn't intend to tell him she'd landed her

living quarters through a rental agency. Other single women, total strangers, looking for someone to foot a quarter of the sky-high rent. Not exactly home sweet home, but at least it wasn't too awfully far from the design studio. Unfortunately, there had been talk of disbanding when the lease was up at the end of March, so she might soon be beating the bushes for another housing option.

"Guess I don't need to ask if your heart's still set on going back."

She smiled at him, shoving away the memory of Bryce's embarrassing comment about a possible involvement with Trey making her reconsider. "Everybody keeps asking me that, like I'm going to change my mind. But there's an energy there. A vitality. Something new and exciting always happening."

"I get the feeling you don't feel that 'energy' when you come back to Canyon Springs."

She pursed her lips in thought. How honest could she be with him? "This is a sleepy little place where everything always stays the same. Each time I enter the city limits, it's like the world grows smaller. Moves in slow motion."

"And that's a bad thing?" He leaned back on the sofa, studying her with a lazy smile. "That's why tourists come here. Pay good money for it, too."

She hooted. "Too much in my opinion."

"Maybe. But they dream about cutting their ties to the rat race and settling down in a town like this. The forest surroundings. Rustic atmosphere. Peace and quiet. The friendly faces of people who know you and call you by name."

She laughed again. "That is precisely what drives me

nuts. Makes me claustrophobic. Everybody knowing me, knowing my business even before I do."

"Seems kind of reassuring to me. Like people care. You forget, I moved all over the West while growing up. New faces, new places. Never in one place long enough to call it home. Same thing on the rodeo circuit."

She studied him, stretched out on the sofa. "So you see the same thing in Canyon Springs that the seasonal visitors see?"

"I see real people. People who aren't cookie cutters of each other. People who take the time to relate on a personal level. Make an effort to get along." His smile warmed her more than it should have, and her heart gave an unexpected flutter. "Folks who are willing to help out when the occasion arises. Aren't afraid to get their hands dirty with what life deals out to them. People who aren't perfect and cut others some slack."

"Kind of idealistic, don't you think?" she teased.

"I've recently been informed by a former local," he said, his own smile tugging, "that my vision of Canyon Springs is a myth."

"But you're not buying that, are you?"

"Seems to me that most people can be about as happy as they make up their minds to be, no matter where they live."

With a shrug she maneuvered away from his pointed comment. She was happy, wasn't she? Just *happier* when she wasn't in Canyon Springs. She stood and moved to the filing cabinet. "So you're giving up rodeoing like Meg says?"

He twirled his pen with his fingers. "Didn't have a choice. Not once that bull all but pried my kneecap off on the side of a chute a year and a half ago."

She cringed. "Ouch."

"Yeah, ouch just about says it all." He chuckled and slapped his leg. "Gate was as wide open as a Kansas prairie, but he just kept ramming my leg into it again and again. So mad at having me on his back he couldn't even see the way out."

"I'm sorry." He'd fallen in love with horses, ranches and rodeo as a kid, back when his folks were filling in at a church outside Tucson. It might not be a way of life that held any attraction for her—or her mom—after her dad left, but it had meant the world to Trey. She remembered that much from their high school years. Years she'd tried in vain to push out of her memory.

His smile broadened. "But you know, it all works out. You don't see a lot of old bull and bronc riders around. So it's not like I thought rodeo was something I'd be doing until I qualified for Social Security. It was good while it lasted."

"But it has to be disappointing. To give up a dream. I know how I'd feel if I had to give up my life at Garson Design."

He held her gaze for a thoughtful moment. "I didn't like it back then, but my folks made me promise to finish college before I hit the circuit. I felt like I owed them after all they went through with me. Here in town, you know?"

How could she forget?

"Anyway," he continued, "I rodeoed on the side until I got a business degree, then full-time. Now I've come back full circle. Canyon Springs."

"Managing Duffy's place."

"When he died, his wife put the property on the market. A dozen guys who'd rodeoed with Duff back in the good old days pooled their resources with a few others to buy it. They didn't have anyone to bring it up to speed, though, until they heard I'd been put out of commission."

"So now here you are."

"Man's gotta eat." Lines crinkled around his eyes. "Besides, once I clear my name—"

That again.

"Or rather," he corrected himself, "after God clears my name—it will be pretty sweet. Settling down near family. Watching my nieces grow up."

Courting some hometown honey?

"Plan to buy property, too," he added. "You may remember I always wanted to train quarter horses."

He'd totally bought into the small-town fairy tale. As much as he hated people lying to him, why'd he keep lying to himself?

"You think this town," she warned as gently as she could, "will embrace you even if God flushes out the bad guy?"

A spark of hurt flashed through his eyes. "I'd like to think so. You don't give people here enough credit, Kara."

Why was he so willing to forgive what Canyon Springs had done to him? She sure wasn't that generous. "I guess I just have to wonder what makes a tumbleweed kind of guy think he can be happy in a place like this. My dad sure couldn't. Not even after his big talk about being a family man. What a joke."

Inwardly Kara cringed. Why'd she say that? It sounded so harsh. Bitter.

His forehead creased. "Every man isn't like your father, Kara. And even a good man can make mistakes."

"I didn't mean to imply—"

"Knock knock." The booming, cheerful words came from the landing at the top of the stairs, accompanied by a door-rattling series of fist pounds.

Irritated at the interruption, Kara watched the knob turn, the door open and Trey's brother peep in. His gaze swept the room, then focused on her with a gleam of interested surprise. He stepped inside, a ponytailed Mary balanced on a hip and a pink backpack clutched in his free hand.

"Sorry to interrupt, bro. Didn't know you had company." His gaze lingered on her again, eyes twinkling. Jason had always been full of teasing humor, but right now wasn't a good time. Maybe he read it in her expression, for he deposited Mary on the floor and turned to Trey, motioning to the papers scattered across the coffee table. "Is that paperwork on a place you've been looking at?"

"No, not that far along yet." Trey sat up and tossed his pen to the table. "Had to let Marilu go yesterday. Kara's filling in so I can make a deadline."

Jason nodded approval in her direction, eyes dancing once again. "Well, aren't you an answered prayer?"

She forced a smile and waved a hand toward the computer. "If I can meet the deadline."

"So what can we do for you?" Trey drew his brother's attention once more.

"Could I drop off Mary for an hour? Maybe ninety minutes?" He looked hopefully from Trey to her, then back to his brother. "Reyna's got her hands full with Missy. She's definitely come down with something. Running a fever now. But I have a counseling session I can't miss."

"Reyna's mom—"

"Is still out of town. Her sisters are at work. Or nursing sick ones of their own. Wouldn't want Mary to be exposed."

Trey sat back, gazing at the paperwork. "I don't know—"

"I wouldn't ask if I had an alternative. You know that."

Trey rubbed the back of his neck. "Sure. Leave her here."

"Thanks. I—"

"Yeah, I know. You owe me. Another one. Running up quite the tab aren't you, Jas?"

"Right." Jason grinned, then crouched to help Mary out of her coat and boots. In a flash he pulled bunny-faced and cottontailed house slippers from her back-pack and snugged them onto her feet. Looked like he'd come to town kid-equipped. And if Kara wasn't mistaken, the pink T-shirt jammies she'd given Mary poked out of the bag, as well. It looked as if Uncle Trey was being set up for a sleepover.

As much as he claimed he wanted to settle down in Canyon Springs, how long would it be before the charm of that wore off? Before it got old. Irritating. Before he'd had enough of pseudo-daddy duty, saddled up and rode out of town again.

Just like her dad.

No big surprise, once her daddy was out the door Mary beelined for Kara who'd again seated herself at the computer. It was like the kid was magnetized or something. Couldn't say he blamed her. Kara was a mighty appealing woman. At times.

He watched Kara's expression soften as she turned her head so his niece could pat her silky ponytail. Listened as she oohed and aahed over Mary's beribboned hair, as well. Heard Mary giggle, then watched her crawl into Kara's lap. Looked like work was on hold until Mary got her first keyboarding lesson.

"Mary. M-A-R-Y," Kara's sweet, soft voice spelled out for the youngster as she guided a little finger to each letter.

He ran a hand through his hair. So Kara didn't think the townspeople would find it in their hearts to accept him even if he proved his innocence.

"Missy. M-I-S-S-Y."

But wasn't it more likely that they'd be grateful? More than happy to have a bad apple weeded out, to welcome another solid citizen into the community?

"Kara. K-A-R-A."

He wasn't buying her pessimistic take on it. No doubt in his mind God had brought him back to town. Even if God was taking his own sweet time about it, he was here to resolve unfinished business, to prove himself innocent of wrongdoing. What other reason could there be?

He studied the gentle curve of Kara's cheek. The silken swing of her red-gold hair caught up in a sea-green satin ribbon. The soft, smiling bow of her lips... He swallowed, remembering how sweet they'd tasted that night long ago.

No, he didn't fear the community's reaction when he cleared his name. Not even if the culprit was the mayor himself. They'd come around. Eventually. No, it was the other thing she'd said that gut-kicked him. When she spoke the word that still rang in his ears. That exposed his insecurity. Voiced his secret doubts.

Tumbleweed.

She'd without reservation pegged him as a drifter. A transient. A rolling stone. Didn't believe him inherently capable of putting down roots. Was openly skeptical that he could make a commitment to a community.

And to a woman as well?

Was her thinking all tangled up because of her folks' divorce? Or could the thing he most feared about himself be true? Was blatantly clear to others?

"Trey. T-R-E-Y."

His ears barely registered the feminine voices. Maybe Kara was right. His ex-girlfriend had said the same thing. T-U-M-B-L-E-W-E-E-D.

A laughing Mary spun in Kara's lap and pointed at him. "That's you, Uncle Trey!"

Chapter Eleven

"Will you come to my Valemtime's Day party, Kara?"

She didn't correct Mary's sweet mispronunciation of the holiday. As she'd predicted, the little girl stayed the previous night with Trey. He'd told his niece this morning that Kara was working and not to bother her. But now, with her uncle dashing out to his truck to retrieve more paperwork, the little girl wasted no time crawling into her lap.

"Thank you for inviting me, sweetheart, but I'm going back to Chicago next week."

"But you gotta come."

"I wish I could."

"Daddy kissed Mommy on Valemtime's Day when they were in high school."

"He did?"

"Uh-huh. They were sixteen. Then they got married. How old are you, Kara?"

"Twenty-eight."

Mary's forehead puckered, then she nodded as if coming to a conclusion. "Me and Missy want Uncle Trey to stay in Canyon Springs. If you kiss him, he'll stay."

Oh, my. Memory flew to the one time she *had* kissed him. Thoroughly.

"Mommy says he needs to kiss a girl and get married and stay here."

How to respond to that? "I imagine there are lots of girls in this town who would like to kiss—and marry— your uncle."

"But I want you."

"I'm afraid I live a long, long way from here. In a big city. I'm just visiting my mom while she's sick."

"But if you kiss Uncle Trey you can live here, too." Her dark eyes emphasized the sincere appeal. "You won't have to be so far away from me and Missy."

"Sweetie, I—"

At the sound of heavy footsteps on the landing outside the door, Mary's eyes widened and she scrambled off Kara's lap. Dashed across the room and threw herself on the sofa.

Just as Trey entered the apartment, the phone vibrated in the purse nestled at Kara's feet. She snatched it up, hoping Lindi was returning her persistent calls. They could set a time to meet in private.

But the caller ID wasn't Lindi's.

"You are aware, aren't you, Kara, that I'm holding this position open for you?" The voice of Spencer Alexander III of Garson Design echoed through the receiver. Her heartbeat accelerated and she glanced at Trey as he and Mary, hand in hand, headed to the kitchen.

"Gabrielle won't wait much longer," her boss continued, and she pictured his aristocratic countenance indulging in a frown. "She's afraid with the economic uncertainty that the board will nix the upgraded position altogether."

"I'm sorry, Spence. I had no idea when I left Chicago that my mother was as bad off as she was. But she's on the road to recovery, and I have my flight booked for next Monday."

"Excellent. You've been working on the NuTowne project, I assume? I told Gabrielle you were."

"Every spare minute." Minutes that only materialized after a late dinner and into the wee hours of the morning. Thank goodness for design software and the ability to log into the company system remotely. And for caffeine.

"Excellent. That will work in your favor."

"I appreciate all you're doing for me." She tightened her grip on the phone, knowing how much it meant to have a designer of Spence's caliber in her corner. "Once I get back, I'll make it up to you. I promise."

She glanced toward the kitchen from where Mary's childish voice scolded Trey for inadequate jelly on her peanut butter sandwich. Caught herself smiling at his indignant, rumbling response peppered with good ol' boy cowboy jargon he exaggerated to make his niece laugh.

"Kara?" Spence's voice drew her back to their conversation. "Text me your flight info and I'll pick you up at O'Hare."

She agreed, then with a smile returned the phone to her purse. The promotion was hers. And not even a frowning Trey, now watching from where he leaned against the wooden door frame of the kitchen, could steal away the tingle of anticipation.

"Looks like a lot of work to me." Trey flipped through a few more pages of the spiral-bound workbook. Then he tossed it back on his brother's desk. A premarital counseling workbook. One like Meg and Joe would be completing in the coming weeks.

He nudged a stack of related videos. "I mean, if it's right, if God's in it, why all the boot camp stuff? If it takes all this not to end up in a divorce court, maybe people should be rethinking the whole shootin' match."

Which is what his once-upon-a-time girlfriend, Tanya Tyber, had done three years ago. Hit the door running when after twenty-two months and fifteen days—yep, she had it figured down to the days—he still hadn't put a ring on her finger.

"That's why we do this." Jason tapped the workbook cover. "Separates the goats from the sheep, so to speak. Or at least alerts the starry-eyed to the realities of wedded bliss."

Even after all this time the memory of Tanya's departure left him shaken. Her words still wounded. Scarred. He'd heard them echoed, in more gentle tones, in Kara's evaluation of him yesterday. But Tanya had believed him incapable of settling down. Keeping a commitment.

The very thing he, too, feared.

"I only wish more would take time to build a stronger foundation," his brother continued. "Everyone's in such a rush. Afraid if they don't tie the knot and tie it fast, their life's ruined. If only they knew the half of it—what ruin looks and feels like once you're in the middle of a bad marriage."

Trey picked up the doll he'd come to retrieve for his niece, having left Mary in Kara's company. "Don't kid yourself, Jas. It's not easy being single, finding someone who shares your values. Your beliefs. Hard enough without others judging you."

"Easier than being unhappily married."

Trey snorted. "Won't argue with that, but there are people—even church people—who make sure you know you're not up to their standards if you don't have that ring on your finger. Or a certificate of divorce in hand to show that you at least 'qualified' at one point in time."

"You don't mean people like Reyna, do you?"

He frowned. Where'd he get an idea like that? His brother was as dense as a rock sometimes. "No, not Reyna. She wants me to be happy. To settle down near the girls."

He moved to the open office door, then swung around again to face his brother. "No, I mean the ones who disregard that it's either not God's timing or not his best plan. Insinuate there's something inherently wrong with you."

Jason pushed back in his chair, donning his irritatingly benign, pastor-like countenance. "I'm sensing dormant hostility here. Residual Tanya? If you want to talk about it, I have a cancellation on my schedule at—"

"Sense whatever you want to, Jas. I'm done talking. I've got to get back to work."

Pulling the office door closed behind him, Trey exited the building by the back door. Now why'd he have to go getting irritated like that? Jas meant well. It wasn't his fault women didn't trust his older brother.

He pulled up his jacket collar against the buffeting wind, then headed for his truck. His heart felt pounds heavier than it had a few days ago. He shouldn't have asked Kara to help out. Handed her the opportunity to voice her opinion of his Canyon Springs dream. To label him a drifter. Forced him to overhear her talking sweet to some big-city hotshot she worked with.

At least they'd made the deadline with room to spare. She'd get back to her own business at the Warehouse now and he'd look for other office help. But why, of all things, did he have to go thinking about Tanya for the second day in a row?

And why was he foolish enough to think he could somehow prove to the pretty Miss Dixon that she was wrong about him?

Late Friday afternoon Kara pulled out a drawer on her mom's home office desk, searching for a stamp. But her mind wasn't on dropping a postcard to her Aunt Tammy.

Lindi still wasn't answering her phone or responding to text messages. Nor had she been in when Kara stopped by her office. Out on catering business she'd been told. So what was stopping her from telling Trey? Nothing. Right this minute she could barge into his office and get it over with. But she'd already ruined Trey's life—now it fell to her to ruin Lindi's as well?

She pulled open another drawer. Where were those stamps? They used to be in that wooden, decoupaged box. The one she'd made in grade school for Mom's birthday. She shut the drawer and tried another. No luck. The next drawer stuck for a moment, then slid out. Empty, except for an eight-by-ten photo frame facedown at the bottom. Curious, she turned it over.

The room dimmed as a cloud obliterated the sun that only moments before had beamed through the western-facing window. Kara stared down at the photograph. There they were. The happy family. Or at least the ten-year-old decked out in cowgirl gear had thought they were. Seated on the fence rail between her parents, she looked close to bursting with it, grinning from ear to ear.

Eighteen years ago. Just three years before Dad hit the road. Three years wasn't a very long time. People didn't just wake up some morning and decide to betray the trust of those around them, did they? Pull up stakes? Had he already been floundering financially? Scrambling to make good on the investments entrusted to him by friends? Restless. Impatient. Ready to move on even as he stood there smiling for the photographer, his arm wrapped around his daughter's waist.

Her grip tightened on the frame. Had Mom sensed he wasn't a home-and-hearth kind of man? That one day he'd leave her behind? How years of hard work on his behalf would mean she'd never find a way back to her own dream? A dream of teaching kindergarten that Aunt Tammy once confided she'd had since childhood.

She flipped the frame over and closed it in the drawer again. She hoped he was proud of himself. Him and his second family over there in New Mexico.

Now where was that stamp box?

She pulled open the remaining drawer. Ah, there it was, peeping out from under a stack of haphazardly crammed, overflowing manila file folders. She lifted out the fat wedge of folders and retrieved the stamp box with her free hand. But the smooth surfaces of the stack slid against each other and one dropped to the floor, scattering papers.

Setting aside the little box and folders, she then knelt to clean up the mess. Looked to be business stuff. Invoices and bills. Receipts. She scooped them up, straightening them to be returned to the folder, when one caught her eye.

OVERDUE.

Stamped in red block letters on the face of the bill. She didn't mean to snoop, but couldn't help but take a closer look. She shuffled through the other documents. Insurance papers. Medical bills. Invoices for Warehouse inventory.

Overdue. Final Notice.

Tons of them. What was going on? With a sense of uneasiness, she scooped them into the folder and headed to the kitchen where her mother sat sewing a button on a shirtsleeve.

"Mom, what's this all about?"

Her mother looked up with a smile. "What's what all about, doll?"

Kara placed the overflowing file folder in front of her. At the look on Mom's face, her heart stumbled.

"What were you doing in my things?"

"Looking for stamps."

Mom set aside the sewing, then pulled the manila folder toward her. "Guess you found more than you bargained for, didn't you?"

"What's going on, Mom?" Her mother's flat, unemotional response scared her more than the bills. The weariness, the resignation, in her tone. "There's all sorts of stuff here. Late payment notices. Letters saying you're going to be turned over to a collection agency."

Mom frowned. "It's mostly a cash flow problem. You know, when insurance hasn't paid yet but everyone wants their share up front."

"Cash flow? Mom, there are dozens of letters asking you for payment. And it looks like you were late on the mortgage for the Warehouse the last several months, too."

"Late, but it got paid. Everything will get straightened out. Don't go getting worked up over this."

"Are you kidding?" Weak-kneed, she dropped into the chair across from Mom. "You're being threatened with legal action. And what about these overdue bills for the Warehouse? I guess this explains why the delivery guy refused to leave that shipment. Roxanne said Trey had to pay him cash or he wouldn't leave it. How can we stay in business if we don't pay our bills?"

"It will all work out."

Kara gripped the edge of the table to still her shaking hands. "Why didn't you tell me? I could have sent you money."

"Honey, I didn't see any point in worrying you about it. I know how much the job and promotion mean to you. You bought that new car. May be looking for your own apartment. You're working hard and I didn't want this to be a distraction."

Kara slumped back in the chair, anger building. How could God have let things get so out of hand?

"It's more than a distraction now."

"I'm aware of that, Kara," her mother said quietly. "I'm working with the hospital and the doctors to see if I can pay it off gradually. It will all work out."

"You keep saying that, but these medical bills are huge. You could lose everything. Your house. The Warehouse."

"I won't lose the house. I've got my business to fall back on—and if I need to sell it to keep my home, so be it."

An invisible fist punched Kara in the midsection.

Sell the Warehouse? Had her mother gone insane? "Did you think you could sell it and I wouldn't notice?"

"I don't intend to file for bankruptcy, if that's what you're thinking. I pay my debts."

Kara smacked the table with the flat of her hand. "No way are you going to lose the Warehouse, Mom. You almost lost it when Dad left us and you worked your tail off to keep it. I'm going back to Chicago. If I have to, I'll live out of my car. I'll get a second job—selling hot dogs on a street corner if that's what it takes. You are not losing the Warehouse."

Mom rose to her feet, then braced her hands on the back of her chair. "This is exactly why I didn't tell you. It may be that this is all for the best. The Warehouse has gotten to be a handful in recent years. Maybe it's time to let it go. Retire."

Kara scoffed. "You're not old enough to retire."

"Then maybe I need a desk job. Regular hours. I've been at the Warehouse since before you were born. That's a long time, honey. Someone will be willing to take it off my hands."

Kara's breath caught. "Does anyone else know about the bills? I mean, Mom, if it comes to selling the Warehouse and people know you *have* to sell or go into foreclosure, they're going to make a low offer. Super-low. Please tell me this isn't common knowledge and that I'm the last to find out."

Mom pulled the chair out and again sat down. "I've never been one to broadcast my personal affairs and you know it. I'd intended to cancel that standing order, the one Trey probably had to pay cash for. It slipped my mind. But I make sure local vendors get paid on time."

Kara let out a gust of pent-up breath. "Good, good. That gives me some time. I can—"

Mom laid her hand over Kara's. "Honey, just relax. Everything's going to be fine. I'll pay my bills one way or another and if that means letting the Warehouse go— making a change in lifestyle—well, if that's what the good Lord wants, I'll do whatever is necessary."

Kara pulled her hands free and staggered to her feet, almost knocking over the chair. "Quite frankly, Mom, I don't care what the good Lord wants. I'm telling you right now, you're not going to lose the Warehouse. I won't allow it."

Chapter Twelve

By the time he'd gotten his horses tended to and headed into town on Saturday morning to complete much-needed manual labor at the horse facility, Trey had a hankerin' for a cup of coffee. Warehouse coffee.

The door jingled its usual welcome as he entered, but he didn't make it to the coffeemaker before Kara came out from the back of the store. He halted and, without even thinking, gave a low whistle. "Whoa. Look at you."

Kara's face pinked as she self-consciously glanced down at her just-above-the-knee skirt and fitted, sage-green jacket. High, strappy heels. That may be standard business attire in Chicago, but oh, man, did she stand out in the casual capitol of the world, Canyon Springs.

He couldn't take his eyes off her. The way she'd looped her hair on top of her head. The glint of gold studs in her ears. The fine chain at her throat. He caught a whiff of faint, woodsy perfume as she slipped past him to the checkout counter, her spiky heels tapping on the wooden floor as she avoided his gaze. His heart beat a little faster.

"So what's the occasion?"

"I'm running to Show Low this morning just as soon as Roxanne gets in." She glanced at him. "Business. That meet with your approval, Cowboy?"

Anything having to do with Kara this morning would meet with his approval. Looked like it was going to be his lucky day. "I'm headed that way myself. Care to ride along?"

"I—" Alarm flickered in her gaze, and he glanced down at his hay-matted jacket, worn jeans and scuffed boots. *Good goin' there, Kenton.* Like a woman dressed like *that* would want to be seen with someone who looked like they'd just walked out of a barnyard. Which was exactly where he'd been.

He scrubbed a hand across his jaw. Forgot to shave again, too. Doggone it. He mustered a wink. "I take that as a no?"

Her sweet as honey-butter-on-a-biscuit smile surfaced. "Thanks for offering, but I need my own transportation today."

"Offer stands anytime. I head over that way about once a week." He grinned. "Generally clean up before I go."

"Thanks, but I'm leaving town on Monday."

"Right." Like he could forget.

She hugged her arms to herself and moved away from him, the floor creaking under her dainty feet. She looked around the rustic expanse as if seeing it for the first time. Beamed ceiling. Earth-toned Navajo rugs hanging on the walls above the merchandise. The faint scent of wood smoke and coffee. Early morning sunlight pouring in the windows to dapple the worn, planked flooring.

"You can't believe all the memories I have of this

place." She turned to him with a wistful smile. "Bet you didn't know this is where I took my first steps."

He couldn't help returning her smile, picturing her as she must have been as a toddler. Sounded like she was gearing up mentally for her Chicago departure. Feeling nostalgic. "And I'm betting those feet were running straight out the door, right? Couldn't get out of here fast enough."

"Believe it or not, at one time my biggest dream was to grow up and run the Warehouse myself."

He arched a disbelieving brow. "How old were you? Three?"

"Actually, it was something I wanted to do for a long time. Until I turned thirteen."

Up until the time her dad walked out.

She again gazed around the room. "I had all these ideas, you know? Beginner designer-type ideas, I guess. For seasonal displays. Dressing up the windows. A cozy seating arrangement near the woodstove. Reading lamps. A lending-library shelf."

"Sounds homey." He studied her, seeing a side of Kara he hadn't seen since his return.

"As a kid I was the original Wrangler girl. Designer duds?" She motioned to her outfit. "Who cared? Give me my horse and a free Saturday afternoon and I'd be happy."

"You had a horse?"

His expression must have reflected his shock because she laughed. "You think the daughter of a rodeo cowboy wouldn't?"

"I never heard you talk about horses when we were in high school. You never hung out at Duffy's with me." Had he just not been paying attention?

"Cinnabar. Red roan. Registered American quarter horse. The fastest little barrel racer you ever saw."

How had he missed this? "You? A barrel racer?"

Kara laughed. "Rodeo Queen Sharon Dixon wouldn't stand for anything less."

"You're kidding. Sharon?" The image of her mother negotiating her way around a tri-barreled arena on a walker flashed through his mind.

"How do you think she met Dad?" Kara's eyes danced, clearly amused at his reaction to her revelation.

He bumped up the rim of his hat with a knuckle. "Guess I never thought about it. How'd they end up here?"

She shrugged. "They met on the rodeo circuit. Got married. Eventually got pregnant and decided to settle down in the town Mom grew up in. Where she'd inherited her father's business. Renamed it for my dad. And the rest is history."

Now if this just didn't beat all. He stared at Kara as if seeing her for the first time.

"You look like you just got lobbed off a bull." Her teasing laugh echoed in his ears. "And hit the ground pretty hard."

He chuckled. "I'm still trying to get my head around you being a horsewoman. And Sharon, too."

"By the time I met you, Cinnabar was long gone. I didn't talk about him. Didn't want anything to do with horses. It hurt too much. I think it killed Mom as much as it did me when we had to get rid of them after Dad left. He took his, of course." Her expression hardened. "But she couldn't afford to keep ours."

He frowned. Why couldn't Dix have made sure this little gal kept her horse instead of sticking her with an old Ford Mustang she never drove? Maybe he didn't know him quite as well as he thought he did.

"We didn't have time to ride or care for them anyway," Kara continued. "Had to make up for the hours Dad vacated at the Warehouse. It was a huge responsibility for Mom to keep this place going by herself. Came close to losing it."

She turned away, her hand trailing along a rack of jackets.

He remembered the little free time Kara had as a teen. How he'd wanted to spend more time with her, but she'd beg off. Her mom always needed her at the Warehouse. He'd figured it was her mother's way of keeping him at a safe distance. But maybe not.

"Losing your horse, that must have been a blow." He knew how attached you got to those big hairy critters.

She turned again to him, her gaze softening with a wistfulness that tugged at his heart. "I loved that horse."

His jaw tightened. He hated seeing her like this. Sad over something that happened when she'd been a kid. If he could get his hands around Dix's throat right now... Guilt pierced his conscience. She'd get her hands around *his* throat if she found out he was keeping his connection to her father a secret. He had to get ahold of Dix. Talk him into letting him tell her.

"Would you like to go riding? I'll be moving my horses to the new facility tomorrow. Big indoor arena."

He'd never thought to ask her before. Didn't know she'd ever been into horses. The Kara he first met had been, well, sort of prissy. But in a nice way. Refined. Polished. Never would have guessed she'd groomed a sweaty horse, mucked out a stall or hauled hay. The contrast intrigued him.

"I don't—"

"It's hard to keep two once-active horses exercised by myself. Especially in the winter." He gave her an encouraging nod. "They're getting mighty fat and sassy."

She shook her head, her eyes reflecting regret. "Thanks, but I'd probably fall on my fanny. It's been too long. And don't go telling me it's like riding a bike."

He chuckled. "I'm guessing it's something like that. So what do you say? Think you can set aside your citified self long enough to give old Taco or Beamer a good work out?"

"Taco and Beamer? What kind of names are those for a horse?"

"You should know registered names are a mile long. Nicknames stick. So what do you say? Want to go riding Sunday afternoon?"

A smile tugged. "I don't know...."

Sounded like she was tempted. He raised an encouraging brow. "You'd be doing me a favor. Think about it. Then let me know."

She nodded, but the little-lost-girl look still lingered. If he could just pull her into his arms. Hold her until that forlorn expression hightailed it off into the sunset. But that would be a mistake. Or rather another mistake. He was supposed to be guarding his heart. Now here he'd gone and invited her to ride with him just because he didn't like to see her sad.

Coming back to his senses, he tipped his hat in her direction. "Guess I'd best get on the road. Need to haul my horses over to Show Low to get reshod. And see a guy who has a lead on a reliable hay supplier. Lots to do today."

"Me, too."

They exchanged parting smiles, and he headed toward the door. With any luck, she'd forget he'd made the offer to go riding. She hadn't jumped at it, so probably thought being around horses would bring back too many unpleasant memories. Which was just as well because he could hardly take back the invitation now. But he'd learned his lesson. Again. Why couldn't he keep his tongue tied down? Lips always flappin' before thinking things through.

He'd just stepped out on the wooden porch, fixing to pull the Warehouse door closed, when he heard her quick high-heeled steps on the hardwood floor behind him.

"Trey?"

Hand still on the doorknob, he turned to look full in her beautiful face. At those breathlessly parted lips. The bristly-lashed gray eyes wide with uncertainty. And hope.

He swallowed. "Yeah?"

"I'll ride with you."

It was nine-thirty when she pulled into the parking lot of a bank in Show Low. Drove around to the far side where her mom's vehicle couldn't be seen from the highway, just in case Trey or another Canyon Springs local was out and about on a Saturday shopping spree in the "big city." She hadn't wanted to do business with the lone Canyon Springs bank. Didn't want to risk raising curiosity or a slip of the tongue on the part of a well-intentioned—or maybe not so well-intentioned—bank employee.

Approaching the doors of the establishment, she caught herself saying a prayer for success, for a savvy, accommodating banker and a quick in and out and on her way. Unfortunately, forty minutes later she climbed back in the SUV. Empty-handed. Most of the time had been spent waiting for a loan rep, but she'd hardly started the paperwork before the word "collateral" popped up. It went downhill from there.

All she wanted was a personal loan to get the bills off her mother's back. Then, from Chicago, she'd pay off the loan and accrued interest. But the amount she needed went beyond a car loan. And she didn't own any property except her vehicle, which wasn't paid for. Combine that with the bottom dropping out of the economy and the bank was cautious to the extreme.

She squared her shoulders. Okay, next stop.

By one o'clock she'd made the rounds of Show Low's banking establishments without success. Would she have any better luck in Flagstaff? Phoenix? Weren't banks supposed to loan money? Isn't that how they earned their income, off the interest?

Mom said she was in negotiations to allow her to pay off the bills little by little. But gradually still meant taking away from the Warehouse. Reducing stock. Putting off upgrades and repairs. So many things made sense now that she knew the truth. The leaky roof that hadn't been fixed. The minor plumbing problem that became a major repair job in December. Patching, not replacing, a cracked window. Turning down the heat at the house. Renting the Warehouse apartment to Trey.

Had she been paying attention at all, she'd have caught the signs last spring when she'd been here. But no, she was so focused on getting back to Chicago that she didn't look beyond the surface.

So what now?

Returning to Chicago on Monday still seemed her best bet. Maybe she could secure a personal loan there. At least could start pumping funds homeward as fast as she could. But what if Mom lost the Warehouse? She'd never forgive herself if that happened. It had come way too close to that when Kara was a teen.

When she walked to the back door of her mother's house late that afternoon, she paused. Heavy cloud cover had moved in since morning, suggesting another snow system on the horizon. Through the kitchen window she could see Mom moving around in the glow of the interior light. Her hardworking mother. Who'd sacrificed so much for so long. Who always remained cheerful, encouraging, faithful. Did she have any idea how serious this latest situation was?

Kara glanced up at the steel-gray heavens. *Please, God, help me to help her.*

"Now, don't you look nice," Mom said as Kara stepped inside and peeled out of her coat. "Where've you been all dressed up like that, doll?"

She'd slipped out that morning, while her mom was in the shower. "Show Low."

Mom frowned, her gaze questioning.

"Well, someone has to do something, don't they?" Kara heard the defensiveness in her tone. "I told you I'm not going to let you lose the Warehouse."

Her mother's shoulders slumped. "So you got a loan?"

"No." Failure weighed heavily as she tossed her coat over the back of a chair. "The banks are being stingy. But I'll take care of everything as soon as I get back to Chicago."

Her mom moved to the kitchen sink to rinse out a

pan, then reached for a dish towel. "You're mad at me, aren't you?"

"No. Disappointed would be a better word." She gripped the back of the chair, searching for the right words that would make her mother understand. "Why didn't you tell me so we could have handled this together? I'm not a kid anymore, Mom."

Mom turned to her, eyes filled with regret. "Oh, honey, I know you're not."

"Well then?"

"It happened so fast. Got away from me." She twisted the dish towel in her hands. "Last spring after that health setback I reduced expenditures. But when the economic bubble burst, when seasonal visitors dropped off, that's when this latest hospitalization hit. I couldn't have foreseen it. I didn't have any idea…."

Kara longed to open her arms. To pull her mother close. To tell her how much she loved her and that she'd make everything right again if it took her last dying breath. But she hesitated, not wanting to interrupt.

"Fortunately, your dad heard about the heart attack. Sent me a check to cover the Warehouse mortgage."

"What?" A roaring filled her ears as bewilderment and outrage slammed into her. "He did *what?*"

"He does that every once in a while."

"Are you kidding me? How can you think of taking anything from him? We don't need him. Never have."

"He couldn't pay much in the way of child support when you were younger, doll. But he pitched in as best he could. When he could. Always has."

"I'm just now finding out about this? That we're beholden to a man who dumped us?"

"I tried to tell you once, years ago, but you wouldn't hear me out."

Kara jerked her coat from the back of the chair. "From now on, you're not taking another dime from him. Not a penny. Not even if I have to hold down *ten* jobs."

"Kara—"

Kara raised a hand to halt her. Fought back tears.

"You know, Mom, I don't feel like discussing this anymore." She thrust her arms into the coat sleeves. "I'm going out for a while. Don't count on me for supper."

She hastily left the house, shutting the back door harder than she intended. Heard the glass pane rattle in its wooden frame.

How could Mom have let Dad back into their lives?

Chapter Thirteen

What had she gotten herself into?

Looking down at Trey from the chestnut Taco's sturdy back, her stomach churned. Not only due to being on a horse again, but to spending personal time with Trey. It was her own fault. Talking about Cinnabar had made him feel sorry for her. Made him think he needed to *do* something.

He wouldn't feel so compassionate if he knew how she'd treated Mom last night. Tension in her arms increased, and Taco's ears twitched uncertainly until she relaxed her fingers on the reins. How had she not known Dad had been pitching in to help make ends meet? And how could Mom take money from him?

She shouldn't have lost her temper. But on top of finding out Mom's health setback was more serious than she'd let on, discovering she'd kept her dire finances secret and now learning Dad wasn't quite the bad guy she'd always believed him…well, it was too much all at once. And she'd lashed out.

Mom probably felt as bad about their falling out as she did. Things had been good between them since her most recent return. They'd grown closer. Formed a stronger bond. Enjoyed each other's company. That is, until now.

She repositioned herself in the saddle, the sound of creaking leather soothing her ruffled emotions. They'd steered clear of each other this morning. Peggy picked Mom up for church. She herself had sat with Meg and Davy. But tonight they'd have a long talk while she packed for her return to Chicago. Get everything worked out between them.

Trey thrust his fingers under Taco's saddle cinch to ensure she'd gotten it tight enough. Surprised that she had, if the raised brow was an indicator. She'd insisted on saddling up by herself. A little rusty, with fumbling fingers, but there was no point in being more of a nuisance than she already was.

He scratched Taco behind an ear, then fiddled with the headstall. The chin strap. "Looks like you're good to go."

"Feels strange to be on a horse again." She adjusted her feet in the stirrups, thankful Reyna had a pair of same-size boots to loan. "Fifteen years is a long time."

He smiled up at her. "You might surprise yourself."

"Not holding my breath."

"So, ready to roll?"

She nodded. And with a nudge of her booted heels, she signaled the horse forward, alongside Trey, who led Beamer. Down the wide stable aisle toward an indoor arena gate, the horses' shod hooves rang hollowly on the floor. Like a kid in a candy shop, Kara filled her lungs with the familiar scent of horses, hay and leather. Happy smells from childhood.

Before Dad left.

Coming up the drive to the equine center earlier, seated next to Trey in his pickup, she'd avoided looking at the snowy, burned-out acreage. But once inside the newly remodeled space all thoughts of the fire dissipated. Her spirits rose further as Trey opened the gate to the arena and stepped back to let her pass through.

She nudged Trey's horse into the well-groomed arena, then halted, marveling at the arched roof above her head. The vastness of the open space. Taco's ears flicked back and forth, alert to the unfamiliar presence on his back, anticipating further instructions.

She glanced back at Trey who'd again shut the gate and was leaning on it with a booted toe hooked in one of its pipe slats, his folded forearms looped through Beamer's reins and resting on top. He tipped his hat to her and smiled. Guess he didn't plan to join her right off. Wanted her to get a feel for her mount and the space without distractions.

Signaling to Taco, she walked the horse around the perimeter of the arena as she shifted in the saddle, tried to find a comfortable sweet spot. Again tested out the length of her stirrups. Adjusted her reins. Attempted to settle into a world she'd long been away from. Too long.

Although it was the same arena in which she'd worked out Cinnabar when she was a kid and spent time in with her folks, the skylights, the lighting and the other upgrades gave her a sense of being far from Canyon Springs. Far from the past.

She leaned forward to pat Taco on the shoulder. Spoke soothing, conversational words, amused at how his winter-fuzzed ears flicked back and forth to catch her every utterance.

A walk. A trot. A few times around the arena. Then

she brought the gelding to a halt on the far side. Signaled him to back up. Straight line. No fuss. Then moved forward again. So far so good. Maybe it *was* like riding a bike?

Might as well find out.

"Let's see what you've got, mister." She signaled the horse into a gentle lope for a few rounds, then into a wide-open figure eight in the center of the arena.

Her scalp tingled and the sensation spread through her face, down her neck, into her arms. Oh, man, did this horse have a rocking chair gait, flawlessly changing leads as she lightly neck-reined him into a reverse. Push-button perfect.

A respect for Trey's training skills soared as she took the animal through a series of warm-ups, then back to the perimeter of the arena for a full gallop. Ponytail flying behind her, cool air brushing her cheeks, the tingling sensation coursed through each fiber of her body—and deep into her very soul.

Tears pricked her eyes.

Thank you, God. I'm flying without wings!

She'd forgotten him. So totally into the moment that she'd forgotten him.

Trey stood grinning from where he'd remained with Beamer just outside the arena. Amazing. Fifteen years and her basic skills were still intact. Instinctive. Sure, a bit rusty, but that would smooth out with time. Practice. A curious pride and sense of satisfaction welled as his trainer's eye expertly evaluated her impromptu performance.

For the first twenty minutes after she'd entered the arena, he'd noted her trying to get her bearings. Calming down. Connecting with Taco. But was she ever into it now. Ponytail sailing, settling in to the once-familiar rhythms. Taco was settling in, too, responding to her every signal. As each minute ticked by, she transformed before his eyes. From the way her left hand held the reins and her right hand, no longer clenched, rested at her thigh, he could tell she'd relaxed.

A beautiful woman on a beautiful horse.

A sight to behold.

God sure had put together a fine-looking package when he created Kara Dixon. A good-hearted woman, too, putting her dream job on hold to look out for her mom. Helping Reyna with the parsonage. Him with his deadlines. Meg and the other townspeople he encountered thought the world of her, as well.

But how did a man keep from falling in love with her? How did you stop yourself from caring? Involving yourself? It could be done, because he didn't fall in love with his friends' wives or girlfriends. If only Kara had come back to town married. Or at least engaged. It would have been much easier.

Wouldn't it?

Why'd God have to go bringing her back to Canyon Springs? And to add salt to the wound she loved horses every bit as much as he did. There had to be more to it than God deciding he needed a refresher lesson in obedience. But the way things were looking, that's what it was coming down to. She stuck to her belief in a "hands-off" God. Still had the bit in her teeth, determined to shake off the dust of Canyon Springs. Leaving tomorrow.

Hold me steady, Lord.

With one last figure eight, Kara brought Taco back

to a walk and headed toward Trey, unable to hide a beaming smile.

She reined in, eyes sparkling as she leaned forward to pat Taco on the neck.

"Do I ever love this horse." Laughing, she wiped at her eyes with the cuff of her jacket sleeve.

Had she been crying? A sharp pain gored him. "He's a good old boy, that's for certain."

"You trained him, right?"

"Since he first stood on wobbly legs."

"You are amazing. It was like, like—"

"Magic?"

"Yes!"

His heart swelled at her praise. If this kept up, he'd soon be buying shirts a couple of sizes larger. "Helps to have a rider on him who knows the ropes. A horse senses that. Didn't take you long to get comfortable and he responded."

"I'm still so awkward." She patted the horse again. "Poor Taco. You probably wonder why Trey's punishing you, don't you?"

"I don't hear him complaining."

Her eyes smiled into his. Radiant. Open. Vulnerable. He took a deep breath and turned to his own horse. "So what do you say we work them both out for a while?"

Preferably her on one end of the arena and him on the other.

"I'd love to. Oh, just a sec." Still smiling, she fished under the waist of her jacket. "My phone's vibrating."

He looped the reins over Beamer's head, trying not to frown. She'd carried her cell phone with her? Probably expecting a call from that Chicago guy. Spence.

Kara smiled an apology as she answered. "Hi, Meg. Out riding a horse, can you believe it?"

Her smile melted. "When? Where is she now?"

Kara's frightened eyes sought his.

"What?" he mouthed, but she shook her head. He unlatched the gate and led Beamer into the arena.

"Is she going to be okay? All right. I'm on my way."

She turned off her phone and sat stone-like, staring at him. Tried to speak, but tears choked her off.

He dropped Beamer's reins and reached up to her. She kicked her feet out of the stirrups and slung her right leg over the saddle horn. Leaned forward to slip her arms around his neck, then slid down into his arms.

"Trey."

"What is it? What happened?" he whispered, holding her trembling body in his arms. The strong, confident horsewoman suddenly so fragile.

"It's—it's Mom." Her grip tightened on his arms as she pulled slightly back and gazed into his eyes. "Meg says they think she's had another heart attack."

In a waiting room of the Summit Medical Center in Show Low, Kara nibbled at her thumbnail. With ponderosa pines now silhouetted in twilight, the space seemed colder, even more impersonal than it had been in the late afternoon hours when they'd first arrived.

"This is all my fault." Kara shivered, the memory of the tiff with her mother replaying in her mind. What she'd said. How she'd said it. How stupid she'd been to think there would be time to sit down tonight and talk things out like they always did. "I shouldn't have—"

"You heard the doctor—she's going to be all right." Trey placed a comforting arm around her shoulders, his eyes dark with concern. He was such a sweetheart to stay tonight when Meg had to leave. "It wasn't a full-fledged heart attack, Kara."

But he didn't know about the medical bills. About their argument. How she'd been so upset about her father that she'd treated her mother as she'd had no right to treat her. How the upset could have contributed to her mother's hospitalization.

She fumbled with her handbag, rummaging for her cell phone. "I got hold of Aunt Tammy. She said she'd call the rest of the family. Maybe I should call—"

Who? Dad? No, not Dad.

Tears pricked again. "Now I know how scared Meg must have been when she found Mom that first time. When she couldn't get hold of me right away."

Trey's hand tightened on her shoulder.

"You know where I was then, Trey? In Costa Rica. On a shopping trip for a client. I'd been assigned a company phone, so didn't think to add an international plan to my own."

"You couldn't have known something was going to happen to your mom."

She stuffed her phone back in her handbag. "When Meg finally tracked me down, Mom was awake and calling the shots. Wouldn't let Meg tell me how bad it was. When I spoke to Mom she insisted it was no biggie. Not that serious. That I shouldn't rush back. So I didn't."

"Moms can be like that sometimes."

"I almost died when I walked in and saw her at the Thanksgiving dinner at the RV park. In a wheelchair. Oxygen. Frail looking. I'd have come, Trey. I would have."

"There's no doubt in my mind that you would have."

"But why didn't I learn my lesson? I could tell she seemed tired the last week or two. I'd ask her if everything was okay and she'd always say, 'sure, I'm fine, doll.' But she wasn't and I should have known it. I was too busy chomping at the bit to get back to Chicago. Only saw and heard what I wanted to."

He frowned. "You're not a doctor."

"No, but I *am* a daughter. And a daughter should—" Her voice cracked, and her gaze sought his for reassurance. "We had a fight last night. About my dad. Apparently he's been helping her out—monetarily—off and on through the years. Which didn't go over real big with me."

Trey pulled his arm from around her, clasped his hands and leaned forward to rest his forearms on his knees. "You know, Kara, maybe it's not my place to say anything, but when I first met you, it didn't take a whole lot of smarts to recognize your dad's abandonment did a number on you."

"That obvious?"

"Still is." He cleared his throat. "Maybe it's time to set yourself free of him."

"Oh, believe me, I've tried."

"I don't mean shoving him under the rug. Forgetting about him. I don't think you'll ever have much success with that." He took her hand in his, his gaze earnest. "Have you ever thought about letting it go? Forgiving him?"

She jerked her hand away, staring at him in disbelieving silence. Was he out of his mind?

"You and your mom came close to parting ways after a fight about him. Isn't that reason enough?"

With a harsh laugh, she shook her head.

"Forgive him? For what he did to me and Mom?" She stood, trying to get as far away from him as she could. "Do you have any idea what it was like for me? Waking up in the middle of the night and hearing my mom crying? For *years?* To be subject to the curious looks. Hear the whispered—and not so whispered—speculation about his departure. Why he dumped Mom. Didn't he even care enough for me to arrange shared custody?"

"I'm not saying it will be easy." He stood up, as well. "I'm not saying he deserves it. But forgiveness isn't something you do for him. It's something you do for yourself. For your mom."

"You don't know him, Trey, or you wouldn't suggest such a thing."

"Kara Dixon?" A pastel-clad nurse had stepped into the room and they both turned toward her, Kara's heart slamming in her chest.

"I'm Kara."

"Your mother would like to see you. But for just a few minutes, please."

Kara exchanged a quick look with Trey, then on unsteady legs followed the nurse down a long, glossy-floored hallway to the intensive care unit. Behind a curtained-off area, with a blanket pulled up to her neck and a tangle of tubes and wires surrounding her, Mom looked weak and defenseless.

"Hey, doll." Her voice barely registered above a whisper, but her eyes warmed.

With a shaky breath, Kara approached and took the familiar hand in a gentle clasp. Hardly any grip at all in the once-firm fingers. "Hey, Mom. You sure gave me a scare. This is getting to be a habit you're going to have to break."

"Humph." Mom produced a faint smile. "Trey. He out there? Waiting room?"

She nodded. Why mention Trey at a time like this?

"Good man," her mother said, studying her with barely open eyes. "Just sayin'."

"Sayin' too much if you ask me." She tucked the blanket in around her. "We're only allowed a few minutes."

"Telling you, Kara…" She was rapidly losing alertness. Probably the meds.

"I've contacted Aunt Tammy and Brielle. They're coming."

"Heard about…tune up?"

She nodded. "More stents. Tomorrow morning."

"Not good. Warehouse. Bad for business, this being sick."

She patted her mother's hand. "I have it covered, Mom."

"No. You need… Chicago."

"I need to be here."

Mom's grip tightened. Barely. "Don't want…giving up dream."

"Like you gave up yours?" Kara kicked herself for the insensitive reminder even as she spoke the words.

"Wanted other dream. More." A smile touched Mom's lips. "Wife to your dad. Mother to you."

"And look where that got you." She forced a teasing lilt into her words. "Podunk Springs."

"Fond… Podunk Springs." Mom coughed. Another trembling smile. "Got me a daughter…proud of, too."

Pain slashed through her and she drew a ragged breath. "Oh, Mom, I'm so sorry we argued. I—"

Her mother nodded. Closed her eyes. The frail hand relaxed.

Tears pricked as Kara leaned down to kiss her now-sleeping mother's forehead. Proud? Mom wouldn't be proud of her if she knew how deeply she despised Dad. And what she'd done to Trey. Was still doing to him.

And how much she resented being stuck in Canyon Springs.

Chapter Fourteen

"Where are you?" a terse but familiar voice demanded through her cell phone receiver.

Spence. Monday. She glanced at her watch and groaned. Two o'clock. Chicago time. Oh, no.

"Didn't you get my message?" She glanced over at Trey, then at Meg, Aunt Tammy and cousin Brielle who'd driven in from Prescott last night. At Bill Diaz, who'd just walked in. "Mom's been hospitalized. A near heart attack."

"So, when are you rescheduled to get in?"

Did he not hear what she just said?

"Mom came close to another heart attack, Spence. I can't leave until I make sure she's okay."

"So what—a day or two?"

"I don't know. She had a couple of stents placed a short while ago. Hasn't come out from the anesthetic yet."

A lengthy silence echoed on the other end. She took a steadying breath, blinking back the tears forming in her eyes. This was it, wasn't it? He was gathering his thoughts, his words, to tell her to forget the promotion. His mentorship. Maybe even a job.

She uttered a silent prayer. God had been hearing from her a lot in the past forty-eight hours. "Spence?"

His sigh carried clearly over the miles. "Look, I'm sorry. I'm not taking all this in yet. Expected you on that flight."

"I know. I'm sorry. I—"

"No problem. It's understandable. I needed to get out of the studio anyway."

"Gabrielle is still pressuring you?"

"What do you think? But don't worry about it. You have other things to deal with now. I'll take care of Gabrielle."

"Thanks. I'm really sorry."

"Yeah, well, take care of yourself. And your Mom. Get back here as fast as you can."

"I will. I promise. And thanks again." She shut off the phone.

"Your boss giving you a hard time?" Trey's tone held a protective ring. He was all but glowering.

"I can't believe you had to tell him twice about your mom's condition," Bill Diaz, Meg's soon-to-be father-in-law, shook his head. He'd been friends with Kara's mom for years, although Kara had long hoped they'd be more than friends.

"Don't worry. It's all good." At least that's what she kept telling herself. "It's just that he's my supervisor. Mentor. And he's trying to hold a promotion open for me."

"I'd like to give him a piece of my mind," Aunt Tammy mumbled as she looked up from the magazine clutched in her hands. "Don't have any patience with big-city bullies."

Kara laughed. "Honestly, he's a sweet guy. He's just trying to protect my interests."

Trey snorted.

"Is he cute?" Brielle popped the top of her third diet soda and shook back her shoulder-length brown hair.

"Mmm. I think you'd think so."

"He's not blond, is he? I think blond guys look sickly."

Kara laughed again. It felt good. Her thoughts had been so wrapped up with Mom, her nerves stretched to their limits. "He has light brown hair, but he's not blond."

"Good. If you decide you don't want him, send him my way." Brielle winked, then glanced at Trey. "Or any extras you may happen to have on hand."

Meg gathered up her book bag—she'd taken a personal day from work but had been constructing lesson plans at the hospital. "Anyone care to join me in the cafeteria? I could use some lunch."

Kara begged off, but Aunt Tammy, Brielle and Bill departed with her. Trey moved from the most distant chair in their cluster and eased down beside her.

"I'd be happy to pick up something for you to eat if cafeteria food doesn't appeal. Pick any restaurant within a hundred miles. It's yours for the asking."

"Thanks, but I'm not hungry. Feel a little queasy."

"I'll take on that Spence guy if that would help. Don't care much for a man who makes a woman cry."

He'd seen how close she'd come to that?

"I'm okay. A little emotional, I guess."

"Not surprising." He glanced around the room at several other clusters of family and friends waiting anxiously for reports on loved ones. "So, do you still think you'll head back to the Midwest after your mom's latest setback?"

"Like I told Spence, I have to see how Mom comes through this. The way she looked this morning before they rolled her in for the procedure, she's not going to be up to managing the Warehouse anytime soon."

"Maybe you can hire a manager to fill in for you."

"Maybe." But that wasn't likely. A manager would need a living wage, and with Mom's precarious financial situation…well, her daughter could work for free. "I'll stick around awhile longer. See how it goes."

"You doing okay, though? Financially I mean? Being away from your job this long has to be rough."

She dropped her gaze to her hands, fearful he might glimpse the alarm in her eyes. "I'm dipping into my savings. Still have expenses in Chicago even in my absence."

"What I can pay won't foot the bill for a champagne-and-caviar diet, but I could use your continued office help. As much time as you can spare. You type fifty times faster than I do."

She needed the extra money. But could she manage to look out for the Warehouse and Mom, keep up with the Garson Design project *and* pick up additional hours helping Trey, too? Maybe if she gave up sleep altogether.

She smiled at him, forcing herself to meet his concerned look with a reassuring one of her own. "That's sweet of you, but I'll be fine."

It was one thing to have helped him out for a few days when Marilu left as thanks for his assistance at the Warehouse. But she couldn't let herself become further indebted to a man whose reputation she'd all but reduced to rubble.

Nor could she let her heart become more attached to his.

"Not so fast, son."

"It's all right here." Trey tapped the thick folder of papers he'd placed on the city councilman's desk. "Documented. Notarized. Everything you asked for."

And it was only Thursday. Beat the old guy's arbitrary deadline by a full day, even without Kara's help this week.

Reuben Falkner, dressed more for a round of golf than a winter day in mountain country, pushed back in his cushioned office chair. A stocky, crew-cutted guy in his late sixties, he still carried a no-nonsense demeanor left over from his Marine Corps days. Trey had heard he was a former MP—military policeman—a role he continued as a guardian of Canyon Springs.

"This isn't a done deal, you understand. Need to review everything. Weigh the impact on the community."

"You're the only member of the city council who has objections. The documentation here is complete. Thorough."

"Not objections, Mr. Kenton. Concerns."

"Duffy Logan's place was a valued part of the community for years." Trey kept his tone low, respectful.

"And so it was. But times have changed since Duffy first developed that property over a quarter of a century ago. The area's built up around it. There's greater awareness of the environment now. More comprehensive regulations."

"You'll find I've observed those to the letter. I plan

to follow in the footsteps of Duffy's reputation. Build on it."

The man chuckled. "Funny you should mention reputation given that you have quite the reputation yourself."

Realization sliced through Trey. So this was Reuben Falkner's agenda? To let him get this far along in the process only to refuse final approval because of something that happened over a decade ago? Something he didn't have anything to do with?

"I'm known for my honesty, sir. Integrity."

The older man leaned forward. "That's not what goes through the minds of most people in this community when they hear the name Trey Kenton."

He stiffened and met the almost-amused gaze of the councilman. "Would you care to clarify that?"

Reuben adjusted his glasses to peer over the top of them. "It's ironic, wouldn't you say, that you'll be earning your living off the property you attempted to destroy when it belonged to another man?"

"You're opposing this project based on an unfounded accusation?"

"Unfounded? You may not have ended up with a jail term, what with your father being a preacher and Duffy letting you off the hook. But you know starting a fire isn't an easily forgiven offense in these parts. You could have burned the town to the ground. *Unfounded accusation* is hardly the term I'd use for it. You were all but caught red-handed."

"But I wasn't. And that's because I'm innocent."

The councilman made a shooing motion. "I'm not opposing you on this, so don't go whining about it around town. It takes time for a thorough review. That's all I'm saying. I'm a busy man."

"These permits are the final piece to wrap things up. Start the hiring process. Bring jobs and tourist dollars to Canyon Springs by summer."

"I'm fully aware of that, Mr. Kenton. It's a noble cause you're spearheading. Your plan to employ locals is commendable." The phone on his desk rang and he reached for it. "But Rome wasn't built in a day. I'll be in touch."

A sharp retort formed in Trey's mind, but with a brisk nod, he departed. Seething.

Now what, God? He'd done just about everything that could be done on the project until he got the final go-aheads. The men who'd hired him expected the facility to be up and running by the time summer visitors returned to the high country. May. June at the latest. He'd tentatively booked several events for the indoor arena. Riding lessons. Horse sale. Barrel racing clinic. Calf roping classes. Had a waiting list for people planning to board their horses.

Out on the main street, he strode toward his own office. You'd think in a town this size the red tape would be diminished. But due to some obscure law on the books, a single councilman could put the brakes on a legitimate business endeavor even when every other governmental entity under the sun had given it the go-ahead.

"Penny for your thoughts, Cowboy," a melodious female voice called, teasing his ears as he crossed over to the Warehouse side of the street.

He swung around to find a smiling, bundled-up Kara standing outside the door, arms laden with two banker-size boxes.

She raised her delicate brows. "And from the look on your face, those thoughts must be a humdinger."

"You're back." His heart lightened as he hurried forward to take the boxes into his own arms. But up close he recognized signs of fatigue in her pretty face. "How's your mom?"

"Improving by the minute. But even though this episode wasn't as bad as the first one, they want to keep her at the hospital until Monday for observation." She made a face. "Insurance company will love that."

"Then back to physical therapy?"

Kara nodded. "So I'll be sticking around awhile longer."

"Did your boss hassle you about that?" If she said yes, he'd catch the next flight to Chicago and practice roping and tying on the jerk.

She grimaced. "Haven't told him yet. Thought I'd wait until Mom's released and I can get a feel for how things are going."

"So, where're you headed with these boxes?"

"Need to take some paperwork home and get it organized." She pointed to her mom's SUV parked a few doors down and he headed off, with her beside him. She cast him a weary smile. "So what's going on in your world that made you look like a thundercloud?"

"Had a run-in with one of our good councilmen."

Her smile melted. "Reuben? What's he objecting to now?"

"He's not objecting to anything. He has *concerns*." Trey could hear the sarcasm oozing from his own words.

"Such as?"

"Same things he belabored earlier. Repercussions on similar businesses. Signage regulations. Property lighting standards—you know, since this is a Dark Sky City. Wants to take another look at the environmental impact. Drainage. Noise. *Odors.*"

"Like he's a competent judge of any of those things?" She threw up her hands in apparent exasperation. "You got the go-ahead on the environmental impact analysis before you even started. Even the city planner said no problem with retaining the property's original use. And what similar businesses is he talking about?"

They stopped at the back of the SUV where Kara popped the back gate open. He placed the boxes inside, then straightened.

"Seems his prime 'concern' is the reputation of the new manager."

"He said that?" She closed the vehicle gate and steadied herself against it with her hand.

"Thinks I got off scot-free because of my dad's connections. Sees himself as the great benevolent protector of Canyon Springs."

"He's always been that way. Sometimes it's appreciated, but this is harassment. Even if he doesn't believe you're innocent, can't he see you're a grown man now? Deserve a second chance? And look at the jobs this project has already generated."

"He says my intention along those lines is—and I quote—commendable. But I guess that's not enough to overshadow what he's convinced is a blot on my past."

Kara thrust her hands into her jacket pockets. "The mayor is an old friend of Mom's. Maybe I could talk to him. See if he'd light a fire under Reuben."

"Thanks, but I don't want to rile the old guy any more than I have to. He looks like the kind who'd dig in for a siege if he felt challenged." He leaned back on the SUV and crossed his arms. "I'm trying to see things from his perspective. To look at this from a professional standpoint rather than taking it personal."

"Sounds like Reuben's making it personal."

Sounded like it to him, too. But he shouldn't have said anything to Kara about it—whining like the aging former MP warned him against. He took a steadying breath and changed the subject. "You know, Kara, I've been following your advice, backing off from asking questions of locals regarding the fire."

She nodded, but her expression looked wary, as if waiting for the other shoe to drop.

"But I can't stand here twiddling my thumbs and let those old lies abort this project. I have too much riding on it. So do the investors who hired me."

He rubbed his forehead, waiting her for her to jump in with dire warnings. But she only stared at him like a proverbial deer caught in the headlights. "So while I know you and Jason have my best interests at heart, I don't have any choice but to stir things up. See what I can do to smoke out the person who really started the fire before it's too late."

If it wasn't already too late.

Chapter Fifteen

Before she could take in what he'd said, her cell phone went off, playing a merry tune. She grabbed it out of her coat pocket to view the caller ID. Spence.

Just what she didn't need.

"I'm sorry, Trey. I have to take this call."

His eyes filled with concern. "The hospital?"

"No, Chicago." She put the phone to her ear and headed for the Warehouse door. "Hey, Spence. How goes it?"

"That's my question for you," her boss countered. "How's your mother?"

She entered the building, relieved rather than worried that there were no customers this morning. "She's doing well, considering. Will remain in the hospital until next week."

"Then she can come home? And you can get back here?"

Kara wandered among the aisles, straightening displays with her free hand as she moved toward the back of the store. "She can't be left by herself right away. And there's no one to manage her business."

"I know what you're going through. How hard it is to live and work so far from family." He paused. "But sometimes you have to step back and let others take responsibility. Carry some of the load. My dad died last year and I couldn't get away from here to help out in L.A. All his care fell on my sisters."

"I don't have any sisters. Or brothers."

"I'm just saying, Kara—"

"Spence, I'm entitled by law—"

"To unpaid leave time. I know that. I'm just giving you a heads-up. This isn't a good time to be away from the home base."

"What do you mean?"

He lowered his voice, as if wary of eavesdroppers. "I'm hearing layoffs are coming. Deep ones. In this economy, our high-end clientele is cutting back. Even if their finances weathered the storm, big CEOs don't want their names in the paper or faces on TV pointing out that they had a million-dollar office or home makeover the same month they laid off workers or cut benefits."

"They'd be pumping money into the economy. That's good, right?"

"But nobody wants to risk it—you know, fearful of that 'let them eat cake' label. It's bad for business."

"So I'm getting laid off." She should have seen it coming. She'd missed so much work this past year she'd be a prime target, would disappear in an avalanche of layoffs.

"Nothing's certain. But we're all being scrutinized. There's not enough work to go around."

"And I'm one of the newer kids on the block."

"And one who doesn't have a physical presence here

right now, who isn't out on the streets drumming up business."

"I'm laying the groundwork on the NuTowne office project for you. Working on it every free minute I can get."

"Don't waste any more time on it. Just heard they're floundering. Big-time. So the new facility won't get off the ground." Spence sighed. "Sorry to be the bearer of bad news, but you need to get back here, kiddo. Pronto."

Kiddo. No "little cowgirl."

"Believe me, I want to. But I'm needed here. I'll have to rethink things. Figure out my options. See what kind of arrangements I can make for my mother."

"Just don't wait too long. I'm slipping in reminders of your contributions to the team. How you hustled on the design research and presentation to help me bring that Barrington contract in. And Tellmont."

"Thanks. I'm sorry I'm letting you down."

He lowered his voice even further. "You're not letting me down if you get yourself back here ASAP. Like yesterday."

"Spence—"

"Just get back here. Now. Gotta run. *Ciao.*"

The line went dead in her ear.

She shut off the phone and stuffed it back in her pocket. Stared vacantly into space, tears pricking her eyes. What was she going to do? How could she leave now? Mom needed her here. But Mom needed her there, too, didn't she? To funnel money back to pay the medical bills, keep the Warehouse.

"Bad news?"

She whirled to face Trey, standing no more than twelve feet from her. She hadn't even heard the bells above the door when he'd come in. Had he coattailed in right behind her? Heard her side of the whole conversation?

She blinked rapidly and gave a little laugh. "Oh, nothing much. Just that if I don't get back to my job immediately, there may not be a job to go back to, let alone a promotion. Company-wide layoffs are in the works."

He gave a low whistle. "Can they do that? Fire you while you're on leave?"

"I don't know all the legalities. But I'd think if they're having to let others go—" She bit down on her lower lip. *Please, God, don't let me cry in front of Trey.* "Spence says this isn't a good time to be an absentee employee."

"I'm sorry, Kara. I know the job, the promotion, mean everything in the world to you. Your dream ticket out of Canyon Springs."

She swallowed. "Unfortunately, keeping the job isn't all about a dream anymore. Somehow I have to make arrangements for Mom's care. For management of the Warehouse. It's come to the point where I can do more for her for the long term in Chicago than I can here."

He frowned. "How do you figure that?"

"Because—" She gazed around the expanse of the Warehouse, her lower lip trembling. "No way am I going to let my mom lose this place."

"That's a possibility?"

She nodded, a single tear trickling down her cheek. A real possibility.

That tear—the same wistful, lost expression she'd had when reminiscing about the Warehouse Saturday morning before she left for Show Low—ripped Trey open deeper than the horn of a raging Brahma could ever have done. Without hesitation, he stepped forward and opened his arms. She came willingly, her own arms slipping tightly around him, her face pressing against the collar of his jacket.

"What's going on, Kara?" he said softly, laying the side of his face against the top of her ponytailed head.

"Medical bills are eating her alive." Her voice quavered. "She could lose the Warehouse and she didn't even tell me."

"Are you sure?"

She nodded, her hair brushing his cheek. "I stumbled across the papers Friday night. Overdue notices. Threats for legal action. And when I confronted her—" so their argument wasn't only about her dad "—she admitted it." Her words ended with a ragged breath.

He tightened his hold on her trembling body, willing his own strength to be infused into her.

"When was she going to tell me, Trey? When I came to visit and found the Warehouse closed? Under new ownership?"

"She must have had her reasons."

"Oh, yeah. She said she didn't want me to worry." She gave a weak, scoffing laugh. "Said she wants me to stay in Chicago to live my dream. But if she'd said something, I could have been helping all along. Maybe it wouldn't have come to this."

"It probably happened so quickly she didn't have time to think that far." His own mother climbed mountains to keep from worrying him or his brothers about anything. "She probably thought she had things under control. So go easy on her."

The arms around his waist loosened as she pulled back, her fingers tightening on his jacket front. "I didn't go easy on her. At all. I carried on awful, Trey. I was so mad."

"And scared."

She nodded again. "We argued again Saturday night. About Dad. So I stayed as far away from her as I could get on Sunday, trying to get my temper under control. Thought that by Sunday night we'd have both cooled down, could get everything straightened out between us before I left. But then—"

She pulled back and stared at him, eyes filled with fear. "I came a hairbreadth from not having that opportunity, Trey. Will I never learn? She could have died."

"But she didn't. I'd say that's evidence of God's hands-on involvement in your life, Kara, whether you're willing to admit it or not."

She leaned her forehead on his chest. "Maybe."

"It's going to be okay."

"You mean that everything works for the good for those who love God stuff? Sorry, but nice verses and a pep talk won't score any points. This is reality. Mom will lose her livelihood, will probably have to leave Canyon Springs if I can't get these bills paid off."

"That's what you were doing in Show Low Saturday, wasn't it? All dressed up." And looking prettier than any woman had a right to. He felt her nod against him. "So you got a loan?"

She lifted her head. "No. They're stingier than a two-year-old with a favorite toy right now."

"It will be okay," he repeated, mind racing as a plan formulated. He had money set aside. Had practically lived the life of a pauper to save every cent he could to someday buy property. A place to settle down. If he loaned it to Kara, how long would it be before he'd be able accumulate that level of funds again? He didn't doubt that it would be repaid—but it could be years until that time.

But what choice did he have? He couldn't stand to see her like this. "I don't know how much your mom's bills are, but I have a fairly sizable amount of money set aside. It's yours for as long as you need it."

She stared at him, her beautiful eyes searching his. Eyes filled with disbelief. Hope.

And something much more personal.

It slammed into him with the force of a stampeding herd of buffalo.

She slowly leaned forward. Tightened her grip on the front of his jacket. Her mouth inches from his. "Oh, Trey—"

His heart staggered as he lowered his head, his lips barely grazing hers.

This man was so good, so very good. The most decent man she'd ever known and she'd ruined any chance of a relationship with him when she was a stupid teenager.

Nevertheless, heart beating an erratic rhythm, Kara clung to him. Returned his warm, tender kiss with a tentative one of her own. How much sweeter, how much more meaningful than the greedy, demanding ones she'd impulsively pulled him into that night so long ago.

Could there still be a second chance for them? After all the painful detours and guilt-laden years, had God brought them both back to Canyon Springs for a purpose? For her to find forgiveness in Trey's arms? A safe place to come home to? It was as if the stone wall of fear she'd built around her heart crumbled at her feet. Turned to dust.

Thankfulness surged through her. Was this really happening?

After a not-nearly-long-enough moment in his arms, Trey gently pulled back. Stepped back. Released her. His expression troubled.

Just like before.

He swallowed. "I'm sorry, Kara. I don't know what got into me."

That's what he'd said that night, too, even though it had been she who'd thrown herself at him. She stepped back, too, heat flooding her face. What had she been thinking, playing kissy-face right on the sales floor of the Warehouse? What if a customer had walked in on them?

"It's okay," she said softly, as numbness gripped her heart. He nodded, but didn't look at her. "I, uh, I'm serious about the loan, Kara."

"Thank you. But I think it would be better if—"

"It would be strictly a business transaction, but no interest. Or minimal enough not to raise any IRS flags. It wouldn't have any, you know, personal expectations. No strings attached."

But what if she *wanted* personal expectations? Strings attached?

Stop that. You're such a fool. Letting a kiss intended only to soothe and comfort send her off and running down the yellow brick road to fantasies of forgiveness and happily-ever-afters. The minute she confessed her role in the teenage deception that dogged him to this day, he'd be out the door. She couldn't accept a loan of that magnitude without telling him the truth.

"I appreciate it, Trey. And you're a sweetheart to offer." She kept her voice level, impersonal. "But I'll get a bank loan when I get back to Chicago."

Assuming she still had a job.

"Think about it, okay? You could go back at least knowing a chunk of the bills are paid. Get the collection people off your mom's back. The stress off both of you."

It was so tempting. An answer to prayer.

But so wrong.

She could never accept his money. And would never be given the opportunity to accept his love.

What was he thinking when he kissed her yesterday?

That was just it—he hadn't been. He seized the moment—and did something really stupid. Just like with Tanya. Flashing red lights all over the place, but he'd ignored them. Again.

Trey surveyed the room at his brother's place that he'd called home for almost six months, then picked up one of the oversize boxes stacked in the corner. With moving day fast approaching for Reyna, Jason and the girls, he needed to get his own stuff hauled into town. Today seemed as good a time as any to begin loading the truck. In hindsight, however, renting the apartment above the Warehouse was another of his less-than-smart moves. Even when Kara left—no employer in their right mind would lay her off—he'd still have a connection to her through her mom. Probably have to hear updates on her career. Promotion. Spence.

But no way would the good Lord have given him the seal of approval on that kiss. It implied things. Things he had no business implying. He and Kara were on totally different wavelengths. City girl. Country boy. And even more significant, he believed God was involved in the smallest details of his life, and Kara denied He did anything beyond setting her world in motion. Attempting to combine those two extremes was a disaster in the making. He didn't need to take one of Jas' premarital surveys to recognize that.

But when he backed off after initiating that kiss, she probably thought he'd been toying with her affections. Disregarding her feelings. One more reason for her not to trust God. Or him.

"What seems to be your problem?" Reyna appeared in the doorway, arms folded and a don't-lie-to-me expression on her face.

"What do you mean?"

"Since you got home last night you've looked like a sad old hound dog who had his bone taken away from him."

Trey shifted the box in his arms. "No bones lost here."

"Could have fooled me." She eyed him skeptically. "Even Mary says you're no fun."

"Just a lot on my mind. Busy man."

"Yeah, right." She started to turn away, then apparently thought better of it. "How's Sharon Dixon?"

Why was she asking him?

"Haven't spoken with her. Heard she'll probably be coming home on Monday."

"Kara still planning to go back to Chicago?"

"Assume so."

Reyna studied him a moment longer, looking as if she wanted to say more. Then she shifted gears. "I have to run to town. You going to be around for a while?"

"Just loading the truck. Thought I'd take some of my stuff in this evening when I go in to feed the horses."

"Would you mind if I left Missy and Mary with you? I have lots of in-and-out errands to run, and you know how convoluted the logistics get when you have to deal with car seats."

"Yeah, sure. But I don't know that Mary will find my hauling boxes out of the house much 'fun.'"

Reyna leaned back against the doorframe. "You're having second thoughts about making a permanent move to Canyon Springs, aren't you?"

Could she read Jason like a book, too? Must drive him nuts.

"Let's put it this way. I'm not making any headway on clearing my name. As much as I need to do it in order to stay here, there isn't much time for digging up, let alone pursuing, leads while I'm trying to keep the renovation on track."

Even though he'd told Kara he planned to renew his investigation, he wasn't a cop. He didn't have the right to point fingers, pull in suspects for interrogation. Couldn't apply pressure for a full confession like a TV private eye. And she was right—it could backfire on him.

"So if you can't find out who set the fire, you'll hire a replacement manager and that's that? You won't stay?"

"I know you want me to settle down here, Reyna. But—"

"Why are you punishing yourself? Making this silly rule or whatever it is that you have to prove your innocence or it's *adiós?*"

"It's not a rule, it's—"

"What is it about Canyon Springs—" she folded her arms, eyes narrowing "—that you're so afraid of?"

He met Reyna's querying gaze. But he couldn't explain it to her. How he'd long dreamed of settling down in one place. How he wanted to be near family. To end the years of a transient lifestyle and short-lived, shallow relationships. Yet at the same time, how much he doubted his own ability to be a success at it.

She looked him over. "It's Kara, isn't it?"

Her words kicked him in the gut. Where'd she come up with this stuff? "What do you mean?"

"You know what I'm talking about. You were getting pretty satisfied with the idea of returning here until she showed up. I didn't catch on immediately, but now looking back I can see—"

"Whatever you see, Reyna, is in your too-vivid imagination."

"Trey! Why can't you ever admit you care for a woman?" Reyna's eyes flashed a challenge. "There's no shame in it."

He set the box on the bed and drew in a steadying breath. "There is when you know God's not in it."

"And just how do you know this?"

"Believe me, I know it."

"So you're punishing yourself for feeling this way— about a woman who doesn't know a great guy when she sees one—by not making a life in Canyon Springs? That doesn't make sense. Why not do something nice for yourself for a change?"

With a look of exasperation, she turned away and headed back down the hallway.

Reyna made it sound so simple.

But it wasn't.

He wanted to settle down here. But how could he ever find a woman who meant more to him than Kara? He couldn't just pick a substitute. That wouldn't be fair to some poor little gal who'd be a pale shadow of the woman who'd claimed his heart since he was seventeen. Would he find himself still dreaming of Kara as he slumbered next to his replacement bride? Would he look at their kids and wonder what his and Kara's would have looked like? Would he find himself secretly longing to glimpse the ponytailed woman each time he heard she was in town?

That kind of "cheating" went against everything he believed in.

Fire. He'd always be playing with fire when it came to Kara. His inner eye flashed to yesterday at the Warehouse. Holding the woman of his dreams so close. His lips on hers…his imagination taking flight in those brief, sweet moments.

Kara as a wife. A mother.

But even if everything else was different, if they shared the same beliefs and values, even if she trusted him to make a commitment to a relationship, how could he ever make her happy in the one place on earth she wanted nothing to do with?

He picked up the box again. It didn't seem right. Getting your heart broken by the same little gal twice. Didn't say a whole lot for his intelligence. His common sense. How'd he get the idea in the first place that he could come back to this town? *Her town.* Pretend nothing had happened to his heart?

The problem was, now he recognized the truth.

He couldn't live in a Canyon Springs that wasn't called home to Kara.

Chapter Sixteen

"We sure could use a real designer like you on the team, Kara. There's been a paid position opening available for months."

High school English teacher Sandi Bradshaw gave her a pleading look as they stood in the frozen food aisle of the local discount store Saturday night. She'd met Sandi, a friend of Meg's, at the New Year's Eve party just over a month ago.

"There are a number of places going into foreclosure," she continued, "but the ones the organization can afford still need major work. Not only elbow grease, but redesign of the spaces. One is the cutest little bungalow, but the rooms are so chopped up. It had originally been a single-family dwelling, then was carved up into office space. We'd like to turn it back into a family home."

"Wish I could help." And surprisingly, she did. The project sounded worthwhile. One that would bring more satisfaction than sprucing up the home or office digs of Chicago's richer than rich. Was this the same group Trey had mentioned being involved with? "Unfortunately, I'll be leaving town as soon as I finish making arrangements for my mom's care."

"So you're going back to Chicago?"

How many times was she going to hear that question? Surely it had to be all over town by now that returning was her intention. Had always been. Did they think if they asked it enough times they'd get a different answer?

"Chicago's home now." Memory flashed to the cramped apartment she shared with her roommates. Calling it "home" was a stretch.

"Think you'll ever move back?" Sandi's cheeks flushed, as though she'd asked a too-personal question. "I mean, I heard you were seeing someone. Trey Kenton."

"What's this about Trey Kenton?" Cate Landreth, a teacher's aide at the high school and a notorious gossip, pulled a pizza carton from the glass-doored freezer next to them.

Of all the dumb luck.

Sandi flashed a look of apology at her. Working at the high school, she'd no doubt figured out by now that Cate had a nose for news—and fabrication when news wasn't handy.

The auburn-haired Cate tossed the pizza in her cart and focused on Kara. "What's up with you and that good-lookin' guy anyway? The suspense is killing me."

Kara managed a benign smile. "Just friends."

"An ex-cowboy isn't good enough for you now that you're a big-city girl?" Cate gave a sharp laugh and nudged Sandi. "Or the fact that he's a pyromaniac?"

Kara's heart jolted. "That's not funny, Cate. Trey didn't start that fire."

Cate dismissed her with a wave of her red-lacquered nails. "Well, pyro or not, he's easy on the eyes, isn't he, girls? Heard he's thinking of settling down in Canyon Springs after he gets Duffy's old place up and running. That true, Kara?"

"Don't know what he's decided." She wasn't doling out insider information on Trey. She owed him that much.

"Heard he's looking at property, too." The woman kept her gaze pinned on Kara. "Must have done pretty well on the rodeo circuit to build up a nest egg."

When Kara merely shrugged, Cate zeroed in on Sandi, a speculative gleam in her eyes. "You know what Jane Austen said, don't you? 'It is a truth universally acknowledged, that a single man in possession of a good fortune, must be in want of a wife.' So now's your chance, Sandi."

Cate's too-loud laugh echoed as Sandi blushed a becoming shade of pink and darted anxious eyes in Kara's direction.

Kara's throat constricted as an image flashed through her mind of the pretty, satin-clad blonde coming down the church aisle on Trey's arm. Both laughing. Eyes only for each other. Him pausing to lean down for a long, lingering kiss.

"Meg!" Cate waved as she spied Meg McGuire-soon-to-be-Diaz, approaching pushing an empty shopping cart. "We're deciding how to divvy up Trey Kenton among the single female population of Canyon Springs. Care to be included or do you think you'll stick with that Diaz fellow?"

Meg laughed, but the questioning look she turned in Kara's direction was volleyed back at her with a get-me-out-of-here stare. "Trey's a sweetie, but no way am I trading in Joe."

"Kara's turned up her citified nose at him. Sandi's too chicken to make her move." The redhead glanced at herself in the frozen food glass door, fluffing her hair. "I'd go after him myself if wasn't for my Duke. Show that cowboy what a real woman is."

Meg spun her cart in the direction from which she'd come, and for a moment Kara panicked. *Don't leave me here with Cate.*

"Kara? Weren't you going to show me those kitchen accessories? The ones you thought might be nice for the parsonage housewarming?"

Thank you, thank you, thank you.

"Right. I'd totally forgotten."

"Shoppin' for your preacher's place?" Cate stepped back as Kara, shopping basket looped over her arm, slipped past her.

"Just getting ideas." Meg smiled brightly as they turned to head down the aisle. "See you Monday, Cate. Sandi."

But Sandi had slipped off in the opposite direction.

They made their way to the back of the store, sharing only "a look" until they were well out of range of Cate.

"What was that all about?" Meg whispered.

"Cate was feeling me out about where I stood with Trey."

Meg's hand flew to her mouth. "Oh, dear. What did you tell her? Not much, I hope."

"The truth. That he and I are friends."

Her brows knit together. "Do you think that was wise throwing the door open to the competition? Sandi, I mean."

"I'm not competing for—" she glanced around and lowered her voice "—him. Besides, I can't see Sandi as his match."

"Why not? She's a delightful gal. Cute. Better-than-nice figure, too, and don't kid yourself that men don't notice that. You wouldn't believe all the insider stuff I've learned about the male perspective from Joe this past month." Meg rolled her eyes. "She has a sweet daughter and Trey loves kids. Plus it's a small town and she's available."

Kara smiled, determined that her friend wouldn't detect her muddled feelings for Trey. "Then I wish her luck."

"You may smile now, but let me tell you he's ripe for the picking. He wants to settle down. Raise a family. Don't forget, it was only a few months ago that he asked me out. So it's not like he's going to wait around forever for a Mrs. Right."

"We don't think of each other in that way, Meg." Or at least she wouldn't confess to it. But Thursday's kiss still lingered on her lips. Kept her awake at night.

"What do you mean? I saw the way he looked at you at the parsonage a few weeks ago. Haven't you even noticed?"

She had, but Meg didn't understand. Would never understand why there could be no future for her and Trey.

"Look, Kara, Sandi would never horn in on somebody else's relationship. But—"

"I'm going back to Chicago. Like I told you in college—and the story hasn't changed—I have no intention of being tied down to Canyon Springs. By anything or anyone."

Not even Trey.

* * *

Trey looked up from the bedding display just as Meg and Kara rounded the end of the store aisle.

How did Kara manage to look like a knockout even when shopping at a discount place? He'd only glimpsed her a time or two since that memorable morning at the Warehouse, and now, in spite of himself, his eyes drank in the welcome sight of her.

But don't forget, buddy, you're playing with fire.

"Good evening, ladies."

The two women exchanged uncertain glances. Must not have expected to find a man in the housewares department. Or had Kara told Meg he'd kissed her? Didn't best friends tell all?

An unexpected warmth crept up his neck to his ears.

Meg pointed at the plastic-encased, puffy bedspread gripped in his hands. "Pink becomes you, Trey."

He returned her smile, thankful for the distraction, and returned the package to the shelf. "Trying to find something for my nieces' new room. Told Reyna I'd outfit it. There's two of this one in a single-bed size. But I can't find matching stuff."

Meg made a face. "Don't look at me. That's Kara's department."

An unsmiling Kara exchanged a look with her friend, then moved down the aisle to pull out a set of sheets.

"You could always get plain cream. Or white." She met his too-eager gaze with an impersonal one of her own. But he could tell by the way her well-manicured fingers fluttered as she pointed out the wrinkle-free, no-iron labeling, that the kiss wasn't far from her mind either. Had she forgiven him for his impulsive act? Or did she think he was a real jerk?

"You could embroider that same rose design that's on the bedspread along the hems," she continued. "Or trim them with eyelet and weave a pink satin ribbon through the holes."

"Embro? Eye what?" Trey raised his eyebrows and Meg laughed.

"I think he wants you to speak English, Kara."

Kara finally smiled and, even though it wasn't directed at him, his spirits rose. "Since Reyna's mother can make bridal wear, I imagine she can handle embellishing simple sheets."

"Or *you* could," Meg chimed in with a pointed glance in Kara's direction.

"Would you have time?" Trey looked to her for confirmation, trying not to appear too much like a starving man hoping for a handout. What was wrong with him? He shouldn't be asking her for help. Shouldn't be setting the stage to see her more often than necessary.

She studied the package again. "I don't know. Mom will be coming home Monday. And I have a lot to do to get ready to leave."

"Come on," Meg cajoled, "you're a marvel at this stuff."

Kara cast him an uncertain look as she put the sheet set back on the shelf. "I guess it wouldn't take too long. Especially if I did the eyelet. Except for threading the ribbon, it would be mostly machine sewn."

"You'd make some little girls very happy." And a big boy even happier. He didn't know anything about this girlie stuff.

"There now, we're all set," Meg chimed in once more, sending a knowing glance darting his way. His ears warmed again. *Had* Kara told her? "Look, you two,

I have to run. Need to pick up Davy from his grandpa's. But you can check out the sewing department and pick out the supplies tonight."

He caught the dismay that flashed through Kara's eyes. Came to her rescue. "I need to run, too. I, uh, have to—do some stuff."

"You can't beg for help, then expect the woman to do everything." Meg grabbed two of the bedspreads he'd been looking at and dropped them in her still-empty cart. Pushed it at Trey. "Get the sheets and there you go."

Kara met his look with one of amused resignation.

A smile tugged as he gripped the cart handle and gave it a shove. Paused to pick up two white sheet sets. Then offered his arm as a chivalrous gentleman might. "Shall we?"

She didn't take him up on his offer, but gave Meg another "look" and took off for the sewing department. Reluctantly, he followed at her pretty heels.

She must have been keen to get this over with, too, for in no time at all she'd checked the measurements on the sheets and pillowcases, and pulled out an oblong roll of three-inch wide white fabric. Kind of puckered, with rounded, holed ridges on two sides and a series of square holes down the middle. She held it up.

"Eyelet." Then she reached for a roll of pink shiny ribbon. "And this is what I'll weave through the square holes. Then sew it down along the hems of the pillows and sheets. Voilà!"

"Voilà!" he echoed, like he knew what she was talking about. "Thanks for doing this. I know you don't have a lot of free time."

"Actually, I have more time than before. Spence said

to stop killing myself on the project I've been work-ing on. Guess the client is backing out due to finan-cial issues."

"Rough times for a lot of people."

"That's an understatement."

He absently rearranged the bedspreads in the cart as he considered how best to reapproach an issue he'd given additional thought to. "You know, Kara, I was se-rious about a loan. Even if it's just enough to cover the Warehouse mortgage for a while until you get back on your feet in Chicago. One less thing to worry about."

She met his questioning gaze with an unsure one of her own. "I think that would complicate things, don't you?"

"You mean because of what happened this past week." He cleared his throat. "Between us."

Color rose in her cheeks and she nodded.

Why was he pushing this? Riding to the rescue just like he'd done with Tanya when she'd fallen behind on her car payments. Now here he was trying to get him-self tied down to Kara when he knew better. Needed to let her go.

He grasped the cart handle. "But we're both grown-ups, right?"

"Right," she agreed, although her tone remained doubtful.

"Well, then?"

"I may not have a job when I get back there. Chicago is overflowing with big design firms, and I'd try to get on with another one of them. But in this economy I'd likely be hired at entry level again. Which means en-try-level salary, too."

"Yeah, but—"

"Thank you, Trey." Her beautiful eyes, filled with regret, held his. "I can't tell you how much I appreciate your thoughtfulness. But no. And please don't ask again."

Chapter Seventeen

"Shh." A smiling Reyna placed a finger to her lips as she ushered Kara into the newly remodeled parsonage the following Wednesday afternoon. "It's nap time."

"I'm here to drop off something for Trey," Kara whispered, inhaling the "new house" scent as she maneuvered a festively wrapped copy paper box through the door.

"The bedding?" Reyna silently clapped her hands. "He told me what you were doing. It's a surprise, so I'll hide it in my bedroom."

Reyna took the box from her arms. "Be back in a minute."

When she returned, she again placed a finger to her lips and motioned for Kara to follow. What was up? They all but tippy-toed through the house, then at a wide arched doorway Reyna stepped back and motioned her forward.

There in the middle of the family room, under a quilt-draped card table, lay a sleeping Missy and Mary—and Trey. All three snuggled up together, their heads pillowed on a folded blanket.

Whoever would have thought to find the rough-and-tumble cowboy so vulnerable? The lion beside the lambs. "How precious."

"I just got back from running errands and found them like this," Reyna whispered. "I think they were pretending to camp while they watched *The Little Mermaid*. Fell asleep."

They stood gazing down at the scene for a few moments longer, then Kara followed Reyna back to the living room.

"You should take a picture of them like that."

"Already did. It will make Trey a great Christmas present."

"He'll love it." Kara reached for the screen door latch and let herself out onto the front porch.

"Trey said you're heading back to Chicago."

"As soon as I can."

"I'd hoped you'd stay even after you get your mom back on her feet. You'd be a good distraction for Trey." Reyna stepped out on the porch and closed the door behind her. "You know, from this so-called investigation of his."

"I'm afraid nothing or no one can distract him from that."

"Well, he's getting discouraged. Maybe it's a bargain between him and God or something, this proving his innocence obsession. Who knows what's going on in that man's head. But he's having second thoughts about staying in Canyon Springs after Duffy's is up and running."

"Surely he won't let that stop him. He's said so often how much he wants to be close to his nieces."

"They love having him here, too. But somehow he

thinks if he stays but isn't vindicated, it will negatively affect them."

Like her dad leaving town under a cloud did her? Goodness knows she'd hammered that into Trey's head. No wonder he was second-guessing his decision to stick around. Was there no end to how she could mess up this man's life?

"Do you think you could talk to him, Kara? Convince him he's not thinking straight? I think he'd listen to you."

"He won't, Reyna." And she needed to keep out of this. Just because Canyon Springs wasn't her dream, that didn't mean it couldn't be Trey's. Although she still doubted it would work out for him in the long run.

"Maybe I shouldn't say anything, but—" the pretty brunette glanced back at the door "—I have to admit I was thrilled when Mary started talking to him about kissing in connection to ponytails—and you."

Kara's eyes widened and a warm sensation pulsed through her neck as last week's kiss flashed through her mind.

"Oh, I'm sorry. I didn't mean to embarrass you. But I was kind of hoping—I mean, I know for a fact he hasn't been involved seriously with a woman in years. Not since Tanya."

"Tanya?" Her heart contracted with a jealousy she denied at once.

"Oops. I'd better shut up before I get myself in hot water. He'll kill me for talking behind his back. He's such a great guy and I want him to be happy. Right here in Canyon Springs."

"Then you'd better look for a lady love for him elsewhere, Reyna, because as soon as my cousin Brielle gets here to watch over the Warehouse and I can take Mom down to her sister's place in Prescott, I'm out of here."

It sounded so hard-hearted. Selfish. She knew that's what Reyna—and others—would think. That she was abandoning her responsibilities. Her Mom. Just like her dad had done. But what choice did she have? No place in Canyon Springs would pay her nearly as much as Garson Design did. She needed to get those bills paid off. Save the Warehouse.

And keep her heart out of harm's way.

"Hey, there, gal!" Jason Kenton stepped through the store's door during the noon hour the next day, carrying a large clasped envelope. "Where's my brother gotten himself off to?"

Kara looked up from where she'd been stocking shelves near the front counter. "I haven't seen him in days. He's not upstairs?"

"His place is locked up tight." Jason set the envelope on the counter. "Found this on the top shelf of his closet when I did a walk-through of the cabin this morning. Looks like business papers. Didn't want to leave it on the landing where just anyone could find it—do you mind hanging on to it until he shows up?"

"Be happy to. So, are you glad to be back in town again? Not having to haul water anymore?" That was a disadvantage to living outside the city limits in many high country Arizona locations. Having to transport hundreds of gallons of water in huge poly tanks secured in the beds of pickups or trailers.

"Definitely won't miss that, but sure did appreciate the Phoenix resident who offered his summer cabin to us. So what's your timetable for getting your mom situated at her sister's?"

Reyna must have filled him in, and she braced herself for a sermon on honoring your parents. "I'll take her to Prescott on Monday, then catch a flight to Chicago the next day."

"I'll get over to see her before she leaves then," he said, heading toward the door.

"Great. She'll love that."

That was one thing she *did* like about a small town. The concern and personal attention when illness or injury struck. She'd gotten calls from at least half a dozen friends of Mom, wanting to know what they could do to help.

Shortly after five she was closing up when she heard the creak of the floor upstairs and remembered Trey's envelope. She grabbed it, locked up and headed to his place. Still seemed strange to have him living up there now, even though he'd been working out of the office for almost a month.

The door off the landing stood partially open and she could hear Trey's voice. Sounded like he was on the phone. She peeked in and saw him standing by the window, his back to her. No need to bother him, she'd just leave her delivery on the desk and slip out.

"Good point," he said, as she pushed the door open wider. "I'm thinking we should set up a conference call next week, get the rest of the investors' take on it."

She tiptoed across the room behind him. Sounded as if he had one of the guys who'd financed the equine center on the line. One of his bosses.

"No, no, I'll handle it. Get it all set up."

She placed the envelope on his desk, then turned to go.

"Well, I appreciate that," he continued. "Sure, sure. Talk to you later, Dix."

With a sharp intake of breath, she halted.

Dix?

Everybody called her father "Dix." Dix's Woodland Warehouse was even named after him. But there could be lots of people, cowboy-type people, named "Dix." Right? He could even be talking to a "Dixie" for all she knew.

At that moment Trey turned from the window, pocketing his phone as he started across the floor. Then he saw her standing by his desk and stopped dead in his tracks. She'd always heard of blood draining from someone's face, but now she'd seen it with her own eyes. And recognized the truth.

"You know my dad."

He took a deep breath. "Oh, man."

"My dad—he's one of the investors, isn't he?"

Trey ran a hand through his hair. Then nodded, an unhappy man if there ever was one. "I'm sorry, Kara. I—"

"How long have you known him?" Her mind raced to all the times she'd dissed her dad in Trey's presence. She'd made it more than clear how she felt about that man. How could he have kept his connection to him a secret from her? Betrayed her like this?

"Quite a while."

"As in days? Months? Years?"

Trey cleared his throat, his forlorn gaze never leaving hers. "I met him on the rodeo circuit when I was starting out. He sort of took me under his wing—"

A little cry escaped her lips. His confession sickened her.

"I wanted to tell you right out of the chute, Kara. When you first came back. But I'd promised Dix I wouldn't tell anyone in town he was partnering in the business."

She shook her head in disbelief.

"He was afraid with what went on here before that if his name was associated with our project there would be resistance from the community. That it might be harder for us to get it off the ground."

"So you couldn't tell *me?*"

"Dix said you might—"

"Rat him out? Throttle *you?*"

He stretched out his hand in appeal. "He's trying to make it up to the town, to the investors of that earlier debacle. Make things right."

"Like that's possible?" She took a step back. "I don't want to hear any more of this."

"Believe me, I understand—"

"Obviously you don't or you wouldn't have deceived me. No wonder you've been at me to kiss and make up with him—he's been badgering me for years to let him back into my life. Now you're on his payroll, paid to do his bidding."

"Kara, that's not—"

"You may like to think of yourself as a man of integrity. A man of honesty. You may not tolerate anyone lying to you—Marilu, Mary—but you're lying to yourself, you know that? How could you betray me like this?"

Tension hung almost tangibly in the silence.

"You should talk," he said at last, his words devoid of emotion. "You know all about deception yourself."

Her heart all but stopped. Had he found out about Lindi and the fire? About her part in it? "What—what do you mean?"

"You know what I'm talking about." He took a few steps in her direction. "Your dad hurt you and now you think you can hurt him by not forgiving him. But you're deceiving yourself. Hurting yourself even more than you are him."

"You don't know anything about it, Trey. What he put me and my mother through. The shame I had to live with because of him."

"Maybe not. But I can see how your attempts to keep him at a distance reflect in all you do. I mean look at your career choice—your pursuit of the dream in Chicago."

"What's that have to do with anything?"

"You've chosen a career far from Canyon Springs so you don't have to be reminded of your dad. A career where you can control the outcome, paint things any color you want, gloss over anything you don't want to look at. Make it all pretty." He shook his head and took another step toward her. "And you think that by denying that God has anything to do with the details of your life that you can shut Him out, too."

"You have no right—"

"Friends have rights, Kara."

"Friends? Is that what we are? You could have fooled me at the Warehouse a week ago. Or was that part of a standard comfort-and-care package you hand out to women like me? Like Tanya."

Something flickered through his eyes and she knew

she'd struck home. Her gaze faltered as he took a step closer. Too close.

"What is it you want from me, Trey?"

"I want—" He stared at her, warring emotions sparking in his eyes, fighting their way to the surface as he searched for words.

She placed her hands on her hips and took a step to close the remaining distance between them. "Spit it out, Cowboy."

"I want—" He took a breath, his gaze locked on hers. "I want you to stay in Canyon Springs, Kara. Stay here. Call this home. Not Chicago."

Her mouth went dry. She hadn't expected that. Not anything like that. What was he saying? That he cared for her more than as a friend?

"Why?" she whispered.

He paused, indecision in his eyes. Then without warning he gently captured her face in his hands. "This is why."

Before she could react, he closed his eyes and leaned in. Lips parting, poised a mere breath away from her own as if waiting for permission.

Without hesitation, her lips met his. The barest whisper of a touch. With a breathless sigh, she gave in to the kiss she was more than ready to share.

He wanted her to stay. With him.

Time stood still as she relaxed into the kiss. Saw in her mind's eye every one of her Chicago dreams drift out the window. But she didn't care. Nothing else mattered but this moment right now. Twelve years in the making, coming home to Trey seemed so right. So inevitable. Her heart soared with hope. Possibilities.

New dreams she didn't even know she had. A home. A family.

Maybe God did have a few good surprises in store for her after all?

When at long last the kiss ended and Trey drew back, she looked shyly into his face, expecting to see the same revelation in his own eyes. The same dreams. The same giddy sense of wonder.

The same love.

The hands that had so gently cupped her face now moved to her waist, but he didn't meet her gaze.

With an uncertain smile, she reached up to touch his cheek. Felt the stubble along his strong jaw. "Wow, Cowboy. That's a mighty persuasive argument."

She wet her lips. Closed her eyes and tilted her head to brush her mouth softly against his once more. But he didn't respond.

"Trey?"

He finally looked at her. Eyes filled with pain. Regret.

She swallowed the lump forming in her throat. "Tell me what's wrong."

"I'm not sure I can."

"So what *was* this to you?" Her words came softly, but with an edge. "Another feel-good moment? Or a way to take back control? To shut me up about my dad?"

He glanced away again and she pried his warm fingers from her waist. Stepped back.

"We've kissed three times in our life, Cowboy— twice in the last week. And every single time you stomp on the brake and shift into reverse. That Tanya woman must have really done a number on you."

Then the truth dawned. "Or couldn't you make a commitment to her either?"

"Kara—" He reached out his hand.

She backed away, her eyes boring into his. "Thanks for the invitation to make this town my home. But you know, Trey, I think it's best I do leave Canyon Springs. Staying here wouldn't do either of us any favors. And for a split second you almost made me forget something very important. I have a dream—and Canyon Springs isn't it."

Chapter Eighteen

The humiliation of those moments with Trey washed through Kara the next morning as she pulled sweaters from the dresser drawers and threw them on the bed. She wasn't in the mood to fold them so they could join everything else she'd crammed into the two open suitcases on the floor.

How could Trey show so much concern for her? Take such good care of her and kiss her like that—only to crawl back in his tight-lipped man cave and act like nothing had happened between them? And how on earth, for those few fleeting moments of insanity, had she tossed away her forever dreams and embraced racing back to Canyon Springs? All because some good-lookin' cowboy knew how to kiss.

She shoved the drawer closed. Trey couldn't make a commitment if his life depended on it. He said he wanted her to stay in town. Make Canyon Springs her home. But why? Let's hear it, mister. Silly her, for a few lunacy-ridden minutes she'd actually let herself believe it might be for a little more reason than that she was a good typist. Met deadlines. Made a good cup of coffee.

Mom was right. Cowboys were nothing but trouble.

"Packin' up, doll?"

She glanced up at her mother leaning on her walker in the doorway. Her coloring was much better now, her eyes brighter, voice stronger.

"Sorry I woke you up."

"You didn't wake me up. Wide awake. Thinkin' about things."

Kara sighed. "You know if I could do this any other way, I would. But you can't stay by yourself just yet. Aunt Tammy's is the best option. Hopefully we can get you resettled when I come for Meg's wedding in March."

Her mother waved her off. "That's not what I've been thinking about. Visiting my sister will be good for body and soul. Never could get away from the Warehouse often enough to do that."

"What's bothering you then?"

Mom moved in closer to the bed. Leaned over the walker to snag a sweater. "You. And that cowboy."

Kara broke eye contact with her mother. "Go ahead. Say 'I told you so.' I should have listened when you warned me about cowboys. You'd think I'd have gotten a clue after Dad."

"I was wrong about that, doll. It's you I should have been warning *Trey* about."

Kara stared at her mother.

"That day he had lunch here with the girls, I should have given him a heads-up. Let him know you were running so fast, so hard, to get out of Canyon Springs that he'd be left sittin' in the dust."

Kara gave a short laugh. "I'd stay, Mom, if he'd give me a reason to stay."

"That's what you're telling yourself?"

"If he had any feelings for me, he'd have told me. Trey Kenton's never been shy about speaking his mind."

Her mother scoffed. "But what about speaking his heart?"

"Believe me, he's had plenty of opportunities to verbalize it." Like when he crowded in close last evening for a kiss that still made her heart quiver. "Mom, I know how much it would mean to you, but I'm not coming back to Canyon Springs on a permanent basis. And certainly not with Trey. He has his own issues. I have mine. I have dreams, and I'm not going to come back here and rot for the rest of my life waiting for him to get around to 'speaking his heart.'"

"I know you have your dreams, doll. And none of them involve Canyon Springs."

Kara wadded up a sweater and tossed it at an open suitcase. "You grew up here, too, so it's hard for you to understand. But it's like my whole life is an open book in this town. I mean, this is a place where everyone remembers which kid threw up on the first day of kindergarten or got caught making out in the church parking lot or fumbled the ball two seconds before the homecoming game ended—even if that 'kid' is now fifty years old. People remember it like it happened yesterday. Nobody gets to grow up. Reinvent themselves. This is a town where everyone knows—"

"Whose dad botched a business deal that cost friends thousands, then ran off and left her and her mom?"

Kara drew in a sharp breath. "It wasn't easy, Mom."

"No, it wasn't. Still isn't. But you gotta forgive him, doll."

Kara's jaw hardened. "I've heard this same song and dance from Trey, thank you."

"The boy's right. If you can't find it in your heart to forgive your dad, you can't be happy inside yourself. And if you can't be happy inside yourself, chances are you won't find happiness anywhere else either. Not here, not Chicago."

"Maybe you can forgive and forget, but I can't."

"Forgiving and forgetting are two different things. I haven't forgotten. But with God's help I choose to forgive—not in the past tense 'chose,' but in an active, continuing tense. Not because it's letting your dad off the hook but because it would destroy my life if I let it. Like you're letting it destroy yours."

"My life hasn't been destroyed."

"Maybe not instantaneously like an imploding building, but you're letting this chip away at your happiness. Allowing it to color your decision making. Cast a shadow over your future. Push that fine young man away."

"I didn't push him away, Mom. Trey and I—we're just not meant to be."

"My, my, doesn't that sound noble."

"Mom, please, I don't want to remember our last day together like this. That we argued."

"Sorry to burst your bubble, but relationships can be messy. You can't keep avoiding life, running away."

"They say you can't go home again, and Trey and I proved it. Coming back here didn't do anything for either of us but open up old wounds."

"Sometimes you have to open up a wound to let the infection drain. Allow it to heal over, to leave a scar that gradually fades away. But you can't keep picking at the scab. Talking about it. Dwelling on it. Opening it up again and again. Which is exactly what you've done with your dad."

"Mom, *please?* You and I have come so far since I was a teenager. The relationship we've developed means so much to me. Don't let Dad and Trey ruin what we've found together."

"I want you to be happy, doll."

"I know." Kara stepped forward and pulled her mother into a warm embrace. "Don't worry, Mom, I will be. Just as soon as I can get out of here."

I have a dream and Canyon Springs isn't it.

If he wanted a sign from God that the door had closed, you couldn't get much clearer than Kara's own words. She was a city girl through and through now. Didn't want any part of small-town life. Or him. But if she'd have stuck around another day or two, maybe he'd have gathered the courage to risk a slap to the face for kissing her on Valentine's Day. Like Mary insisted was the key.

Followed by Rowdy, he slipped into a box stall where Taco rummaged for the last remnants of his Monday morning breakfast in the bucket anchored to the wall.

"You're thinkin' I could have stopped her, aren't you, old boy?" The horse leaned his head into Trey, looking to have the sweet spot behind his ear scratched. "You're thinkin' I should have told her. You know, that I…love her."

There, he'd said it out loud.

Taco stomped a hoof and heaved a contented sigh.

"You're thinkin' that's why she left, aren't you? Because I couldn't say it." He brushed his fingers through the coarse hairs of the horse's mane. "But I can't. Not with her acting the way she is about her dad. Blaming God for everything. Not believing I can keep a commitment—just like Tanya."

But could he keep a commitment? He'd long asked himself that. Had he used all the years of transient living as an excuse to keep his heart at a distance? Always moved on when he started to get too close. Before expectations of a long-term relationship were raised. Tanya had stuck around two years before giving up on him. Looking back, he probably *had* been a jerk. Should have been up-front with her to begin with about his reservations about them. But it had been good to have someone to hang out with. Not always having to do things on your own. Alone. And it's not like he didn't care for Tanya. He did. But why hadn't he fallen in love with her?

Was it because of Kara?

He looked out the open portion of the half door leading to an adjacent paddock. In the dim morning light the moon hung between the clouds in the western sky, casting shadows on the frozen white ground.

As always when he looked up at the craggy, illuminated orb, he couldn't help but be aware that was the very same moon Jesus had gazed up at two thousand years ago. A comforting connection. And the same moon that shone on him now would be gazing down on Kara in Chicago tomorrow night.

A little tune played through his memory. One his mom used to sing to him when he was a tyke. About how the moon could "see" somebody you yourself would like to see. He hummed the few bars he could remember, then rubbed the back of his neck.

What he'd give to see Kara every day for the rest of his life. To hold her in his arms. To whisper his love in her ear. To take care of her. Share his life with her. But God—and Kara—had a different plan. So there was no point in kickin' at the traces. Fightin' the bit.

Why'd he have to go and fall for her all over again? But sure as shootin' he had. As easy as a calf jumpin' over a caterpillar. And all the while his common sense kept hauling on the reins, trying to get him to pull up, but he kept on going.

He glanced again at the moon, then shook his head. Gave Taco a pat. "Besides, what's the use in sayin' anything about love to her? I'm not movin' to Chicago. And if you'd have heard her, you'd know wild horses couldn't drag her back here."

No, there wasn't anything he could do about it. It was what it was. God closed the door.

But he could still lend her a hand. Make things easier for her to pursue her dream. And he knew just the person who could help him do it.

"I see a member of our team has returned at long last," Garson Design's Gabrielle Dubois announced with a condescending smile at Kara. The department head stood overlooking the gathering in the main conference room. "Welcome back, Kara—from ridin' and ropin' or whatever else it is you cowgirl types do in your spare time."

The mocking words stung.

"Yee haw," someone in the back of the room said quietly. But everyone heard it. Snickered.

Kara sent Spence a questioning glance. He returned

it with a thin smile. Betrayed. By the one person she thought she could count on at Garson.

"Actually, ma'am," Kara said with an exaggerated drawl. "Spare time's spent pickin' out the best chewin' tabaccer money can buy."

Everyone laughed. With her. Not at her.

So there, Gabrielle.

Spence.

But a queasiness in her stomach persisted as the meeting settled into its usual routine. She looked around the room filled with the familiar faces of those she'd worked with for almost five years. Served together on teams. Faced mutual challenges. Celebrated accomplishments. But if she walked out the door right now, would she miss any of them?

The soaring ceiling with open ductwork caught her eye. A sweep of angled windows. Recessed lighting. Bold, colorful artwork. A design studio on the cutting edge. How it had thrilled her twenty-two-year-old heart when she'd come to do a preprofessional residency the summer between her junior and senior year of college. And how unbelievable when postgraduation she'd been invited to interview. Electrifying to be hired right into the heart of the Chicago design world.

But how could the heartbeat of the company that once had her dancing to its rhythm suddenly no longer appeal? She'd been gone a few months, yet no one asked about her mother's health that morning. Or said they missed her. It was almost as if she'd never been gone. But that's what she'd always liked about Garson Design, wasn't it? Everyone focused on the moment. No one knew her past, stereotyped her. She could be anyone here she wanted to be.

Until Spence told someone about her cowboy dad.

She'd been labeled now. No longer sophisticated metro Phoenix, but cowboy's daughter. Hick. She'd been careful to keep up an urbane image. The clothes. The shoes. The hair. The nails. She'd eliminated conversational references to screaming deals at Walmart and her love affair with pickups. Watched her diction and guarded against regional colloquialisms—although she'd slipped back into those recently.

She sat up straighter. She was the same designer this week that she was before she left for Canyon Springs at Thanksgiving. She could still do the job. Clients would still like and respect her. Maybe she could use the cowgirl slant to her advantage. Like a product "brand." Play up Arizona. The West.

After all, her future was wide open now. Nothing to tie her down to Canyon Springs. For as much as she resented her mother mentioning the situation to him, Dad stepped in with a loan. Called Mom at Aunt Tammy's house Monday afternoon. But although she may now be indebted to her father financially, you couldn't buy someone's love. Or forgiveness.

Even as she mentally pumped herself up with thoughts of a Garson Design future, however, memory flashed to the day she'd worked out Taco as Trey watched. The clank of the bit, the squeak of leather, rhythmic hoofbeats. Trey's satisfied grin and a tip of his hat as she rode back toward him.

With effort, she refocused on Gabrielle, but as the team leader droned on about the conditions leading to recent layoffs, Kara glanced up at the clock—11:00 a.m. Ten o'clock in Arizona. Had Trey stopped in for his morning coffee after he'd completed his chores? Had a little chat with cousin Brielle? Or now that Kara wasn't there, would he drift over to Camilla's? Or Kit's? Or replace the defunct coffeepot in his office?

Was Brielle getting the hang of things at the Warehouse? Had Sandi found anyone to help out with the housing project? Did Mary like the pillowcases? Had Trey made up his mind if he'd stay in Canyon Springs or not?

Their last meeting had ended on a bad note. She still resented his shallow kiss. His deception about her dad. But maybe she should call him. Assure him she was settling back into Chicago life. Let him know that while awaiting her flight at Sky Harbor she'd found cute hair accessories for Mary in one of the shops.

"—and in conclusion," Gabrielle continued, "I think we all recognize that tough times call for even tougher measures, more focused attitudes. A willingness to invest the extra time and effort that will keep Garson Design in the game."

Kara joined in the light smattering of applause.

Yes, she'd call Trey tonight.

Chapter Nineteen

Trey checked the caller ID of his ringing cell phone.
Kara.

With renewed determination, he let it go to messaging and added another piece to the puzzle he and Mary were putting together on the Warehouse apartment dining table. He glanced over at Missy playing quietly with her dolls on a corner of the sofa, talking animatedly to herself.

Kara had called twice that week. Once on Wednesday night to tell him she was safely in the Windy City and that she'd found hair doodads for Mary. Was sending them priority mail. Then Thursday she called to ask if he could give her Reyna's cell phone number.

Now it was Saturday night. He'd finished up at the equine center. Showered. Flopped on the sofa, too tired to even turn on the TV while he'd awaited the arrival of his nieces. He'd volunteered early in the week to give Jason and Reyna a date night without the girls—one of those things Jason's premarital guides recommended. At least the prior commitment gave him a good excuse to dodge an unanticipated volley of demands on his free time.

A single gal at the church had invited him to a dinner gathering at her place, but he'd begged off. And another of Meg's friends, Samantha Couldn't-Remember-Her-Last-Name, called to remind him of a moonlight cross-country ski outing with other singles from a sister church in Pinetop-Lakeside. He turned down that one, too. Sure seemed with Kara gone that the unattached ladies of Canyon Springs had come out in droves.

Is that what life would be like if he settled down here permanently? Not that the attention wasn't flattering, but he'd rather be hanging out with Kara. Listening to her talk. Watching the sway of her ponytail down her back. How her gray eyes sparkled when amused—or flashed when she was really into something. Like giving him what for.

Rather be remembering how her soft lips tasted on his.

Which didn't exactly explain why he'd let the phone go to messaging instead of picking up.

"It's your turn, Uncle Trey."

"Oh, sorry." He selected a colorful piece of shaped cardboard and slid it into place.

"That's not where it goes. That's an eye."

"It fits."

"No it doesn't." She shoved the piece back at him.

"Are you tired, princess?" She hadn't been her usual perky self tonight. Maybe she was coming down with something. "Ready for bed?"

She gave him a dirty look. "No."

He reached across the table and put his hand on her forehead. She jerked back.

"I just want to see if you have a fever."

"I'm not sick."

"Then what's the problem?"

With an obstinate jut of her chin, she folded her arms. "It's your fault Kara left. You didn't kiss her on Valemtime's Day."

Oh, boy.

"Kissing doesn't always make everything right, Mary." He should know. And if Kara kept calling and he kept answering, he'd never get over her. Never be ready to see what God had in store for him next.

Not that he had much interest in a love life right now.

With the High Country Equine Center set to launch in a couple of months—he was still determined to get that final approval from Reuben Falkner—his goal was nearly met. But without the extra cash he'd saved up it would be hard, if not impossible, to embark on and promote his long dreamed of horse training venture on the side.

But he'd figure out a way to do it. One of these days. If he ever felt like it.

"If you'd have kissed her, she would have stayed." Mary's cheerless tone echoed his own unenthusiastic thoughts. "Are you going to stay, Uncle Trey?"

Was he? He stared down at the now-silent cell phone on the table. "I don't know, Mary."

"But you've got to." Her lower lip protruded.

You're not making this easy on me, God.

Even before Kara had returned at Thanksgiving, he'd sensed her presence in her hometown. Had known better than to come back to Canyon Springs. But once he was spending time with family—with Missy and Mary—he'd convinced himself he could make a go of it. That old memories would be overlaid with new ones. That he'd clear his name, find himself a nice hometown girl and start his dreamed-of family.

But he'd been wrong. Kara had come back just long enough to lasso his heart, throw it to the ground and tie it up with a pigg'n string.

Again.

Mary stood up. "I don't want to do a puzzle anymore."

He wasn't much in the mood for it either. "Then come here and give me a hug."

He knew she was mad at him. Saw her hesitation. The war going on within. Then her ever-soft heart won out and she came around the table to wrap her arms around his neck. Man, did he love this little girl. Wanted to make her happy. Wanted to be there for her. But—

When she pulled back, her dark solemn eyes gazed into his. "You should have kissed her, Uncle Trey."

She patted his leg, then all but dragging her feet she moved off to join Missy on the sofa. Her body language spelled out a heaviness in her heart that rivaled his.

He glanced again at the cell phone.

Guess he'd better see what Kara had to say. Make sure there hadn't been an emergency. Something he needed to take care of for her. He retrieved the message.

"Um, hi, Trey. It's me," the familiar voice began, her tone light and lilting. "Nine o'clock Chicago time. Eight o'clock Canyon Springs. Guess you're working late tonight. No rest for the wicked, huh? Or maybe you're out on a hot date?"

A soft giggle warmed his heart. But she'd guessed

wrong. There was only one woman with whom he was interested in sharing a hot date.

"Anyway," she continued, "I just thought I'd check in and see how things went at the meeting with old Reuben yesterday. Well, guess that's all for now. Bye."

He listened to the message two more times, then placed the phone back on the table. Slid back in his chair, stretched his legs out. Bumped Rowdy curled sleeping at his feet.

No, things hadn't gone well with "Old Reuben."

He wouldn't return Kara's call tonight. Didn't feel like talking about the councilman's continued insinuations about his past. He'd text her tomorrow. Let her know how things stood. But could she be lonely? Missing home? Him? Was that why she'd called three times since returning to her dream world?

Naw. She was where she wanted to be. Probably just felt sorry for him. *Dumb old cowboy, thinking you could win her heart. Be enough to keep her from going back to Chicago.*

Maybe he could have if he'd spoken up? *Kissed her on Valemtime's Day?* But after Tanya he'd promised God he wouldn't get involved with a woman who didn't put a lot of stock in faith issues. Who didn't share his beliefs.

Or was he hesitating because of what she'd done to him as a teen? Didn't quite trust her for letting him take the fall for something she knew he hadn't done. Had he forgiven her as he'd told her he had? Or did that still stand between them?

Whatever the answer, it was a moot point. An old cowpoke like him couldn't keep her happy in Canyon Springs. And he sure as shootin' couldn't be an urban cowboy. So where'd that leave them? Same place they'd been since the first night they ran into each other outside Kit's Lodge.

Worlds apart.

Kara leaned her forehead against the cool window of the darkened apartment, gazing down at the street far below. Bumper-to-bumper traffic. Headlights and streetlights. Glowing neon signs and lit windows of other apartments across the way.

How could you be sitting in the middle of a teeming city of millions and feel so all alone?

She'd been back three weeks now. Three long weeks. Her roommates were out for the evening again and she had the place to herself. Time to think without interruption. To celebrate her freedom far from the confines of Canyon Springs.

But Trey hadn't returned her recent calls. Any of them. He did send a brief text message telling her things remained hung up with Lindi's grandpa. Which only made her feel worse. His business wouldn't have hit a logjam if she'd defied Lindi and just told him the truth.

Why should she be surprised, though, that he'd texted and not called? She'd lit into him good about knowing her dad and keeping it a secret from her. Questioned his honesty, his integrity—two things he was ultrasensitive about because of the low-down thing she'd done to him as a teen. What a hypocrite she was. While it angered her, the promise he'd made to her dad didn't come close to the one she'd made to Lindi. His offense paled in comparison to hers.

But still, he'd kissed her, hadn't he? Even after she argued with him about her dad. He said he wanted her to stay in Canyon Springs. But of course, he couldn't come up with a good reason—the only reason that could have changed her mind about what she did with her future.

Nevertheless, she'd called a couple of times. An excuse, really, to hear his voice, sort of smooth things over. He'd been polite, but not talkative. Then he'd stopped picking up on her calls. She'd left a few messages, then took the hint—didn't call even to tell him she'd been giving thought to what he'd said about forgiving her father.

Even praying about it.

After all, what else was there to do when you came home to an empty apartment? Oh, sure, she could have gone out with the after-work office crowd. Joined her roommates at a trendy nightspot. But after a few evenings of that the first week, the crowds, the noise, it seemed so pointless. Artificial. Forcing herself to smile. Laugh. Pretending to have a good time when all she wanted was to slip off for a quiet walk under the stars. Preferably with Trey.

She stared out the apartment window at the sky above, but couldn't even see any stars from here. At least she glimpsed what might be the moon overhead, rising above the buildings down the street. But it seemed more hazy and far away than it did back home.

With a sigh she drew a finger across the cold plate of window glass. This was just a phase she was going through, right? An adjustment period before she got back into the swing of things. She'd gotten too used to her sleepy hometown the past few months. To seeing people she knew on the street, in the shops and restaurants. At church. People asking how she was. Chatting about old times. Hoping she'd come back.

Now she found herself missing the fresh pine air. The brilliance of a high country Arizona sky. Mom's laughter. Meg's friendship. Mary and Missy's giggles.

Trey's smile.

Seems to me that most people can be about as happy as they make up their minds to be, no matter where they live.

Could he be right? Mom seemed to think so. Was it something she could just make up her mind about? Could she be happy in Canyon Springs by *deciding* she would be? If she turned her life back over to God—stopped dredging up the past, replaying it in her mind, repeating it with her mouth—would the pain of her father's abandonment gradually fade away? Could the past, tied so closely to Canyon Springs, stop overshadowing her future if she trusted God to make it happen?

She needed to think more on this one. Pray. Forgiving her father, though, seemed minor compared to the other obstacle to her happiness. She stared out the window for several more minutes. Then picked up the cell phone from where she'd placed it on the upholstered arm of the chair. She had to tell Trey the truth.

But how would she convince Lindi, who'd been so opposed?

Nevertheless, for the hundredth time since they'd breakfasted together at Kit's, she punched in the speed dial for Lindi's number.

And listened to it ring.

Chapter Twenty

Kara headed to the rental car she'd parked in back of Mom's house an hour ago. She'd flown into Phoenix early that morning, then picked up her mother in Prescott and was now headed to the Friday night wedding rehearsal for Meg and Joe.

Thank goodness the weather looked to be perfect for her friend's special weekend. Sunny and temps almost to fifty. March, traditionally a big snow month in mountain country, could make for dicey travel conditions. But even though a layer of snow still piled one to two feet deep in unmelted shady spots, the roads were clear and dry where sunlight warmed the pavement.

She glanced over at the garage, paused, then took a few more steps toward the rental car. Paused again. Mom still kept Dad's old Mustang in drivable condition. Even drove it when she wasn't in need of the SUV's hauling capacity or the weather didn't require four-wheel drive.

She took another hesitant step, then abruptly changed direction. Strode to the garage and let herself in the side door. Flipped a switch on the wall. The cream-colored Mustang shone in the bare-bulb illumination of the overhead light.

She stood undecided for a moment, then approached to run a gloved hand along the glossy hood. Dad's pride and joy. How she used to love to go riding in it, around town or out in the country with the windows rolled down. They'd always stopped for an ice cream cone in the summertime. Her, Mom, Dad. Back when they were a family.

The Mustang's paperwork was in her name. Why hadn't she sold it before now?

She opened the driver's side door, retrieved the keys from where Mom always left them in the ignition, then opened up the trunk. Even in the dim light she confirmed the translucent, plastic bin was still wedged in the back corner where she'd left it. Filled with unread cards and letters from Dad. For whatever reason, even in her most angry and anguished moments as a teen, she hadn't the heart to tear them up and throw them away.

Maybe she'd get them out this weekend. Read them. It would be a start. After all, she'd told God on the flight to Phoenix that not only was she coming home to Canyon Springs for a wedding, but she was coming home to Him on a permanent basis.

Moved by a sudden impulse, she shut the trunk, tossed her purse to the passenger seat, then slid in behind the wheel. Pulled the door shut. Fastened the seat belt. She reached up to the remote control clipped to the sun visor, pressed the button and heard the garage door rise on its tracks.

Closing her eyes for a brief moment, she turned the key in the ignition. The engine jumped to life, and with an unexpected sense of liberation she carefully backed the car out.

So far so good.

With each block she drove to the church, the car's engine humming, a weight lifted from her shoulders. And by the time she pulled into the parking lot, she'd come to a decision.

She'd call and talk to Dad.

Of course, that was assuming he still wanted to hear from her. She'd spent the past fifteen years keeping him out of her life. Told him he'd made his decision to walk out on her and he could just live with it. She'd refused his calls. His correspondence. Had hidden out at Reyna's house when he'd shown up out of the blue on her sixteenth birthday. She must have finally made her point. He hadn't attempted to contact her in person since then.

She still wasn't sure how much she wanted him back in her life now. Maybe not much. But she wouldn't slam any doors.

All thoughts of her father, however, flew out the window as she stood at the front of the church watching Meg almost float down the aisle on a wave of happiness. Clad in jeans and a tunic sweater, but carrying a paper plate plastered with ribbons and bows, she looked every bit as beautiful as she would the following day. With a pang of melancholy, Kara couldn't help but notice how from the front of the church Joe's warm, loving gaze locked on his bride to be.

What would it be like to have a man look at you that way? To see your faults, know your weaknesses, yet have the courage to commit to you for a lifetime? Would she ever experience that for herself? And would she ever want the man waiting for her at the front of the church to be anyone other than Trey Kenton?

You're such a ninny, Kara.

She'd glimpsed him seated in one of the back rows—Meg had asked him to serve as an usher seating guests—but she kept her attention focused on the bride and groom. On Davy the cute ring bearer. Giggling flower girls Missy and Mary. Listened to the teasing, encouraging words shared by the minister, Jason Kenton. Before she knew it, she was trailing the couple back down the aisle to the fellowship hall for the rehearsal dinner.

Repeatedly throughout the dinner and festive celebration, she'd start to approach Trey, only to have someone else pull him aside for a few words. Missy or Mary often drew near him for a hug or to be picked up. Over and over she herself got sidetracked for informal pictures and "welcome home" conversations with longtime friends.

And then she saw her. Lindi. Crossing from an outside entrance into the kitchen adjoining the meeting hall, a metal warming tray in her mittened hands. She was catering the event? Her cousin had evaded her for weeks. But tonight Kara would have some answers.

To her relief, the kitchen was empty except for Lindi. The handful of teenage waiters and waitresses were busy with their duties in the fellowship hall. She slipped inside and closed the sliding door.

Lindi turned. "I was hoping you'd find me here."

"Where have you been? I've called you for weeks and weeks. Texted. Left messages."

"I was mad at you."

"No kidding."

"I don't want to argue, Kara."

"Neither do I. But you need to know I'm going to tell Trey the truth tonight, no matter what you say. Your grandfather is refusing to sign the final papers for Trey to launch his business. Blames him for the fire. I can't allow that. I can't continue to live this lie."

Lindi's words came barely above a whisper. "Neither can I."

Had she heard right? Was this an answered prayer—or wishful thinking?

"You asked where I've been." Lindi adjusted the lid of a warming tray. "Avoiding you, to begin with. But the past two weeks James and I've been in California. In intensive marriage counseling. Got back yesterday."

"Counseling? You're working things out?"

"I think so. But we still have a long way to go." She rinsed off her hands in the sink, then dried them on a dish towel and looked Kara in the eye. "I, um, told him about the fire."

"And?"

"He's the only person I've ever told besides you. He was shocked, of course, but says he'll stand by me."

"Thank God."

"It was…freeing. We plan to move to Phoenix. Together. Surprised?" She laughed, then sobered. "Last night I told Grandpa about us moving and it didn't go over well. But I've come to realize what a chokehold on my life maintaining this lie has been. Not only how wrong of me it was to allow Trey to take the fall for something I did, but for me to hold you to that promise."

"So I do have your permission to tell him?"

She nodded. "I ran into Trey yesterday afternoon. Asked him if he'd talked to you recently. If he knew when you'd be getting back for the wedding. Within minutes, I knew he was one miserable man—without you. It was as if blinders had come off my eyes and I could finally see clearly that my lying, and my forcing you to lie, had possibly cost you the love of your life. I'm so sorry, Kara. Can you ever forgive me?"

How could she not, when she so badly needed to be forgiven herself? She hurried to her cousin's side and pulled her into a hug.

"I need to talk to Trey," Lindi said, holding her tight. "But I wanted to tell you first."

"And I want to talk to Trey before you do. Apologizing of my own is in order."

Lindi gave her another hug. "On Monday, let's go see my grandpa, okay? Tell him the truth. Get him to sign those papers."

"Thank you, Lindi."

And thank you, God.

It had been a long evening, beginning with watching from the back row of the church as the ponytailed Kara had walked up the aisle to await Meg's arrival. How'd she keep getting more and more beautiful? And how'd he ever think not returning her calls would be a cure for his…heart problem?

He now leaned against the door of his pickup in a darkened corner of the parking lot and stared up at the full moon rising in the eastern sky. Had it been a month since he'd seen her? A month since he'd kissed her?

Man, why couldn't he get that out of his head?

With Sharon Dixon in Prescott, he hadn't heard any updates on how things were going in Chicago. Except, of course, for the calls he'd gotten from Kara herself that first week after she'd left. The calls he didn't return. As he'd intended, his lack of response put a halt to her attempts to contact him. So why'd he still persist in getting his hopes up each time he checked his messages? Set himself up for disappointment?

You'd have thought she'd at least have spoken to him tonight. But she appeared all caught up in the excitement of the eve of Meg and Joe's wedding. Into the moment. Focusing on her maid of honor duties. Enjoying chatting with old friends.

Or rather, *some* old friends.

Not him.

With a heavy sigh, he unlocked the pickup door and climbed in. Started the engine.

He couldn't go through this every time Kara came back for a visit. It had been a hard lesson to learn, but he'd finally come to the right decision.

To leave Canyon Springs.

Chapter Twenty-One

❧

Trey was nowhere to be found.

In desperation, Kara slipped away from the festivities, out a side door and into the stillness of the night. As was typical of the high country in March, the night air was cold and clear. Stars sparkled overhead, the moon's face glowed low on the horizon, barely filtering through the trees. Even with the fixture over the door and a single streetlamp lighting the parking lot, it was too dark to tell if Trey's truck was still there. She suspected he'd left.

But he'd have to come back for the wedding tomorrow, wouldn't he?

She leaned against a post by the side door and gazed up into the moon-silhouetted pines. Only a month ago she'd said her goodbyes to Canyon Springs. Goodbyes to the dreams that were never to be. Maybe it was just as well that Trey hadn't lingered tonight, that she hadn't caught up with him. How could she face him without making a fool of herself? Without letting him see the humiliating truth that she cared for him far more than he'd ever cared for her?

How could she look him in the eye and tell him that she'd known all this time who started the fire? Had let him pay the price for it?

But that's what she had to do. Would do. Tomorrow.

"Kara?"

A distinctive male voice spoke from the darkness. Her breath caught. She momentarily closed her eyes, turning to grip the support post to steady herself. She hadn't anticipated this. Hadn't prepared herself.

"Dad?"

A tall man emerged from the shadows and slowly approached, his familiar rolling gait confirming her recognition of the gravelly voice. The dim light illuminated his Western felt hat and suede jacket, the craggy features of his face. He had to be pushing sixty now, but she'd have known him anywhere.

"What are you doing here?" she said softly, her mind still not comprehending that the man she hadn't wanted anything to do with since she was thirteen stood before her. Had he driven all the way from New Mexico to see her? Or happened to be in the neighborhood on equine center business?

"Your mom said you were comin' back for a wedding." He pulled the hat from his head and clutched it in front of him with both hands, like a schoolboy called on the carpet. "I know you never wanted to see me again. You have every reason in the world not to. I brought a shame down on my family that still grieves me. That's why I didn't have the heart to demand shared custody. Visitation rights. But—"

"Dad—"

"Saw the Mustang." He jerked his head toward the parking lot.

She hugged her arms to herself, both to keep warm and to stop her hands from shaking. "Drives pretty good."

He gave what sounded like a relieved chuckle. "Does it?"

"Mmm-hmm."

Both stared, drinking in the presence of the other as if coming across a stream in a water-parched land.

A numbness seeped in around her heart.

Dad. He was here.

"I, uh, don't want to keep you from your wedding responsibilities. Know you have lots going on tonight." He shifted his weight, glanced at the ground, then back at her. "But when I saw the car, I thought if I waited long enough maybe I'd catch a glimpse of you. And when you stepped out with that long ponytail, I knew it was you—all beautiful and grown up. I couldn't hang back. I mean, just look at you. The spittin' image of your mother when she was your age."

"Dad—"

"I couldn't wait one more day to tell you how sorry I am for what I did to you. To your mom."

"Dad—"

"I've no excuses. Not one. I can't go back and change anything. I can't erase the pain. I can't make it up to you. But I want you to know—" His voice cracked. "Know I'm sorry. And that I love you, little girl."

He held open his arms.

She hesitated. Did he think he could walk back into her life as easy as you please, just like he walked out? That he could pick up where they left off and she'd be good with it? That he only had to—

And forgive us our trespasses as we forgive those who trespass against us.

The words of the Lord's Prayer she'd memorized as a child pierced her conscience. She needed Trey to forgive her. *As we forgive...*

A whimper escaped her lips. "Oh, Dad, I'm so sorry. I love you, too."

She stepped into his welcoming embrace. The smell of leather. His familiar aftershave. Stepped back into time. Time before he left. Time before she'd hardened her heart against him, built a protective shell to keep him out.

They stood together for some time, his calloused hand patting her hair. Her soaking his jacket front with tears.

"Trey was right," he said at long last, his voice not yet steady. "He said it was time. Said we needed each other."

She pulled back and he handed her a handkerchief. "I forgot. You know Trey."

"Known him since he was in college, cuttin' his teeth on rodeoin' in the summer." He chuckled. "He said you were madder at him than a bull on a rampage for not telling you he was working with me."

She dabbed at her eyes. "I let him have it, that's for sure." He chuckled again. "That's my girl. Don't let him get away with anything."

He scuffed a booted toe at the ground, his next words spoken in a more serious tone. "But don't place the blame on him, missy. That was my doing. I made him promise not to say anything to anyone in Canyon Springs long before you showed up to take care of your mother."

So Trey hadn't lied about that.

"That young man thinks the world of you, little girl."

A wistful sigh escaped her lips. "Don't I wish."

He gripped her arm and gave it a light shake. "Hey, now, what's it take for a young buck to get your attention? Giving up his own dream isn't enough?"

She crumpled the handkerchief in her hand. "What do you mean?"

"He loaned your mom the money to pay off her medical bills. That's a pretty clear marker of serious interest in my book."

"He offered to pay the bills," she clarified, "but I turned him down. You paid them off."

"Who do you think gave me the money? Handed over his nest egg so you wouldn't be under pressure when you headed back to the big city."

Her grip tightened on the handkerchief. "What?"

"He didn't want you or your mom to know. But after seein' him moping around today like a stray in search of the herd—and puttin' two and two together and comin' up with *you*—I can't keep my mouth shut."

She stared at him, trying to take in everything he'd said. "You're serious, aren't you?"

"Sure am. Just as sure as I'm standing here and you're standing there with that same dumbfounded look you used to get on your face as a kid when someone pulled a fast one on you."

"I don't understand. Why would Trey give you money to loan me and Mom?"

"I told you." He lightly pecked his index finger on her forehead. "He's head over heels in L-O-V-E. All I can say is you'd better wake up and smell the coffee, 'cause soon as he finds another property manager to take over our project, he's lightin' out of here."

"No, he'll find a way to stay in Canyon Springs. He wants to be near family. His nieces."

"Could if he wanted to, I suppose. But it looks like he can't stomach the place without you."

She gripped her dad's arm to steady herself.

"Do you have feelings for him, Kara?"

"I—" She stared into her father's eyes but it was Trey who filled her mind. Her heart. Trey whom she'd betrayed. Trey who'd forgiven her for what he thought she'd done to him. Trey who'd supported her, encouraged her. Who enabled her to return to Chicago with Mom's medical bills paid. Saved the Warehouse. "I think—I love him."

Her dad raised a brow. "Well, then?"

"It's not that simple, Dad. There's so much you don't know. So much no one knows. Not even Trey."

"I don't know what you're frettin' about, sugar, but if you have any feelings for him at all, I'm thinkin' you'd better get a move on. You and I can talk later. Go on now, git!"

The apartment above the Warehouse was dark, but she hit the gas and cruised on through main street. Then past the glowing lights of residential neighborhoods and on toward the other side of town. Rounded a familiar curve and broke through the stand of trees where the still-frosty, burned-out acreage of Duffy's place stretched out in the moonlight.

Heart drumming, she slowed, searching for the iron-arched entrance. Turned the car up the drive. Said a prayer. No matter what happened when she saw Trey, when she made her confession, she'd drive back down the lane knowing she'd come clean. Broken free of the shackles of her twelve-year deception.

The indoor arena lights blazed, and she parked next to Trey's pickup. Then slipped inside. Drank in the smell of horses, grain and hay. Could hear the rhythm of shod hooves on the groomed floor of the arena. The squeak of leather. Rattle of a bit. A horse's snort.

Standing in the shadows, Rowdy brushing up against her leg, she watched in fascinated silence as Trey put Beamer through his paces in the center of the arena. His expertise made her own feeble performance of a month ago fade in comparison. This man knew his stuff. Knew his horse. Would be a great trainer.

It was only when fifteen minutes later he stepped down from the saddle to lead Beamer back to the stable area that she made her presence known.

"Quite a ride, Cowboy."

His head jerked up and he stared, unseeing, in her direction, the arena lights blinding him to where she stood.

"Kara?"

She moved to the gate where he could see her, then opened it and slipped inside, Rowdy at her heels. Trey paused for a long moment, his expression uncertain, then turned Beamer in her direction and limped across the expanse toward her. She met him halfway, willing her heart to quiet.

Please, God, get me through this.

He came to a halt a few feet away, but Beamer stretched out a muscled neck, nostrils quivering, to check her out. She scratched the big bay under the chin. What to say? Where to start? "I saw Dad tonight."

"And?"

"And while I don't know what kind of relationship we'll have in the future, it's a start."

He nodded. "Glad to hear it."

"He said you told him it was time. And you were right."

"Could I get that in writing? Maybe in liquid gold?"

She heard the smile in his voice and returned it as she patted Beamer's neck. "You were right, too, about God being involved in my life all along. For fifteen years I've been so angry at Dad, at myself—and even at God—that I couldn't recognize it. Recognize Him. Until I had time alone this past month to rethink— pray—about a lot of things. Things you'd said. Mom. Things God's been saying to me for a long time and I refused to listen. Until now."

Trey nodded his understanding.

"God and I are on the same team again. I made a decision to forgive Dad. Now I need God to teach me how to work it out in my heart. Through action. How to work through the roller-coaster emotions."

"It'll take time."

"Dad told me something else, too." She pinned her gaze on Trey. "That you gave him the money to loan to me and Mom."

His brows lowered as irritation flashed. "You weren't supposed to know that. He wasn't supposed to tell."

"Well, he did. So you can take that up with him." Beamer nibbled at the hem of her jacket and she gently pushed his head away. "But thank you. You shouldn't have done it, Trey. It's too much. I don't deserve it."

"I wanted to do it, Kara, or I wouldn't have."

She took a deep breath. "When I get back to Chicago, I'll get a second job. Get you paid off as fast as I can."

"No hurry. Take your time." He toyed with Beamer's reins. "So you're still determined to go back to Chicago."

"That's where my job is." She forced a smile. "If you'd like to see your money in this lifetime, you'd better hope I keep it."

"Your job's there. Is that where your heart is, too?"

Ever since Trey's return to town, she'd sang the praises of her life in the city. Her career. The promotion. The dream. Took every opportunity to put down the community she'd grown up in. Belittled his hope to settle here.

Was her heart still in Chicago?

"Not so much anymore." She glanced at the ground. "Ironic, isn't it? The past month I've been there has been quite an eye-opener. Small-town America is looking better and better."

He looped the near side stirrup over the saddle horn, then loosened Beamer's cinch, but didn't respond.

Guess that was that. Her lips tightened. "Well, I guess I'll see you tomorrow. At the wedding?"

"Right."

He continued to fiddle with the saddle. She turned away and with leaden legs headed back toward the gate. Dad had it all wrong. Trey wasn't head over heels for her. Never had been. Loaning the money had been one of the many do-gooder deeds of a man who couldn't make a long-term commitment if his life depended on it.

Loner. Tumbleweed.

With a jolt, she halted. Her business wasn't done

here yet. Fortifying herself with another silent prayer, knowing what she was about to tell him would seal the distance between them forever, she turned.

And came face-to-face with Trey.

Chapter Twenty-Two

He'd startled her, his turning Beamer loose and coming up behind her like that. Just like the night at Meg's when he'd found her in the laundry room cleaning off soda cans. Gray eyes wide and beautiful.

He swallowed the lump in his throat, still not quite believing his own ears. What she'd just shared with him. That God had led her back home. To His heart.

Come on, Kenton. It's now or never.

"If you're no longer sold on Chicago, Kara," he spoke the words softly, reaching out to catch her hand in his, "why don't you stay in Canyon Springs—"

Her gaze met his uncertainly and he realized she'd heard that identical invitation before. The night they'd had their falling out because he couldn't—

Spit it out, Cowboy. Isn't that what she'd said?

He took a steadying breath. "Why don't you stay in Canyon Springs, Kara—with a man who loves you?"

The look sweeping across her face caught him off guard. Belted him squarely in the gut. He expected to see surprise. Maybe bewilderment. But not panic. Fear.

He loosened the grip on her hand, certain she'd feel

the wave of cold coursing through his limbs. "I take it that's not what you wanted to hear."

She tightened her fingers on his, eyes pleading. "It's exactly what any woman would dream of hearing from you, Trey."

"Any woman." His voice sounded hollow, expressionless. "But not you."

"I'm sorry, Trey. I—"

"Don't be." His jaw hardened as he took a step back, but she held fast to his hands. If she'd let go of him, he'd put them both out of their misery, make himself scarce.

"Hear me out, Trey. Please? Your words—they're what I've dreamed of since I was sixteen years old. But I'm not the person you think I am. You don't know me. Not really."

"I know you, Kara, probably better than you know yourself."

"No." She shook her head, her eyes filling with a sadness he couldn't comprehend. "There's something that I've been wrong to keep from you."

His heart shuddered. He should have seen this coming. "You're marrying that Spence guy, aren't you?"

Confusion flitted across her features. "What? No. He's not the kind of man I'd ever want to marry."

Relief shot through him. "Then what?"

She wet her lips and he could feel her hands trembling in his. "I know who started that fire twelve years ago."

He frowned, not sure what this had to do with what they'd just been talking about. He'd tried for months to discover who'd started the fire. Got nowhere. Had given up. "How'd you figure it out?"

"I didn't have to." She lowered her gaze, as if with shame. "I've known all along."

"What are you talking about?"

She looked up at him again, her eyes searching his. "I've known who set the fire all along, Trey. Even before you were arrested."

This didn't make any sense. He tried again to pull away, but she tightened her grip.

"Someone confessed to me. I promised not to tell. But I didn't know when I made that pledge that you'd be blamed."

"I must be some kind of dimwit, Kara, but I don't understand any of this."

He finally pulled his hands free of hers, trying to get his head around her words. She'd known who set the fire even before he'd been accused? Is that what she was confessing?

She'd apologized the night he and the girls camped out at the Warehouse. Asked for his forgiveness for leaving him to the law. He'd given it to her—willingly—when he thought she hadn't come forth because he'd rejected her. But she'd lied to him?

His memory flashed to the times she'd tried to talk him out of pursuing his investigation. Tried to convince him he'd do himself more harm than good. He hadn't understood her adamant stance. Now it made sense.

"So a promise trumps truth?"

"Yes. No. I mean, I vowed from the time I was thirteen that unlike my dad, who said he'd always be there for me, I'd never break a promise. I made a stupid, stupid mistake. A mistake you've paid for. It was a decision, Trey, that I've regretted with every breath I've taken since that night."

Her eyes begged for reassurance. Comfort. But even as compassion attempted to claw its way to the surface, still reeling from the shock of her confession he had none to give.

"Who were you covering for?" A list of suspects rowed themselves up in his mind. If it was her "friend" Bryce Harding…

She nibbled her lower lip, avoiding his gaze. "You have every right to hate me. I don't even expect forgiveness."

"Tell me who it was, Kara."

She closed her eyes. "Lindi."

He groaned. A cousin who hadn't even hit his suspect list. He'd never have pegged her. Never in a million years.

"She'd found your lighter in the parking lot after a basketball game that week. Intended to return it. But she'd sneaked down the road from her grandparents' place for a smoke, dropped it and didn't get a cigarette extinguished. I'm convinced it was an accident, Trey."

"This news comes a little late, don't you think? Why are you telling me this now? After all this time?"

"Because I can't live with it anymore. God doesn't want me to live with it anymore. Tonight I finally persuaded Lindi to release me from the promise. Or rather God persuaded her." Her pleading gaze never left his. "She says she'll face whatever she has to in order to clear your name. She's already told her husband. And on Monday we'll tell Reuben. You'll get your paperwork signed."

He stared at her. *The woman he loved.* Absorbing her pain. Her grief. Her guilt and shame. He'd forgiven her once before. Before he knew the truth. Did he have it within him to forgive her now? For the reality of such betraying deceit? Her lies.

A breathless pain twisted through him, mind, body and soul.

Why are you making this so hard on me, Lord?

"I'm sorry, Trey," she whispered. "I don't know what else I can say."

He drew a breath and stepped forward to again take her hands in his, certainty welling in his soul. "How about 'I do'?"

Confusion flitted across her features. "I do—what?"

He quirked a smile at her bewilderment. "How about 'I do take thee, Trey Kenton, to be my lawfully wedded husband'?"

She stared at him, obviously not comprehending a word he'd said. "What are you talking about? I ruined twelve years of your life."

He tugged her in closer, his heart swelling. "Then, darlin', don't you think you owe me not to ruin the rest of them?"

"But—"

He put a shushing finger to her soft, full lips. Lips he intended to kiss just as soon as he could get her to shut up. It wasn't Valemtime's Day, but it would have to do. Seal the deal on a second chance courtship.

His gaze flicked from her mouth to her eyes. "What part of 'I love you' don't you get, Kara? Are you trying to tell me you don't feel the same?"

She stood speechless as Rowdy danced around them, tail wagging. But from the look now glowing in her eyes, he knew for certain what her next words would be.

Epilogue

"What else can I say?" Trey concluded as he forked up another bite of the Diaz wedding cake and winked at Kara from the far side of a towering bride-and-groom-topped bakery confection. "I had to persuade her to marry me so I could get my hands on that sweet '63 Mustang."

"Bet that's not the only sweet thing you want to get your hands on," Pastor Kenton mumbled under his breath. "Premarital counseling starts Monday. My office. Ten o'clock sharp."

Everyone laughed and Reyna elbowed her ministerial hubby. Kara's face warmed. What an ornery brother-in-law Jason was going to make.

She leaned over to Meg who stood beside her, decked out in white satin and lace and looking every bit as beautiful as any bridal magazine photo. "I can't believe Trey made a big announcement right in the middle of your reception. I'm so sorry. I didn't want him to say anything today. He wasn't supposed to take the spotlight off you and Joe."

"Are you kidding me?" Meg hugged her. "I'd have

killed you if I didn't hear the news until we got back from our honeymoon. If everyone knew except me."

"But still—"

"No buts. I'm so happy for you both I could just explode. Do you know what this means? You're going to be living in Canyon Springs, too. Remember? You told me not to hold my breath, but my dream did come true! So when's the wedding? And what are you going to do when you quit your Chicago job? Run the Warehouse?"

"No date set yet. We don't want to rush things."

Meg smirked. "Twelve years is rushing things?"

"You know what I mean. But I'll be working at least part-time at the Warehouse until Mom gets back on her feet. Once we're married, we'll probably be living in the apartment above it for some time to come. But I'm also going to check with your teacher pal, Sandi. She once mentioned a paying designer position was open with a regional affordable housing group."

Her friend sighed happily. "Now wouldn't that be an answered prayer?"

Meg's handsome new husband slipped an arm around his wife's waist. "Warnin' you, Kara. Nobody outprays this little lady."

Both women laughed and exchanged a look born of years of friendship. Then as Kara's mother passed by with a pink satin-clad Missy Kenton in her arms, the little flower girl reached out to her. Kara hesitated, then with a smile took Missy into her own arms. The little girl giggled.

"I may be getting off to a slow start with this full-fledged praying business," Kara admitted, enjoying the feeling of the trusting child snuggling in close, "but I think I'll get lots of practice considering what—and who—I'm committing to."

"Now, is that a fact?" Eyes dancing as his gaze skimmed appreciatively over her Grecian-cut maid of honor dress, Trey set aside the fork and cake plate, then made his way to Kara's side.

Her breath quickened as she met his challenging gaze. "You don't think it will require extra help from the heavenly realms to rein you in?"

"Could be, darlin'. Been runnin' loose on the free range for quite a few years." He eyed the family and friends circled around them, a confiding smile tugging at his lips. "Guess you might say I'm her 'cowboys ain't nothing but trouble' nightmare come to life."

He got the laughter he was aiming for.

She shifted Missy, then slipped her free arm around his waist and momentarily pressed her ear to his chest, listening to the rhythm of a heart she loved. She lifted her head and met his smiling gaze.

"I'm thinking that's a nightmare I'm more than ready to handle, Cowboy."

"You think so, do you?" He cast a deliberately doubt-ful look at those surrounding them. Gave them a comic I-give-in shrug.

Then lowered his head for a kiss.

* * * * *

Dear Reader,

Welcome back to Canyon Springs!

Nestled in the more-than-mile-high mountain country of north-central Arizona, this is a community where ex-rodeo cowboy Trey Kenton longs to settle down. However, his teenage crush, Kara Dixon, can't wait to see the town in her rearview mirror.

Old feelings rekindle, but Kara harbors a guilty secret that can split them apart for good. One wants to call Canyon Springs home. The other wants to hit the door running. One hungers for roots, the other wings. But both must learn that only by trusting in God and following His leading can their hearts be set free to find a second chance at love.

While writing this book, I was reminded of how all too often we build internal walls to protect ourselves from the hurts of life. In doing so, we often build walls between ourselves and God, as well. We refuse to see Him, refuse to hear Him. But He's right there. Waiting for us to open our eyes and ears to His presence. To allow Him to draw close and to help us gain a victory over the hard times that come in life so that we may help others.

I know I've been personally blessed when I'm open to following God's leading, which is how I came to know the wonderful readers of Love Inspired. Hearing from readers of my first book, DREAMING OF HOME, has been such a joy! I hope SECOND CHANCE COURTSHIP touches your heart, as well. Please contact me via email at glynna@glynnakaye.com or c/o Love Inspired Books, 195 Broadway, 24th floor, New York, NY 10007. Please also visit my website at www.glynnakaye.com.

Glynna Kaye

QUESTIONS FOR DISCUSSION

1. Kara was barely sixteen years old when she made a promise to keep a secret. Trey later challenges her: "So a promise trumps truth?" Would you as a teenager have made the same decision Kara did? Have you ever done something that you later regretted and wished you could have a second chance to "do over?"

2. Trey bore the burden of having few people believe he wasn't responsible for an incident that occurred when he was in high school. Have you ever had a time when you spoke the truth and weren't believed? How did that affect you?

3. How do you think Kara's father's abandonment affected her decision making? Her career choice? Her determination to get out of Canyon Springs? Do you think she was pursuing a dream in Chicago—or running away?

4. How much of Kara's dislike of Canyon Springs was inside of her and had nothing to do with the town itself? Despite his past experience in the community, Trey looks at Canyon Springs far differently than Kara. Is it possible for people to legitimately "see" the same place or situations differently than others? Why is that?

5. Trey tells Kara: "Seems to me that most people can be about as happy as they make up their minds to

be, no matter where they live." Do you agree with that? Why or why not?

6. Trey longs for roots. Kara longs for wings. Trey asks her: "So you see those two values—roots and wings—as polar opposites? They can't complement and support each other?" What are your thoughts on that?

7. Was Kara's mother right to keep the seriousness of her financial situation from Kara? How could this have been better handled on both their parts?

8. Why do you think it was important for Trey to settle down in one place? What do you think was missing in his life because of the transient nature of his growing up and rodeo years? How might that lifestyle have enriched his experiences in a way that, living in the same place, he may otherwise have missed out on? Have you always lived in the same place? How do you think that shaped and molded you?

9. Both Trey's old girlfriend and Kara let his background convince them he couldn't make a commitment. How do you think that played a part in Trey's doubting his ability to settle down? Have you ever let someone's opinion of you influence your actions or perception of yourself?

10. Do you think Kara was hurting herself more than she was hurting her father by keeping her anger stirred up against him? Kara's mom tells her for-

giving and forgetting aren't the same thing. What are your thoughts on that?

11. What did Kara's mother mean when she told her: "With God's help I choose to forgive—not in the past tense 'chose,' but in an active, continuing tense."

12. Do you think Trey was justified in thinking he couldn't settle down in Canyon Springs because of the "shadow" of Kara hanging over it? Have you ever had a time when your past overshadowed your present and your future? Were you able to resolve that? If so, how?

13. In what ways did Kara and Trey finally have to step out and trust God in order to allow Him to open the doors to a second chance at a lasting love?

WE HOPE YOU ENJOYED THESE TWO

LOVE INSPIRED®

BOOKS.

If you were **inspired** by these **uplifting, heartwarming** romances, be sure to look for all six Love Inspired® books every month.

Love Inspired®

www.LoveInspired.com

Love Inspired®

Save $1.00

on the purchase of any
Love Inspired® book.

Available wherever books are sold, including
most bookstores, supermarkets, drugstores
and discount stores.

Save $1.00

on the purchase of any Love Inspired® book.

Coupon valid until July 31, 2018.
Redeemable at participating retail outlets in the U.S. and Canada only.
Limit one coupon per customer.

52615199

5 65373 00076 2   (8100)0 12313

Save $1.00

on the purchase of any

Harlequin® series book.

Available wherever books are sold, including
most bookstores, supermarkets, drugstores
and discount stores.

✂

Save $1.00

on the purchase of any Harlequin® series book.

Coupon valid until July 31, 2018.
Redeemable at participating retail outlets in the U.S. and Canada only.
Limit one coupon per customer.

52615203

Canadian Retailers: Harlequin Enterprises Limited will pay the face value of
this coupon plus 10.25¢ if submitted by customer for this product only. Any
other use constitutes fraud. Coupon is nonassignable. Void if taxed, prohibited
or restricted by law. Consumer must pay any government taxes. Void if copied.
Inmar Promotional Services ("IPS") customers submit coupons and proof of sales
to Harlequin Enterprises Limited, PO Box 31000, Scarborough, ON M1R 0E7,
Canada. Non-IPS retailer—for reimbursement submit coupons and proof of
sales directly to Harlequin Enterprises Limited, Retail Marketing Department,
225 Duncan Mill Rd., Don Mills, ON M3B 3K9, Canada.

U.S. Retailers: Harlequin Enterprises
Limited will pay the face value of
this coupon plus 8¢ if submitted by
customer for this product only. Any
other use constitutes fraud. Coupon is
nonassignable. Void if taxed, prohibited
or restricted by law. Consumer must pay
any government taxes. Void if copied.
For reimbursement submit coupons
and proof of sales directly to Harlequin
Enterprises, Ltd 482, NCH Marketing
Services, P.O. Box 880001, El Paso,
TX 88588-0001, U.S.A. Cash value
1/100 cents.

5 65373 00076 2 (8100)0 12314

HSCOUP0318

Get 2 Free Books,
Plus 2 Free Gifts—
just for trying the
Reader Service!

Love Inspired®

Looking for inspiration in tales
of hope, faith and heartfelt romance?

Check out **Love Inspired**®,
Love Inspired® **Suspense** and
Love Inspired® **Historical** books!

New books available every month!

CONNECT WITH US AT:

www.LoveInspired.com

Harlequin.com/Community

 Facebook.com/LoveInspiredBooks

 Twitter.com/LoveInspiredBooks

www.ReaderService.com

LIGENRE2017

Inspirational Romance to Warm Your Heart and Soul

Join our social communities to connect with other readers who share your love!

Sign up for the Love Inspired newsletter at **www.LoveInspired.com** to be the first to find out about upcoming titles, special promotions and exclusive content.

CONNECT WITH US AT:

Harlequin.com/Community

 Facebook.com/LoveInspiredBooks

 Twitter.com/LoveInspiredBks

LISOCIAL2017

LOVE
Harlequin
romance?

Join our Harlequin community to share your thoughts and connect with other romance readers!

Be the first to find out about promotions, news, and exclusive content!

Sign up for the Harlequin e-newsletter and download a free book from any series at **www.TryHarlequin.com**

CONNECT WITH US AT:

Harlequin.com/Community

 Facebook.com/HarlequinBooks

 Twitter.com/HarlequinBooks

 Instagram.com/HarlequinBooks

 Pinterest.com/HarlequinBooks

ReaderService.com

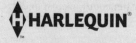

ROMANCE WHEN YOU NEED IT

HSOCIAL2017